THE TIME
IS
NOW

---

by

Maxwell Maltz

SIMON AND SCHUSTER
NEW YORK

Designed by Irving Perkins
Manufactured in the United States of America
By The Maple Press Co., Inc., York, Pa.

1   2   3   4   5   6   7   8   9   10

Library of Congress Cataloging in Publication Data
Maltz, Maxwell.
The time is now.
1. Tagliacozzi, Gasparo, 1545-1599—Fiction.
I. Title.
PZ4.M2613Ti   [PS3563.A4337]   813'.5'4   74-16020
ISBN 0-671-21859-X

To my wife, Anne,
whose love, faith
and encouragement
made this possible

Author's Note

Many of the main characters and events are historically authentic. Some persons and events are fictional, and in some cases chronology of dates has been altered to further the narrative.

Chapter 1

It was an era in which the mutilating specter of war clashed fiercely with the healing vision of peace. It was a day in which actors on the stage prayed to God for salvation or cursed Him in their despair. It was an hour in which human lives were worth everything or nothing. It was a time like our own.

Post-Renaissance Italy in 1555 was a land seething with restlessness and conflict. Its people, proud and buoyant, struggled to survive political instability. Strange crosscurrents whipped through its cities, and the winds of change were at the same time refreshing and chilling. The scalpel of the Renaissance had carved out a spirit of free inquiry, an impassioned championing of individual rights, an irrepressible idealism that would not die. A counterforce was the Holy Church, demanding that the populace gaze heavenward and plan for the Hereafter. God was King, and in His Name the Church was determined to reign supreme.

In the City of Bologna the sun blazed down from a cloudless blue sky. Three young boys ambling down the Mercate de Mezzo turned into a large public square, the Piazza Maggiore. They stopped by the stately Church of San Petronio and looked out across the square at the Lambertacci Palace, with its dazzling painted windows, and the imposing Cathedral of San Pietro, partially destroyed by earthquake.

They crossed the square to a high tower that had once belonged to the family of the nobleman Catalino Catalini, denounced by Dante for his life of debauchery and greed.

No one was watching so the youths moved quickly inside the tower, and though stairs were available, they scrambled up a ladder to the top. From their pockets they pulled beanshooters and small pebbles. Their mission was common for ten-year-olds throughout the universe: to wage a war on adults.

Through the open window they could see the Palace of the Pepolis, solid stone walls lighted by the pure sun, and adjoining it the tower of the Castellis. The Pepoli and Castelli clans had battled for centuries, an interminably bloody feud. Nearby was the massive Prendiparte Tower, prison for ecclesiastical offenders, spires jutting skyward, an impenetrable fortress secluding inmates from the world. And the Asinella, erected in the twelfth century by a family of Crusaders. The Bolognese worshiped the Asinella, which had stood firm during the catastrophic earthquake of 1503. In the distance, visible in the clear air, were the Apennine mountains, hideout for marauding lords who, with gangs of outlaws, would swoop down to rob and murder unwary travelers and rape their women.

Gasparo Tagliacozzi, the son of the pious weaver Giovanni Andrea, looked out at the scene with large probing brown eyes, his mind afire with questions. He wondered about the terrifying secrets of the mountains, so alien to his upbringing, and about the ruthlessness of the Pepolis and the Castellis. He reflected upon the nature of God and the causes of human suffering. His father, on the other hand, was famed as a weaver of silks, satins, and damasks, traveling to faraway cities to sell his wares to members of the aristocracy. He was an aggressive, combative man with stern moral principles. More sensitive and contemplative, Gasparo would not submit to dictation and an independent mind was shaping behind his mild-mannered countenance.

Flaminio Vulpi was his most treasured companion. Like Gasparo, Flaminio was rather shy and quiet. His mother was dead, and his widowed father was an honored figure in the community—a doctor.

The third youth, Lorenzo Desiri, descended from a family of soldiers. Impulsive, stubborn, intolerant, Lorenzo saw one side of every question. Tall and muscular for his age, he was bursting with confidence and in love with power. His father was captain of *bravi* for the predatory Abizio Pepoli, and no one challenged Lorenzo's right to assume command of the day's adventure.

The boys prepared to launch their barrage from the tower. Though harmless enough, it was against the law, and they had heard of other children being imprisoned and having their hands cut off for this minor infraction. They were playing soldier, however, and would take their chances.

The City of Bologna was a volcano—quiescent, explosive by turns. A century earlier, the Bolognese, outraged by the massacre of the Bentivoglio family, killed the murderers and nailed their hearts on the doors of the Bentivoglio mansion—this appalling act symbolizing their love for the slain family. This was followed by a dreadful vendetta. The Pepolis and the Castellis, slaughtering one another then, were still at one another's throats.

Incredibly, intellectual refinement walked hand in hand with uncontrolled violence in 1555. The civilizing idealism of the Renaissance was shedding light, but upon a populace darkened by schemes for revenge and lust.

The cultured, yet decadent Italian people found themselves locked in an internal war. Troops on the march, fighting, killing, dying—generally without clearly defined purpose. The nation was partitioned into embattled states that were further weakened by invading hordes from France and Spain. Families and individuals engaged in their own private wars, with the average person stockpiling an arsenal of weapons in defense of his home. There were no extradition treaties between states, so thieves and murderers would terrorize the law-abiding and escape punishment by crossing into another state. Ruthless *bravi* served the nobility, protecting their lives and property and dealing harshly with enemies. Luigi Rimini Desiri, Lorenzo's father, was inhibited by no scruples or laws.

Thus the youths, about to besiege the unwary pedestrians below, were merely imitating their elders, and Lorenzo, their general, did not trouble himself with the age of their victim, an old man with long gray beard and stooped shoulders, plodding down the Piazza Maggiore.

Gasparo and Flaminio missed but Lorenzo's pebble struck the old man in the back. Wheeling around, startled, he stared in their direction but they were hunched up behind the window. Lorenzo and Flaminio were snickering softly but Gasparo was suddenly fearful. *If he catches us,* he worried, *the military will arrest us, and the judge will order my hands cut off as a lesson to other children.* Crouching, he peered down at the street. The old man resumed his stroll, moving away from the tower.

"You seem nervous," said Flaminio, who was uneasy himself.

"No," said Gasparo.

"You are white as a ghost," said Lorenzo.

"No. This is not so."

"Coward," taunted Lorenzo. "You are a coward."

"You are the coward. You think you are brave, but you are not."

"I *am* brave. Would you take me for a weakling like you and Flaminio? I am the son of a soldier. My father is an illustrious warrior."

"There are other soldiers," said Gasparo, "who must be braver than your father."

"No. My father is a man of courage; he is the stoutest-hearted soldier in the City of Bologna. Is this not so, Flaminio?"

"I do not know."

"You cannot recall how he almost died protecting your father? Is your memory so feeble?"

"He received a minor flesh wound in the shoulder."

"From a *bullet.* But, my friend, suppose he had been hit in the chest. Why—"

"Look," yelled Flaminio. "Below."

In the public square a trio of musicians was striking up a martial tune. The drummer was flailing away in harsh tattoo and the trumpeter was rocking the air with rhythmic, strident insistence. The third man, a lute player, was signaling people to come watch the entertainment.

"Let us go," said Lorenzo, and catapulting down the ladder, they ran to the Piazza Maggiore, passing on their way the Lambertacci

Palace with its huge windows, a decorated frieze with angel by Michelangelo below the balcony of one window; the Palace of the Notaries, housing offices of the money-changers; and the Palazzo Accursius, containing the grain market, in whose statuesque tower Copernicus had studied astronomy.

The drummer was lashing out, whipping at his instrument, deafening listeners with the abandon of his assault. He was a gigantic bearded man, wearing a turban of red sable, his powerful body draped in a bright-yellow gown swirling with arabesques, a black sash girdling his ample waist. The trumpeter joined in and the pair unleashed an alarming volume of sound at the people flocking toward the spectacle. When these musicians stopped, the lute player began a gentle love song as two individuals in flamboyant costumes pushed through the crowd and instructed assistants on placement of a chair and a table with medicines.

Merchants had closed their establishments and clustered in small groups talking shop. A haughty Spaniard was standing next to a solemn-visaged Jew—members of this religion, driven out of Spain along with blacks, had emigrated to Bologna's celebrated sanctuary of learning. Ladies in gay rustling silks and ornate white ruffs chatted animatedly, while a prostitute, pale face inflamed with rouge and powder, eyes mascaraed, was whispering to a young artisan. Her hair was piled high, her natural tresses supplemented by a thick mass of yellow silk false hair, and the odor of her perfume was overpowering.

Flitting quickly through openings, the three boys, led by Lorenzo Desiri, moved to the front of the crowd, alongside a couple of Dominican friars in white robes and black hoods, hands clasped in resignation. To the rear, mounted on a handsome stallion, was Abizio Pepoli. Guarded by two horsemen in black tunics, accompanied by a retinue of grooms and footmen, Pepoli's appearance was grotesque. He was magnificently attired in a black doublet and a feathered hat of cerulean velvet with white plume—but his nose was missing, the result of a duel. And yet he was not alone with his terrible affliction. A ragged beggar in the crowd had also lost his nose—to the dread disease syphilis.

Gasparo's eyes bulged. To his left was the old man pelted with the pebble. The boy felt like hiding; the man was old, his hair was very gray, and lines etched on his face seemed to record the misery of a suffering world. And then Gasparo realized who he was; yes, he had visited his father's place of business the day before. He was a gentle, courteous man who had purchased expensive damask and tablecloths, napkins, bed sheets, and pillowcases of the finest linen. His father had said the man was Michelangelo, returning to Bologna to recapture the memory of his fiery youth; preparatory to leaving for Rome, he had bought these goods as gifts for his nephew.

The incomparable Michelangelo! Fascinated, Gasparo stared, his fear and shame dissolving beneath the intensity of his desire to converse with the wise old man, to ask him questions about life and to drink from the well of his sophistication.

Michelangelo spoke—but to himself: "How many years ago was it that I threw away hammer and chisel, leaped on my horse, and left the City of Florence? And then here in 1494—oh, but I was young— I stayed at the home of Aldovrandi, who commissioned my first sculptoring: two figures of saints and an angel at the shrine of Saint Dominic. Ah, they are fine pieces of work. And my frieze at the Lambertacci Palace. Oh, the memories.

"I returned to Bologna again—was it in 1506? My memory fails me. Pope Julius had marched unopposed into Bologna at the head of his army. I etched him in bronze, and the statue adorned the entrance of San Pietro—but Julius was defeated and my statue was destroyed."

Gasparo continued to stare at the old man. Michelangelo, his father had informed him, suffered a permanent kink in the neck from his intense labors in immortalizing the ceiling of the Sistine Chapel. Michelangelo, his father had marveled, pounded life into a mass of marble to bequeath the inimitable statue of David to the City of Florence. And it was he, this elderly man, the energy of his youth spent, who had slashed granite throbbing to life in his masterpiece, *Moses*. With his burning drive and savage incisiveness, he had painted the *Last Judgment*, which had caused such controversy because the figures were nude—and Giovanni Andrea had been scathing in his denunciation of this immodesty.

Gasparo turned away to watch the entertainment in the public square. A wire had been fastened to two upright poles and a comic, pretending he was drunk, weaved on the wire, first one foot on, then the other, reeling, horrified, always about to fall, eternally regaining his balance. Next, a pair of acrobats, somersaulting, alone, together, on the ground, on the wire. Applause.

"Quiet, please."

A gargantuan individual in flowing velvet robe addressed the throng. His cheeks were two florid tomatoes separated by a flabby lobster-red nose with spacious tunnels. His girth was stupendous; his stomach was a mountain. Benignly, he smiled at his audience, but, for all the buffoonery, his eyes were hard and cunning, searching out which was the sheep and which was the fox.

"I am the Great Van Zandt, and I will demonstrate to you my unparalleled skill. I am the Great Van Zandt," he bellowed, his voice booming out to every corner of the public square, his speech betraying a foreign accent, "and I remove stones in the head, which cause headaches, imbecility, and insanity. Traveling the length and breadth of this world, I have cured thousands of pitiful suffering people, and many offer testimonials to the effectiveness of my skill. I cure the exalted and the lowly. If you are dizzy from headache, pray step forward and I will render you assistance. Who is suffering from headache?"

There were no volunteers. The Great Van Zandt scanned the crowd like a starving lion searching for his lunch, but no one stirred.

"Is it possible," asked the Great Van Zandt, "that no one wishes to take advantage of my marvelous skills and never again suffer from headache? Headaches come from stones in the head, and I am a specialist in removing stones from the head. Do not be afraid, my friends; I will not harm you. And, for a few paltry centesimi, I guarantee to cure anyone of the scourge of chronic headache."

A shabbily dressed man in the crowd shuffled forward one step but reconsidered. The Great Van Zandt reacted instantly. With a few quick strides he was in the crowd and out, pulling the fellow by the shoulder.

"What is your trouble, my good sir?" he demanded, shouting into his subject's ear.

"Headache. I have a headache."

"Stones in the head," diagnosed the Great Van Zandt. "Ladies and gentlemen, this man suffers from a terrible affliction: stones in the head. These stones are painful but I will remove them and render relief. He will be a new man—and for merely a few centesimi."

In one fluid motion, the charlatan settled patient in chair, warned him to hold tight to the arms, whirled behind him, and yanked his head backward. Snatching a dirty knife from his belt, he made a small incision without anesthetic in the wretch's forehead. The unfortunate man howled.

The wound bled slightly. Dexterously, pretending he had taken them from the man's head, the faker palmed a few stones and dropped them into a receptacle held by an assistant. He bandaged the wound with rags.

"Ladies and gentlemen," announced the Great Van Zandt, bowing in courtly fashion, "I have removed stones from the head of this good fellow and never again will he suffer from headache. I shall pass the stones amongst you so that you can verify the truth of my claim."

The assistant carried the receptacle into the crowd to exhibit the stones.

"Twenty-five centesimi," whispered Van Zandt to the headache sufferer, staring horrified at the stones.

The patient searched his pockets. "I have but five centesimi," he said.

"I will accept this as payment," said Van Zandt.

The three youths were impressed but the Dominican friars disapproved. "He should be hung," they commented. "He is a blasphemy in the eyes of God."

Michelangelo had seen and heard everything during his lifetime. He had listened to Savonarola condemn the depravity of his countrymen and he had witnessed the unchristian brutality of the Borgia Pope Alexander VI. Savonarola was burned at the stake for honoring principle. He had known the unscrupulous Cesare Borgia, who, determined to become another Julius Caesar and rule a united Italy, had murdered his enemies, aided by the infamous Machiavelli, whose only principle was that there were no principles. And he had lived with full knowledge of the unbridled depravity of Lucrezia Borgia, Pietro Aretino, and Benvenuto Cellini, to whom no foul tactics were alien. Their immorality and ruthlessness lived on, constituting the heritage of his countrymen, of the assemblage in the public square, fooled by the cunning of itinerant medical quacks.

"Ladies and gentlemen," the charlatan proclaimed, "let me introduce you to the greatest surgeon in the world. He is a man of fantastic, unbelievable skills. He gives people new noses and new faces, enabling them to live again. Ladies and gentlemen, Professor Bartoli."

A slender man with lean cheekbones and furtive brown eyes, hawk nose looping over a curlicued mustache, manicured beard framing his chin, Professor Bartoli bowed and shook hands ostentatiously with the Great Van Zandt. He was wearing an elegant arabesqued black silk robe with puffed sleeves, a medallion of gold circling his neck, on his head a crimson hat with velvet plume, but underneath the robe was a tattered doublet and a rusty dagger in a filthy sheath.

"Ladies and gentlemen," he thundered, "I repair noses lost in wars or from the French disease. I am a great artist; this may sound immodest but I swear it is the truth. I fashion new noses handsome beyond belief. I have learned this art, which no other doctor understands, from the great Vianio. And I have surpassed the genius of my master. I have cured one emperor, two kings, four dukes, and seven princes, and the brother of the Turkish emperor. I have traveled to every corner of the earth to give the afflicted and the deformed the benefit of my skill. My fame has spread over the world. If you need me, higher or lower persons, step forward and I will assist you."

The crowd was silent, for they had witnessed the Great Van Zandt's incision in the forehead of the sufferer from headache. But Professor Bartoli glimpsed the noseless syphilitic beggar.

"You," he cried, "come here and I will restore you to your former status as a human being. Do not be afraid, my dear fellow. I will give you a new nose, and once more will you hold up your head with pride."

The beggar tried to run away but it was too late. He was caught by one of Pepoli's *bravi* who hurled him to the ground and straddled him. Abizio Pepoli had ordered him to block the escape route. Astride his stallion, Pepoli was thinking: *Let us see if this rascal knows what he is about. If he does, he shall make me a new nose.*

Screaming, praying to God, the beggar was dragged along the ground to the operating chair. Professor Bartoli called for the acrobats to hold the arms of the squirming, kicking patient. Bartoli loosened the beggar's rags and examined the man's left arm, pinching it to aid the circulation. Then he handed the poor fellow a glass of wine.

"Here. It will give you courage."

The beggar swallowed the wine in one gulp and the charlatan pulled the rusty dagger from its filthy sheath, waving it triumphantly.

Reluctant to watch, Gasparo observed the old man again. Michelangelo pitied the noseless syphilitic and identified with him, too, for his nose had been deformed since he was sixteen. Then, studying under Ghirlandajo, he had quarreled with another pupil, the bully Torrigiano, who had struck his nose fiercely, breaking it. For a long time the sight of his nasal organ crushed his spirit. Trained in the ways of Plato, idolizing beauty in the human form, Michelangelo was depressed by his ugliness and enclosed himself within a shell, but his misfortune induced him to worship the good in life all the more ardently and he vowed to use his art in the service of mankind.

"What ails you?" Lorenzo taunted Gasparo. "Do you fear to watch?"

"No."

"Unless you are a coward, you will witness the operation."

Gasparo turned back to the exhibition. With his rusty dagger, Professor Bartoli started cutting into the beggar's arm to prepare skin for the nose. The patient screamed and both acrobats could not hold him steady. He cried out in terror, struggling to wrench free. Taking a pistol from beneath his robe, the charlatan clubbed him over the head. The beggar was unconscious, and Bartoli quickened his pace. Handing the pistol to one of the acrobats, he used his dagger to cut out a cylindrical area of skin from the arm to fit the defect of the nose. While his assistants held the unconscious patient, he placed the skin graft over the defect, then from the lapel of his black silk robe he took a needle with a long waxed thread and sewed the graft onto the nose, bandaging it with layers of rags.

The medical quack worked feverishly, and as the onlookers applauded his apparent deftness, he bowed from the waist in acknowledgment. "In two weeks," he announced, "I will remove the bandage and this wretched beggar will have a new nose."

Gasparo was fascinated. *Is this the truth?* he asked himself. *How wonderful if it is. To remake a man's face and help restore his destiny.*

The Dominican friars did not agree. "This man is an enemy of the Church," said one. "He is bewitched, and the blood of the Devil flows in his veins. As with any sorcerer, he should be burned at the stake for defying the will of Our Lord."

"He is possessed," said his companion. "His conscience is impure, and he is plagued by the Evil Eye."

Townspeople were mumbling apprehensively and crossing themselves, sending up fervent prayers to God, hurling themselves to their knees to plead for mercy. A shoemaker pulled an amulet of theriac from beneath his clothing, holding it reverently in his blackened hands. Many reposed their trust in the compound theriac, reputedly a preventative of the plague. Its contents, mostly the flesh of vipers, were a subject of great controversy during this age.

Abizio Pepoli had watched the operation carefully and he whispered instructions to his *bravi*. "See that this Bartoli does not leave town. If he speaks the truth, he shall give *me* a new nose."

Michelangelo said nothing. Aged, mind weary, skin shriveling, still he was indestructibly wise, blessed with an unshakable belief in himself. Symbolically, he stood alone, high above the crowd—as the towers stood high above the houses and the mountains in the distance stood high above the plains surrounding the City of Bologna.

Young Tagliacozzi, ten years old, could not know that someday he would emulate Michelangelo and model human flesh as brilliantly as the Renaissance artist sculptured in marble, restoring lost beauty to the human face and assisting in reincarnation of the human spirit. He could not know that he would become one of the great medical innovators—in a sense the father of modern plastic surgery.

His companions were also oblivious to what the future would bring. Flaminio Vulpi, adopting the philosophy of the Dominican friars, would climb to a prominent position in the hierarchy of the Church. Lorenzo Desiri, like Pepoli, would establish his reputation as a ruthless warrior—arrogant and egotistical, yet heroic and loyal—living for the moment, taking his pleasure, asserting his will.

In the morning the beggar was sick in bed. His face, inflated like a balloon, was flushed. His eyes were swollen and he moaned as, unable to sleep, he tossed and turned. He felt feverish and itched all over, and his pulse beat rapidly. The bandage was loose and ineffective. The pale graft was now bluish in spots.

Professor Bartoli, panic-stricken, perspiring, worked on the patient. He gave him a cathartic and forced him to drink water, but the beggar continued to moan. Bartoli tightened the bandage and applied soothing ointments and hot fomentations to the flushed face. But the syphilitic did not improve. Desperate, Bartoli thought of sending for the Great Van Zandt, then he remembered that Van Zandt knew even less than he did.

The graft became progressively worse. On the fifth day after Pepoli's *bravi* had tossed the unfortunate wretch onto the operating chair, the skin sloughed off from the emaciated body hot with fever. Bartoli removed the bandage and revealed a nauseating sight.

Dr. Vulpi, hired by Pepoli to watch the patient's progress, reported to his employer.

"Bring the charlatan here," bellowed Pepoli.

Forcefully, a quartet of *bravi* escorted Professor Bartoli through a huge door leading into the turreted Pepoli Palace. With a few shoves, they encouraged him to walk down a long dark narrow corridor and through the entrance at the end of the hallway.

Abizio Pepoli, seated in a majestic leather chair, was not smiling. He was dressed in a black velvet doublet, golden chain dangling from his neck, and as the *bravi* pushed the fearful Bartoli into the room, Pepoli's fingers were toying with the chain.

"You claimed you could rebuild a nose," raged Pepoli. "But you lied."

"No."

"Yes, you lied."

"No," said Professor Bartoli. "I learned my art from the famous Vianio family."

"You all but killed the wretched beggar."

"He had syphilis, the abominable French disease. How can I be blamed if I did not have the salves and inunctions for his syphilis? I would have given him a splendid nose, sire, I assure you of this."

Abizio Pepoli's eyes were ablaze; he did not care about the pitiful beggar, but when he speculated on how this faker might have operated on him—

"You should have thought of that before," roared Pepoli, springing to his feet, the noseless hole in his face hideous.

Dr. Vulpi, Flaminio's father, listened glumly at the far end of the huge room. His eyes roved listlessly up to the high ceiling and down to the belligerent gaze of Abizio Pepoli's father, staring from his portrait framed in gold. Behind Abizio a carmine-red banner displayed the chessboard emblem of the clan; to his left was a golden crucifix.

"I can assist you," pleaded the charlatan. "I promise you a magnificent new nose. It will be exquisite."

"Take him away," roared Pepoli, signaling his *bravi*.

"No." Bartoli dropped to his knees. "I can show you testimonials."

Pepoli's laughter was chilling. "Do you think I would allow you to murder me as you nearly did this poor devil? You are a practitioner of witchcraft. Take him to the torture chamber."

"Peccato," screamed Bartoli, "have pity." But he was dragged out of the room and down the corridor.

"Vulpi," said Pepoli, when the charlatan was gone, "I have consulted the stars and decided. Cut the impostor's nose off."

The doctor departed silently. He hated himself more than he hated Pepoli. In the torture chamber, Bartoli was bound with stout ropes to a straight-backed chair. A *bravi* was stationed at each end of the room, which contained tables with knives, scissors, tongs, and other instruments, and Vulpi had no illusions about their reaction if ordered to cut *his* throat. With a razor-sharp dagger he amputated the nose of Bartoli, who howled terribly and slumped unconscious, blood gushing from his face to drench his clothes and spill out over the cold stone floor.

He was cut from the chair. Then, at the command of Captain

Luigi Rimini Desiri, the impostor was hanged. The corps of *bravi* stood at attention during the execution. At their head was Desiri, in his splendid suit of Milanese armor, gilded, exquisite, engraved with swirling arabesques, standing erect in his military finery, unconcerned about the fate of the charlatan.

The corpse of Professor Bartoli was suspended from an open window of a tower of the palace. His stylish curled mustache was coated with blood beneath the ugly stump that had been his nose; his magnificent robe of black silk was soiled and ripped; his darting eyes were forever closed. It was a clear warning to people of the community: *Beware the Pepolis!*

Flaminio and Lorenzo agreed that the scoundrel had received justice. Gasparo was not so certain.

"Father," he asked, "why should they hang this man? His sole crime was in attempting to fashion a new nose for an unfortunate beggar who looked like a monster."

"He would not honor the will of God," said Giovanni Andrea Tagliacozzi, the pious weaver of silks and satins. "The beggar was afflicted with the French disease as punishment for his sinful ways. The charlatan was a sorcerer in league with the Devil. He would not abide by the judgment of God."

"But the beggar looked so miserable," said Gasparo, "and his nose was so ugly. Everybody laughed at him, and Lorenzo called him names. Even Flaminio made jokes. And, Father, suppose Professor Bartoli *had* given him a new nose?"

"It would still have constituted an act of insubordination to the will of God."

Is this so? the boy asked himself, alone in his room. If the charlatan had been an honest man, a surgeon of excellence, utilizing his skills to assist people, could this be wrong in the eyes of God? Had not Saint Cosmas and Saint Damian healed the deformed and the crippled? Was this improper? Were they lacking in faith? Or could his father be wrong?

This thought disturbed him. No, Giovanni Andrea could *not* be mistaken. On little things, perhaps, but not on so crucial an issue. His

father was so famed a craftsman that even Michelangelo had purchased linens from his shop; with shame, he recalled how he and
Flaminio and Lorenzo had sniped at the old man from the tower.

But it had been Lorenzo who had struck him, he recalled, and the
thought was sufficiently comforting to carry him off into sleep.

Chapter 2

Six years passed and Gasparo found a gulf widening between himself and his childhood companions Flaminio Vulpi and Lorenzo Desiri.

Reading was a vital force in post-Renaissance Italy, with literature a platform from which leading thinkers announced their ideas. Judgment Day, Paradise and Hell, and the conviction that immortality in a more perfect world constituted the meaning of life on earth, these religion-oriented issues absorbed the minds of people. Is the soul immortal or corruptible? Philosophers and theologians debated this heatedly.

The adolescents read hungrily, their eyes feasting on a banquet of concepts, as three totally different personalities were shaping. Seldom would the boys study the same books; if they did, their reactions were at odds. Gasparo, long antagonized by Lorenzo's arrogance, was now irritated by qualities in Flaminio that he could not comprehend.

Young Vulpi loathed his father's medical books—and, indeed, he detested everything about his father. Dr. Vulpi, depressed by his lifetime of compromise and surrender, appalled by the inhuman acts Abizio Pepoli had compelled him to perform, was turning inward. He was horrified by life and hated himself for his cowardice. Where were his dreams? Gone, gone forever, and he could find no way to satisfy the hell of his outraged conscience. There was no happy laughter in the somber, dispirited Vulpi home. The widowed head of the family was helpless to brighten the atmosphere for his son. As a doctor, Vulpi was respected by many, but he could not erase from his memory the terrible deeds Pepoli had forced upon him. He considered himself a failure as a human being.

Flaminio was taller than his father, a young man whose classic features were marred by a habitual expression of petulance hovering around his lips. "Always," he would scold the doctor, "you are fatigued. Why is this?"

"I do not know, my son."

"An abomination. Can you never act as the fathers of Gasparo and Lorenzo do? As if you *were* alive?"

These accusations would distress Dr. Vulpi. Silently, he would withdraw, resenting his son for not appreciating his sacrifices. Why had his wife died, leaving him as mother and father to this boy since infancy? For long periods Flaminio and the doctor did not speak to each other.

A brilliant, articulate student, Flaminio focused his energies on religion. He became convinced of the existence of God, of His beneficent nature and lordly attributes, of the creation of the Promised Land; he believed in Paradise, Hell, angels, and devils. Faith in the immortality of man relieved his unhappiness, for, feeling betrayed by his father and fearing the looming responsibilities of adulthood, he was frequently obsessed by visions of an early death.

Young Vulpi worshiped the writings of Thomas Aquinas. A former Dominican friar, Aquinas was a skilled logician who had brought the teachings of Aristotle into harmony with the Christian religion in books constituting the theological ramparts of the Middle Ages.

The philosopher had attempted to answer the objections of non-Christians by distinguishing between reason and faith. Both, claimed Aquinas, were concerned with the same thing—but in different ways.

Strolling with Gasparo through narrow cobblestone streets, dodging the bantering students and soldiers on horseback, side-stepping ragged beggars sleeping under the archways, Flaminio would enunciate the views of Thomas Aquinas.

"Do you not see that reason begins with the senses and then on to a knowledge of the unity, the goodness, and the will of God? Dependent on revelation and authority, faith acknowledges God as a completely spiritual Being, one with a trinity of persons. These approaches may be different but they are not contradictory. Can you not understand this, Gasparo? Faith is more basic because it allows man a knowledge he could not otherwise possess; therefore, faith transcends reason. But here is the main point, my friend; reason and faith come from one source embodying all truth—God, the absolute Ruler of the Universe—and are *not* contradictory. Do you not agree with me?"

Gasparo did not know. "Truth," he said. "What is the truth, Flaminio?"

"Surely you believe in God?"

"Of course," said Gasparo.

Every year a group of renowned university professors would assemble at the Vulpi residence. They traveled from the great cities of Florence and Rome and Milan, and one celebrated scholar made the dangerous journey from Madrid. Dr. Vulpi would be a different person, bustling about to greet his old friends, refilling their wineglasses, stocking his table with fine meats and cheeses and breads and fruits.

His son would not share in the festive spirit. Critically, he would listen to the learned men discourse on dissection of human corpses. Sacrilege. Did they not believe in the resurrection of the human body after death? Was it possible that they failed to understand the necessity of human beings arriving at Heaven whole? How could they live with their consciences and advocate such a practice toward members of their own species?

They will be punished, Flaminio comforted himself. *They will suffer in the Hereafter. My father, too. Yes, he will not escape punishment for his blasphemy against the will of God.*

He realized that Dr. Vulpi expected him to follow his example and attend medical school. *He is a fool,* thought Flaminio. *I feel my vocation. I shall become a priest. At the proper time, I will inform my father.* He suffered from headache, feeling faint and a trifle nauseous. No matter; he would tell his father his decision.

Fantasizing, Flaminio would identify with the religious zealot Savonarola, whose father had also been a doctor, and who, destined for the medical profession, had rebelled, becoming a Church reformer. As a boy, Savonarola, too, had been fascinated by the teachings of Aquinas. Repelled by the vulgarity of court life, disheartened by an unhappy love affair, he had decided to adopt a religious vocation, entering the monastery of St. Dominic in the City of Bologna. His novitiate was marked by the fervor of his humility and the fire of his visions.

Flaminio would see himself as Savonarola. He, too, would hear supernatural voices proclaiming mercy for the faithful and vengeance for the guilty. He, too, would hear thunderous cries announcing that the wrath of God would strike down blasphemers.

Lying on his bed, head on his pillow, suddenly frightened and perspiring, he would close his eyes and picture the day of reckoning for the guilty. The sky would darken, the lightning would flash down, showering white fire on the sinners below, as the thunder boomed, crackling drumbeats announcing the purifying anger of Our Lord.

Young Vulpi envied those privileged to have heard the magnetic voice of Savonarola, denouncing the sins of the common people, the impurity of the clergy, the unscrupulousness of the nobility, pledging that the wrath of God would visit itself upon all evildoers. In Florence, the monastic avenger had declared war on pomp and vanity, forcing citizens to observe the ascetic regimen of the cloister.

Flaminio vowed to purify the sinful Bolognese. He would order the destruction of ceremonial gowns and masks and robes, and all the carnival finery of the decadent nobility. He would insist on burning indecent books and pictures and eliminating filthy songs. The townspeople would lift their faces to God and raise their voices in hymns and psalms to celebrate His glory.

With tears in his eyes, Flaminio had read of Savonarola's persecution by the Borgia Pope Alexander VI. The monk had upbraided the Pope, accusing him of polluting the Vatican with a harem of prostitutes. Retaliating, the Pontiff had ordered the monk's death.

Over and over, the youth read about the execution of Savonarola. It was humiliating, and the account would make him tremble with rage. Two Dominicans had stripped off the monk's sacerdotal robes, hurling them to the ground, crying out, "I separate thee from the Church Militant and from the Church Triumphant." Savonarola had answered, "Militant, yes; triumphant, no; that is beyond thy powers." And the hangman had tied the rope around the martyr's neck while, undaunted, Savonarola gave the sign of the benediction with his right hand. Then the noose was tightened and he was dead. The pile of timber was ignited, the Church reformer's body was burned to a shapeless mass, and the corpse was unceremoniously dumped into the River Arno.

Propping himself up on his elbows, Flaminio listened to Dr. Vulpi padding back and forth in the next room. *My father,* he mused, *is a pathetic fool.* The youth did not know that the doctor mourned the death of his wife and the loss of his self-respect and that he felt guilty toward him. Flaminio's temples throbbed and the taste in his mouth was acid. He would not inform his father of his trouble with headache.

At the age of sixteen, Lorenzo's philosophy was simple; nothing— and nobody—would interfere with his pleasures. He read the Arab scholar Averroës' interpretations of Aristotle, arguing against immortality of the soul. Lorenzo agreed. He hurled the book to the floor and lay back in bed, flexing his muscles. *I will enjoy life,* he promised himself, *assuredly.*

One day he walked with Gasparo and Flaminio. "Why should one worry about the morrow? Is not Judgment Day an illusion?"

"You blaspheme," said Flaminio, tight-lipped. "You cannot mean this."

"Paradise," answered Lorenzo, "is a product of the imagination, like Hell. Who has seen Hell?"

"You must retract your statement or face the wrath of Our Lord."

"You are a fool and a coward, Flaminio. You fear to live so you dream up illusions. But I do not fear. I will seek power and win the hearts of beautiful women. I will dedicate my life to enjoyment. Is this not proper, Gasparo?"

"How can one be certain? But should one not attempt to make existence more palatable? Open your eyes, my friends; can you fail to see the human suffering?"

"Who concerns himself with me?" responded Lorenzo Desiri. "I must look out for myself. Ah, yes, my friends, with the blessings of the stars, I will win."

The three youths continued their stroll in the parish of San Giacomo de' Carbonesi, not far from the Archiginnasio. They arrived at a tavern and Desiri winked.

"Talk about Heaven and Hell, Flaminio—this is the establishment of Signora Rinaldi, and many delights abound here."

"I do not imbibe," said young Vulpi testily.

"You do not grasp my meaning, my dear friend. On occasion I take my pleasure in this—tavern."

"It is a brothel—a house of sin. This is your prerogative, Lorenzo, but I warn you that you defy the will of Our Lord and face eternal damnation."

Lorenzo laughed. "Gasparo, will you accompany me?"

Young Tagliacozzi hesitated. "I have not your will power, Flaminio. I must confess that my flesh is weak and I am tempted by sin."

Without a word, Flaminio stomped away, and Lorenzo and Gasparo entered the brothel. It was a wild night at Signora Rinaldi's. The youths were entertained by two courtesans imported from Paris. Later in the evening, they changed partners, and then the girls playfully staged an exhibition of homosexual lust that inflamed Lorenzo to new heights of sexual frenzy. Gasparo, however, was satiated and succumbed to sleep.

Flaminio, returning home, proceeded to his room and, fuming with impotence, threw himself upon his bed. "They will burn in Hell," he stormed, but he was almost weeping in his frustration.

Finally, against his will, he thrust his hand under his clothes. His penis responded to his touch; fondling his erect organ, he hated himself and his Devil's tool, but then—he imagined that God understood his need and sanctified it. After his orgasm he napped, but fitfully, and sullenness clouded the contours of his face.

Lorenzo's favorite author was Pietro Aretino; since his works were subject to ecclesiastical interdiction, he read them in secret. He also admired Benvenuto Cellini, the sculptor; Niccolò Machiavelli, the statesman-philosopher; and Cesare Borgia, the soldier. They shared a contempt for the law and an absolute lack of conscience. Idealizing the use of force, they symbolized a driving, ruthless egotism that suited Lorenzo's personality. He, too, was adventurous and would live by *his* rules—like his father, Luigi Rimini Desiri, captain of Abizio Pepoli's *bravi*. No one dared boss his father; even the belligerent Pepoli respected him.

Why study Latin and Greek? Lorenzo would ask himself. *Aretino ridiculed this, and why not? Let Flaminio and other fools study these useless languages.*

Instead, Lorenzo indulged his sexual appetites at Signora Rinaldi's, in willing imitation of his idol Aretino, famed for his sensual capacities.

Lorenzo's conceit was as gross as was his courage. Neither Gasparo nor Flaminio could vanquish him in tests of physical strength and no peer could subdue him. He loved to brag about his physical superiority and about the incomparable strength of his father.

With admiration, he perused a letter written by Aretino:

> I am now in Mantua with the Marquis and am held by him in so high favor that he leaves off sleeping and eating to converse with me and says he has no other pleasure in life. It was at Bologna that they began to make me presents. The Bishop of Pisa had a robe of black satin embroidered with gold cut for me; nothing could be handsomer. So I came like a prince to Mantua.

Aretino was on cordial terms with princes and other leading figures in Italy. A bosom companion was Giovanni de' Medici, a general of the Renaissance period. They had been rollicking companions on the battlefields and in brothels. In 1526 the general died in battle at Mantua; he breathed his last in Aretino's arms.

The most formidable weapon of Aretino was not the sword, but the pen. Was he the first to realize the power of the printed word? Perhaps. His verses were venomous, when he wished, and admiring, when this was profitable. Dreading his slashing attacks, the nobility would seek out his purposeful praise.

From every corner of Europe, people journeyed to visit him, bringing gifts and paying homage—to avoid slander or to invite praise. Princes, scholars, and artists flocked to him; one admirer was the brilliant Titian. The most gorgeous Venetian prostitutes arrived, gowned, perfumed, faces mascaraed and rouged, dyed hair piled high. In his home he maintained a harem for his pleasure and that of his friends—never was there a shortage of females. Aretino was father to a number of illegitimate daughters whom he dowered, and his ego was as inflated as were his sexual desires.

Identifying, his imagination burning with lust for power, Lorenzo digested the words of Aretino:

> I swear to you by the wings of Pegasus that, much as may have reached your ears, you have not heard one half the hymn of my celebrity. Medals are coined in my honor, medals of gold, of silver, of brass, of lead, of stucco. My features are carried along the fronts of palaces. My portrait is stamped on comb-cases, engraved on mirror handles, printed on majolica. I am a second Alexander, Caesar, Scipio. Nay more, I tell you that some kinds of glasses they make at Murano are called Aretines. Aretine is the name given to a breed of cobs, after one Pope Clement sent me, and I gave to Duke Frederick. They have christened the little canal that runs beside my house upon the Canalozzo, Rio Aretino. And, to make the pendants burst with rage, besides talking of the Aretine style, three wenches of my household, who have left me and become ladies, will have themselves known only as the Aretines.

Francis I and Charles V were his patrons; so were other princes. Pope Julius III made him a Knight of St. Peter with a pension. King Henry VIII sent three hundred crowns for a dedicatory epistle.

Lorenzo was fascinated by Aretino's life—adventurous, bold, extravagant. He would appraise an engraved portrait of his mentor, a portrait alongside a wolf whose grinning snarl and narrowed eyes mirrored the expression on Aretino's face. There he was as a youth, arrogant, hot-blooded, wearing a black satin mantle embroidered with gold cut for him by order of the Bishop of Pisa, mounted on a stalwart white charger, preparing, no doubt, to flirt with a luscious prostitute.

To Lorenzo, history was one-dimensional. Cesare Borgia, Machiavelli, Cellini, Aretino—nothing stood in their way, for they were victors. Aretino was a liar and a bully; he was debauched and corrupt—and he lived like a prince.

Why worry about the Hereafter? reflected Desiri. *Flaminio talks about it incessantly, but is he not a weak coward? The Church is corrupt. And what is the value of moral principles? Or the worry of a conscience? I will learn from Aretino and taste my pleasure. I cannot write but I am courageous and will become a great soldier. The sword will be my pen.*

What has happened to Flaminio? Gasparo asked himself. Vulpi had been his inseparable childhood companion; they had shared each other's secrets. Gasparo was accustomed to Lorenzo's arrogance and it did not bother him, but Flaminio, sensitive and loyal as a child, had changed. He had not expanded with adolescence, shrinking, instead, into a hard shell of bitterness. Gasparo found conversation with him difficult. Once he had confided to Vulpi his inner turmoil over emerging sexual feelings. His old friend had advised renunciation and praying to God for deliverance. Their relations further deteriorated after Flaminio knew that he had visited the brothel of Signora Rinaldi with Lorenzo.

Young Tagliacozzi, lean, of average height, with curious brown eyes, was an amalgam of his mother's passive obedience and his father's aggressive self-righteousness. Still, one thing about Isabetta: she could be pushed only so far. Gasparo, too. Like his mother, he tended to be passive but with a fierce sense of justice, and he would not submit to bullying.

Into his studies he poured the aggressive drive of his father in pursuit of the ethical aims of his mother. Seeking truth and meaning and justice and goodness, he read voraciously; his range was wider than that of the other boys. Their reading reflected the rigid channels of their solidifying personalities. But Gasparo was in conflict. He saw two sides to every question.

Sometimes he saw no answers at all, merely additional questions.

He had completed his study of dialectics, digesting Thomas Aquinas and Aristotle, plus Machiavelli and Aretino. In addition, he had perused the writings of Cicero, Seneca, and the Greek philosopher Plato. Most impressive were the writings of Pietro Pomponazzi, a man of virtuous conduct, who was a forerunner of modern scientific thinking. He preferred Pomponazzi's interpretation of Aristotle to those of Aquinas and Averroës. Pomponazzi waged a brave war against superstition and ecclesiastical despotism, positing that the soul was perishable, as mortal as the human flesh, and that Eternity and the Hereafter did not exist. Virtue, he argued, was man's proper goal. "Virtue is its own reward as vice is its own punishment."

With Aquinas, Pomponazzi agreed that faith and reason were two aspects of human beings that did not necessarily corrupt each other. Even if antagonistic, they could coexist in the same individual. Aquinas was convinced that faith was more basic than reason; Pomponazzi did not agree. As a philosopher, he could not believe in the immortality of the soul; as a Christian, he could accept it. Aiming at moderation, he was willing to compromise, but he could not place credence in the multitude's avowal of demons, miracles, angels, and devils; nevertheless, as a Christian of good will, he could grant them token recognition.

Increasingly, Gasparo found himself interested in the twin conflicting forces of the age: scientific thinking as opposed to miracles; superstition as opposed to realistic physical study. He could not repose faith in ideas for which he could find no foundation in the world of hard facts. That his father believed and he could not pained him for he loved his father. Still, he would control his own life and think his own thoughts. This was not an easy position; inside him, his mother's desire to please clashed with his father's strident assertiveness.

Someday, reflected Gasparo, *I will do good. I will fashion new faces, giving hope to the deformed.*

In sixteenth-century Italy, independent thinkers were attacking ecclesiastical authority, but the Church was a relentless foe and those whose opinions ran counter to its teachings endangered their lives. Gasparo's classmates would whisper of men tortured, their tongues cut out to silence them, and then killed.

Gasparo would never forget the hideous death of Michael Servetus.

Giovanni Andrea had taken him along on a business trip—to Florence, Mantua, Verona, Milan, and across the Alps to Switzerland. High adventure for the youth, then ten years old. With the third passenger, a teenager named Galileo, Gasparo for the first time gazed at the magnificent City of Florence, marveling at the splendor of Brunelleschi's dome rising over the skyline near the spire-topped tower of the Palazzo Vecchio.

Shortly, Galileo left for his native Pisa. He never returned to Bologna but, decades later, his son, the astronomer, fleeing Jesuit persecution, came in his place.

Giovanni Andrea, accompanied by his son, transacted business at the palace of the Medicis, delivering merchandise for Cosimo I. "Someday you will be a weaver of fine silks and satins," the elder Tagliacozzi told his son, "and noblemen will be your customers."

With fresh horses for the carriage, the pair departed for Mantua, haven of the banished Romeo, where the father sold his wares to the distinguished house of Gonzaga. Then Verona, and Milan, with consignments for the Sforzas. Finally, across the majestic Alps to Switzerland; in the Protestant City of Geneva the trial of Michael Servetus was being concluded.

As a medical student, Servetus, with his ally Vesalius, had performed dissections on corpses of criminals hanged on the scaffold. The anatomical dissections had uncovered flagrant errors in current medical thinking, and Servetus had contradicted the teachings of Galen.

For these researches, and for a manuscript denying the Trinity of God, the physician had incurred the wrath of the powerful John Calvin, Protestant leader, and of the Roman Church as well. Ironic, because Servetus had joined Calvin in rejecting Roman Church doctrine, choosing Protestantism; now he was persecuted by his own sect.

In the public square of the City of Geneva, Gasparo viewed the spectacle. A platoon of Swiss soldiers ringed the square, wearing breastplates and helmets, armed with halberds. Nearby, the tribunal was seated in chairs on the hotel porch.

Two soldiers on horseback blew lustily on trumpets, silencing the crowd, as a court official read from parchment. The condemnations seemed endless, with fifteen accusations of heresy and blasphemy against the faith.

The verdict of the judges: "These and other causes moving us, desiring to purge the Church of God of such infection and to cut off from it so rotten a member, we, sitting as a judicial tribunal in the seat of our ancestors, in the name of the Father, Son, and Holy Ghost . . . we condemn thee, Michael Servetus, to be bound and taken to Champel and then, being fastened to a stake, to be burned along with thy books, printed as well as written by thy hand, until thy body be reduced to ashes."

Then the march to the hill of execution. In front, officers of the guard, mounted on white stallions, armed with golden daggers. Then a prominent official with a cordon of guards and the weary prisoner, followed by the crowd screaming obscenities, hurling stones, threatening to overpower the guards and murder the condemned man.

"Renounce your heretical views," bellowed the official. "Confess."

"I have *nothing* to confess," responded Servetus. "God have mercy on you, for you know not what you do."

At the hill of execution, the prisoner hurled himself to the ground. "God have mercy on my soul," he cried out. "I love thee, Jesus Christ."

The executioner yanked him to his feet, leading him to a pile of greenish faggots alongside the stake. He was placed against a block, feet brushing the earth, and, fastening an iron chain around his waist and a thick rope about his neck, the guards tied him to the stake. To his side they tied copies of his book, so that the fire would destroy human body and doctrine together, reducing both to ashes.

A wreath of straw and green twigs covered with brimstone was placed around his head. The executioner applied the torch to the green faggots, and the brimstone was aflame.

Servetus screamed in agony as the fire whipped through him; then, mercifully, he lost consciousness. Crackling, sizzling, writhing, his corpse was licked by the terrible flames. The body was gruesomely charred; Servetus might have been a tree trunk after a forest fire.

Gasparo had been shocked by the brutality, but his father defended it. "The man sinned; he defied the Will of Our Lord."

The son questioned his father, for the first time—but said no more. Still, he dreamed of being a surgeon, and someday he would realize his dream.

Gasparo realized that if he became a surgeon he would face persecution; the Church would consider him a sorcerer in league with the Devil. Its officials would not bother to differentiate him from the charlatan Bartoli, no matter the sureness of his skills.

Like Pomponazzi, he felt that he could be a scientist true to reason as well as a Christian true to faith. *If I make the mutilated normal, if I make the ugly beautiful, will I not be fulfilling the wish of Jesus?*

His father was a major obstacle. Sternly religious, Giovanni Andrea would fill with rage when he learned that his only son wished to attend medical school. How would he confront him?

Gasparo was impressed by Pomponazzi, who observed men and the world as they *were*, not as they *should be*. He enjoyed Machiavelli, who studied human nature realistically, not in the rosy glow of the Church's idealism. Machiavelli's prose was admirable—simple, direct, free of flowery ornamentation. But, unlike Lorenzo, he detested Machiavelli as a man who had no conscience and who utilized his talents for evil. With Pomponazzi, he believed in the existence of human goodness, and regarded religion as useful to society only when contributing to development of this goodness. He also agreed with the Greek philosopher Epictetus that giving is a precious sustaining act, and he resolved to develop his surgical skills and give them to the afflicted.

He also liked Castiglione, the counterpart in literature of Pomponazzi in philosophy. Castiglione's *The Courtier* was a fascinating analysis of a gentleman's proper conduct in relation to the needs of society.

As his thinking expanded, Gasparo felt restless and doubted his courage to support his growing identity and the threats that might challenge it. He was lonely, wondering where Flaminio's sweetness had gone, wishing Lorenzo would acquire humility, and fearing the punishing wrath of his father.

Giovanni Andrea, glowing with prosperity, purchased a farmhouse in Roffano, outside the city in the Apennine mountains. One day Gasparo proposed a picnic, inviting Lorenzo and Flaminio and two young ladies, Giulia Carnali and Caledonia Bargillini, as well as the son of Giulia's servant, Scipio, a small black boy whose parents had fled Spain to escape the persecutions sweeping that unhappy land.

They clattered through the narrow streets lined with tight-packed brick structures joined by colonnades, ground to a halt at the city's twelve-gated outer wall, then resumed on signal of the sentry, galloping toward the rich greenery of the countryside. Gasparo anticipated a pleasant day. His mother, Isabetta, had packed a tasty lunch and the weather was sunny and mild; in spite of their disagreements, he felt content to see Lorenzo and Flaminio once more.

He stole a look at Giulia, seated opposite him in the bouncing carriage. She lived two streets away from the Tagliacozzi residence, and he had conversed with her every now and then in a casual vein. She was gracious in a reserved way and, being timid, he had needed to muster up his courage to ask her to the picnic. *Oh, she is beautiful,* thought Gasparo, and his excitement at her physical presence embarrassed him.

Giulia, aware of his feeling, glanced sideways at the trees lining the road and at the Apennines towering in the background. She was wearing an exquisite full-length pale-pink gown and her hair was pinned into an upsweep of auburn tresses. She seemed older than her fifteen years. Her large green eyes were reflective and sedate and mirrored her quiet self-assurance.

Noting the direction of Gasparo's gaze, Flaminio blushed, for, though he found Giulia attractive, he was obsessed with combating his impure desires. "Have you read the passage from Thomas Aquinas that I underlined for you, my dear friend?"

"No, Flaminio, but I will study it on the morrow."

"It is not unreasonable to have faith in matters of the spirit. For the honorable will be rewarded in the Hereafter, and sinners will fall to Hell."

Lorenzo snickered. "Always the Hereafter. I do not concern myself with the Hereafter, Flaminio, I take my pleasure today."

"You are evil and Our Lord will punish you."

"Why do *you* not punish me, Flaminio?" asked Lorenzo, cocking his fist and punching it into his palm. "Do not be afraid." Knowing Caledonia was watching, he puffed out his chest and flexed his muscles. "What delays you, Flaminio?"

"Your insolence will not be tolerated," said young Vulpi. "The Lord will strike you down."

Gasparo's glance was straying to the full lips of Giulia Carnali. His blood warmed on beholding her firm young breasts swelling against the pink silk of her gown. He felt almost dizzy with the intensity of his desire and, fearing she would be affronted, averted his eyes. He scanned the sky, the sun was still shining. They would arrive shortly at the farmhouse.

But first there was a furious fight between Flaminio and Gasparo, and it symbolically represented a turning point in the life of young Tagliacozzi.

It centered around Scipio, who was not only black, but small for his age and afflicted with harelip. He looked as if someone had taken brace and bit and bored a hole in the middle of his face. This snout-like formation made him resemble a dog, his front teeth visible through the hole. Growing up in a tiny village in Spain, Scipio was ridiculed by playmates, who made jokes at his expense, calling him "Dogface."

He was morbidly shy and flinched when anyone stared at him. Always frightened, he hated to speak because when he stuttered the other children would laugh. He would remain silent, developing the habit of covering his mouth with his hand.

Before the birth of Scipio Africanus Borzani, his mother and father were very happy, and awaited his birth with rapture. If he were a boy, they would name him after the eminent Roman Scipio African-us. And so they did—but his harelip shocked them.

Exhausted from childbirth, the mother looked at Scipio and began to cry, insane with despair. Her son would be more fortunate dead than looking like a monstrous dog. But Scipio suckled her breast and lived.

The formerly compatible parents bickered constantly. Husband and wife attacked and counterattacked like armies on the fields of battle, accusing each other of bad blood. Drunk, the husband stormed into his wife's bedroom one night screaming incoherently that he was aware of her infidelity—was this not the explanation for Scipio?—and then began punching and kicking her.

Succeeding months were unbearable. The husband, obsessed with his wife's unfaithfulness, planned to poison her. Once he had loved her passionately; now she enraged him and he commenced to hate himself too.

A Franciscan friar came to the rescue, convincing the husband that his suspicions were unfounded. "It is the will of God," said the friar of Scipio's deformity. If they raised him properly and prepared him for his lifework, Scipio would be like all good Christians in the next world.

Amazingly, the child now cemented the abrasive relations of husband and wife. They were determined to make him happy, and the harelip that had nearly destroyed their love ended up intensifying it.

Fleeing the Terror in Spain, the family journeyed to Bologna and were employed as servants by Giulia's family. But wary parents would not allow their children to play with Scipio, whispering that he had been besieged by the Evil Eye while in his mother's womb. Some said the boy had syphilis, and others claimed his mother was bewitched.

Self-conscious, undersized for his age, Scipio was lonely, but eventually, realizing that he was harmless beneath his frightened defensiveness, the neighborhood parents permitted their offspring to associate with him.

Still, the troubles of Scipio were far from over. As in Spain, the lad had to endure the other children's jokes about his deformity.

"He resembles a homely dog."

"No, he is a rabbit."

"My mother says he was scared by a lame horse."

"Not a horse, stupid, a witch. Is it not true that the forces of evil have possessed him?"

Said Filipe, Caledonia Bargillini's brother, "Your name is Scipio Africanus? Africanus was a great man and handsome—nothing like you. Open your mouth so we may observe whether you have a hole in there too."

Infuriated, Scipio rushed at Filipe yelling "I will make a hole in *your* lip" and struck him on the mouth. Cuffing each other fiercely, the youths wrestled to the ground. Finally, dirty, bleeding, they separated and went home crying. Filipe received no sympathy from his sister Caledonia, who liked the black boy.

In time, the other children accepted Scipio, who needed their friendship and tried to please them. Gasparo, three years older, protected him from bullies, and reflected on how someday he would give him a normal lip. Lorenzo tolerated him; the deformed lad was no threat.

But Flaminio Vulpi loathed Scipio. *Is not the boy owned by the Devil,* he asked, *punished for the sins of his ancestors?* One had been a cruel witch, concocting poisonous potions over a cauldron in the inky night blackness, as the winds shrieked their anger and the thunder roared, propelling rain from the sky.

He could not have been deformed, reasoned Flaminio, if his ancestors had been devout Christians. There must have been a harlot in his family, a diseased creature making hideous charms of hair, skull, ribs, teeth, dead men's eyes, and navels of little children. This witch had doubtless enchanted children and ruined cattle and crops with her evil incantations. Was she one of the forty-one witches burned by the Dominicans at Como after the Bull of Innocent VIII in 1484? *How I hate Scipio and his sinful lip,* mused Flaminio. He was sitting next to the black youth in the carriage, but he moved as far away as he could manage without attracting attention.

The carriage was rumbling over the dusty country road, with Lorenzo bellowing a ribald song and Caledonia giggling. Then a wheel of the speeding vehicle passed over a rock, causing the carriage to swerve and throwing Scipio against Flaminio. Their faces touched briefly, cheek to cheek, and Vulpi, enraged, punched the black youth on the temple. "How dare you come near me, you creature of the Devil!" he shouted, as Scipio tried manfully to hold back the tears.

Gasparo had been fretting about how to impress Giulia. His desire had continued to mount; he could no longer look in her direction. While Lorenzo, singing and bantering, had been exhibiting himself to Caledonia like a strutting peacock, Gasparo and Giulia had conversed little. How could he overcome his shyness and win her admiration?

Then Flaminio lashed out at Scipio, and without thinking, young Tagliacozzi pounced on his childhood chum and pummeled him in the face. It was a wild scene, with the girls screaming and Scipio crying; the coachman reined in the horses, Lorenzo opened the door, and the pair, scratching at each other, tumbled onto the dirt road. Gasparo hammered Flaminio on the nose, which started bleeding, and Flaminio fiercely clouted Gasparo in the eye. Seizing each other, they rolled over and over on the dusty ground, Vulpi digging his teeth into Gasparo's arm, the latter yelling in pain and yanking Flaminio's hair, until Lorenzo pulled them apart.

Wiping his bleeding nose, Flaminio shrieked, "Our Lord will punish you for this."

"You know very well that you started this fracas," said Gasparo. "What induced you to strike him? He is smaller than you and younger."

"He is a heretic and descends from a family of sinners. Possessed by the Devil, his deformity dooms him to suffer for their sins."

"Nonsense."

"Witches and sorcerers contaminate his family. Demons inhabit his bloodstream. A demon escaped from his mouth grasping a lance and cut his lips with the lance."

"Flaminio, you are a fanatic."

"You pretend to possess virtue, Gasparo, but I am aware of your playing dice and cards with Lorenzo, telling each other filthy jokes and visiting brothels. Our Lord will punish you for your sins."

"I do not sin," said Lorenzo. "I take my pleasure. I do not consider this sin."

"You read the forbidden books of Aretino and your sins are countless. Repent, Lorenzo, or you will go to Hell."

"Aretino is a great man. Can I help it if fools like you wish to undermine his writings?"

"When I am a Dominican friar like Savonarola, I shall wipe out heresy and devote my life to the glory of God. I will rise to Heaven. But you, Gasparo, are doomed with Lorenzo to Hell."

"I believe in God," said Gasparo.

"You incur His wrath, cramming your head with blasphemous writings. You study Pomponazzi and parrot his evil teachings. Why do you not read the saintly Thomas Aquinas and appreciate the beauty of his thinking? But no, you choose to become a barber surgeon, dissect corpses, and bring on the wrath of God."

"I have faith in Our Lord, and He would wish me to assist the suffering and the afflicted like Saint Cosmas and Saint Damian."

"You will kill them—like Bartoli."

"I will assist them," said Gasparo, his left eye discolored and half shut, glaring at Flaminio. "But I warn you, my dear fellow, do not strike Scipio again or I will kill you."

Clambering back into the carriage, he seated himself next to Giulia. She nestled against him and he was astonished to note the admiration shining from her eyes.

"You are courageous," she said softly, "and a young man of inestimable character. I feel respect for you—and I do like you."

The Tagliacozzi household was stormy. "You want to become a barber surgeon?" yelled Giovanni Andrea.

"It was my duty to inform you of my intentions," responded his son.

"You want to become a barber surgeon—like Bartoli?"

"No, not like Bartoli, Father. I wish to become a skilled surgeon. I will attend the university and learn the art of giving people new faces. Is this not a worthy ambition?"

The elder Tagliacozzi's face blazed with anger. "My son will not dissect bodies. It is sinful and unchristian."

Gasparo marveled at his calm; for the first time he did not fear the rage of his father. "It is good work," he said simply. "I am proud of my desire."

"You dare defy me? Where is the respect due your father? Have I not slaved so that you might receive a fitting education? Have I not persevered so that you might own your business?"

"Yes, Father, and I do revere you for your sense of responsibility. But my lifework, is this not my decision?"

"You violate the sacred teachings of the Church, and God will not tolerate your irreverence."

"The Church should approve of my easing human suffering."

"You will obey my command. Over my dead body will you become a barber surgeon."

That night Giovanni Andrea was unable to sleep. Sitting up in bed, he marveled that Isabetta was breathing deeply. *I addressed my dear son rudely,* he reproached himself. *I must ask his forgiveness. But I cannot, for he has broken my heart. How can I sanction his ignoring my teachings and defying the will of Our Lord? How may I forgive this?* Toward morning, a happier thought—*Perhaps he will change his mind*—and he drifted off to sleep.

Gasparo, too, was sad, for he loved his father. Should he ask Giovanni Andrea for forgiveness or should he bow before his will? He would do neither. Approaching manhood, he recognized that the responsibility for the decision was his.

Still, he felt relieved, for at last he had confronted his father directly, casting aside all evasions. A new strength surged through his body, for he had met *the* challenge. Never would he turn back from his objectives, and no one could repulse him—he was, indeed, a man.

An inspiring vision filled his heart, lovely, enchanting, firing every nerve end of his body. Giulia. He throbbed with a desire overshadowing any feeling he had ever experienced. It was more than he could bear; she was virtually a stranger, yet, awed, hypnotized, he realized that he adored her.

Chapter 3

Flaminio's bleak voyage away from life had accelerated. His mother-less home was no comfort, lacking both the soft touch of a woman and the hearty vigor of an unvanquished male—as well as the companionship of a sibling. Dr. Vulpi, more than ever agitated by an overpowering sense of failure, would pace the floor till almost dawn before succumbing to a tense uneasy sleep. He and his son were annoyed at the sight of each other.

Moreover, the passing months had accentuated the clash in their personalities; the youth had become addicted to an endless series of cleanliness rituals, and since his father was increasingly careless and absent-minded in his habits, their infrequent exchanges were tense and disagreeable.

Flaminio began spending huge periods of time in the Church of St. Dominic, studying its paintings, reading and rereading the works of Thomas Aquinas, meditating in the solitude of its chapels and tombs. His friendship with Gasparo had cooled and he and Lorenzo detested each other; in compensation, he turned to adoration of the memory of St. Dominic, the saint of medieval times, who had walked the cobblestone streets of Bologna as he now walked them—alone, deprived, contemplative.

Of noble Spanish lineage, St. Dominic had from an early age determined to enter the Church. Flaminio believed in the story of how, shortly before the saint's birth, his mother dreamed that her child would appear in the shape of a dog, a lighted torch clenched in its teeth, fleeing from her to set the world on fire. Perplexed as to its meaning, the expectant mother would pray at the tomb of an abbot at the monastery of Silo Domenico near Calaroga; receiving comfort there, she called her son Dominico. Did her dream refer to the Dominican Order? The dog was black and white, and the Dominican friars wore white robes and black hoods; furthermore, the name Dominicani was a play on the words *"Domini Canes"* (hounds of the Lord).

St. Dominic founded an order that emphasized preaching, waging a relentless war against heretics. Eighteen years old now, Flaminio decided he would join this order and preach the gospel of God, exterminating heretics and consigning evil books to the fire. *Gasparo must be forced to repent,* mused Vulpi. *His desire to restore mutilated faces is inspired by the Devil. If God ordained such mutilation, facial features should remain as prescribed. My old friend conspires against the will of God.*

He continued to mull over the sweetness of his revenge against his former companion. When he was a Dominican friar, he would preach against the dissection of dead bodies and resist the restoration of facial deformities. If Gasparo insisted on performing surgery, he would summon him before the Inquisition on charges of heresy. *At his trial I will prove that he is a practitioner of witchcraft, in league with the Devil,* exulted Flaminio. *Tortured for his crimes, his hands will be chopped off so that never again will he use them to defy Our Lord. He will be tied to the stake and burned alive for his sins.* But, at this last, young Vulpi felt contrite. Memories of their shared childhood adventures surged into his mind. They were intolerable, so he pushed them away and returned to his religious concerns.

A painting on the church wall portrayed Hell: hairy devils with tails and horns, demons with long, pointed ears, bodies encircled with snakes, were torturing the damned with tridents.

For hours, Flaminio would sit in one of the chapels and meditate before the sarcophagus containing the mortal remains of St. Dominic. The panels of this beautiful shrine had been completed by Nicola Pisano in 1267. The first showed the saint raising to life the youthful Napoleon Orsini, killed by a fall from his horse, restoring him to his mother. The second depicted the "trial by fire," with heretical books consumed by flames while those of the saint remain unharmed. Another panel illustrated the miracle of St. Dominic, angels bringing bread to the starving brotherhood.

I must reform Lorenzo, too, Flaminio reminded himself. *He must discontinue his gambling and keep away from brothels or he will burn. Bologna will be purified. Those who follow our precepts will be treated with kindness; other cities will see our nobility and join our crusade against evil.*

Head bowed in what he considered humility, he strolled through the church. In another chapel was a monument to the renowned Taddeo Pepoli; on the altar was the Archangel Michael surrounded by angels and by pictures of the Blessed Virgin and St. Dominic; on the left, the tomb of Taddeo Pepoli, decorated with an armorial black-and-white chessboard insignia. An adjoining chapel boasted exquisite inlaid work depicting stories of the New and Old Testaments, a labor said to have consumed twelve years of the saint's life.

Flaminio looked at it adoringly, but his thoughts were of when he would be a powerful cleric. *All women appearing in public immodestly dressed will be flogged,* he fantasized, *and prostitutes will be rounded up and expelled from our city to the accompaniment of trumpets. I will close taverns, suppress racing, forbid dancing, and outlaw gambling. All shops except that of the apothecary will be closed on Sundays and on saints' days.*

But something was wrong. The image of his inconsolable father interrupted his pleasant reveries. His temples started throbbing, a feeling of nausea invaded him and Flaminio worried about whether, after all, he would take sick and die young, unfulfilled. And another image, equally unwelcome, infiltrated into his mind: Giulia Carnali, in the carriage, gazing admiringly at Gasparo, sitting close to him. How he hated Giulia. She, too, must suffer.

It was in the same year that young Tagliacozzi faced the most dreadful ordeal of his brief life.

One morning, early, Giovanni Andrea moved about in his garden at the rear of the house. From his bedroom window, Gasparo watched as his father plucked the branch of a bush from the earth, watered it, and transplanted it into the earth to grow again and flourish. He then removed a branch from a big tree and transplanted it elsewhere. Estranged from his son, he seemed to gather comfort from his garden. *I am content,* thought Gasparo, *that he finds peace in his misery. But someday he will understand that what I wish is good, and once again he will be joyous.*

It was not to be. A few hours later, his father departed in a carriage for the Florence of the Medicis to sell his merchandise.

Isabetta, sobbing, waved good-bye after embracing her husband, but Gasparo's sister, Cassandra, winked at her father as if this was silly and they shared a little joke. Had not Giovanni Andrea always returned safely from his journeys?

He did return—but the following morning, prematurely. It was a terrifying sight: the horses skittering in panic; the bundles of satins and silks and damasks ripped open and emptied; on the carriage floor, crumpled like a shapeless mass of fabric, the lifeless body of Giovanni Andrea Tagliacozzi, throat slit, dried blood caking his chin and coating his shirt front, eyes sealed forever. Sprawled on the front seat was the dead coachman, stabbed in the chest. Brigands had swooped down from the Apennines to plunder and kill.

Horrified, unbelieving, Gasparo tried to calm Isabetta, who was sobbing hysterically. He cradled her in his arms as if she were a small child, but she kept moaning and rocking and finally burst away to fling herself near her husband and embrace his bloodstained body.

Gasparo ran up to his room, but it was too confining, like a prison, so he retraced his steps and seated himself in the garden. Never had he felt so isolated; his mother and sister were inside the house yet he felt alone, cut off, an unbridgeable chasm separating him from them. He looked around the garden encircled by the white fence, and suddenly the fence took on a new meaning, for it seemed to separate him from the rest of the world and curtail his movement. He remembered climbing the tower with Flaminio and Lorenzo and wondering about the vast universe beyond the Apennines. And now in his despair, his world had constricted; it was tiny, lonely, limited to the garden and to the white fence, and he felt separated from the world of his father, from the world of his university, from the world of his mourning mother and sister, and from the world inside himself. His fright mounted, and his feelings terrified him, for he felt empty and uncertain, stampeded into a retreat that threatened to lead to disaster. He was too young to know how to cope with his overwhelming grief and was so besieged by despair and guilt that he feared he would never recover. He felt helpless. The white fence around the garden continued to alarm him. Was this fence growing, enlarging into the bars of a prison? And was he the prisoner, restricted, denied his freedom? In his agony, he had difficulty breathing. Finally, he stumbled to his feet, re-entered the house, took one last look at his father in the living room now, and started to walk. *It was my fault,* he agonized. *If my father had not been so upset by my stubbornness, he would have been alert and, with his coachman, would have repulsed the robbers. I am an unworthy son, and truly I am responsible for the death of my father.*

Dazed, he plodded on through the narrow streets. At the approach to the public square, the great Fountain of Neptune, to be fed by ninety jets of water, was under construction. The sculptor Gianbologna was working on the gigantic statue, which was to be surrounded by dolphins, sirens, and shields bearing the arms of Pope Pius IV.

Unseeing, Gasparo walked past. *I must bear the guilt,* he tormented himself, *for I was a disobedient son.*

A light rain was falling as he trudged past the Lambertacci Palace. *I will not study medicine,* he vowed. *I will become a weaver.* Magically, his mood lightened. A smile of relief lighted up his father's face and Giovanni Andrea was embracing him—*No.* He was daydreaming. His father was gone forever; his son had betrayed him. Gasparo's eyes welled with tears when he recalled the lifeless heap, once the proud figure of Giovanni Andrea Tagliacozzi. *Am I losing my mind?* he reflected. *Oh, who will render me comfort now?*

Instinctively, he found the answer. Like the horses that, leaderless, had obeyed their instincts and dragged the vehicle to the Tagliacozzi household, Gasparo's feet unerringly carried him to the home of Giulia Carnali. The girl had heard the terrible news and her arms were open to him. She pulled him to her ripe full breasts, for the moment a child to comfort, and he sobbed in her arms while she hummed a lullaby and stroked his hair and kissed his cheeks and reassured him that it was not his fault.

But, later, he reminded himself of the bitterness festering inside his father before his death. *Oh,* he mused, *would that I had brought happiness into his heart in his last hours.*

His room was a cage for the pacing of a tortured animal; he would have escaped its confines, but downstairs Isabetta and Cassandra were still weeping. As with the fence around the garden, he felt a sense of separation—from the world, from himself. So he lay down on his bed and submitted to the brutal images whirling through his brain, kaleidoscopic, abrasive, bolts of lightning: Professor Bartoli hanging from the Pepoli tower; the brave Michael Servetus in flames; his father dead on the carriage floor.

I will attempt to do good in this chaotic world, he promised. *I am so sorry, father, that you did not understand this.*

Gasparo absented himself from his undergraduate courses for many weeks. During this period he translated from Latin into Italian the chronicles of the history of Bologna from the year 104 to the time of writing.*

Depressed, he would take long walks, often with Torquato Tasso, the poet. Tasso's life had been chaotic. His father, condemned as a heretic, had escaped to France when Torquato was a young child. Tasso was then educated by Jesuits, but his father's exile rendered him suspicious of religious teachings. Later, his mother was poisoned.

Still, his poetic gifts were outstanding, and at nineteen he was famous. Monsignor Pier Donato Cesi, appointed by Pope Pius IV to supervise the city's public education, invited him to Bologna.

Sensitive to Gasparo's moods, Tasso at this time was a loyal friend and the youths exchanged views on a wide range of questions.

They would stop at the Fountain of Neptune and watch Gianbologna molding the statue as horse-drawn carriages rattled past and pedestrians strolled by, and students of art would join them in observing the sculptor's technique.

"A masterpiece," proclaimed Tasso. "Someday perhaps I will write a poem to equal this statue in majesty. Does this sound conceited, my friend?"

* This book may be seen today in the library of the University of Bologna.

"Ambitious."

"I would like to capture the First Crusade in epic form. This era fascinates me and—oh, years of research will be required. It will be a formidable undertaking, but this magnificent sculpture—the scope, the sweep—it fortifies my resolve."

"Your ardor reminds me of my deep desire to become a surgeon and help the deformed."

"Your plans, my dear friend, are inspiring. But the Church? Do you not fear the Church? I must confess that if I were you I would live in fear of the Roman Church and the Inquisition and would proceed with caution. Promise me that you will be careful, Gasparo."

"I have no desire for martyrdom, Torquato, but to be a surgeon is my dream. It is the reason for living, a veritable lust—such as I feel for Giulia."

Oddly enough it was Tasso who lacked caution, fleeing to escape prosecution for libel, a charge leveled at him for ridiculing with biting epigrams the literary judgment of Monsignor Cesi and his other teachers. Gasparo was once more alone, another void in his life, coming so soon after the poet had helped him endure the grim days after his father's death.

But the void was filled almost immediately.

"I heard about the death of your father," said Flaminio Vulpi, visiting the Tagliacozzi residence. "I wished you to know that I am very sorry."

"Thank you," said Gasparo, reserved. "It was thoughtful of you to pay your respects."

"I liked your father; he was a devout man. I feel the full weight of your loss."

"I appreciate your call."

"I would have come sooner, but my duties—Gasparo, I must confess that I, too, have suffered a deprivation. I have lost the dearest friend of my childhood. You, Gasparo. I regret our misunderstanding. For fortnights have I loathed the rude memory of our argument and I will do penance to Our Lord for my wickedness on that occasion. I hereby apologize to you, for I realize that I was to blame. Will you once again become my friend?"

Gasparo had listened warily at first but Flaminio's sincerity was obvious. "Gladly," he responded finally. "You, Flaminio, were also the dearest companion of my childhood."

"I was fanatical," said young Vulpi. "On reflection I see this. I have always admired you, Gasparo. Certainly, granted a minimal amount of flexibility, Our Lord must understand that you are really a good Christian."

Chapter 4

And so Gasparo and Flaminio were once again friends. Their relationship was not as when they were children—they had grown too far apart in their philosophies of life—but each attempted to adapt himself to the other. Crushed by the death of his father and saddened by the departure of Torquato, young Tagliacozzi learned to overlook his companion's religious fanaticism. As for Vulpi, he arrested his flight inward, making one final effort to harness the sweet innocence of his early youth and use it in pursuit of adult goals. Troubled, never able to bridge the gap between himself and his father, he would writhe with guilt at his fleshly desires, tormented by the fear that he was in league with the Devil.

After their reconciliation, they planned an outing. On a warm sunny day they set out on horseback for a small lake near the Tagliacozzi farmhouse, in Roffano, with lunch baskets and a bottle of wine, joking as they galloped through the countryside. Flaminio had enjoyed a night of restful sleep and was in a hearty mood. "Do you recall that time—we were ten years old, my dear friend—when we climbed the tower and you hit that poor old man with a pebble?"

"I remember." Gasparo laughed. "But *your* memory does not serve you well, Flaminio. The culprit was Lorenzo."

"Lorenzo, the artist of high sin," gibed Flaminio, with uncharacteristic tolerance. "I do not know why, Gasparo, but it is as if a great weight has been lifted from my shoulders."

"I rejoice in your return to happiness and confess that I, too, feel splendid. I have been seeing Giulia Carnali and shall ask her to marry me."

"Giulia?" said Flaminio, his smile vanishing. "Whatever do you see in her?"

"She is beautiful and adorable."

"Ah yes, the flesh is weak."

"Her eyes are luminous and lovely and her breasts—"

"Your talk is sinful. You mouth obscenities and term this love. In truth, she is silly and trivial, a girl of no substance."

"Let us not engage in disputation. Open the wine, Flaminio, and we shall celebrate the resumption of our friendship in spite of our differences."

The afternoon commenced peacefully but its conclusion was ugly and the overtones would be ominous. For Flaminio, it represented his last hungry attempt to reach out toward human warmth; for Gasparo, the birth of a lifelong enemy, committed to destruction of his dreams.

At first the climate between them was festive. Removing their clothes and folding them on a blanket on the grass, they ran, yelling cordial insults, into the lake to swim and float and splash each other gleefully. Then, after feeding the horses, they sat down naked on the blanket, surrendering to the joy of gluttonously devouring thick juicy meatballs on fresh-baked bread and passing the wine bottle back and forth while the sun warmed their bodies.

Gasparo was pleasantly tired—the horseback ride, the cool lake water, the food, the wine. He lay back on the blanket and squinted at the sun framed in the blue sky.

"Life is fine, Flaminio," he said yawning. "Ah." Perhaps he would close his eyes for a moment.

Young Vulpi, too, was feeling mellow. *Am I mistaken?* he reflected, tilting back the wine bottle. *Could it be that there is no Afterlife? Must one live for today and take one's pleasures as they come—as Lorenzo does?* He looked fondly at his companion. How wonderful that Gasparo was again his friend. Breathing gently, lying naked on his back, Tagliacozzi's serene face was pointed toward the blazing sun. Flaminio admired the lithe, slender body. *Is he not handsome? Perhaps desires of the flesh are not dishonorable.*

Gasparo was sleeping and as Flaminio watched, fascinated, his penis began to rise and, stiffening, remained erect. *I love Gasparo,* mused Flaminio drowsily, *so why should this part of him be considered sinful?* The strength of his impulse staggered him, pushing aside his defenses.

Gasparo stirred. He had been dreaming, and segments of his dream lingered in his consciousness. *Ah—Giulia.* He would return to sleep—what had roused him?—but, raising up on his elbows, he opened his eyes.

He was horrified by what he saw. Flaminio was caressing his thighs, gently, with trembling fingers, and kissing his penis adoringly. He was salivating in his passion, his eyes bright with excitement, and he leaned over, flicking out his tongue to lick the throbbing penis.

"Stop it," Gasparo yelled, shocked, disbelieving. "Get away from me."

"No. I love you."

With the palm of his hand, Tagliacozzi shoved Flaminio away from him. Then, leaping to his feet, he flailed out with both fists as his childhood friend covered his face with his hands and sobbed, "I love you, Gasparo."

But Tagliacozzi, numb with outrage, scooped up a rock and hurled it at Vulpi, striking him just above his left eye, on the eyebrow, and blood started flowing over the eye down Flaminio's cheek.

"You bastard," yelled Flaminio. "I am blind."

"You are perverted and evil."

"It is you who are evil. Your thoughts are contaminated by the Devil and the Devil's instrument."

Of a sudden, Gasparo felt saddened. He might merely have rejected the advances of his old friend. Why had he thrown the rock? Blood poured down Flaminio's cheek, dripping down to stain the naked skin of his torso. "You are sick, Flaminio," he said more temperately. "It is not your fault. Please forgive me."

"Never," shouted Vulpi, hysterical, seething in an amorphous welter of rage, guilt, and confusion, hating Gasparo and loathing himself.

"You have deprived me of my eyesight and I will take my revenge."

"You are not blind, Flaminio. I apologize for my action, but I assure you that you are not blind."

"You have insinuated the Devil's wiles into me—or why should I have behaved in such manner? You have implicated me in your compact with the Devil and you will be punished."

Drowsy with wine, shocked by the train of events, repentant at the sight of the blood dribbling down Flaminio's cheek and torso and leg onto the blanket, Tagliacozzi felt immobilized. *What should I say?* he wondered. *What would my father have said?* But he knew the answer, and perhaps this is why he had hurled the rock.

"You are a heretic," yelled Vulpi, "but you will be punished in the name of Our Lord."

Gasparo dressed and climbed on to his horse. "You should not have forced yourself upon me, Flaminio," he said, measuring every word, trying to rise to wisdom and compassion, and to back off from his instinctive violent reaction, "but I am truly sorry and never will I forgive myself for the wound I inflicted upon you."

"I will take my revenge," sobbed Flaminio, dazed, shaken by his homosexual act, unable to understand or accept it. "You hypnotized me with the Devil's wiles, seducing me to evil. But someday I will take my revenge and I swear by Almighty God that you will burn to ashes at the stake."

Weary, dispirited, Gasparo gentled the horse into motion.

A few weeks later, Isabetta Tagliacozzi had a vision. She was attending early Mass in commemoration of the death of Giovanni Andrea. Her husband was standing in front of her, smiling, attired in his most splendid jacket.

"Isabetta, darling," the apparition said, "I am well; do not worry about me. You are a good mother to Gasparo but he is troubled because of me. So, my beloved, tell him I was wrong, that with my blessing may he study medicine. Surely he who aids the afflicted is on the side of Our Lord. If the stars are favorable, Gasparo will become a great surgeon."

When Isabetta returned home, she found her son brooding in the kitchen. The death of his father, the flight of Tasso, followed by this nightmare with Flaminio. He felt indecisive; should he flout the will of his father and attend medical school?

"I cannot bear to see you so sad," said his mother. "But we are indeed fortunate. A vision came to me today at Mass, a marvelous vision, praised be Almighty God. Your father has relented. He admitted that he was mistaken to have interfered with your desire to be a surgeon."

Poor Mama, thought her son, *she believes in her vision.* He did not believe, but he *was* comforted. His mother wished him to be happy. Yes, he would go to medical school.

"Thank you, Mama," he said, embracing Isabetta. "Your vision was lovely. You have given me a gift of peace."

At medical school Gasparo was hazed by a group of students. Surrounding him in a lecture room, they pretended he was a horned monster with an abominable smell. They handled him roughly, pushing him against a wall, while one lad commanded him to stand motionless for inspection. Another youth suggested calling a physician to pluck and shave the loathsome monster and make him presentable for student society.

One hazer, dressed like a ludicrous doctor, walked into the room with surgical instruments. Tormenting the initiate, he pretended that he was drawing the tusks off the monster and cutting off the deformed nose and flabby ears. Then, laughing wildly and cheering, the students pushed Gasparo onto the floor while the "doctor" pulled hair from his nose and head.

A lather compounded with manure and water was applied to the victim's nose and cheeks. Young Tagliacozzi's face was scraped with a wooden razor; screaming, he tried to wrench free from his torturers but they pried his mouth open and forced him to swallow a loathsome cathartic.

Poor Gasparo felt faint and, pretending that he was dying, the hazers called for a "priest" to administer last rites. "You are a thief," yelled the "priest." "Your crimes are known to us. You have also ravished virgins, committed adultery, and offended the student body with your endless blasphemies. But you will receive absolution if you repent and do penance. And your penance is that you provide food and drink for the student body of this great university."

And so Gasparo, pulled to his feet by his persecutors, now his friends, was escorted to a local tavern where everyone feasted and drank and sang and joked—at his expense.

Afterward, he accompanied several students to their quarters, and his companions introduced him to the dubious joys of the opium pipe, a popular diversion at this time. Tagliacozzi was bewildered by the hallucinations he experienced: weird visions of crackling flames and stampeding horses and dying men, interposed with a terrifying image of Flaminio sucking his penis and in his rage biting his organ, drawing blood. On the morrow, he endured an attack of migraine headache and vowed that never again would he smoke opium.

In this day, medical practice was bound in with superstition. Physicians would make diagnoses merely by inspecting a urinal. Many prescribed herbs as cure-alls for almost any ailment with little concern for their properties. Some practiced astrology and indulged in their love of amulets or in bloodletting through conjunction of the planets; they would devise fortunetelling almanacs and would appeal for aid to the heavens.

The barber surgeons who shaved criminals condemned to death or dressed the wounds of heretics tortured on the rack were themselves considered felons and often, in truth, they were. Some, like Professor Bartoli and the Great Van Zandt, traveled through the countryside, staging their fraudulent exhibitions.

Only in medical schools was there any attempt to make medicine ethical, but even men graduating as accredited physicians might surrender to practices involving astrology and uromancy. Those who tried to achieve more potent cures through experimentation with forms of hypnotism or what passed for psychotherapy were called magicians by the ignorant populace, and some were persecuted as practitioners of witchcraft.

The Rector was head of the medical school at Bologna. A matriculated student elected by the other students, he was of necessity generally wealthy, for he was required to finance public festivities at which he presided. Gasparo appeared before the Rector, paying his registration fee of thirty ducats.

"You are now admitted to the corporation of the university. Therefore, Gasparo Tagliacozzi, you may now receive all advantages and privileges of the great University of Bologna.

"The men who sell to the students, lend them money, or copy manuscripts for them are under the regulations of the university and pay taxes to it. I can suspend them or deprive them of their privileges if they indulge in sharp practices. If you have any complaints, come to me.

"I am the supreme head of the university; both professors and students are under my jurisdiction. You may find that students—and even professors—may fight for their beliefs, even with sword or dagger. In any civil or criminal affair, students and professors have a special court of law, over which I preside, aided by the bishop and a few professors who are elected. Minor violations will be subject to fines; major violations, such as selling opium, may result in dismissal from the university. So you must be careful.

"Take my advice: go about your business without interfering with others. Avoid serious disputes. More than one student has let his temper control him and has killed in anger and suffered the consequences. If you are sensible, you will seek me out for advice when you need it.

"You will be excused from military service and taxes, and during any period of shortage, you will be permitted to buy grain for yourself and your family. As a student, you become the child of Bologna and the city will defend you and your possessions. Signor Tagliacozzi, please accept my wishes to you for good luck, and may Our Lord bless you."

Gasparo commenced his study of practical and theoretical medicine, reading the works of Greek and Arabic authors. Among his professors, three were world-renowned: Girolamo Cardano, theory of medicine; Ulisse Aldrovandi, natural history; and Cesare Aranzio, anatomy.

Quickly, Tagliacozzi demonstrated a mastery of anatomy, and Professor Aranzio selected him as assistant at autopsies. On one occasion, for amusement, the other students blindfolded Gasparo, testing his skill by handing him, one at a time, bones of the human skeleton. With his sensitive fingers, Gasparo felt each bone and identified all correctly.

He enjoyed his classes in the theory of medicine; probing, earnest, he was instantly one of Cardano's favorite pupils.

The eminent sculptor Gianbologna completed his great statue of Neptune, and the ruling powers of Bologna decided to celebrate with a carnival preceded by a public anatomical dissection. Carpenters erected a temporary amphitheater to accommodate the audience.

At the ceremony, the Cardinal Legate, the Vice-Surrogate, and the Archbishop of Bologna occupied the front seats; they were flanked by the august Senate of Forty. The Rectors of the university were in special boxes, hoods of gold brocade topping their caps of red cloth, professors in long robes, business officials, and students of prominence behind them. In another box were Abizio Pepoli and his *bravi*, including Captain Desiri and Lorenzo. In the rear, in white robes with black hoods, blending into the crowd, were Fra Chiari, head of the Order of Saint Dominico, and Flaminio Vulpi, a member of the order.

A human corpse was carried in and deposited on a table in clear view of the notables. It was the dead body of a criminal hanged for murder.

The cadaver was given "respectability" by the reading of an official decree, stamped with the university's seal. Then the body was beheaded in deference to the universal prejudice against opening the cranial cavity, which was believed to hold the seat of the soul.

Assisted by Tagliacozzi, Professor Aranzio proceeded with the dissection, while the painter Bartolomeo Passarotti sketched him. The stench of decayed flesh insinuated itself upon the spectators and a fastidiously attired dandy poured perfumed oil from a bottle into his palm, applying it to his mustache. Aranzio finished the dissection, the audience applauded, and the remains of the unfortunate murderer were removed.

The other activities were on a lighter note. A quartet of two flutists, trombonist, and lute player performed popular songs of the day and a troupe of actors staged a drama.

The City of Bologna was bedecked for the carnival. Banners and tapestries, as well as velvet and silk coats of arms, fluttered from windows of the buildings surrounding the public square. The Fountain of Neptune, with its ninety jets, spouted streams of water into the air. Fireworks streaked through the sky, while confetti snowflakes swirled around, falling lightly on the heads of the costumed masked populace. Laughing, shoving, cursing humanity, exultant, wretched, imperious—it was the voluptuous carnival spirit of the post-Renaissance period.

Flaminio had watched the dissection and the entertainments with a quiet rage, the sight of Gasparo igniting his desire for revenge. He looked as if he had two left eyebrows now, for, healing, the gash seemed to have produced a duplicate.

It was three years since that fateful afternoon in the country. Vulpi had eradicated the incident from his memory; he recalled only that Gasparo had wounded him, body and soul, but absolved himself from all blame.

For months he had been ill, suffering from headache and dizziness, sometimes overpowered by such fury that he feared he was going mad; during this period Fra Chiari had comforted him.

Flaminio would build fantasies about girls like Giulia or Caledonia. He longed to possess them, but, in panic, driving their images from his mind, he would feel even more terrified at the strength of his sexual desire for other men. Repentant, he would bang his head against the wall of his lonely room and pray fervently with other members of the Dominican Order. Then desire would sweep over him in a frenzied encore and he would flagellate himself with a whip to drive out the Devil.

Fra Chiari hit upon a wise choice of cure, appointing the young man as his assistant reader. Hurling himself into his work with an aggressive sublimated passion, Flaminio stopped brooding.

But, moving through the carnival crowd with Fra Chiari, Vulpi obliterated from his mind the scene before him and saw himself instead, in flowing regal robes, before a snapping bonfire reaching halfway to the stars, directing his followers to cast the heretical books and pamphlets into the flames, along with the idolatrous pomps and vanities infesting the world.

The Dominicans moved slowly through the packed mass of people, past the public square, to a carriage that would take them back to their monastery. Vulpi could not endure the image of Gasparo assisting at the dissection.

Still, his day would come.

Tagliacozzi was progressing in medical school but his personal life was frustrating. After a brief period of courtship he had asked Giulia Carnali to marry him. He enjoyed her companionship and longed to consummate a deep, permanent relationship. Dating, they would take walks, eat at inns, and attend public celebrations, and on occasion they would join Lorenzo and Caledonia Bargillini. Then he would escort her home.

In the shadowy corners of the courtyard, they would embrace passionately and he would run his fingers through her flowing red hair and lose himself in the green pools of her eyes. When his hands caressed the soft round contours of her breasts through her gown, he would feel mad with desire, but, trembling, he would stop, for his stern conscience warned him that it was his duty to marry her first. He would stumble home in a frenzy; once, he met Lorenzo and they went to Signora Rinaldi's brothel, but this would not do. No, he must marry Giulia.

"Yes," she said when he asked her, "I will marry you. I love you, but we must wait."

"Why?"

"I must not interfere with your medical studies. They are too important to you and I could not bear the thought of upsetting you with my demands. But I shall wait for you."

They would kiss good night and Gasparo, more impatient than ever, would clomp noisily on the cobblestones, booting rocks and sticks with an avenging fury, arriving at his home in foul humor. Once he slammed the front door uncontrollably, waking up his mother and Cassandra. Isabetta was indulgent but it was too good an opportunity for his sister to miss, and the next morning she reprimanded him at the breakfast table while he sulked.

Nevertheless, he applied himself to his studies and his schoolwork remained on a high level; indeed, Tagliacozzi was such an exceptional student that, two years before receiving his degree, he was allowed to practice in the medical clinic. From here, and from the prison, the bodies of those about to die were scheduled for the public dissections that enriched his knowledge of and skill in dealing with anatomy. His fellows elected him class anatomist. Soon after, he cemented his growing friendship with Professor Girolamo Cardano, who supported his desire to become a surgeon.

Three weeks before completing his medical studies, the family fortunes having declined since the slaying of his father, Gasparo addressed to the college a petition in which he asked for exemption from the customary graduation expenses, pleading poverty.

This was recorded as follows:

> There was summoned and gathered in an assembly, reverend heads and esteemed doctors of medicine and philosophy in the Sacristy of the ancient church of the Cathedral of Bologna, in the accustomed meeting place of their assembly for the purpose of undertaking and completing the following business:— . . . The testimony of the witnesses was heard, who had been examined in the name and on behest of Gasparo Tagliacozzi concerning the alleged poverty of Gasparo to observe the constitution in a different way from its reading.
>
> No citizen of Bologna can become a doctor without paying the fee because he pleads poverty except by an action in court of poverty, which poverty should be attested to by at least two witnesses worthy of trust, to be approved by two-thirds of the doctors; they came to this decision, *viz.:* Those shall deposit a white bean who vote that the said Gasparo has legally proved his poverty. Those against this decision shall deposit a black bean. The beans were distributed among the full professors and they were then collected and inspected. Five were white and three were black. Thus they said that the decision was not favorable.
>
> A vote was taken on another decision, *viz.:* All those who approved or disapproved the following resolution should vote with affirmative or negative beans, to wit:

Resolved, That an extension of one year be granted to Gasparo Tagliacozzi for the payment of twenty-three scudi in addition to the sum customarily paid by the citizens of Bologna who are to be promoted in medicine alone.

The beans were distributed, collected and counted; all were favorable.

Then Gasparo Tagliacozzi appeared in the apostolic palace before the Vice-Surrogate and the Archbishop of Bologna to take an oath of fidelity to the Roman Church.

Kneeling before the officials, Gasparo, his hand touching the Scriptures, was asked by the Vice-Surrogate: "By the Gospel of the Holy Lord do you swear that you are a Christian and belong to the Catholic faith?"

"I do."

The Vice-Surrogate continued: "Since you desire as a citizen to be promoted by the Faculty of Medicine to the degree of Doctor of Medicine in this your beloved fatherland, the City of Bologna, do you solemnly swear in accordance with the form and content prescribed in the Bull of His Holiness Pope Pius V published in Rome that you will not treat a patient for more than three days if during that time the patient has not confessed to a confessor of the Roman Church?"

"I do."

"As Surrogate, I pronounce and formally declare that you, Gasparo Tagliacozzi, citizen of Bologna, residing in the street Delle Lame, subject to observing all the other presumptions in law and in form contained in the canons of the Council of Trent, shall and may be admitted to an examination and trial for a degree or degrees only in said Faculty of Medicine, to be effected in every way possible. May God bless you!"

The ceremony was over, and Gasparo breathed a sigh of relief. Delivering the prescribed affirmations on cue, he was still tense, fearing he would be adjudged an unworthy Christian.

The next day he invited his close friends and relatives to attend his examination, as well as some students—the university limited their number to ten.

The rituals continued. Before the examination, Tagliacozzi was required to swear that he had not given or promised anything to his examiners, and that he had never acted against the university and its ordinances. Then his teachers Ulisse Aldrovandi, Girolamo Cardano, and Cesare Aranzio presented him to the examiners. He gave each professor a cloak, a cap, and a hood. On the Prior he bestowed wine, sugar, coated almonds, a ring, a cap, and a pair of gloves.

Gasparo detested the formal ceremonies, wondering what relation they had to the practice of medicine. Grimly, he endured them. He was slightly dizzy and alarmed by his pounding heartbeat when the first examiner began to interrogate him. At this, he rallied from his anxiety, summoning his knowledge to restore his confidence and his powers of concentration. Lucid now, articulate, he addressed himself in disciplined fashion to the barrage of questions directed at him by the examiners. His command of his subject matter was unmistakable, and finally the audience rewarded him with spontaneous applause.

After receiving his degree, Tagliacozzi was named lecturer in surgery at the university, his salary one hundred pounds per annum. In those days it was a handsome income for a young man, and Isabetta could not suppress her tears of happiness.

A great bell tolled in celebration, and well-wishers awaited Gasparo in the courtyard fronting the university building. Isabetta was with Cassandra and Giulia, accompanied by Scipio Africanus Borzani. The young doctor was hoisted onto a black stallion as a procession formed, marching past the Cathedral of San Pietro, filing through the crowded streets, trumpets and fife serenading him all the way home. Lorenzo Desiri was striding alongside Scipio, the latter unwilling to smile for fear that this would make his deformity more visible. Gasparo recalled a passage on lip surgery from a book by the French surgeon Ambroise Paré. *Despair not, Scipio,* he vowed, *I will give you a new lip, and your life will begin again.*

Shortly thereafter, Gasparo married Giulia, daughter of Giuliano Carnali. On their wedding day, music and games at the home of the bride preceded the religious ceremony and the signing of the marriage contract, which was followed by refreshments and dancing.

Then the newlyweds journeyed to the City of Florence for their honeymoon.

For a while the groom was despondent, for he recalled the trip with his father when he was ten years old, and felt grieved that Giovanni Andrea was not alive to see him receive his degree and marry. But Giulia revived his spirits.

The lovers would rise early to tour the thriving commercial city, home of the Medicis, haven for culture, citadel of idealism. Breakfasting on ripe sweet melons, thick slices of fresh bread and cheese, and cups of a steaming beverage, they would set off to see the city that had contributed so gloriously to the Italian Renaissance.

They marveled at the brick and stone wall encircling the city. It was a massive protection for the citizenry; five miles long, forty feet high, about six feet thick, flanked by seventy-three towers and a deep moat, it was a mighty fortress.

Next, the Palazzo della Signoria, whose bell would summon people to meet for emergencies, and Giotto's splendid marble campanile, whose bell would ring out to assemble the Florentines for prayer.

They viewed the four stone bridges linking the main section of Florence to the Oltr'arno and, arm in arm, strolled down its narrow twisting streets, bordered by heavy stone houses with overhanging balconies.

With young Galileo, Gasparo had marveled at Brunelleschi's spectacular dome, rising majestically over the city, and he viewed it again with his fascinated young bride. It was an incredible piece of architecture; since A.D. 125, the date of the Pantheon, no dome had been constructed to rival this in size and Giulia felt that it towered above the mountains surrounding Florence.

"To think," said Gasparo, "that this structure was conceived by one man—Brunelleschi—and that he alone supervised its construction. Brunelleschi was so respected for this that when he died, in 1446, a wax model of his face was commissioned—this honor has customarily been reserved for saints and eminent military and political leaders."

"Io ti voglio bene, I love you. Because you know so much."

"I do?"

"Yes, but you also forget that my feet ache and my stomach is empty."

"Ah, lunch. I love you too. For your ideas are splendid."

In the afternoon, more sightseeing. About one hundred churches abounded in Florence, and the outside walls of some were decorated with an extraordinary boldness—geometrical patterns of deep-green or rose-red marble inlaid on a white background. Other churches were Gothic style, and this bold design was interwoven with statuettes and vague floral motifs and delicate traceries. They observed the severe rectangular outlines of the fourteenth-century Palazzo Davenzati, contrasting them with the more ornate Palazzo Rucellai, built in the fifteenth century, featuring pilasters and a carved cornice.

On the Ponte Vecchio, they surveyed the rows of butchers' shops with clean fresh meat, and walked to the business district near the Signoria. Bankers set up outside offices here: on chairs and tables in the street they made loans and changed money—in fair weather. The cloth and silk merchants' offices were also in this district; nearby were the fruit and vegetable markets and the bread market, to which bread from more than one hundred ovens was delivered fresh daily. The establishments of furniture makers, goldsmiths, and feather merchants were here—and the higher-class prostitutes lived in the candle-makers' shops.

Back to the inn for dinner. The tablecloth was of fine white linen and the waiter served heaping platters of veal, a basket of fresh rolls, and a flask of red Trebbiano wine. For dessert, large reddish dates and sweet cakes with tiny cups of strong tea.

And then they would be alone in their room—to make love and to sleep, waking up refreshed, to savor more fully the wonders of this spectacular city.

For hours they would appraise the endless artistic masterpieces: Leonardo da Vinci's geometrically constructed *Adoration of the Magi;* Piero della Francesca's *Baptism of Christ,* featuring the Tuscan landscape; Pollaiuolo's *The Rape of Deianira,* vigorous and rhythmic, a mighty river surging beneath the principals; Botticelli's *Magdalen at the Foot of the Cross,* with shields protecting the City of Florence while fiery brands are launched from Heaven. Gasparo was intrigued by Pollaiuolo's *Battle of Nude Men* and by da Vinci's drawings, which indicated anatomical knowledge gleaned from the dissection of human corpses. Giulia would marvel at the realism of Botticelli's *La*

Derelitta, depicting Queen Vashti, bedraggled, despairing, symbolizing the mood in Florence after the French invasion.

In their room at the inn they would rediscover each other. The
quiet, reserved Giulia was wildly passionate; protected until her marriage by her proper parents, chaperoned, she was a virgin on her
wedding day, and experiencing the miracle of sex for the first time,
with a man she loved dearly, she gave herself to him with an intensity
that almost frightened him. Her need to give, to receive, to love, it
was inexhaustible and radiant, and Gasparo worshiped her. Giulia
aroused in him passions so strong that he feared he was depraved.

The young bride loved to sing. Undressing, she would begin to
hum and then she would sing, caressing the notes mischievously.
When she was carefree and craved sex, she would sing with abandon,
signaling her mounting excitement and enticing him to her.

"Do you love me?" she would ask coquettishly.

"Ah." Gasparo would bury his face in the sweet softness of her
neck, his fingers exploring the nipples of her firm young breasts, swollen, stiffening with ecstasy. "Ah." Adoringly he would nuzzle the
smooth velvet of her belly and stroke her gentle quivering thighs, and
waves of lust would rise in him, building, roaring, consuming, until he
exploded inside her with a volcanic power that seemed to him a
miracle.

"I love you, Gasparo." Her green eyes were drowsy. "I love you."

"You are evil," joked Gasparo. "You have the Devil inside you."

"No, Gasparo. Just you."

"Then I am the Devil."

"You are wonderful. And I will be a good wife to you."

Tenderly, Gasparo would run his hand through her flowing red
hair and kiss her cheeks and her eyes and her nose. "You are lovely,"
he would murmur but her breathing was rhythmic and her eyes were
closed. "Lovely," he would almost sob, so intense was his pleasure in
her.

He would rest, head on the pillow, cheek brushing her cheek. *Perhaps we have made a baby,* he would muse. *How can one know? If we have
a boy, I will teach him to take responsibility and never will I force him to adopt
my occupation.* The thought, critical of his father, made him uneasy. He
reflected on his long-time submissiveness in the face of his father's

aggressiveness, on his new-found strength to assert himself, and, sadly, on Giovanni Andrea's violent death. *Father, I am so sorry that you did not live. We might have come to understand each other. And you would have found my wife charming.*

Giulia was sleeping. There was a slight smile on her lips and her breasts heaved gently. *You look so soft, my Giulia,* Gasparo thought. *So soft. And, discovering your sweetness, your goodness, have I found my manhood.*

Chapter 5

Returning to Bologna, the newlyweds installed themselves in the Tagliacozzi household—in mourning since the death of Giovanni Andrea. The youthful surgeon, with his wife's assistance, laid out an
office within his residence, furnished and equipped with the tools of
his trade. Then he performed his first operation—on the harelip of
Scipio Africanus Borzani. The field of surgery was shrouded in the
twin fogs of ignorance and superstition, and this operation and others
by Tagliacozzi represented attempts to penetrate these fogs and
search areas of practice beneficial to humanity.

Gasparo had long planned to reward Scipio, who had endured
countless humiliations caused by his disfigurement. Giulia would often ask if he could correct a harelip, and her interest sharpened his
incentive. Still, surgery wobbled on unsteady infant legs, and prior to
the operation, uncertain of procedure, he bolstered his confidence by
seeking out the most competent professional advice available.

At the University of Bologna, he paid his respects to Professor
Girolamo Cardano, bringing a copy of a book on surgery by the
Frenchman Ambroise Paré.

"We visited Agostino Solario in Florence, as you requested."

"Thank you, my friend. And how did you find him?"

"In prime health, and his spirit is buoyant. He wished you good
fortune and, what is most remarkable in these troubled times, his
statement bore the stamp of sincerity."

"My loyal colleague Solario—a noble man, truly. But, Gasparo, you have changed. Delight gleams from your countenance and flesh hangs heavy on your bones. Marriage agrees with you?"

"Yes."

"Yes?" roared Cardano, eyes gleaming mischievously. "Yes?"

"Yes."

Seated behind his desk, Girolamo Cardano tilted back his head and his lusty laughter thundered through his office, ricocheting back to lose itself in the space overhead, the ceiling perhaps twenty feet above their heads, outside the room a wide solid stone staircase. "Gasparo, you have bathed yourself in sensual delights. Like documentary evidence, this fact is etched into your face."

"Is it?" Meek, boyish-looking, Gasparo felt frightened in spite of his professor's bantering tone. "Am I so transparent?"

"I tease you, my dear fellow. Please forgive me. It is an abhorrent quality. But I am gifted with psychic powers, and they inform me that you seek my advice."

"It is about a harelip, Professor. I intend to operate on a young man horribly afflicted since birth. My wife is solicitous about his welfare, and I must feel on sure ground before proceeding. Professor, what is your view of the recommendations of the surgeon Paré?"

"A great man," responded Cardano wryly, "a seeker after truth, destined for punishment by the Church, certainly. A brilliant, constructive innovator. The Inquisition will focus its avenging wrath on Monsieur Paré."

"And his procedure for harelip? For a large, deep wound, with the lips considerably separated, he suggests a three or four square needle, with wax thread; you must insert this needle through the lips of the wound and leave it in the wound. Then, says Paré, you must wrap the thread eight or ten times around it, like women fastening a threaded needle upon their sleeves or tailors to their headpiece, so as not to lose it. Until there is perfect agglutination of the wound, you leave the needle in this position. But one must be careful not to leave any skin between the lips of the wound; otherwise, this form of suture will not aid agglutination. Then, as a preliminary precaution, any such skin must be cut away."

"This procedure seems flawless."

"In his book, Paré illustrates his technique, emphasizing that other kinds of sutures may not be effective because they will not contain the movement of the lips in eating and speaking and so on."

As if patting an affectionate kitten, Girolamo Cardano stroked his long gray beard. He was a tall, angular man, with penetrating eyes, sharp-pointed nose, and a firm chin hidden beneath the great bush of his beard. "This technique sounds logical; valued colleagues vouch for its efficacy."

"I cannot gamble," said Gasparo earnestly. "Scipio is a decent fellow, and I could not bear to harm him."

"Gamble? My dear Gasparo, life itself is a gamble. When I adopted this profession—and you, too—I wagered my chips on the proposition that the powers that be would comprehend the truth underlying it, but the Church hierarchy sees only the Devil, and these fanatical lunatics desire solely to prosecute me and burn me to ashes. But as for Paré, he is a superb surgeon and a magnificent teacher; naturally, his enemies formulate daily prayers to God for his destruction. One may measure the eminence of Monsieur Paré by the caliber of his enemies. He advocated treatment of hemorrhage from new wounds by tying the vein and the artery with a thread while his adversaries insisted on treatment by cautery, or the burning iron. Paré was correct; oh, his wisdom is considerable. Therefore, how can the Church allow him to live unchastised? His book will be burned, for he courageously and indiscreetly pursues truth. Oh, he is braver than I, my friend. I talk with bite and give my tongue free rein, but at heart I am a cowardly old man who craves meat and wine and the sweet flesh of women, so I discipline my pen, governing my rebellious thrusts, evading the vengeance of the baying hounds of Heaven. They hate me for my learning and fear me because I will not hide my views, but in print I am an ostrich and save my skin so that my life of debauchery may continue. For the joys of the flesh give meaning to existence."

"May I request your further counsel, Professor?"

"Perform this operation, Gasparo, for otherwise this unfortunate fellow will be always degraded. And yes, I would follow Monsieur Paré's advice, but, my boy, let me add this. If you fail, you will feel unhappy, and if you succeed, the Church will punish you. But, as the

French claim, *c'est la vie.* I am seventy years old, and human existence seems less rational to me with every day. Is this what you wished to hear?"

"My dear Professor, I wished to fortify my resolve and to reassure myself that if I failed in my endeavor, it was not because of negligence."

"Someday you will be famous, my friend; an old man feels this in his bones. You are truly a unique phenomenon—a human being who against all reason desires to assist humanity—but, son, the Church will resist you to the last gasp."

Entering the Tagliacozzi residence, Scipio Africanus Borzani was apprehensive. He had not been able to sleep soundly for a week. Excited at the prospect of looking like a normal person, he was terrified of the pain accompanying the surgical procedure. In Spain, as a small boy, he had heard the shrieks of a wounded soldier whose leg was being amputated. The soldier had returned from the wars to the house adjoining that of the boy's family and the doctor had operated in the man's bedroom. Scipio was all too aware of the terrible pain endured; never had he been able to eradicate from his mind the soldier's screams. Only his trust in Gasparo plus the urging of Giulia had induced his consent. Faint, dizzy, heart palpitating, he feared for a moment that he was dying. Death seemed a welcome solution to his problems, releasing him from the agony of the operation.

Gasparo greeted him, ushering him through the beautifully furnished consultation room to the operating room, seating him in a straight-backed chair flanked by a long table filled with surgical instruments. "We will undertake surgery shortly," he said, "and you will have a beautiful new lip."

"Will it be painful?"

"Yes, but it will be tolerable. I will cause you as little pain as possible, I swear this. My dear Scipio, drink this tumbler of wine."

Scipio gulped the wine and glanced nervously about him. "I do not know if I can bear the pain," he whispered, miserable at the scrutiny of the big, brawny Lorenzo Desiri, whose eyes filled with contempt.

Gasparo had confided his plans to Lorenzo, who, always eager for adventure, had volunteered to assist. Tagliacozzi had hesitated—his old friend, now a Pepoli *bravi*, was brutal and unsympathetic—but Desiri had promised that he would obey instructions. Now it was too late to reconsider, and Lorenzo and Scipio were antagonizing each other.

"Drink another tumbler of wine," said the surgeon, adjusting the candlelight. "You will find this relaxing. Hold firmly to the chair arms and raise your head. Like this—excellent. Lorenzo, stand to my left."

Rolling up the sleeves of his gown and washing his hands, the surgeon extracted a long knife from his satchel. Plucking a hair from his own scalp, he sliced it with the blade as a test for sharpness.

Scipio jumped from the chair. "You will harm me."

"It will be endurable. I promise to keep your pain to a minimum."

"No, I do not wish the operation."

Gasparo continued to soothe the terrified patient but Lorenzo decided upon more direct methods. "You are a coward," he thundered, pushing Scipio back into the chair. "I feel shame for your lack of manhood."

Motioning Lorenzo away, the surgeon bent over his subject, who gripped the chair arms with desperation. Scipio's eyes were closed, perspiration oozed from his forehead, and arteries throbbed in his neck. "In the name of God," he moaned.

"Raise your head," whispered Gasparo, internally tense, making a supreme effort at gentleness. "You must do this so that I can operate on your lip."

"No."

The surgeon signaled his assistant. "Hold his head steady, Lorenzo." As Desiri seized the patient's head, yanking it backward, Gasparo leaned over him, his knife poised to cut the edge of the harelip.

"No," screamed Scipio, struggling to squirm free from Lorenzo's grasp. "No."

Gasparo drew back his knife. "This is difficult, my friend, but think of your pride when your face is normal and—"

"Please." The patient's eyes widened with terror.

Lorenzo had been restraining himself. "We will try my way," he bellowed finally, releasing his hold on Scipio, and, cocking a fist, clouted him fiercely on the chin. Unconscious, the black youth slumped in the chair.

"In the name of God, Lorenzo, what is the matter with you?"

"I could endure this cowardice no longer. He is a man—let him act like a man. In any case," smirked Lorenzo, twirling his mustache, "I prepared him for surgery."

Tagliacozzi stared at the inert patient. *Did this really happen?* he agonized. *Did Lorenzo, as if slaughtering an animal, club my first patient unconscious? Mother of God, was this not how the charlatan Bartoli prepared the syphilitic beggar for the knife? Perhaps my father was right, and I, too, am a charlatan.*

"Now you can operate," said Lorenzo.

Gasparo stared at him. "Lorenzo," he reasoned, "he is a human being."

"A coward, a woman. You wished to assist him? Proceed."

There was an insane logic to this. "Let us lift him up in the chair," directed the surgeon.

And, with Lorenzo holding Scipio's head, he leaned forward to commence the procedure. Deftly, he pared the edges of the harelip, which started to bleed. "Hold his head steady," he reminded his assistant, and quickly snatched a three-point needle with thread from his instrument table. Then, driving the needle precisely through both edges of the wound, he waited until its point appeared externally through the lip, winding thread around needle like a figure of eight, approximating the edges of the wound. The bleeding ceased.

He stepped back to survey the lip. "You may release him. The operation is concluded."

"Praise the Lord," said Lorenzo, subdued. "You are mad to do this work."

The young surgeon set about waking up the patient, slapping his cheek until he opened his eyes, mumbled a few phrases, and dropped back to sleep. Numbed by Lorenzo's blow, drugged by the wine, harelip sutured, Scipio, shocked awake time and again by the insistent slapping, would relapse into slumber. Finally, his eyes remained open.

"Listen to me," said the surgeon. "I do not wish you to speak—to anybody—for a week. And you must not smile during this period.

This will be difficult, but it is essential to the success of the operation. You will stay in my home until you have recovered, and we will give you juice and warm fluids. If you wish anything or desire to say something, write it down on a piece of paper. But remember: do not talk or smile, or you will tear the stitches on your lip and the operation will have failed. Do you understand?"

The dazed patient nodded. "Am I all right?"

"Fine. But do not speak. I will prepare warm compresses for your lip. I must warn you again: do not talk or smile. You must not feel too happy or you might forget yourself and smile. Understand, my friend?"

Scipio nodded, his eyes alive with anticipation, but he said nothing, for the first time relaxing in the operating chair.

"You were an excellent patient," said Gasparo. "Is that not correct, Lorenzo?"

His assistant massaged his bruised hand affectionately. "Oh, yes." He smiled. "During the whole operation you did not say a single word. It was as if you were not even aware of the pain."

The surgeon slept little that night. He answered his wife's questions abruptly, and later, in their room, he warded off her embrace, choosing to pace the floor. *Why did I allow Lorenzo to assist me?* he reproached himself. *My first operation—a disaster. I might just as well have instructed Lorenzo to shoot him.* Then a brighter thought. *My technique was sure. Paré could not have done better.*

He drifted off for a few hours and, awaking, rushed to examine the patient. His appraisal was not reassuring. The lip was inflated to twice its normal size. Scipio, unable to open his mouth, seemed to beseech him.

"Do not worry," Gasparo said, applying hot compresses, "you will feel better. You must have sleep, and in a few days you will be a different person."

Accustomed to suffering, unthreatened by pain now, Scipio was compliant. On a piece of paper he scribbled: "I hope you are not angry with me. Was I a terrible patient?"

"You did not cry out once during the operation," said Gasparo evasively.

Tagliacozzi began to worry about the swelling, though it was not uncommon at this stage. On the fourth day after the operation, the inflammation began to go down and the lip assumed more normal proportions. He was overjoyed; the recovery from his initial operation was proceeding splendidly. He hastened to tell Giulia, and she celebrated by preparing the patient a thick soup with beans and rice and barley and rich dry peppers and fresh tomatoes.

After ten days, Gasparo unwound the thread in the lip and extracted the needle. Adjusting the lighting he examined the lip minutely. *It is perfect,* he whispered to himself. *Never have I seen anything so beautiful. Oh, Father, you were wrong. Surely God must see that my work is good.*

"Look, Scipio, you scoundrel," he yelled, exultant, "in this mirror. You can talk now. You can smile. You can dance. You can sing. Scipio, my good fellow, that is you. The handsome fellow in the mirror is *you.*"

Somberly, Scipio admired his face. He could talk now; he could smile. But he did neither. It was too wonderful for that.

Scipio was a new person, and people were electrified at the change. Dramatically, he shed his defenses overnight. The cleft was gone, and no longer were his front teeth visible through his lips. He could smile or laugh without fear that a bully would call him "Dogface" and that everyone would join in the laughter.

"Can it be," he said, "that I am handsome?"

"You are a fine-looking man."

"It is a miracle. I feel reborn, like a baby, into a fresh exciting world."

"You do not hiss anymore," said Gasparo. "Repeat after me: embrace."

"Embrace."

"Kiss."

"Kiss."

"Now say face."

"Face."

"Hiss."

"Hiss."

"Congratulations, my friend. You hiss no longer because your lips are whole."

"Yes, and how can I ever repay you?"

"By enjoying your life, for then I will have helped you and may face my God without fear or guilt."

Radiant at beholding the new Scipio, Giulia insisted on a party. It was perhaps the wildest, most irreverent celebration in the history of the Tagliacozzi household, traditionally disciplined by the dogmatic Giovanni Andrea. Lorenzo came with his father and Caledonia Bargillini, whom he continued to court between visits to the emporium of Signora Rinaldi. Captain Desiri made a grand entrance in his handsome suit of Milanese armor, bowing with courtliness, striding to a table packed with bottles of liquor and glasses. In a few moments he was belching out ribald songs, composed, doubtless, by a graduate anatomist. Professors Aranzio and Aldrovandi, invited, could not (or would not) attend, but Professor Girolamo Cardano was present, announcing his opinions on the Roman Church and the wretched condition of humanity at large.

Gasparo was annoyed. The party was to have been an affair honoring Scipio Africanus Borzani, but it resembled a Roman orgy. Lorenzo, intoxicated, was demonstrating to Cardano his anesthetizing technique. *A great boon for my reputation,* mused the surgeon. Meanwhile, Luigi Rimini Desiri was stumbling around like a blind elephant in a thick forest, crashing into furniture and glassware impartially. The captain of Pepoli's *bravi* had spilled wine on Isabetta's favorite armchair, wiping it with a handkerchief that might have been used to pick up horse manure. His wineglass always full, he stopped drinking only to pat Caledonia on the behind or to stare lustfully down the front of Giulia's low-cut gown. Gasparo was furious but said nothing.

The affair was redeemed in part by the sparkling presence of Scipio. The black man, now grown tall, was broad-shouldered and strikingly handsome, yet until this moment his defensiveness and apprehensiveness had so negated these features as to render them invisible. A smile broke constantly over his lips, a scorching sun bursting from behind a cloud. Looking at him, Gasparo felt privileged, for Scipio was proof that his surgery could bring happiness to others. Thus he consoled himself, managing a wan smile at Lorenzo's father, who seemed to be contemplating rape, weighing the merits of Caledonia against those of Giulia, before passing out, vomiting quietly on the living-room rug.

Exhausted with liquor, bloated with Isabetta's succulent roast, plus sweet cakes and figs from Smyrna and large purple grapes, the guests departed, proclaiming it an occasion *molto bello*. Luigi Rimini Desiri, awaking to seize the black man's hand in congratulation, pumped it enthusiastically, then lurched out the front door.

"A splendid occasion," gibed Cardano, leaving. "The Inquisition has in writing the guest list, I assure you."

"And the crime?" asked Gasparo.

"The crime is the pursuit of truth and justice, and a regard for the sanctity of the individual. It is obvious, my friend, that the Church will not countenance such heresy."

Isabetta was angry. "Barbarians," she stormed. "Thank God my good husband was not compelled to entertain these impious people." She swept around the living room with her cleaning rags, wiping, dusting, then used broom and mop on the soiled carpeting. The views of the Antichrist Cardano rang in her ears, but still worse was the horrifying Captain Desiri, and she was disgusted by the memory of his spilling wine on her chair and throwing up on her finest Persian rug. The virtuous Isabetta was furious at her son and refused to talk to him. Disgustedly, she scrubbed at the rug; she would erase the last traces of the abominable Captain Desiri.

But the party was not over. Lorenzo, delighted with the new Scipio and apologetic for knocking him unconscious, invited the black man to accompany him home for a nightcap. They helped Captain Desiri to bed and escorted Caledonia home and then, whistling and singing, strolled to the parish of San Giacomo de' Carbonesi.

"Have you been with a woman?" asked Lorenzo.

"No," responded Scipio. "I have always been ashamed of my lip and—"

"I understand," said Lorenzo, unusually tactful. "I will take you to the establishment of Signora Rinaldi."

It was a memorable experience, and for once Desiri played second fiddle. The courtesans were wild about the handsome black man, and, flattered by their admiration, glowing at his good fortune, Scipio felt his lust mount. One of the girls stripped off his clothes and there he stood, naked, his penis huge and erect, surrounded by the prostitutes, who complimented him lavishly on his magnificent organ. The novitiate set about compensating for a lifetime of abstinence and his efforts were stupendous. For, amazingly, so strong was his good feeling that no sooner did he satisfy one of the Signora's hostesses than his penis would spring erect almost immediately and he would give a repeat performance.

"My nobility exalts me," murmured Lorenzo, intoxicated, drowsy, "for it is I who prepared him for surgery."

It was three in the morning, and the surgeon walked in his garden. He was still too excited to sleep. Giulia had retired and only Isabetta was awake, silent, upset, washing the dishes and stowing them with a strident clatter in her impeccable cupboards.

His first operation had been an unqualified success, and shortly he would operate on a wealthy nobleman, Aurelio Morisini, whose nose had been deformed in a duel years back. He had been debating with himself whether to accept Morisini's case and, discussing it with Cardano at the party, he had decided in the affirmative. The professor was lavish in complimenting him for his work on Scipio, though he ended up warning about the punitive wrath of the Roman Church.

Which reminded the surgeon of Flaminio Vulpi. He and his fellow Dominicans claimed that harelip symbolized evil in one's family, witches, an affliction preordained by God to punish sin. They would insist that Tagliacozzi, interfering with the will of God, was practicing an evil magic gleaned from Girolamo Cardano, eternally under investigation by the Inquisition. Glumly, he recalled Flaminio's threat of revenge.

The moon was shining and Gasparo remembered how his father, enraged by his son's disobedience, would turn for comfort to his garden. *If only you could see Scipio, Father,* he mused. *No longer does he hiss like a snake. With my hands have I made his face splendid. If you were alive, you would rejoice with me.*

What had Giovanni Andrea done in the garden? Oh, yes, he had scooped the branch of a bush from the earth and, after watering it, transplanted it back into the rich soil. Meditating awhile in the shade cast by his finest tree, he removed a branch from the tree and emerged to transplant it elsewhere. In his shirt sleeves, dirt under his fingernails, he would assist nature with his hands.

My father and I, thought Gasparo, *with our hands we have created. He has helped plants to grow, and I have helped a human being to grow.* Excitement filled him at this, and he felt his father's vigorous presence behind him. Giovanni Andrea's eyes were gleaming with pride on beholding his son. It was amazing, but his father was still alive. Awed, he could not turn around to confirm the miracle. *Do you not understand, Father? I do for human beings what you did for plants. And you have given me an idea. If you could take the branch of a bush or a tree and plant it in another section of ground, why can I not take some skin from a healthy area of the body—say, the arm—detach this skin partly from the arm, and while it is still attached to the arm graft it onto the face to correct a disfigurement?* He imagined that his father was smiling at him. *Father, we are both artists—you with cloth and I with faces.*

And he turned around to embrace his father. But no one was there—he was alone in the garden. The light from the moon beat down upon him and, despondent, he shuffled into the house. He did not tell Giulia about his hallucination but, awaking, she pulled him into bed beside her and caressed him, whispering her admiration of what he had done for Scipio, kissing and fondling him until he felt the power surging through his blood and, adoring her tenderness, worshiping her softness, he inflamed her with the fierce thrust of passion and they came together, afire, separating contentedly to drift into sleep.

The lip of Scipio is magnificent, Gasparo mumbled to himself, losing consciousness. *And I will give Aurelio Morisini a fine new nose.*

His enemies—and they were legion—did not share his sanguine mood. Indeed, in spite of the glorious transformation in Scipio, they would not relent in their antagonism.

Their ranks numbered not only Flaminio and the officials of the Roman Catholic Church. At the university, a number of professors were opposed to his work; most bitter was the renowned anatomist Cesare Aranzio.

With Aranzio, it was a matter of personal egotism. He had been a professor at the university for many years, his reputation was considerable, and Tagliacozzi was one of his most gifted pupils.

But the professor's ire had been aroused by a public dissection of a criminal's corpse. It was his understanding that he would perform this dissection; to his surprise Gasparo was selected for this function.

And now, with his former pupil's name on everyone's lips as a result of his operation on Scipio, Aranzio was overflowing with resentment. Tagliacozzi, he vowed, must be required to observe limitations and respect authority. Influential, the anatomist drew other faculty members to his side.

In spite of the enlightenment and idealism accompanying the Italian Renaissance, and following in its wake, these years were characterized by much superstition. Flaminio Vulpi and the Dominicans and other Roman Catholic groups were not alone in their belief that Tagliacozzi was an instrument of the Devil, inviting the wrath of God by restoring Scipio's face to normal, when it had been preordained that he should remain deformed as punishment for his sins or those of his ancestors.

Many townspeople would avoid the surgeon, pretending not to see him when passing in the street, and they shunned his wife and his mother. More than one of his friends stopping talking to him after the successful harelip operation.

Chapter 6

In the morning, Gasparo visited the home of Aurelio Morisini, who lived in a stone mansion on the Via Castiglione. Once a proud cavalier, Morisini had lost the greater part of his nose in a duel ten years before, and for a decade he had lived in the past, filling his mind with glorious memories of his formerly handsome appearance and his conquests—on the battlefield, in tournaments and hunts, and in the boudoirs of female admirers.

But the glory began to fade and Morisini, unable to bear the sight of his nose, cultivated a splendid thick beard, letting his sideburns grow till his face was framed in a matting of fierce black hair. But this did not help because his deformed nasal stump was still visible, and even strangers would feel fascinated, making a game of seeing through the crude disguise. Ladies avoided him, and only his cellarful of choice wines brought him blessed oblivion—for a while.

He summoned the youthful surgeon, who hurried to the Via Castiglione to accept this case.

"Splendid," said Aurelio Morisini. "I have been informed of your marvelous work with Scipio."

"Tomorrow morning, ten o'clock?"

"Yes. Doctor Tagliacozzi, your credentials are excellent and I have supreme confidence in your ability, but I must admit that my knowledge in such affairs is limited, and with grave apprehension do I recall an instance many years ago. I cannot remember the principals, but this surgeon attempted to rebuild this fellow's nose and almost killed him, making the hole in the nose even deeper. He was hung by Abizio Pepoli from his tower. Ah, yes, his name was Bartoli, and this knave deserved to die."

"I must reassure you," said Gasparo, "I am not a charlatan. I have attended the medical school of the University of Bologna and I am confident I can help you."

"Did not the son of Captain Desiri assist with your prior operation?"

"Yes, but Lorenzo tends to be callous—"

"May I request his participation? He is but a casual acquaintance but, like myself, he is a warrior."

"Agreed," said Gasparo, trying to hide his ambivalence. "Tomorrow at ten, at my office."

The disfigured, bearded nobleman arrived on time, and the surgeon, seated at his desk, conversed with him briefly in the consultation room, then ushered him into the operating room. "Take care, please," he whispered to Lorenzo, who was ready.

"Aurelio Morisini is a man," said Desiri haughtily. "My services will not be necessary."

Rigid, a soldier at attention, the patient sat in the operating chair while Tagliacozzi adjusted the lighting and instructed his assistant to pour Aurelio a tumbler of wine. Then, after asking the patient to strip to the waist, Gasparo assembled his instruments on the table: knife, forceps, pair of scissors, needle holder, curved needles, and waxed thread. Rolling up the sleeves of his white silk robe, he threaded the needles. "How do you feel?" he asked Morisini. "More wine?"

"Yes. Yes."

The surgeon washed his hands, then waited while the patient swallowed another tumbler of rich red Trebbiano. "Hold his hands, Lorenzo—on the chair arms—and make certain his shoulders remain in position."

Grimly, Lorenzo pinned the patient into the chair, and Gasparo, inspecting what was left of the nose, measured the approximate amount of skin needed to fill it out. Taking a surgical knife from the instrument table, he made an elliptical incision in the hairless area of Morisini's left arm. Howling like a wounded animal, Aurelio struggled to burst out of the chair.

"Hold steady," said Gasparo, and the muscular assistant tightened his grip.

Deftly, the surgeon separated the peninsula of skin from the underlying muscle, leaving it attached to the arm at one end. Then he applied hot fomentations to the arm to control the bleeding and, sighing with relief, stepped back.

"*That* is finished," he said. "Lorenzo, pour him another tumbler of wine."

Morisini, trembling, gulped the wine. His eyes were feverish, but he was fighting to maintain his composure.

I do not know, Gasparo agonized. *The pain is gruesome.* He stepped into the consultation room, opened the door leading to the rest of the house, and yelled for Giulia. His wife came and held the patient's hands while Desiri grasped him firmly by the head. The surgeon then focused the lighting on the nasal stump.

With the knife he pared the edges of the nasal wound and Morisini, shocked awake from his wine-induced stupor, tried to wrench free but Lorenzo was too strong for him. Blood oozed from his nose, rolling over his mouth and chin onto his bare chest, and Giulia, holding onto his hands, was compelled to avert her head.

"Now," yelled Gasparo. "Lorenzo, lower his head to his arm. Quickly."

Nimbly, the surgeon sewed the skin flap of the arm onto the open wound of the nose. One stitch—two stitches—three stitches.

"Hold his head and arm. Firmly, Lorenzo. Help him, Giulia. He must not move a muscle."

Eighteen stitches, and the nasal stump and the arm skinflap were joined.

"Do not move, Aurelio," commanded Gasparo. "I will be finished in a moment."

Using yards of satin, he bandaged head and arm to keep the graft in position. "There," he said finally, mopping the perspiration from his face, "it is over."

The two men helped Morisini from the operating chair and led him to a bed in one of the adjoining patients' rooms. Breathing heavily, shivering, half-blind with his left eye covered by the bandage, Morisini sprawled miserably. "Wine," he murmured.

"He earned it," said Gasparo wearily to his assistants. "You too. And Lorenzo, you rascal, fill mine to the top. The result should be fine, my friend. Bartoli detached skin from the arm completely. But this will work, for while the graft is still getting nourishment from the arm, it will certainly grow into the stump of the nose."

That evening Morisini's face was swollen. His left eye was completely shut, his face was flushed, and he complained that his skin felt hot and then chilled and that there was a terrible taste in his mouth. "I am dying," he moaned. "In the name of God render me assistance."

"Do not worry," said the surgeon. The head bandage had loosened, so he tightened it to prevent further motion or pulling apart of the graft of skin. All night he remained with his patient, applying hot compresses to the skin flap to keep it alive—but it turned darker blue.

The next day, Aurelio continued to complain about fever and raved deliriously. The skin flap had become partly detached from the nasal stump and was now black.

It was clear that the operation had failed and Tagliacozzi could not understand why. His idea for the skin graft from arm to nose, inspired by his father's work in the garden, had proved a disaster. But why? He felt confident that his reasoning was sound.

Removing the bandage, and separating the dead flap from the nose, he cut it away from the healthy skin of the arm. Then he applied hot fomentations and healing salves to both wounds and forced the patient to drink liquids. For ten days the doctor hovered over Aurelio, sleeping rarely and for but a few hours, fighting to save his life. At last, the infection was controlled and the fever subsided as the swelling disappeared from the bearded face of the nobleman. But the nasal stump remained—red, ugly, ludicrous.

"Why did the operation fail?" Gasparo voiced his bewilderment to

Giulia. "The skin graft, why did it die? Morisini was somewhat underweight. Perhaps, before I operated, I should have advised him to nourish himself with fattening foods for a few weeks; then he might have gained weight and felt sufficiently strong to withstand the shock of surgery. Do you think I am correct?"

"I do not know."

"My knowledge of tree grafting should have taught me that only the branch of a healthy tree cut off can grow when transplanted; a rotten plant dies. Therefore, as a corollary, one should build up the health of a patient before attempting a skin graft. And one should prepare the graft in a different fashion. Why did it die? Because taking it from the arm and transferring it immediately to the nose was too profound a shock and the body could not endure it? Can this be the reason, Giulia?"

"Perhaps, darling. Gasparo, you expect too much of yourself—"

"I could experiment with another procedure. In advance of the operation, I could measure the width of skin needed on the inner hairless aspect of the left arm, where I could make two parallel incisions into the skin, raising this strip of tissue from the underlying muscle, leaving it attached to the arm above and below. Then the skin bridge could be kept separated from the underlying parts with linen, and bandaged with a salve of olive oil and turpentine. After an interval of a week—or possibly, two weeks—the graft might be strong and healthy and at this point I might transplant it to the nose. My dearest, I think I know why I failed. And, if I am correct, next time I will not fail, and my patient will be a new person. Do you understand?"

"No, but I love you, and I wish you would go to bed. You look so tired, my poor darling."

"Sleep? Giulia, can you not understand what I am telling you? I have found the answer. I do not know how, or why, but, *Dio,* this is the greatest discovery of my life. It will spare my patients excruciating agony. Done in separate stages, the operation would be less painful, since each stage would be a week or two apart. Alas, if we could put the patient to sleep beforehand—but we do not know how."

"Oh, it must be torture for them."

"I must lessen their suffering by refining my techniques. I require a strong broad forceps to hold the skinflap in position so that I can cut and separate it instantly from its attachment to the underlying tissues. I need sharper knives and scissors as well as needles and more durable thread. Perhaps I can commission a silversmith to fashion special instruments for me."

"Go to sleep, my love. You must forget your work and rest or you will take sick."

"Never has my thinking been more clear. And I realize another mistake. Aurelio's head bandage was too loose, permitting the arm to pull the skin flap away from its attachment to the nose, and this may have caused the death of the graft. Yes, I have located another costly error. An apparatus must be constructed to keep the head, arm, and chest rigidly in position to prevent any movement of the skin graft. It must consist of a cap to fit the head, a jacket to fit the chest, and an arm sling to fit the arm carrying the graft. With laces, they could be secured to each other to hold the graft immobile after attachment to the nose and to freeze the skin flap. Then, Giulia, when the transplant has grown into the nose, the apparatus can be removed, the graft completely detached from the arm, and the nasal surgery completed. Do you see what I mean, my dearest? Oh, you are my inspiration; I adore you. Do you understand what I have been saying?"

"I understand that you no longer eat and sleep and that you are raving like a man who has driven himself beyond his endurance."

"But, my Giulia, you are wrong. This is the greatest discovery of my life. No, that is not true. You, Giulia. You are my greatest discovery."

"I love you, Gasparo."

Suddenly, visibly, a change came over the surgeon's face. His delight vanished as guilt overwhelmed it, driving it into hiding. *I am a monster*, he reproached himself. *I have ruined the life of Aurelio Morisini. Never should I have attempted this operation without additional preparation. I loathe myself for my egotistic self-congratulation and will pray to God for forgiveness. Flaminio is right; the Devil is inside me. My father was right; I have flouted the will of God.*

He massaged the temples of his forehead; his skin felt tight and uncomfortable and he itched all over. He stood up, and he felt dizzy and feared he would faint.

"Come to bed," said Giulia, slipping her arm around his waist. "Come."

Forgive me, Morisini, he whispered to himself, his head on the pillow. *I am so sorry.* But his next thoughts were more consoling: *I have made valid discoveries today, and I will not fail again. I will give people new faces— as I did for Scipio.*

But he had three avowed enemies: Flaminio Vulpi, Cesare Aranzio, and now Aurelio Morisini.

Enraged, the nobleman studied his features in the full-length mirror of his bedroom—his bushy beard, so carefully groomed, and his exquisite, aristocratic-looking sideburns—spoiled by the grotesque nasal stump.

Hysterically he recalled the sheer anguish of the operation. And for nothing. *Oh no,* he proclaimed. *The charlatan Tagliacozzi will discover that one does not trifle with Aurelio Morisini. He will regret his treachery. I will see that he receives his just deserts.*

With desperation mobilized from despair, Gasparo had rallied from the Morisini operation to a creative surge that was to revolutionize the history of plastic surgery. Shortly, he would validate the theories he had wrenched from himself to defend his ego against the realization that he had failed and, in failing, had jeopardized a man's health, his sanity, and his slim chance to build a meaningful life.

But, in the weeks following, he succumbed to the most severe depression of his brief life. *My father was right,* he reprimanded himself. *I should have been a weaver.* Flaminio Vulpi would take revenge upon him, and he deserved it. He was arrogant and his wrongheaded feeling of omnipotence had caused him to challenge the will of God. If only his friend Torquato Tasso were still in Bologna; he could converse at length with the poet, unloading the burden of guilt devouring him, but Tasso had not returned.

Isabetta had not been herself since the party for Scipio; always tidy, she was now obsessed with cleanliness, washing, scrubbing, mopping, dusting, chasing dirt with a frenzy comparable to Flaminio's monomaniacal pursuit of the Devil. She could not help her son in his spiritual agony.

And for the first time, even Giulia's ministrations were futile. Her lovely body, naked in his bed, awaiting his touch, failed to rouse him now. Her efforts to console him were equally fruitless. Gasparo wanted no sympathy and reacted to her commiserations with a fury that drove her away from him into a void, weeping silently, for Isabetta was no company these days and her sister-in-law, Cassandra, engaged to marry a merchant from Milan, had traveled there to meet his family.

Head lowered, shoulders hunched, the surgeon would plod through the cobblestone streets. Once, fearing that Morisini was walking toward him, he darted into a side alley to avoid detection. But then he saw that the man was a ragged, starved-looking beggar, one of thousands of unfortunate wretches asking alms of passers-by.

One day he blundered into Scipio, and it cheered him to observe the electrifying change in the black man. It was as if a stranger, timid and withdrawn, had all these years inhabited his body, now aggressive and mobile. Scipio talked fluently of his plans, of his girl friends, of his undying gratitude. But his appreciation reminded Gasparo the more poignantly of his negligence toward Morisini and his gloom thickened.

Forgive me, Aurelio, he moaned, *I have committed a grave sin against you.*

Succeeding days and weeks brought new problems. People in the neighborhood were whispering about his failure with Morisini and they would clutch their amulets of theriac at his approach. The young surgeon would pace his consultation room, his boots crunching into the thick carpeting from Smyrna, but no one visited him, and more than once he kneeled before a silver crucifix to pray. Cardano referred patients, but when they heard about Morisini, they vanished. *How can I regain my reputation?* the surgeon pondered, but he could find no answer. At the University of Bologna Cesare Aranzio was publicly speaking out against him, and his student supporters were less enthusiastic since the Morisini operation.

One evening Lorenzo came to say good-bye. He was with Caledonia Bargillini (they were engaged to be married, but Lorenzo still found time to visit Signora Rinaldi's) and he announced that in a few weeks he would depart to fight the Turks. Desiri was laughing and drinking, pounding Gasparo on the back, slipping his hand under Caledonia's dress to pinch her thigh. Caledonia Bargillini fascinated him. She was flirtatious, laughing easily, and, unlike many girls, did not try to moralize with him or control him.

"I shall pierce through the Turkish infidels," he chortled. "Their blood shall transform the color of the soil."

On the battlefield I would have the opportunity to test my theories, mused Gasparo. *I might reclaim my good name and outflank my enemies. I shall discuss this matter with Giulia.*

Chapter 7

In the early sixteenth century the Turks were a formidable naval power, ruling Greece and the islands of the Archipelago, as well as Rhodes, Syria, Egypt, Tripoli, Tunis, and Morocco. Their fleet dominated the Mediterranean, and Austria and Poland constituted the sole barrier to the westward advance of the Turkish hordes.

Intent on preserving her trade with the East, the Republic of Venice had signed a secret pact with the Turks which gave Venice undisputed possession of Cyprus for more than eighty years. An island of great strategic importance, Cyprus was located at the eastern end of the Mediterranean, south of Turkey and west of Syria.

When Sultan Suleiman died in 1566, the nations of Europe, divided, were unable to take effective measures to block the power lust of his successor, Selim II, a semi-imbecile nicknamed the "Drunkard." Turks and Moors ravaged the opposing forces, plundering and taking slaves. On capturing Christian ships or raiding Christian villages, they would carry off captives and enslave them for the remainder of their lives, training them to pull oars in their galleys.

Pope Pius V attempted to band Christendom together to drive the invaders back from the Danube and the Mediterranean, but the bickering European powers could adopt no common course of action.

In 1570 the Turks sent an envoy from Constantinople to the Venetian Senate bearing the message that Sultan Selim was now sovereign on Cyprus, and demanding that Venetian troops evacuate the island.

The Venetian Republic was ill equipped for warfare but the Doge and Senate rejected the Ottoman ultimatum and requested aid from the Vatican. Pius V responded, putting his resources at the disposal of Venice and asking others to help; at last he could mass the forces of southern Europe against the heathen. Cosimo de' Medici supported the Pope, who had crowned him Grand Duke of Tuscany.

Cosimo had instituted the Tuscan Order of Santo Stefano with headquarters at Pisa. Its cross was similar in shape to that of the Knights of Malta, but red instead of white. This naval order of noblemen aimed at ridding the Mediterranean of pirates, propagating the Christian faith, and liberating Christians captured by the Turks.

As Grand Master of the Tuscan Order of Santo Stefano, Cosimo dispatched his mightiest craft to Cyprus, manned mostly by Florentines but including warriors from many sections of Italy. On the lead galley was a bragging, swearing crew of fighting men; it included Lorenzo's father, Captain Luigi Rimini Desiri, and the noseless Abizio Pepoli, as well as Pepoli's lifelong enemy, Felice Castelli, head of his clan, a cool, haughty man said to be more expert with his sword than any of his *bravi*.

Cosimo's galleys landed at Cyprus at night and the soldiers, wading to shore, marched to the aid of the Venetian commander, Antonio Bragadino, defending the Famagusta fortress from the Turkish onslaught.

In the meantime, thanks to the tireless efforts of Pius V, a fleet of Maltese, Genoese, Roman and Venetian galleys had been assembled under the command of Prince Colonna. This force sailed for Crete to join a squadron of Venetian galleys.

But the Turks moved quickly and decisively. In a show of strength, their fleet emerged in the waters of Cyprus, landing an armed force of seasoned warriors to institute the siege of Nicosia.

Colonna was in nominal command of the Christian fleet, but the real control was wielded by a committee composed of the squadron chiefs. Councils of war were stormy, and by the time the Prince took his galleys across to the coast of Asia Minor, Nicosia had fallen to the invaders, who were attacking Famagusta.

Again the commanders failed to agree. Veterans of prior campaigns in the Mediterranean, they squabbled with one another for power and no strong leader was able to take charge. Delay followed delay. Then there was poor weather, and the squadrons sailed to ports in Italy and the west coast of Greece for the winter months. Only a Venetian squadron remained to patrol the harbors of Crete.

Confidently, the Turkish hordes pressed forward on Famagusta, blockading it by land and sea. Their general, Mustapha Pasha, demanded that the defenders surrender, but the Venetian Bragadino, commanding the fortress, refused and, aided by Cosimo's forces, continued to repel the enemy.

By June 1570, the Turks had lost thirty thousand men to the Christian guns—and to the dread fever, but Bragadino's starving, ragged garrison, thinned out by the invaders' fire power and by disease, was in desperate straits. There was no more flour for bread, almost no gunpowder, and no reinforcements were on the way. Finally, Bragadino was forced to dispatch a flag of truce to Mustapha Pasha.

Now a treacherous and vicious deception. The Turkish general, professing admiration for the heroism of the Italians, said he would permit them to march out with honor. They would, said Mustapha, be transported under the flag of truce to Crete and be liberated. The commander, Bragadino, accompanied by his Venetian officers, was received cordially at Mustapha's tent. But then, separated from their soldiers, they were taken prisoner and robbed of their personal property. Some were beaten; others, with cords attached to their genitals, were paraded naked through the streets, humiliated, mutilated. Hands bound behind his back, Bragadino was forced to stand in front of Mustapha's tent and watch the Turks, laughing and screaming abuse, behead his officers. The Bolognese, Felice Castelli and Luigi Rimini Desiri, stoical, silent, were executed and finally, shouting, struggling to wrench himself free, the noseless Abizio Pepoli. "We will take revenge," yelled Pepoli. "Turkish infidels, you, too, will die!" And then Pepoli was no more.

Mustapha Pasha's huge belly was heaving with laughter. The sight of Abizio Pepoli had inspired him with a new idea for torturing his last prize, Antonio Bragadino. "Cut the accursed Venetian's nose and ears off," he commanded.

Bragadino, trembling, did not cry out at the mutilations, but blood poured over his face and dripped down to drench his uniform. He started to fall but two Turkish guards seized his arms and, holding him upright, paraded him through the ranks of the jeering Turkish army, where the coarse soldiers mocked him and launched their spittle to land on the bleeding, exhausted body.

"Flay him alive," roared Mustapha and the horror had barely begun when Bragadino was dead. "Take the skin from his body. Stuff it with straw and send it with the heads of these accursed Christians to Sultan Selim so that he will know what his brave men have done in his island of Cyprus."

News of the atrocities reached Italy and Pope Pius V's pleas for unity were now heeded. Pius warned that the country would fall to the Turks if the states did not band together to repulse them and drive them from the Mediterranean.

Furious at the fate of his father, Lorenzo Desiri volunteered to fight. He, together with Taddeo Pepoli, named for a famous ancestor, and Alberto Castelli, joined the army of Grand Duke Cosimo, all determined to avenge their fathers' hideous deaths.

After saying good-bye to Lorenzo, the surgeon considered whether he should volunteer his services. No patient had consulted him since his operation on Morisini, and he had done little but feel sorry for himself. But with the fighting men on the ships of war, he would be useful. Moreover, he could put his theories to a practical test while giving medical help to the wounded.

"I am in doubt," he said to Giulia. "What is your opinion?"

"The decision is yours."

"We are newly married and certainly I owe you my presence—"

"You owe me nothing. You have given me your love, Gasparo, and is this not all I could expect? No matter what happens, you have made my life beautiful."

"And if you are with child?"

"Then the stars bless me, because he will be part of you and I shall love him."

Feeling guilty, not wishing to desert her, Gasparo had difficulty sleeping. "I will go to the wars," he announced to his wife finally.

"I shall feel sad while you are gone, and daily will I pray to Our Lord for your safe return. But it is necessary for you to go, and never will I stand in the way of your happiness."

"I feel unworthy alongside your shining virtue."

"A woman's trick, my Gasparo. It is I who should feel shame in utilizing a woman's guile and causing you to reproach yourself. *I* apologize for being a woman."

"Ah, but that is my greatest delight, and I shall prove it to you."

"I promised Isabetta I would wash the dishes and dust the furniture." With a flirtatious rustle of silks, she pirouetted to him and, kissing him lightly on the cheek, smiled up at him. "Tonight."

Later, Giulia began to sing as she undressed for bed, and they felt a great tenderness for each other. She did not want to let him go. Attempting to be brave, she would not reveal her deep fear that perhaps he would not come back from the war—or that if he did, his throat would be slit, as with Giovanni Andrea. She recalled the time years before when after the death of his father Gasparo had come to her for consolation and she had hummed a lullaby and had caressed him with maternal solicitude.

On the evenings before his departure, they made love every night, and on the final night her affection was mixed with a terror that she could not suppress. Would her husband return whole from the battlefield? She kissed his hands again and again—the hands of her husband, mightier than those of Michelangelo, for he was a sculptor of the flesh, not of marble, breathing new life into the afflicted. She kissed each finger and prayed that, if he returned, each would be unharmed. For if he arrived with his precious hands, his skilled fingers, mutilated, life would end for him and for her.

At twenty-six Lorenzo, barrel-chested, with muscular legs, was proud of his physical strength. By habit he would bang his right fist into his left palm, as if smashing in the face of one of the heathen Turks who had cut off his father's head. *Oh, I will split open the skulls of those Turkish heathen,* he seethed, tears of rage in his eyes. *I will avenge you, Father.*

Before leaving for the wars, Lorenzo spent one last week in Bologna gambling, drinking, and whoring. One night he was challenged by a fellow in Signora Rinaldi's luxurious living room. He leaped upon the man with both fists, driving him skidding over a walnut serving table to crunch into a figurine of the goddess Venus which shattered, evoking a torrent of wailing from the proprietress. And at the end of the week, fingernails manicured, mustache trimmed, wearing his most elegant robe, Lorenzo married Caledonia in the Cathedral of San Pietro.

Then, blessed en masse by Cardinal Morone, Lorenzo Desiri, Taddeo Pepoli, Alberto Castelli, Gasparo Tagliacozzi, and the other volunteers left on horseback for Pisa to answer Cosimo's call. Thundering down the narrow crooked streets of Bologna, they reached the outskirts of town and headed for Florence, leaving behind the Apennines and the dozens of towers upthrusting over the university city. In formation, the horses pounded down the country roads, dust flying in the air, and the doublets of the fighting men were soon moist with perspiration.

Gasparo spurred his stallion alongside the companionable Taddeo Pepoli most of the way to Florence. He carried with him a black leather case filled with instruments made for him by a silversmith from a nearby hamlet. They included a powerful broad-bladed forceps, razor-sharp knives and scissors, and fine delicate needles. He also packed spools of superb-quality thread and an apparatus sewed for him by Giulia. It consisted of a cap designed to fit the head, a jacket for the chest, an arm sling, and strong-fibered laces. This was a device on which he placed his deepest hopes: if, after operating on a patient, it could keep head, arm, and chest precisely in position, immobilizing the skin graft, freezing the skin flap . . .

In the City of Florence they were received in the Medici palace by Duke Cosimo, his sons Francesco and Pietro, and his huge son-in-law, Paolo Orsini, Prince of Bracciano, who was to command the Tuscan galleys. They and their cause were blessed in the name of the Roman Church.

Arriving in Pisa, they were greeted by the Knights of Stefano, dressed in flowing robes with red crosses. After Mass, they manned the galleys, stowing their meager possessions on board and almost immediately sailing for Messina, where they were to join the great armada of the Holy League under the command of Don Juan of Austria.

At Messina a tremendous fleet was massed. In the wake of the atrocities at Famagusta, Pope Pius V had assembled an awesome naval force from a Holy League composed of Spain and Malta as well as Rome, Venice, Naples, Sicily, Tuscany, and other states of Italy. Two hundred and seventy-eight ships jammed the harbor, 202 of them galleys, with a force of thirty thousand men aboard, including five hundred gunners and thousands of stalwart oarsmen.

Again, there was little time, and the fleet of ships put out to the open sea, reaching Corfu ten days later.

Meanwhile, the Turkish fleet in the Cyprus waters had been reinforced with galleys from the arsenal at Constantinople and with a squadron of corsairs under the leadership of Pasha Ulugh Ali, one of the Turks' ablest naval commanders. Ulugh Ali, like many of the Turkish admirals, was more pirate than officer. He would at times dissipate his strength, making sorties aimed at injuring the trade of the Christian states. One Ottoman task force landed on the western shores of Greece, plundering villages and capturing merchants.

Early on the morning of October 2, the Christian armada, having sailed from Corfu to the coast of Albania, moved out of the Bay of Gomenizza, heading south, passing through the straits between Cephalonia and Ithaca, where just a few years before the Christians had fallen before the Turks. A storm arose and the fleet took shelter for two days in the Bay of Cephalonia. On October 6, the violent waters calmed somewhat and the craft put out to sea without sail. The winds were still fairly savage and the waves more turbulent than usual, but the men at the oars pulled mightily until they reached an island where they anchored for the night. The opening of the Gulf of Corinth was nearby, and not more than twenty miles away, in the Bay of Lepanto, was the Turkish fleet.

The commander of the Ottoman armada, Ali Pasha, a veteran of Sultan Suleiman's victorious campaigns, was anxious for the battle to begin. Ali Pasha had received a distorted estimate of the Christian strength. One of his most trusted spies had cruised the Sicilian waters and, painting his ship black, had slipped into the harbor of Messina at night before Don Juan's arrival. He had counted the Christian galleys, frigates, and galleasses but his strength report was inaccurate because the fleet had not yet fully assembled. At Corfu he had tried to confirm his estimate, but had been unable to infiltrate close enough to do so; this time he conveyed a belief that the Turkish fleet was superior to that of the enemy. Ali Pasha strained for an early engagement.

In actuality, the Ottoman fleet was approximately the same size as the Christian armada, ranging from two hundred and fifty-four galleys with sails and oars to twenty smaller craft. Under General Porter Pasha were twenty-five thousand soldiers. They included Greek and Calabrese renegades, Arabs and Syrians, residents of Rhodes and of the Greek islands, and men from Tripoli, Tunis and Algiers.

Ali Pasha divided his force into four squadrons. The right wing of fifty-six galleys was under the command of Mohammed Scirocco. The left wing of ninety-three galleys was under Ulugh Ali of Algiers. Ali Pasha himself led the central squadron of ninety-three craft. A reserve of thirty smaller craft was under the leadership of Murad Dragut of Constantinople. But, with hundreds of his sturdiest warriors suffering from fever, Ali Pasha's ships were undermanned. This increased the manpower advantage of the Christians and, further, though a handful of their rowers were captured Turks, most were hired mercenaries or convicts, chained to the oars, who would be released to fight on the day of battle and would receive pardons in case of victory. The Turks had no such advantage to claim: rowing their craft were thousands of starved, beaten, humiliated Christian prisoners who, when exhausted, were often hurled overboard. Moreover, their soldiers were armed, in many instances, with bows and arrows rather than muskets and their contingent of arquebusiers was not equal to the Christian complement.

Nevertheless, overconfident on receiving the misinformation, Ali Pasha, disregarding the advice of some of his admirals, acted. He issued orders for his fleet to embark from the Bay of Lepanto and pass through the narrow straits into the Bay of Calydon, in the Gulf of Corinth, anchoring there for the night.

Nearby, the Christian armada was anchored. At dawn on the morning of October 7, a red sun was rising and a temperate breeze was rippling the cloth on the ships' sails as a Christian patrol reconnoitered the narrow channel between Oxia Island and Cape Scropha, moving into the wide mouth of the Gulf of Corinth.

"The enemy," the commander of the patrol was yelling, his craft returning to the main body of the fleet. "We have sighted the Turkish fleet."

On the *Reale,* Don Juan of Austria was alerted, and the patrol commander boarded the flagship to deliver his report.

"They are to the east," he said. "One of my men counted two hundred and fifty sails."

"Can you be certain of their number?"

"No. But, sir, they are heading directly toward us. Of this I am positive."

Don Juan issued the order to prepare for battle. For a moment he vanished, reappearing on deck in his finest suit of plated armor decorated with swirling arabesques, his peaked helmet jutting forward over his sharply pointed chin, on the back of his helmet a velvet plume. In his hand he clutched the consecrated banner given him by Pope Pius V, a large square flag embroidered with the crucifix and the figures of Saints Peter and Paul. Lowering himself over the side of his flagship, he descended into a brigantine, which then toured the fleet he commanded. Erect, standing in the bow of the brigantine, holding high over his head the banner, Don Juan of Austria proclaimed to his fighting men, "If every man does his best, we will win. I swear it in the name of Our Lord and as representative of our Holy Church."

The brigantine moved past each ship of the armada, the commander standing at attention, saluting his men, bidding them take courage. "Free the Christian galley slaves," shouted Don Juan. "Give them weapons to fight for us and for their freedom. This is an order. Free them now."

And, returning to the flagship *Reale,* the young leader gave the signal, and the Christian fleet, in formation, moved forward to engage the Turkish forces.

Agostino Barbarigo's division had positioned itself to the left of the armada. Two brothers, Ambrogio and Antonio Bragadino, cousins of the martyr of Famagusta, captained the galleasses leading this division. The sails of all ships were furled, the long yards hauled fore and aft, and Barbarigo stood at the extreme left peering ahead for sight of the Turks.

The central division of the fleet was aligned as planned, with Don Juan in the middle, Veniero and Colonna to the left and right in their galleys, and a pair of powerful galleasses in front.

On the right, the commander Doria directed his men to hold to their stations and watch for the enemy, while the reserves maintained their role in backing up the files of front-line naval vessels.

"The heathen approach!" A lookout on one of the lead galleasses shouted this, and the cry gathered momentum as thousands of men repeated the words, pulling out their pistols, unsheathing their daggers, waving their swords above their heads, screaming out their eagerness to revenge themselves upon the barbarians who had butchered their countrymen so mercilessly. The wind was favoring the oncoming Ottoman fleet.

On Barbarigo's right wing, Lorenzo Desiri and Gasparo Tagliacozzi were on the deck of their galley.

Lorenzo was banging hand into fist in the gesture that had become habit. "I shall slaughter the infidels," he bellowed. "I will avenge the death of my father. Every Turk who comes near me will be a dead Turk."

"I pray for your safety."

"Pray? And you, Gasparo? You will not fight these inhuman heathen?"

"No, Lorenzo. I came to heal, not to fight. If you are wounded, my friend, I will do everything in my power to assist your recovery."

Suddenly the wind favoring the Ottoman fleet died down, and the turbulent waters became as placid as the waters of a lake.

"It is an omen," shouted Don Juan of Austria from the flagship *Reale*. "We shall repulse the attack of the Turkish renegades. Fear not, my brave fighting men."

Furling their sails, the Turks moved straight at the Christian navy. At noon, in the heat of a blazing early October sun, the Battle of Lepanto commenced.

First to fire were long-range cannons mounted on the Christian galleasses. The roar of their shells almost deafened the men nearby, and one, landing on Ali Pasha's flagship, exploded in the middle of a group of the Turks' most dreaded troops, the fearsome Janissaries. Screams of anguish rent the air, and, splitting up into disorganized configurations to escape destruction, the Ottoman galleys surged past the galleasses toward the main body of the Christian fleet.

At close quarters now, the noise was overwhelming. The blare of Christian trumpets was answered by the roll of Turkish drums, and the arquebusiers and grenadiers showered death upon the invaders as Turkish muskets retaliated.

With Barbarigo's fighting men, Lorenzo clenched his teeth so fiercely that he drew blood from his lip. He beckoned to Taddeo Pepoli and a group of Christian warriors near him.

"Let us board the heathen galley and butcher the Turkish swine," he bellowed.

An Ottoman galley was so close to his own craft that he could discern the brown eyes and close-cropped beard of a huge fellow in blue caftan and high white cap, a lance waved aloft in his right hand, dagger clamped in his teeth. *This Turk will die,* vowed Lorenzo. *I will slaughter him for you, Father.* The air vibrated with the explosions of gunpowder and the cries of men in pain, and penetrating through them the harsh summons of the trumpets and the rhythmic roll of the counterattacking drums. *I shall kill him for you, Father. I swear this, and may the stars desert me if I fail.*

Oars splintered and timber flew in the air as the Christian and Turkish galleys collided.

"Forward," yelled Lorenzo. "Let us attack the pigs and slit open their throats."

He leaped over the side onto the enemy galley and there was the enormous Turk, eyes blazing with fury, brandishing his sharp-tipped lance, a jagged scar running down his cheek almost to his beard.

"Ha," the giant screamed. "I will cut you open and pierce you through. Come and fight, Christian coward."

He had removed his dagger from his teeth and, lance in one hand, dagger in the other, he stalked Lorenzo, who threw himself upon the Turk and wrestled him to the deck, then wrenched free, hurtling to his feet with a bloodthirsty yell. As the giant struggled to rise, Desiri lunged forward with his sword and pierced him through.

"Ah," he shrieked, "you bleed, you swinish infidel. I revenge you,

Father." And Lorenzo slashed the enemy warrior—and again and again.

Blood was pouring from the man's left eye and from his neck, his blue caftan was drenched, and with his body immobilized forever, only his blood still lived, oozing out onto the deck to stain Lorenzo's fine leather boots.

Taddeo Pepoli was struggling with a pair of Turks and Lorenzo rushed to his aid. "Ha, I will slay all of you wretched barbarians." Feigning a thrust at one enemy's face, he slashed him in the belly, then joined Taddeo crossing swords with the other.

"He is mine, Lorenzo," shouted Taddeo Pepoli. "I will dismember his head from his body."

"And I will hurl him overboard to the sharks," yelled Lorenzo. "*In nome de Dio,* it is what these illegitimate sons deserve."

Elsewhere, Barbarigo's left wing had cornered the galleys of Mohammed Scirocco. The Egyptian pasha's ship locked oars with those of the Venetian flagship and the Turks fired their muskets and launched their arrows point-blank at the Christians. Barbarigo, with an open visor, was struck in the face by an arrow and was carried below, where he died. His nephew assumed command and drove the boarding party from the flagship's decks. Then he was killed by a Turkish musketeer. His warriors commanded the arquebusiers to fire and, reinforced by Venetians and Spaniards, charged onto Scirocco's flagship with swords and pikes. Scirocco was pierced in the chest and the Christians moved in on the leaderless enemy, slashing them till blood flowed like a river over the entire deck of the flagship, then, at the height of their rage, lifting the corpses and dumping them overboard.

The fighting men of Barbarigo's left wing celebrated their victory by hauling down Scirocco's standard, stamping on it with their bloody footgear and spitting on it. A group of Christian criminals, freed from being chained to the oars to battle the Turks, set an enemy galley on fire; losing heart, other Ottoman galleys escaped, vanishing to faraway ports.

In the center, the skirmishing was fierce. The cannonading of the advance Christian galleasses had wreaked destruction upon the Ottoman command. Ali Pasha's ship, an extravagantly large galley, flying a white pennant embroidered in gold with verses of the Koran, was damaged by shot. Quickly, Ali moved on Don Juan's flagship *Reale,* flying the standard of the Holy League. At the same time, General Porter Pasha, on the right, was storming Admiral Veniero's galley, flying the lion flag of St. Mark, while on the left, the Pasha of Mitylene was heading for Prince Colonna's craft, decorated with the ensign of the Papal Keys.

At close range, Ali Pasha's cannons fired, the iron shot crunching through the bow barrier of the *Reale* and raking the rowers' benches, killing and wounding dozens of oarsmen. The guns of the *Reale* thundered back, but the bow of the Turkish flagship plowed through the smoke and stench of gunpowder to crash solidly into Don Juan's vessel. The captured Christian rowers screamed out in horror, legs and ribs and heads broken, chained to their oars as their own blood poured over them, oars splintering and fragments of wood shooting through the air like sharp needles to sting their tortured dying flesh.

Ali Pasha's ship rebounded from the collision, then glided alongside the *Reale,* a boarding party of caftaned, white-capped Janizaries hurling aside their muskets and pulling out their broad-bladed, one-edged swords, daggers clenched in their teeth, behind them armored Turks with visors open clutching lances and roaring out their hate for Christians.

"Fire!" yelled Don Juan, and his force of four hundred Castilian arquebusiers loosed a salvo straight at the massed boarding party. "Fire!" And the Turks were crumbling on top of one another. "Fire!" And the invaders were writhing in agony on their deck a few feet away, blood pouring from one dying body to another, survivors imploring the heavens to help them.

But Ali Pasha's musketeers answered back, and one hundred Ottoman archers launched arrows upon the crew of the *Reale,* inflicting casualties upon the massing Christian boarding party.

"Our advantage," yelled Don Juan. "Their decks flow with their lifeblood. Now. Now." Waving pike and sword, the Christian force clambered over the side to trample the bodies of the dying Turks and to challenge those who still lived.

But Ali Pasha had rallied his men. With scimitar and sword, dagger and lance, they ran through the boarders, and on the deck of the

Turkish flagship, Christians and heathens were dying in one nauseating pile of bodies, Turk moaning to Christian for aid, the Pope's warriors pleading to God for intervention, all bathed in an ocean of blood that soaked through their clothing onto one another's mutilated bodies.

And, waving his sword above his head, the muscular, swarthy, bearded Ali Pasha launched his laughter into the atmosphere. "We will drive you into the sea," he mocked. "Christian blood will turn the Mediterranean crimson."

Will this horror never end? Gasparo, alone on the deck of his galley, had never witnessed such carnage. Though one memory twisted back into his mind, perhaps in natural association to the savagery of the battle raging around him: the inhuman burning of Michael Servetus at the stake, the idealist Servetus on fire, howling in agony, as the mob taunted him.

Why? Gasparo asked, and he recalled how his father had justified the atrocity. What had Servetus done to merit such a fiendish death?

Is there an answer? Pacing the length of the narrow galley, the young surgeon stopped to scan the deck of the Ottoman galley nearby, where Lorenzo and his victorious comrades were stooping to heft onto their shoulders the bodies of dead Turks, hurling them into the waters of the foul, polluted Gulf of Corinth. The Christian warriors were filling the air with profanities, blood from their wounds escaping as they chanted of their courage and shouted praise to the justice of Our Lord.

I see no answer, mused Gasparo, *but must there not be one?* Was it the influence of Isabetta that caused him to continue to search for order and neatness and reason in the universe? He did not know. But he would keep on looking.

Meanwhile, in the center, directing the Christian armada during the Battle of Lepanto, the twenty-four-year-old Don Juan of Austria had regrouped his forces and awaited the counterattack of the Turkish admiral Ali Pasha.

Chapter 8

Screaming their derision, the Turks hurdled the rails of the flagship *Reale,* surging into the bow. Crouching at the sides, Don Juan's warriors waited until the invaders were concentrated there, leaping to their feet then and attacking with swords. Surrounded, the enemy struggled to break out of the trap but Christian steel pierced them through and shortly the boarding party was a mass of writhing, agonized dying human flesh, shrieking obscenities and prayers in their last hours on earth.

"Forward," commanded Don Juan. "This time when we board the flagship of Ali Pasha the bullets and arrows of the heathen will not turn back our onslaught."

The young leader was first over the rail and onto the Ottoman flagship. With his sword he slashed the first Turk in his path, then turned to wave his men onward. Half the fighting men on board were dead and the Christian swordsmen butchered the remainder—four hundred Turks were corpses. Last to die was the courageous, sadistic Ali Pasha, who slit his own throat with a dagger. A Christian warrior cut off the blood-drenched head and presented it on a pike to Don Juan along with the captured standard of Mecca.

Nauseated, Don Juan of Austria turned away, shouting "Throw the head into the sea."

To the side, Admiral Veniero, seventy years old, was leading the Venetian forces to victory. Standing erect near the poop rail of his galley, he ignored the cannon balls and bullets and arrows whistling past and repeatedly fired his blunderbuss into the Turks crowded on board General Porter Pasha's ship. His servant would reload his weapon and he would fire it again, aiming directly at the deck. Veniero and his men, from noble families of Genoa, Urbino, Parma, Milan, Mantua, and Rome, subjected the Turkish ship to a relentless barrage, sinking the galley, with Porter Pasha escaping in a smaller craft. Despite a bullet wound in his leg, the Pope's elder commander remained at his post until the enemy on his flank was defeated.

The Spanish writer Miguel Cervantes was twice wounded in this engagement. A musket ball mutilated his left hand. The bleeding wound had to be cauterized by fire and iron, but Cervantes managed to endure the pain.

While the papal forces were victorious on the left and center, on the right wing Admiral Doria was sailing with his fifty galleys southward to the open sea in a line parallel to Ulugh Ali's powerful force of ninety-three galleys. He figured that Ulugh Ali would surround the right wing of the Christian armada and overwhelm it with superiority of numbers.

But the Ottoman admiral outsmarted Admiral Doria. He maneuvered his rearmost craft close to the central wing of the Christians and, with a forty-three-ship margin over Doria, he assaulted the center at the same time that a group of his galleys attacked the right wing.

On the right flank of Don Juan's central division was the flagship of the Knights of Malta, and Ulugh Ali's warriors saturated the knights of the white cross with bullets and arrows. Many died under the barrage and then the Turkish hordes charged onto the ship, slashing the survivors and bringing back to Ulugh Ali as a trophy the standard of the Knights of Malta.

Still, this was the Turks' final stand during the Battle of Lepanto. Recovering from his surprise, Admiral Doria rushed to the battle from the south, followed by the reserves, and Don Juan dispatched twelve galleys to contain the attackers, soon vanquished.

Ulugh Ali escaped with fourteen ships, steering northwestward for Cape Oxia and the wide channel between Ithaca and the mainland. Doria started out in pursuit, but a strong gale from the southeast buffeted his ships and he decided to give up the chase and return to formation.

It was a great victory for the men of the Christian armada; finally, the Turks had been set back on their heels. Aside from the few galleys that escaped and those fleeing into the Gulf of Corinth headed for Lepanto, the Ottoman fleet was decimated, and Don Juan of Austria and his navy ruled the Mediterranean.

The battle, joined at noon, was over by four o'clock. Seventy-five hundred Christian fighting men lost their lives—five thousand soldiers and twenty-five hundred oarsmen. Deceased were noblemen from Italy and sections of Spain, as well as German mercenaries.

Almost all twenty-five thousand men comprising the enemy armada were dead, including Ali Pasha and most of his captains. Fifteen enemy ships had been sunk or burned; the papal forces captured more than two hundred vessels. One was the huge, luxurious flagship of Ali Pasha, laden with rows of bottles of fine wine, crates of sweet golden dates, figs from Smyrna packed into jars, dried fish from Egypt preserved with salt, and honey cakes and spices. A golden curtain, bearing inscriptions from the Koran, was on the door of Ali's room, and inside, on a table, was a purse overflowing with gold and silver coins, and on the wall, a medallion engraved with the Muslim profession of faith: "No God whatever but God; Muhammad is the messenger of God."

There was much to do. First, the survivors hoisted up the bodies of the dead and hurled them overboard to clear the decks and stave off disease. Then they helped the wounded below; there was a surgeon on a number of the ships, and the injured were transferred to these craft for treatment.

On one of Cosimo's ships, Tagliacozzi had set up a little office belowdecks with a cot, a chair, an instrument table, and a cluster of lighted candles. For hours, the seriously wounded were brought in and grimly the surgeon examined their injuries, attempting gallantly to lift their flagging spirits. *Pieta, Dio,* Gasparo murmured to himself. *Have pity.* One poor fellow's right side was half blown away by a cannon ball; he was gone before the surgeon could commence his operation. Another unfortunate had been pierced through by an enemy swordsman, the blade almost severing his stomach. The surgeon listened for his heartbeat, which was faint; the man's breathing was irregular and his skin was pale, almost green. *How can I save him?* Gasparo asked himself, but the question was needless, for the man's heart, too, had ceased to function.

Abizio Pepoli's son Taddeo was carried in with a bullet near the left groin and Gasparo was pleased to use his medical skill to aid him. He washed the open gash, cleaning off the dried blood with a clean cloth and then, with a probe, he tried to locate the direction and position of the bullet immersed in the fleshy part of the groin. Taddeo sat erect in the operating chair, gritting his teeth to keep from crying out, biting his lips, eyes shut so that he could not see what the surgeon was doing. For half an hour Tagliacozzi manipulated the probe until he had verified the location of the bullet. Then, enlarging the wound, he inserted a sturdy pair of forceps into the gaping wound and extracted the bullet as finally Taddeo screamed with pain. Following this, the surgeon dressed the wound: Taddeo Pepoli, at least, would recover. And he would return whole to his native Bologna. Others were not so fortunate and Gasparo worked far into the night doing what he could for them. Yet sometimes this was so inadequate.

Early the next morning, the battered victorious fleet sailed through the Oxia Channel where a fierce gale roused the waters to swell and roll and bounce the craft up and down and sideways. Then the rain poured down upon them and they were compelled to anchor with their prizes in a sheltered bay.

Gasparo had finished working on the worst emergencies. Now Lorenzo was scheduled to come in. Sleeping only three hours, unshaven, the surgeon cleaned his instruments and waited for his old friend, hoping that his wounds were superficial.

He was shocked at the sight of his boyhood chum. Lorenzo's cheek and the corner of his mouth had been slashed open by a Turkish swordsman; the wound was jagged and ugly, running downward from left to right across the corner of his mouth to his chin. Even more startling was his demeanor. Lorenzo slumped in the chair after shuffling into the room. He said nothing and stared blankly at Gasparo, almost without recognition.

And yet it was a wonderful moment for Gasparo, and he would never forget the thrill of it. *I can help him,* he was thinking. *He looks like a man with two faces. You were wrong, Father. I am doing the work of God; I*

*am sure of it now, because I can give Lorenzo a new face and he will laugh
again.*

Aloud, he said, "Cheer up, my friend."

Lorenzo did not answer for he had looked into a mirror after the
battle. Caledonia would no longer love him. The girls at the brothels
would mock him. All that remained was to spend his life killing
Turks—and even they had vanished.

"Once again you will be handsome, Lorenzo."

The warrior's eyes brightened for an instant, then he frowned.
"You are certain of this?"

"Yes."

Lorenzo hesitated. "What about Morisini?"

A cloud seemed to blot out the sun in the surgeon's mind but he
rallied. "I am certain."

The long, jagged slash remained, irritated-looking and seeming to
cut his face in half, but the old cocky Lorenzo reasserted himself.
"For what do you wait?" he demanded. "Operate." Then Tagliacozzi handed the patient two full tumblers of wine and Desiri
downed them. Preparations for the surgery were complete.

Finding assistants was not difficult. Lorenzo's bold leadership
against the enemy had made him popular with the other fighting
men.

Gasparo washed the angry wound with a cloth dipped in astringent while his aides pinned the patient into the operating chair.
Inserting waxed thread through the needle, the surgeon approxi-
mated the edges of the wound with interrupted stitches. For thirty
minutes he worked intensely, Lorenzo gripping the chair until his
hands were white, and finally crying out in agony. Then the surgeon
stepped back for a while as the patient drank another tumbler of
wine. Another fifteen minutes or so and the wound was neatly closed,
with the corner of the mouth restored to its normal position and the
cheek intact. But for the thin line of thread Desiri looked like his old
self. On each side of the sewed-up gash Gasparo placed pieces of
adhesive plaster; then he sewed these strips together with interrupted
stitches. This would prevent the stitches from tearing the skin of the
cheek.

"The operation is over," said Gasparo. "Was it endurable? No,

Lorenzo, I am sorry, you must not talk or laugh or smile. I shall remove the stitches in ten days."

His heart was singing, for he had helped a friend, and in a world where most men seemed bent upon destroying one another.

In a different sense, he found another case more exciting. Tomasso Antinori, a nobleman from Florence, had lost part of his nose to the scimitar slash of a Turkish warrior. His nose was not as deformed as Morisini's but the principle was similar and the surgeon was confident that he could apply the techniques he had developed after the failure with Morisini.

This time, he thought, *I shall work up gradually to the operation. Today I shall measure the width of skin needed for the nose and I will nourish the skin graft on the arm for two weeks before transplanting it to the nose.*

He made two incisions into the skin of his patient's left arm, lifting the strip of tissue, but leaving it attached above and below. Then he used a clean linen cloth to separate the skin bridge from the underlying muscle, bandaging the graft and applying an olive-oil-and-turpentine salve.

Ah, he breathed, surveying his handiwork, *in two weeks I will transplant this skin graft to the nose of Tomasso.*

Aloud, he said, "Tomasso, you will go on a diet specially prescribed for you. You will strengthen yourself with fresh fish, and as soon as we are in our native land we will see that you eat prime-quality beef and oranges and green beans and that you drink milk with sweet honey. In two weeks I will operate and you shall have a beautiful new nose."

Meanwhile, the Christian fleet was crossing the Adriatic Sea en route to its destination: Messina. Don Juan dispatched a convoy of galleys as an advance party to bring news of the victory over the Turks to the Italian people.

When the triumphant armada arrived in the port city, a huge crowd lined the docks and the bells of the churches pealed out their salute while the cannons roared in welcome. Leading the way into the harbor, Don Juan of Austria waved to the mob, holding aloft the standards captured from the enemy. The crowd responded with waves of cheering, and for three days the Christian fighting men enjoyed the adulation of the populace.

Taddeo Pepoli, wounded in the groin, had been worried about his potency in spite of the fact that the surgeon had removed the bullet.

At the pier were two prostitutes, and, with Lorenzo, they strolled to the brothel; here Taddeo felt reassured, for he found he was still a man.

After a night of abandon, the warriors returned to their comrades.

Cosimo's ships then departed with numerous trophies for the port of Pisa. Here, too, the crowd was wildly enthusiastic, and a carnival spirit radiated from it to the men on the ships and back again.

After Mass, the Church of Santo Stefano was made repository for Moorish banners and for the figureheads of Turkish galleys.

Later, at his elegant palace, Cosimo presented his fighting men with a golden medal. Dressed in the robes of the Order of Santo Stefano, he wore underneath a doublet of red satin and red stockings. A huge sword dangled from his waist and in the velvet lining of his scabbard, hidden by a gilded hilt, were a tiny dagger and a few small stilettos with points as fine as needles stuck onto the lining as into a needlecase. On his head was the crown with which he had been named Grand Duke of Tuscany by Pius V a year previous. This crown glistened with the Florentine lily, its points curving outward like the blades of the iris. In front was a large, red, heavily jeweled iris. His scepter was surmounted by the Medici *palle* adorned with the Florentine lily, as laid down in the Pope's Bull.

Near Cosimo stood his sons Cardinal Ferdinando, Pietro, and Francesco with his homely wife, Archduchess Joanna of Austria, and alongside them the enormous Paolo Orsini and his lovely wife, Isabella.

Afterward there was a huge supper and ball. The knights were dressed in elegant robes and wore the red cross of their order. The ladies were ravishing in their silk and satin gowns, hair upswept, powdered necks adorned with white ruffs or pearls, lips and cheeks crimson with rouge.

Don Juan of Austria bowed in most courtly fashion and assured

Cosimo that the Turks would no longer terrorize the inhabitants of Italy.

In the morning, Gasparo, with Lorenzo and others, galloped toward Bologna. Tomasso Antinori rode with them so that the surgeon could continue his operation. The celebrations of their conquest of the Turkish navy were endless. People from tiny villages would gather to congratulate them on their exploits. Young girls would rush to embrace them, and their mothers would prepare lunches of Italian rolls and thick juicy sausages; their good fortune would also bring them a bottle of refreshing wine, tucked away beneath a fine cloth napkin in a corner of the lunch basket.

In Bologna, their reception was tumultuous, and Giulia, impatient, had driven Isabetta to the outskirts of town so that she could greet her Gasparo an hour sooner.

For many weeks, Tagliacozzi had seen little but bearded angry men plotting to butcher other bearded angry men, and feasting his eyes once again on his Giulia, he told himself that he was the happiest man alive. Leaping from the stallion, he hurled himself at her, kissing her cheeks and her neck and her nose and her lips and then holding her in his arms as he buried his face in her lovely red hair. For days, then, they scarcely left their bedroom, firing each other with their passion, and Gasparo, fresh from witnessing such carnage and such human misery, asked himself how he had been singled out to be so fortunate.

Standing before her dresser mirror, Giulia would sing of her happiness, brushing her flowing hair and letting it fall back on her naked shoulders. She would look up delightedly at the face of her husband, reflected from the glass, his mustache tickling her shoulder as he kissed it gently.

His absence had intensified her desire, and in bed she was inexhaustibly passionate. His hands, his fingers, his body, his soul—he had come back from the wars unharmed and, grateful, she kissed his fingers and his cheek and his neck and he pulled her into bed and they made love.

His spirits rose to new heights. Lorenzo came to his office and he removed the stitches from cheek and mouth. The results were superb—there he was, the old Lorenzo. Desiri was so moved that he seized Gasparo in a bear hug, tears streaming down his cheeks as he vowed eternal loyalty.

It was time to transplant the skin graft from Antinori's arm to his nose. Tomasso, a guest in the Tagliacozzi household, was well nourished—Isabetta had seen to that.

Three days after removing the stitches from Desiri, the surgeon requested that Tomasso sit in the operating chair. Scipio was there to assist. Giulia fetched the head, chest and arm apparatus that she had sewed. Though Gasparo had packed it for his trip to Messina, he had not had occasion to use it during the Battle of Lepanto. This would be the first time, and he sighed as he placed the apparatus on the patient, for he was counting on this brace to insure the success of the operation. Morisini's head bandage, he reasoned, had been too loose, and in allowing the arm to yank the skin flap away from its attachment to the nasal wound, had it not caused the death of the skin graft and the failure of the procedure?

That would not happen this time. Deftly he pared the edges of the nasal wound; he then detached the distal end of the skin flap from the arm and raised the arm toward the nasal defect.

"Hold his hand and forearm over his head, Scipio. That's it. Now pin his arm close to the nasal stump."

Skillfully and artistically Gasparo sewed the skin flap from the arm onto Tomasso's nose. Then he quickly tied the laces connecting the head, chest, and arm apparatus to immobilize the graft attached to the nose and freeze the skin flap in position.

After an interval of about two weeks, he removed the apparatus, detached the remainder of the skin graft from the arm, and completed the operation on the nose. The skin graft on the nose was strong and healthy, and when the final nasal dressing was removed, Gasparo looked at his handiwork and then cried out: "Giulia! Giulia! A mirror, quick. A mirror for Tomasso. *In nome di Dio,* hurry up, my Giulia."

His wife turned to peer at Tomasso. "Oh," she said. "The nose is beautiful."

"Yes," said Gasparo, "but think of Tomasso. He has not seen his new nose in the mirror. Hurry, my Giulia."

And Tomasso Antinori, proud, stoical nobleman from the City of Florence, wept when he saw his handsome new nose and rushed to embrace the surgeon. "You are a superb craftsman," he said. "I'm almost grateful to that Turkish knave who pierced my nose, because now it is more handsome than ever before."

"*Grazie*," said Gasparo.

"I will spread your reputation far and wide, my dear friend," said Tomasso. "I have many friends of influence, and I am more than slightly acquainted with our former leader, Don Juan of Austria."

The surgeon basked in the glow of his success. He found Isabetta in the kitchen and seizing her around the waist whirled her about in a mad dance that sent them nearly crashing into the oven, in which his mother was cooking fresh turnips and green beans and an aromatic roast.

"Stop it," she screamed, delighted. "You have lost your mind."

"Mama, the nose of Tomasso is beautiful. Though not so beautiful as *your* nose, Mama."

"You *are* crazy. Now let me go; the roast is burning."

Flaminio Vulpi, rising in the hierarchy of the powerful Roman Church, was still obsessed with the idea of destroying Gasparo.

Now Censor of Books, Flaminio was a zealous representative of the Inquisition in its steadfast battle against the evolution of new concepts that might threaten the rigid teachings of the Church.

He analyzed every book submitted to him with a sublimated ardor, ferreting out the writings of religious thinkers that appeared to oppose Catholic doctrine. He investigated prefaces and marginal notes of manuscripts for sacrilegious remarks, reading between the lines to detect even the mildest innuendos against the established order of the sacraments and rituals of the Roman Church. He hunted down books submitted without the approval of the censors and the consent of the Inquisitor.

Although the Index had indicated reservations about scientific observations touching upon navigation, agriculture, and medicine—in which the prognostications might be useful to mankind—Flaminio would exercise his authority to proscribe such doubtful material.

Booksellers, publishers, and printers would come before him to swear that they would conform to the regulations of the Index. But, in his thoroughness, he would tour the bookshops searching for prohibited books.

Trying to force the stream of learning back into scholastic channels, Flaminio sensed that eventually he would engage in conflict with Gasparo, who represented the new scientific learning. *And,* he told himself, *I will see that Gasparo is punished for flouting the will of God.*

For many months, Vulpi had been perusing the works of Girolamo Cardano. The professor was a heretic—there was no doubt of that—and Flaminio underlined passages that might be considered sacrilegious. Flaminio delighted in building up a case against Cardano, knowing that he was a friend of Gasparo's. As yet, the censor could not initiate action against Tagliacozzi for his old friend attended church regularly and had written no books; furthermore, he heard that the operation on Scipio's harelip had been a phenomenal success and therefore the surgeon would be unpopular to prosecute.

But, he mused, *someday I will get my revenge.*

One day a visitor was announced, a man with a hideous void in the middle of his face—only a tiny nasal stump. It was Aurelio Morisini.

Chapter 9

"I have been tortured," said Aurelio, "by a fiend without a conscience, who has utilized gigantic knives to slash into me until I thought he would dissect my face and present it on a golden platter to the Devil Himself."

"The evildoer?"

"A charlatan by the name of Gasparo Tagliacozzi, son of the pious Giovanni Andrea Tagliacozzi. Out of respect for the name of his revered father, I reposed my trust in this young butcher—but you see the result."

Flaminio Vulpi veiled the smile struggling to break out over his face. *Ah,* he thought, *but this is a stroke of fortune.* Opposite him Morisini sat, his carefully groomed beard framing the strong high cheekbones and flashing black eyes of a warrior, but in the center of his face was the red scaly nasal stump, and his image was destroyed; indeed, he was transformed into a monstrous defilement of a human being. *Yes,* mused Vulpi, *with this face will I bring Gasparo to his doom.*

Aloud, Flaminio asked, "You wish to testify against him?"

"I insist on revealing the impostor for what he is—a sorcerer, playing with magic, a man in league with the Devil."

"He operated on your nose?"

Morisini leaped to his feet. "You may call it that if you wish, Reverend Sir. I would call it torture. If not for my splendid physical constitution, I swear, *in nome di Dio,* that I would be dead."

Flaminio fought to hold his delight in check and, frowning gravely, asked for the details, jotting them down in a little black notebook. "I must congratulate you, Signor Morisini, on your nobleness of spirit, which has induced you to present us with evidence for punishing this man who has dared to challenge the authority of Our Lord. And, let me repeat, it is my understanding that you will be available to bear witness against this practitioner of witchcraft?"

"Yes," cried out Morisini, once more jumping to his feet. "The charlatan Tagliacozzi attempted to kill me, and I will testify to this under oath. He is a very dangerous man, and if not for the fact that I always wear my amulet of theriac against my very heart—Well, sir, who knows?"

"Let me assure you that our glorious Inquisition will prosecute—"

"I recall vaguely— Were you not a friend of this Tagliacozzi—as a boy?"

"Yes," said Flaminio stridently, "but that will not stop me in my pursuit of justice. I will not allow the sentiment arising from an old friendship to protect a sinner who has committed blasphemy against the will of Our Lord. I thank you, Signor Morisini, for telling me about this and I will be in touch with you shortly so that this impostor will receive his just deserts."

But Fra Chiari insisted that the evidence against Gasparo was scanty, instructing Flaminio to continue building his case against Girolamo Cardano.

Vulpi was disappointed and yet, to his surprise, he felt relieved. Leaning back in the straight chair in his dank, spare room, he massaged his temples gently with his long, slender fingers and, against his will, he allowed warm, friendly memories of Gasparo to roam about in his mind—how he had loved the lean, sensitive youth who had shared his childish thoughts and dreams. He recalled their walks in the countryside when they were nine and ten years old and then that afternoon in the carriage—when Scipio had lurched against him, the disgust he had felt and expressed, and then he and Gasparo clawing at each other, rolling in the dirt.

The ambitious Censor of Books laughed indulgently. *We were children then—sixteen years old? The father of Gasparo died afterward, and when I offered my consolation, we resumed our friendship.*

But another memory was battling for entrance into his consciousness. A balmy sunny day, by the lake near the Tagliacozzi farmhouse, he and his companion were stretched out sunning themselves
and Gasparo was asleep, his penis erect and— *No. I did not do that. No.
He infected me with the spirit of the Devil. It was not my fault.*

Shoulders hunched, hands clasped together as if in supplication to
God, Flaminio paced the floor. Once again he found himself suffering
from headache. Would this complaint never go away? With his fingers, he applied pressure to his forehead, but his head felt like a rock
and he was somewhat dizzy. *I hate Gasparo,* he told himself, *and I will
revenge myself upon him. But, first, his good friend Cardano.*

Professor Fracantiano of the University of Bologna was an avowed
enemy of Cardano's; they had chatted recently. He would summon
Fracantiano to his office.

"Are you certain," asked the Censor of Books, "that Girolamo
Cardano has treated the sick without confession?"

Fracantiano was smug, and Flaminio wondered briefly if he would
not feel more satisfaction in prosecuting *him* and deflating *his* bloated
ego.

"Of course," the professor answered. "He has long been negligent
in this respect."

"This is a grave offense. Do you have proof?"

"You have my word on this. Cardano is a practitioner of witchcraft. He has tried to lull people to sleep by insinuating false ideas
into their heads. He has exerted a magical power over them, con-
taminating their minds with evil. It is not medicine but witchcraft to
force demons into the consciousness of patients."

"And you have proof?"

"No, but I have seen him practicing witchcraft." Fracantiano
sneered. "He thinks he is a very clever fellow, does Cardano, but I
will show him that nobody can make a fool of me."

"Yes, but do you have witnesses? Will people swear that he has
served as the Devil's henchman?"

"No."

Vulpi snorted and again briefly wished it were the snide, superior

Fracantiano he was investigating. "Has Cardano ever professed a disbelief in witchcraft?"

"Many times."

"Do you have witnesses?"

"No."

"That is the trouble," said Flaminio. "But we must trap the heretic Cardano. We shall openly accuse him of practicing witchcraft and then, hopefully, he will deny it and state, before witnesses, that he does not believe in it."

"And then?"

"And then, my good professor, we will have him. Because an avowed skeptic who denies the existence of witchcraft is more dangerous to our great religion than one who practices it. The Roman Church recognizes the powers of Evil and their manifestations. Witches are the willing, conscious instruments of the malefic forces. Anyone denying this is a heretic and must receive punishment."

"Ah, your point is well taken."

"Leave it to me. Girolamo Cardano will regret his opposition to the ways of God."

Flaminio dispatched three minor officials to visit Gasparo's mentor in his home one evening but the mission was a failure.

"We come, honored professor," said one, "because, appreciating the breadth of your learning and the depth of your philosophical insights, we feel you may tender us precious advice to help a poor mortal in distress."

"Your opinions, honored sir," said the second official, "are revered throughout the great City of Bologna."

"And therefore," said the third, "we beseech you to use your influence and recommend that a poor defenseless woman condemned for blasphemy and witchcraft should be pardoned by both temporal and spiritual authorities."

Cardano's eyes twinkled. "I understand, gentlemen, but who sent you?"

"We come in the name of the Senate and we also represent the judicial officers of state."

"I see."

"You are a world-renowned philosopher, and obviously your word carries overwhelming weight. If you were to state your belief that demons and spirits do not exist for philosophers, you would be extending the hand of friendship and mercy to this poor woman and doubtless she would be released from imprisonment."

"I see." Girolamo stroked his beard and eyed his visitors impishly. "Oh, yes, I see. Gentlemen, I do not feel that I am conceited if I state that my wine cellar is second to none in our illustrious city. And with full heart I offer you to share in my pleasure."

"Yes. But will you help this unfortunate woman?"

"Gentlemen, I am an old man in search of continued longevity, and I regret that I am selfish and self-protective. I offer you the joys of my wine cellar but, my dear sirs, there my offer stops and I must confess that you offend my vanity, for, though seventy years old, I am in full possession of my faculties and your motives are extremely transparent."

"You misunderstand—"

"Oh, come now." Girolamo Cardano was on his feet, tall, erect, his eyes beaming mischievously upon the delegation. "I regret that you have not chosen to sample my delicious wines but I must bid you good night. My servant will show you to the door. Good night, gentlemen."

Realizing the futility of tricking Cardano, Flaminio accused him openly of impiety and heresy and, riding the crest of the Inquisition's authority, forced the secular leaders of Bologna to arrest the professor and imprison him. A lengthy ordeal began for the learned scholar.

His sophistication and genial cynicism helped him endure the first few days of incarceration with good humor but then he felt his very soul suffocated. For days he had talked to no one; every so often, a guard came by to slide a platter of unappetizing food under the cell door and that was the extent of his contact with the human race.

Cardano would look around his bleak cell, a trapped animal lusting to escape, but it was hopeless. The room was tiny, its harsh stone walls pressing in upon him. Only the door offered possibilities but the apertures between the black bars were pencil-thin, and when he grasped the bars with all his strength and pulled, there was no give, and he sank back upon his cot with a strangled sob.

Seventy years have I lived on this arrogant, unjust, insufferable earth, agonized Cardano. *I have suffered from the naïve idealism of my youth and taught myself how to survive disillusionment. No longer can anything surprise me. But this—no human being can live like this.*

He would pace back and forth across his cell—four strides in each direction. Pivoting, turning, striding out—and back, over and over. Evening would come and the professor could not differentiate it from the daytime—his room was always dark, illuminated only by a candle in the corridor outside. And always, he felt exhausted, but sleep would not come to bring him blessed relief.

And this became an obsession. How could he get sleep? Grimly, he would pad around the room repeating the multiplication table; he would interlink his fingers and crack his knuckles; he would resume his pacing, twirling the selenite and jacinth rings on his fingers. Still, he could not sleep.

I will go mad, he told himself. *I will go mad if I cannot get sleep.*

He began massaging himself—his thighs, the soles of his feet, the back of his neck, the smooth expanse of his forehead—but he could not escape into sleep. Now and then he dozed fitfully for a half hour or so but he was semiconscious and, unrefreshed, he would hoist himself wearily from his cot to stumble around the narrow cell.

After the most miserable week of his life, Girolamo had tired of looking for answers. Why should he care if he never had another good night's sleep? He was too spent to worry about this—or anything else. Words and images chased each other through his mind; he saw the sneering countenance of his rival Fracantiano, whispering behind his hand to Cesare Aranzio, and mingled with this were exercises in multiplication and the word "sin," which he kept repeating to himself—*sin, sin, sin.* Of a sudden, the pale, strained face of his only son, replaced by the intense, eager features of Gasparo Tagliacozzi and then by the lush body of his deceased wife—they were in bed together and he hungered for her—but this image vanished and he found himself eating dinner in his home, ah, rich red wine in his glass, with veal and melted yellow cheese and fresh-baked bread hot from the ovens.

Cardano jumped up from his cot. *I am starving to death,* he moaned to himself. *I cannot go on. Let them burn me at the stake. It does not matter.*

He heard violent noises outside his cell—then silence. Rushing to the bars, he peered out but could see nothing in the dim light. *What was that?* he asked himself. *Ah, of course, it was my guardian angel, appearing at God's bidding under the disguise of these horrendous sounds, telling me that I am to receive divine favor and escape the wrath of my enemies. My guardian angel will aid me.*

The professor shuffled back to his cot and sank down on it, holding his head in his hands and stroking his forehead with slender, long fingers. "My God," he muttered, aloud. "I am hallucinating. My sanity, where has it gone? They need not try me and convict me; they have driven me insane."

And finally he slept. For many hours he rested on his cot, unconscious of the tyranny of his small, cheerless cell or of the machinations of the people in power who were attempting to force him to his knees.

Awaking, he felt refreshed and almost calm. Clasping hands behind his head, he stared up from the cot to the bleak stone ceiling. "Life is like this ceiling," he whispered, aloud. "It is confining and hard. People come into this world ignorant and powerless and, as children, they dream of a happiness-to-be that is nothing but a mirage. I have been fortunate. I have known the flesh of many women and the companionship of many good men. For seven decades, I have lived comfortably, interested in my lifework, animated by a desire to help mankind, disillusioned by the hopelessness of this objective—but I have enjoyed good days. Oh, yes.

"Never will there be any rest for poor suffering mortal man. History, when it is truthful, discloses to us an endless chain of calamities and near-disasters. In the time of Polybius, murder was an everyday event, the great mass of people was enslaved, and ruthless dictators, unopposed, appropriated the property of many hard-working noble men.

"Death is inevitable, of course, but I have lived well, and is this not the answer to accepting death? 'He who passes a large stone from the bladder suffers less, by contrast with his preceding pains, than he who passes small gravel and he is less likely, therefore, to perish.' Who said that? Some doctor, was it not? Yes. And what is my point? I do not know. I cannot remember my train of thought. Oh, but I am so tired."

And Girolamo Cardano rolled over on his stomach and escaped again into sleep.

The next morning, a trio of men filed into his cell, unlocked by a stone-faced guard who slammed the door shut behind them. The men wore long, flowing black robes and their faces were covered with hooded masks. Cardano recognized one of the intruders. It was the Censor of Books, Flaminio Vulpi.

"We have come for your confession," said Flaminio. "Confess that with your pen you have written words of blasphemy denouncing our beloved Church. Confess that you practice witchcraft, and that you have sinned by treating heretics who have not submitted to—"

"I am a medical man and—"

"—confession."

"—I treat the infirm when they seek my help and when I feel I can assist them."

Vulpi stood erect, his back against the cell door, hands clenched at his sides. "You know perfectly well, Cardano, that the Church will not tolerate this."

"I have done no wrong. All my life I have tried to serve my fellow man."

"Yes, but what of God?"

"I have also tried, in my way"—and for a moment Cardano's eyes twinkled, as of old—"to serve God."

"You lie. You have challenged the will of God and heaped scorn upon His sacred authority."

"That is not so."

"I condemn you," cried out Flaminio. "I condemn you for your arrogance!"

Leaping forward, his assistant seized the prisoner, pinning his arms behind his back, holding him immobile while the third man, the prison executioner, fastened screws on Cardano's fingers and

tightened them until the professor's screams pierced the air and pal-
ing, almost green, perspiration flowing down his face, he went limp.

"He has fainted," said the executioner.

"He is a swine," said Flaminio. "Leave him on the floor."

When Cardano regained consciousness, he was instantly aware of
the searing pain in his fingers, swollen and discolored. On hands and
knees, he crawled to his cot and, with great effort, climbed up onto it.
Did they injure my fingers, he asked himself, *because I used them to help the
sick and the afflicted? Are they lacerated because they wrote on paper my ideas?
Ah, yes, this is a strange world, and this should come as no surprise to me. I have
asked little of life—good food and wine and books, a civilized spirit of inquiry,
and fine lusty females. For this, will they cut my hands off or rip the tongue from
my mouth? No longer do I care. If my good friend Pope Pius IV were alive—oh,
no matter.*

He fell asleep, dreaming that a tall man in black was thrusting his
sword at him, charging forward on his horse, wheeling around and
attacking again, the sword piercing his chest, blood pouring from him
as he shrieked in terror, while the horse, stumbling, collapsed on top
of him.

Blindly, the prisoner shot upright from the cot, plunging out of his
nightmare sleep into the real world of the dark, bleak, lonely stone
cell. "A dream," he gasped. "I was dreaming. Thank God for that."
Not that reality was much better—and surely Flaminio Vulpi would
conjure up new tortures for him.

But Flaminio changed his strategy again, taking the prisoner out of
solitary confinement, authorizing him to receive visitors. It was a sly
maneuver, actually, for the censor knew that Gasparo would come—
and frequently. Rudolfo Sylvestro, a former pupil, was first to console
his old teacher, and then Tagliacozzi appeared at the thick stone
fortress to offer his comfort. From then on, Gasparo visited each day.
He signed his name on a sheet of paper each time, and Vulpi chortled to himself, *The evidence against him is building. Oh, yes.*

The days passed, and the weeks. Each day Gasparo presented
himself to the guard at the front gate, signed in, and walked to his

friend's cell. His heart was heavy, for the damp, dreary solitude and the threat hanging over his head were destroying one of the finest human beings he had ever known. Oh, the old man hated pity and loved to laugh at life but the wit and good nature were draining out of him and—yes, he looked like an old, old man.

"When will they hold your trial?" asked the surgeon, trying not to notice the paleness of his friend's face or the deepening lines on his forehead or the stoop to his once-proud shoulders. "Surely it must be soon."

"They are waiting for the rats to eat me," said Cardano, attempting a smile, but his eyes were angry, "to absolve them of guilt."

"This is no joking matter."

"I am not joking, my boy—not really. I am expressing the rage I feel in a subtle way. Because I am a product of civilization, a civilization that brutalizes its members and forces them into deception and evasion and finally self-deception and arrogance— Oh, I am raving like a madman, Gasparo. You must once again find it in your heart to forgive me."

"No, you are not mad." Gasparo fought to keep the tears out of his eyes at the sight of Cardano's hair turned white, fingers swollen and discolored, face lean and starved-looking, eyes bloodshot and furious. "Others are mad. The Roman Church, perhaps, is mad. You are quite sane, and I will always be grateful for your friendship and your warmth toward me."

"I ask myself if their accusations are true. But always have I believed in God and tried to honor Him."

"And I, too."

"Yes." Sitting on his cot, the prisoner leaned over to regard a cockroach crawling on the floor. He raised his right leg a few inches off the floor and brought it down, crushing the roach under the heel of his boot. "Civilization is leaving me, my friend. I am becoming a barbarian, and doubtless the Church will kill me for this too."

"Let us hope not."

"I refuse to deceive myself. It will. But I would rather die by the hand of the executioner or by the torch than remain in this squalid prison, hungry and miserable, confined and dehumanized, filthy and ragged, for the remainder of my life. Because, my good friend, existence without freedom is a wasteland and the wise man fears not death but life without meaning or fulfillment."

Seventy-seven days after Girolamo Cardano was seized and imprisoned, his trial got under way. Pale, thin, trembling slightly, he was led from his cell, so bare and cold, into a long, rectangular room with high ceilings and a huge table behind which, in straight-backed chairs, sat six Dominican friars, thin-lipped, in their fine white robes with black hoods. At the other side of the room was the judge of the Inquisition, a tall, disdainful-looking man who seemed bored by the proceedings. Circling the courtroom were soldiers on guard duty, with bows and arrows and halberds and pistols. Two guards escorted Cardano to a small table to sit alongside his defense counsel, an appointee of the Inquisitor General.

Sighing, the prisoner seated himself and glanced at his counsel. He had not met him, and the sight was not reassuring. He was an inordinately repulsive-looking man, with hunched back, a cleft chin, and prominent cheekbones that jutted out from his face like twin peaks on a mountain. Worst were his eyes, mirroring his treacherous and self-seeking nature. *Oh,* mused Cardano, *this man hates me and he does not even know me yet.*

Flaminio paced the room slowly. He was tall and good-looking, but a petulance hovered about his lips and he had what appeared to be two left eyebrows, from the gash inflicted by Gasparo many years before.

This is what I have lived for, Flaminio told himself, walking with self-satisfaction toward the defendant. *First Cardano, then Gasparo. I will purge Bologna of these degenerate heretics. I will, like Savonarola, declare war on sin and on the ways of the Devil.* He saw himself as the Great Avenger, like the infamous Torquemada of the Spanish Inquisition, who, aided by the Dominicans, had butchered more than one hundred thousand people.

Assured, almost pompous, the Censor of Books announced the charges against the defendant, then, wheeling, began his assault. "Did you, Girolamo Cardano, write the manuscript *De varietate rerum,* printed at Basel in 1557?"

"Yes."

"And did you not state in Chapter Eighty that the Dominican brotherhoods were composed of rapacious wolves who hunted down reputed witches and despisers of God, not because of their offenses, but merely because they possessed great wealth?"

"No, I did not write this," said Cardano. "The printer, Petrus of Basel, added that statement in Chapter Eighty—without my permission. You may recall that I disclaimed it when the book was issued almost fifteen years ago."

"That is a lie."

The prisoner's eyes were gleaming with mischief. More than two months of imprisonment had deepened the furrows in his forehead, turned his hair white, and just about driven him insane, but now, on trial, he felt more like his old self, as if he were addressing a lecture hall full of students.

"No," he said urbanely. "I am telling the truth, and you are quite aware of this. Your statement is—and I will express myself delicately—not in conjunction with the facts."

At this, the six Dominicans cried out against the defendant, and the judge motioned them to remain silent.

"He accuses the pious Flaminio Vulpi of lying," roared Fra Chiari.

"Quiet, please," bellowed the judge. "The trial must proceed in an orderly manner."

"The prisoner should be flayed alive," said Fra Chiari, "for falsely accusing monks and nuns of sexual vices."

"This charge has not yet been made. You must remain quiet in this courtroom."

Flaminio was striding back and forth, hands behind his back. "Signor Cardano, may I ask if you believe in the immortality of the soul?"

"I do, and I can prove this. I wrote a book entitled *The Immortality of the Soul.*"

"Ah, yes, but before its publication did you not write a heretical book on the mortality of the soul?"

"No."

"Which you exhibited in secret to your intimate friends?"

"I did not."

"You lie."

Wearily, Girolamo Cardano palmed his forehead with his right hand and massaged his temples, which were starting to throb. He had once planned such a book, but his prudence had won out over his unorthodoxy and he had not published it. "I am not lying," he said. "Can you support your statement with evidence?"

Flaminio studied a sheet of note paper. *It is my ill fortune to face an antagonist such as this,* he thought. "In your book *The Immortality of the Soul* did you not attempt to cast the horoscope of Jesus Christ with diagrams?"

"Yes, but—"

"You are in no position to equivocate, Signor Cardano. Answer Yes or No."

"Yes."

"You admit this blasphemous interpretation? You admit your attempt to prove that the actions of our blessed Jesus Christ resulted from the position of the stars at the time of his nativity? This is sacrilege."

"It is sorcery," shouted Fra Chiari. "This man is a practitioner of witchcraft."

En masse, the Dominican friars leaped to their feet, heaping abuse upon the prisoner.

"You are a vile heretic."

"In league with the Devil."

"Quiet," warned the judge. "I insist on quiet."

"I will proceed," said the Censor of Books, as order was restored, "to a consideration of your blasphemous book *De subtilitate rerum,* which contains a passage on the tenets of Islam and another on the birth of Christ. Both passages are offensive to me and to all devout members of the Catholic faith."

"False," said Cardano. "I am a devout Catholic."

"You slander the name of God and of the Catholic religion. You demonstrate your heretical arrogance in book after book when you describe the divine principle as one that animates wise men alone— wise men and philosophers throughout history. We will not tolerate your irreverence toward your faith. If you admire Aristotle so much, when do you pay homage to Our Lord?"

Cupping his chin in his hands, Girolamo suppressed a moan of pain. What was he to say? The age of the humanist popes was over, and anything he had written would now be considered an offense. *Yes,* he reminded himself, *I have praised Averroës and Plato and Aristotle and Pomponazzi with impunity in the past, but no more.* Aloud, he said, "Young man, I pay homage to God in my own way and with as much sincerity as you profess to feel."

"I demand an apology for this outrageous insinuation," yelled Flaminio. "Immediately."

"I apologize," said the defendant softly, but his eyes were twinkling. "I retract my statement."

"He means not what he says," shrieked Vulpi. "It is two-faced disbelievers like this prisoner who have made our great City of Bologna a hotbed of heresy. Medicine and philosophy and free thought flourish here and religion declines. Since the reign of Pope Pius IV, heretical thinking has infected Italy like a spreading plague, and nowhere more than in our illustrious city. The Compendium of the Inquisitor states that Bologna is in peril. The evil Rotto, benefiting from the support of wealthy noblemen, has been collecting money and distributing it to blasphemers of the faith. We must decontaminate our beloved city, as our pious brother Savonarola did in Florence. We must save the world from sorcerers like Girolamo Cardano, who, in the name of knowledge, poisons the minds of the young."

"I deny that, my good young man."

"I am not your good man," screamed Flaminio, losing his temper when he saw that the defendant was still wearing his benign smile. "I accuse you of heresy and hereby petition this court for your conviction and death. Your life has been sordid. You were an illegitimate child, cursed in the name of Our Lord. You were not permitted to enroll in the College of Physicians at Milan because of your experiments with magic. And you were a friend of the infidel Vesalius, who mutilated not only corpses but a living person and who was saved from our blessed Inquisition only by Emperor Charles V, who stipulated that he must embark on a penitential pilgrimage to the Holy Land. Vesalius died after a shipwreck off the island of Zante—a just end for a sinner."

"Poor Vesalius."

"He was spared the righteous punishment of the Inquisition—but not you. You would dare prognosticate the future? You would deny the supernatural origin of disease? And disbelieve in witchcraft? And, then, you would incur the wrath of Our Lord by treating sick people who have not offered confession?"

"I have not sinned. I am not a saint and I do not believe in saints, but I have lived trying to respect the rights of the other poor suffering people on this wretched earth."

"You feel you have given to the world?"

"Yes. At best this world is an insecure and perilous home for man and beast, but I have done my best to cope with the absurdities of life."

"You admit it is absurd?"

"I insist on it."

Enraged by Cardano's composure, Flaminio exploded again. "You egotistical maniac, what have you given to the world? A drunken son, whom you yourself sent to jail? A malicious son, who poisoned his wife and was beheaded?"

The defendant leaped to his feet but was hurled back into his chair by two soldiers on either side of him. "You dare to—"

"I dare to ask this court for a sentence of death, by burning at the stake. You claim to love God but you love gambling more, and dicing, and wine, and the flesh of women.

"Your books—your more than two hundred books—are monuments to the Devil and show your disrespect for Our Lord. I stop here. Your books alone condemn you as a dangerous heretic. I need not make use of my other evidence. Your books show your admiration of Plato and Pomponazzi and your contempt for the supreme goodness of God. Can you deny that?"

"Yes."

"Then state your case."

"I submitted my books to the Index and received approval."

"Only because of your friendship with Pope Pius V. They were read superficially. Your writings stand as the evidence that brands you unmistakably a heretic. Formally, I do accuse you and ask the court for the death penalty."

Vulpi, exhausted by the debate, shuffled to his chair and sat down, and Girolamo Cardano, feeling despair creeping back into his heart, glanced helplessly at his counsel, who had said nothing during the trial. It was not a cheering sight. In this ugly situation, the tribunal had given him the ugliest counsel in the history of mankind—hunchbacked, deformed facially, eyes shifty and totally selfish. Cardano wondered whether he should laugh or cry, and while he was debating with himself, his counsel announced that he could not dispute the case of the prosecution and therefore committed it to the mercy of the judge.

"Have you anything to say in your defense?" asked this official.

"The accusations were unfounded," mumbled Cardano, and his eyes were sad and filling with tears, for he realized that the court would condemn him to die.

Indifferently, the judge recited the charges against the defendant, concluding: "These and other causes moving us, and desiring to purge the Church of God of such contamination, and to cut off from it so rotten a member, we, sitting as a judicial tribunal in the seat of our ancestors, in the name of the Father, Son, and Holy Ghost . . ."

The white-robed, black-hooded Dominicans bowed and crossed themselves, murmuring supplications to God. In his splendid suit of armor, a sword clanking against his waist, the captain of the guard directed his soldiers to stand at attention.

". . . we condemn you, Girolamo Cardano, to be bound and fastened to a stake, to be burned alive together with your books."

Cardano, slumping in his chair, was hauled to his feet by two guards, one at each elbow. His stomach bulged and his shoulders sagged, and his eyes were those of a drowning man who no longer wished to battle the power of the waves.

Flaminio's face reflected the joy of his triumph, but when he rose to leave the courtroom, he felt slightly dizzy. *Damned headaches,* he muttered under his breath, *will they never go away?*

The next day the Chief Inquisitor of Bologna was ordered to appear before the illustrious Cardinal Morone, who was wearing his formal red robe. "I have received a letter from Pope Pius V," said the

Cardinal, and his manner was frosty. "Personally, His Eminence has investigated several cases of alleged heresy, including that of Giro-lamo Cardano. The Pope, in his infinite wisdom, suggests the pris-oner be released for the following reasons:

"First, he has demonstrated good faith by refusing to treat the heretical King of Sweden.

"Second, coming from Milan, Pius avers that Cardano has never openly combated the teachings of the Church.

"Third, Cardano submitted his manuscripts to the Index for ap-proval. The Pope does not blame the prisoner but the laxness of the officials serving the regime of his predecessor, Pius IV, for sanctioning publication of these manuscripts.

"Fourth, the prisoner predicted the defeat of Italy at the battle of Cyprus, stating that the Italian fleet lacked coordination. He was the first to suggest that all states of Italy join forces with our Pope in a Christian crusade to subjugate the Turks. The Pontiff respects him for his acute judgment.

"Fifth, Cardano is a superb physician and our leader wishes his services in Rome. Of course, he is guilty of indiscretions, but we will warn him to exercise more caution. We will liberate him and then, unannounced, he will become the servant of the Church for the re-mainder of his life."

When Flaminio heard the news, he felt impotently angry and ut-terly crushed. He could not find a target for his fury so he punished himself instead. He had little appetite for food, and when he did eat, he was nauseated and vomited.

In his room he stripped off his clothes and with a whip flagellated himself until he began to bleed. Exhausted, he collapsed on his bed and stared listlessly at the ceiling. Was he dreaming or was the face of Gasparo on the ceiling? Was the surgeon laughing at him? His ten-sion mounted at the thought of his childhood friend and visions of revenge danced through his mind.

Against his will, Flaminio recalled the country outing when he had revealed his physical feeling for Gasparo. At this, he felt apprehensive and yet he experienced an erection. He began to massage his organ and almost instantly had an orgasm.

He felt more futile than ever now. Again he had disobeyed the will of God, and he could not be certain that the Lord would forgive him. He felt powerless, and, weeping, beat his hands against the pillow.

Late that year Girolamo Cardano was released from prison and escorted to his home, frail, stooped, broken in spirit. Never would he regain his old lust for life.

For eighty-six days he was a prisoner in his own comfortable home, giving the authorities a bond for fifteen hundred gold crowns as security so that he could act as his own jailer.

Then he set out with his devoted former pupil Rudolfo Sylvestro for Rome, where he spent the rest of his life under the protective custody of Pope Pius V.

Chapter 10

With the operations on Lorenzo Desiri and the Florentine nobleman Tomasso Antinori, Gasparo's reputation was re-established. Not entirely, of course, because in these years following the Renaissance, enlightenment and ignorance mingled in the most stupefying fashion. Thus, extremely superstitious people continued to avoid him, relying on their amulets of theriac to protect them from his proximity.

Giulia, too, had many troubles. An old friend confided she could no longer see her because her husband considered her a witch and feared for the health of their children. Sobbing, Giulia had run to her room, burying her head in a pillow until she fell asleep, but she did not tell Gasparo or even Isabetta, nor did she complain when an old woman rushed up to her in the town square to spit in her face and curse her in vile language as an evildoer assisting Gasparo with his magical incantations against the will of God.

At the university, also, Gasparo's miseries were mounting. No longer was his ally Girolamo Cardano there to defend him, and Cesare Aranzio and Ulisse Aldrovandi, backed by Cardano's relentless enemy Fracantiano, warned that his techniques were unconfirmed by science and were opposed to the principles of the Roman Church.

Still, the success of his operations on Lorenzo and Antinori had solidified his support from students at the university. At a large rally on campus, a medical school student delivered a ringing oration eulogizing Gasparo's work, and several university lecturers in the audience applauded his words. Then the students, carrying huge placards, marched, shouting their praise to Tagliacozzi, to the Piazza del Nettuno, where Gianbologna's statue of Neptune, streams of water spouting from the base, towered, the muscular figure of the man rippling high in the air, left hand outstretched, fingers spread, right hand clutching a long, lethal two-pronged spear.

Professor Cesare Aranzio delivered a strident denunciation of this meeting, arguing that Tagliacozzi was a heretic who merited punishment—but the students retaliated the following day.

On every day in which classes were held at the university, students and professors celebrated a Mass of the Holy Ghost in the frescoed chapel of Santa Maria de' Bulgari, off the courtyard on the ground floor of the famed Archiginnasio. Then, students were summoned to class at nine o'clock by the ringing of a huge bell, *la scolara*, for a half hour. Meanwhile, the professors, waiting in high-ceilinged corridors on each side of the chapel, were accompanied by beadles to their lecture halls. Dressed in full-length togas with flowing sleeves and ermine mantles, they climbed the wide staircase, preceded by beadles with silver maces on their shoulders, wearing black hose and jackets and mantles of rich velvet. In the classrooms, the students, waiting, would rise in respect as the beadle led the professor down the center aisle to the elevated lecture chair with its solid desk, topped by a canopy, a frescoed image of the Blessed Virgin overhead. The professor would then commence his lecture to the students, seated now at rows of benches with narrow table boards.

Aranzio, walking down the center aisle of the lecture hall to his chair, was greeted by the sight of students huddled on their benches, refusing to rise respectfully for the professor who had denounced Tagliacozzi. Such a form of rebellion was unprecedented in the annals of the University of Bologna, and, outraged, Aranzio charged the student body with heresy.

"Degenerates have assumed leadership among our students," he cried out to faculty members the day after the incident, "degenerates who defy the will of Our Lord and spend their evenings carousing drunkenly in our taverns, engaging in unspeakable debaucheries in the brothels, and returning to their quarters to smoke pipes of opium and to participate in other obscenities that I cannot trust myself to mention."

But public opinion among the educated favored Gasparo, and

townspeople were increasingly more willing to visit the young surgeon's office. Friends of Scipio and Lorenzo were impressed, and as for Tomasso Antinori, the Florentine nobleman was a friend of the fabled commander of the fleet that had subdued the Turks, Don Juan of Austria.

One day, a servant of Vincenzo Gonzaga, Prince of Mantua, clattered on horseback down Bologna's cobblestone streets to fetch the surgeon. The Prince was suffering from a severe case of erysipelas, his face was red and inflamed, and Tagliacozzi journeyed in his carriage to Mantua. For days he applied soothing medications. After a week, the erysipelas had disappeared and, overjoyed, Vincenzo Gonzaga embraced him and pledged his lifelong friendship. He showered the young doctor with gold pieces and fine silks and announced to anyone who would listen that Gasparo was the greatest medical man in all of Italy.

"I was positive that you would be able to help me," said Vincenzo.

"You were? Why?"

"You were vouched for by a man of unimpeachable integrity. Don Juan of Austria."

"Don Juan?"

"The resourceful commander of the fleet that conquered the Turkish barbarians. He told me of your splendid work during the Battle of Lepanto and of what you have done for Tomasso Antinori. And he did not exaggerate in the slightest, for you have relieved the unendurable itching in my face, and once again I can behold my countenance without loathing myself. I will always bless you."

And with his purseful of gold coins and parcels of silks, the young surgeon returned home to the greetings of Giulia and Isabetta.

But Vincenzo Gonzaga's troubles were not over, and a few years later he called on Gasparo in crisis.

Vincenzo, Prince of Mantua, had married Marguerite Farnese of the powerful house of Parma. The ceremonial festivities were elaborate, and the rejoicing of both families was great. The wine flowed freely, the violins played, the girls in their beautiful gowns danced, and laughter filled the air. No one was happier than Vincenzo's father, Duke Guglielmo, for this union promised the perpetuation of his bloodline.

But six months passed and there was no announcement. One year, and the bride was still not pregnant.

Duke Guglielmo decided on a heart-to-heart talk with his son. He dispatched a servant to bring him to his antechamber. Vincenzo appeared, handsome, graceful, a lean, athletic young man with flashing eyes, trimmed mustache, and carefully cultivated goatee. He was dressed in black velvet with a rich embroidered collar, a silken sash encircling his waist. With the rash gone from his face, he was a striking-looking dandy.

"My son," said Duke Guglielmo, "what is the matter?"

"Nothing, sire."

"Are you sure?"

"I am."

"Then," said Guglielmo, Duke of Mantua, limping slowly across the room—he was hunchbacked and, always conscious of his deformity, walked as erectly as possible—"why is your bride not with child? Why is she not fulfilling a woman's function and producing a child to carry on my family line?"

"I do not know, sire."

"You do not know? My son, if you do not know— You are sleeping with her, are you not?"

"I assure you that—"

"Yes or no."

"Yes, Father."

"Then what is the trouble? Are you impotent?"

"Of course not."

"Then is anything wrong with your bride?"

"I am afraid there is."

"There is?" Guglielmo, agitated, seized his son by the arm. "Tell me."

"I have done my duty," said Vincenzo, Prince of Mantua. "Regularly. Every night. But, apparently, Marguerite has some structural defect which—"

"Structural defect? How do you know?"

"I do not *know*, Father, but—"

"The doctors will examine her."

"No, she will not submit to such an indignity."

"You are right, my son. We will send her back to the home of her parents."

Depressed, the willful Guglielmo dismissed his son from his presence. He had heard rumors of Vincenzo's wild escapades in the brothels. *After all your debauchery with harlots,* he mused, *you might die, my son, before you provide me with an heir. We must dissolve your marriage and arrange an alliance with a wife who can give you children.*

Marguerite returned to Parma, and the families initiated a feud. The Farnesi were prepared to attack every living Gonzaga with sword and dagger but, revising their battle plan, decided to revenge themselves by spreading the news that Vincenzo's impotence had caused the infertility of the marriage. Duke Ottavio Farnese sent a representative to Florence to plant this idea in the mind of Grand Duke Francesco. Word of the feud passed from mouth to mouth throughout Italy and, snickering, people would gossip about it in the courts of nobles, in their homes, in the streets, in taverns and brothels.

Guglielmo, Duke of Mantua, appealed to Pope Gregory XIII and His Holiness delegated Cardinal Borromeo to arbitrate the dispute. Lawyers and doctors were engaged by both families to defend their position in writing, and one medical man suggested that Marguerite obtain the child of another woman and claim it as her own. Each family issued pronouncements and accusations and denials and soon any possibility of reconciliation had become unthinkable.

Anxious to settle the unhappy affair, Cardinal Borromeo advanced the idea that the bride, Princess of Parma, could entertain the possibility of renouncing the secular life and take her vows. Finally, she accepted this and, receiving permission from Pope Gregory XIII, entered a nunnery.

Thus the marriage of Vincenzo Gonzaga was formally dissolved, and the elated Guglielmo, Duke of Mantua, turned his attention to arranging a more suitable union. After a thorough analysis of the field, he concluded that the most advantageous alliance would be with the Medicis. The Grand Duke of Florence could also profit from a union with the Gonzagas, who were favorites of the House of Austria and were related to Archduke Ferdinand of Innsbruck through the marriage of Guglielmo's childless daughter to him. Archduke Ferdinand was a powerful figure in Germany. The court of France offered in marriage the sister of the King of Navarre, but Duke Guglielmo rejected this because France was devastated by religious strife; moreover, he feared that such an alliance would endanger his rapport with the House of Austria.

Thus, Guglielmo, Duke of Mantua, decided on Eleonora de' Medici and initiated the negotiations with Grand Duke Francesco de' Medici.

New difficulties were looming for Vincenzo Gonzaga, Prince of Mantua, and soon he would receive a challenge that would make him the laughingstock of Italy.

Fully aware of the advantages of the match, Francesco de' Medici gave his approval—but there was a catch.

After the wedding ceremony, he would confer upon his new son-in-law the title of "Serenissimo." But rumors of the Prince of Mantua's impotence had reached his ears, and he insisted that Vincenzo give absolute proof of his virility before the marriage plans became official.

Guglielmo accepted these conditions and a conference took place between Cardinal Cesi, Legate of Bologna, representing the Grand Duke, and the Bishop of Casal, in behalf of Prince Vincenzo. What test of potency could they prescribe? Dismayed, they sent for Cardinal Ferdinando de' Medici, imploring his assistance. Ferdinando heeded their request, leaving Rome for Florence to offer his advice.

A conference of notables was then arranged in the Medici palace. There were cardinals and bishops, including Cardinal Borromeo, representing Pope Gregory XIII, as well as secular leaders and prominent members of the business community. It was a stormy meeting.

Grand Duke Francesco addressed the assemblage. "You know the purpose of this meeting. Rumor has it that Prince Vincenzo Gonzaga is incapable of being a father. We know, of course, that this rumor, spread by the Farnesi, is unfounded. Nevertheless, it is of vital importance that we know the truth before my daughter ventures forth into matrimony. I will not tolerate an alliance that may endanger her well-being, and thus I beseech you learned gentlemen for assistance. Perhaps one of you has a suggestion." Francesco's manner was bland, but secretly he was delighted with this opportunity to humiliate the Gonzagas, for Duke Guglielmo had ridiculed his own marriage to Bianca Capella many years before.

Then Cardinal Borromeo spoke. "Guglielmo, Duke of Mantua, has asked his son to provide evidence to eradicate these doubts, and Prince Vincenzo has agreed to do this—but what procedure is advisable? I assure you, my lords, that I do not doubt the manliness of the Prince but, then again, we must leave nothing to chance. A number of people from the Church have questioned intimates of the Prince of Mantua but the reports are inconclusive. Most swear by his manliness, but others are not so sure, and, signors, though Don Cesare d'Este says he will vouch for his friend—I believe, ahem, that they performed certain rituals one chamber away in the town brothels, forgive me, O Lord—this is not absolute proof."

"No," said Grand Duke Francesco, "it is not. And my daughter, gentlemen, is not—"

"Calm yourself," said Cardinal Borromeo, representing the Pope. "I did not mean to impugn—"

"I must remind you that my daughter is a lady of noble character and fine sensibilities and—"

"Yes, Francesco. Please—"

Cardinal Ferdinando de' Medici interrupted. "Gentlemen, we have no time for soothing ruffled feelings. What we must face is reality. It is holy matrimony that we discuss, and I would recommend a formal demonstration of the Prince's capabilities. Does not everyone agree?"

"The morality—" began Cardinal Borromeo.

"We are not interested in morality," retorted Ferdinando. "Our concern is with the establishment of a fruitful union that will advance the interests of the families involved. We must not lose sight of our objective."

"A fruitful union under God," said Cardinal Borromeo.

Ferdinando nodded his agreement. "Under God, sanctified by the powers of Heaven."

"Excellent," said Grand Duke Francesco de' Medici. "This is the only sensible solution. I shall request Duke Alfonso d'Este to arrange this affair in Ferrara, where he will determine the nature of the test and the details of the rendezvous, and the principals."

"Forgive us, O Lord," said Cardinal Borromeo. "Our intentions are honorable."

"Yes," said Francesco, "and may I go on record as believing in the capabilities of the splendid Prince of Mantua. When the arrangements have been completed, I am sure that Vincenzo Gonzaga will pass the test, and that one encounter will be sufficient to offer proof."

"Let us hope so," said the stern Cardinal Ferdinando de' Medici.

"I will apprise Pope Gregory XIII of the agreement," said Cardinal Borromeo, "and assure you gentlemen of his tolerance and understanding. However, in the interests of the Church and to guarantee the benevolent attitude of Our Lord, may I insist that this encounter will not take place on Friday."

"Amen," said Cardinal Ferdinando.

"Mother of God," shouted Vincenzo Gonzaga, Prince of Mantua, facing his father, Duke Guglielmo, in his antechamber. "Mother of God, what now?"

"What?" screamed Guglielmo, Duke of Mantua. "Are you incapable, my son, of proving yourself?"

"No, Father, I am not." The Prince lowered his voice, as he usually did in the presence of the Duke. "But what kind of an indecent and shameful—"

"Oh," leered Guglielmo, "that is the trouble. But, my son, I have learned on the most reliable authority of some of your exploits in the brothels and—"

"Sire," said Vincenzo, his voice rising with an emotion that he could not control. "Do you not understand the absurdity of my position? Sooner would I take to the battlefield and match swords with the barbarous Turks than—"

"You cannot withdraw. I have given my word."

"I will not exhibit myself in so ludicrous a fashion. I will be the laughingstock of all Italy."

"No, not if you succeed. But if you withdraw from this test, people will say that the Farnesi's vile insinuations are true, and *then* people everywhere will scorn you and heap contempt on the House of Mantua, bringing us permanent disgrace. Is this what you want?"

"No."

"Then prove yourself and inflict degradation upon the accursed Farnesi of Parma."

The Prince of Mantua found himself pacing back and forth, stroking his neat goatee, his eyes afire with rage. Then a thought came to him and he stopped and turned to confront Guglielmo. "Perhaps," he said slyly, "this is a plot of Duke Francesco's to revenge himself upon you. He hates you because you ridiculed his marriage to Bianca Capella. Maybe he aims to get even with you through shaming me."

"No. The Grand Duke stands to profit from this alliance, which could gain him the friendship of the House of Austria, and he would not jeopardize this. The Grand Duchess will assuredly select a lovely young lady, charming and beautiful, to participate with you in this great trial—and, beyond doubt, she will conduct herself agreeably and offer her full cooperation."

"Great trial?" screamed the Prince of Mantua, afraid of his father, but seized with an impulse to fasten his hands around his neck and squeeze. "Full cooperation?"

"Yes."

"And judges will be watching?"

"Yes, my son."

"They will be watching me while— Father, can you not understand my feelings?"

"Yes, but you must not dishonor the good name of the Mantuas."

"The good— How many judges will be observing me?"

"I am not positive. Perhaps five."

"Five? Father, listen to me. Let us assume that my partner in this ridiculous adventure is the most beautiful female in Italy and I adore the sight and feel of her gorgeous flesh. Still, how can I forget that five bishops and cardinals are focusing their lecherous eyes on my— Heaven help me, while they are watching me anxiously attempting to penetrate this wretched, unfortunate girl, they will be wafting sanctimonious prayers to God and crossing themselves hurriedly so they can get a good look at what I am doing and— Father, I will fail."

"I know that you will do me honor, my son."

"Honor? And tell me, Father, from what brothel will they dig up a woman who will submit to this obscenity in full view of the entire Italian nation?"

"She will be a great beauty—and a virgin."

"A virgin?" A new terror poured over Vincenzo Gonzaga, Prince of Mantua, and he resumed pacing the floor, over and over, back and forth with increasing speed, and a sob escaped his lips. "You mean that I will be fornicating with a *virgin* before an audience of the most powerful dignitaries of the Catholic Church?"

"Yes."

Agonizing, Vincenzo Gonzaga continued to pace the floor. *Why me?* he kept asking himself. *Why me?* But finally Duke Guglielmo persuaded him to try, on condition that he have three chances.

The Bishop of Casal traveled to Florence to entreat the Grand Duke to accept the Prince's condition, but Francesco remained firm: one trial.

"I will give Vincenzo ten days to prove his manliness," thundered Grand Duke Francesco de' Medici, Duke of Florence. "If he does not pass the test within this time, I will consider myself free of obligation and contract a more suitable alliance for my daughter."

"But this would humiliate the House of Mantua," said the Bishop of Casal. "You must honor his request and give the Prince three opportunities to succeed. You must understand that this is a formidable undertaking before a group of judges."

"One trial."

"I implore you to reconsider."

There was an impasse for a while but then Grand Duchess Bianca Capella urged her husband to recognize how trying were the circumstances and to take a more reasonable position. Yielding, he agreed that the encounter could be staged three times.

The Grand Duchess then proceeded to interview more than one

hundred young virgins before she discovered a girl who combined the same qualities of beauty, charm, and wit of the bride.

"You must," the Grand Duchess instructed the girl, "give the Prince encouragement, for he will feel nervous."

The young virgin, a ravishing teen-ager, blushed. "I will do my duty," she whispered.

"You must not be frightened, my dear."

"Must all those judges watch?"

"It is God's will."

Venice was chosen as the site for the encounter, which fired the imagination of the whole Italian populace, who gossiped and giggled over poor Vincenzo Gonzaga, the beleaguered Prince of Mantua. It was announced that there would be eight judges: four cardinals and four bishops. This news would not inflate the depressed Prince, who, it was rumored, had not experienced one erection since the trial had been scheduled.

Cavalier Belisario Vinta, favorite of the Grand Duke, was selected to supervise the ceremonies and the honorable Vinta headed a strange procession from Florence to the great City of Venice. In the lead carriage were the impeccable Vinta and the young virgin. Following in two carriages were the judges, the cardinals and bishops of the Church.

"Yours is a grave responsibility," Vinta counseled the young girl. "If you entice him properly, the Prince's future is assured, and the House of Mantua will ensure your comfort for the rest of your life."

Nervously, the girl nodded, but said nothing, compressing her lips tightly.

"I have confidence in you, my dear," said Vinta, glancing at her hungrily. "The Prince of Mantua is a lucky man."

Vincenzo Gonzaga did not agree. *Why me?* was all he could say to himself. *Why was I singled out for this absurd affair?* The Prince had not been able to summon up one sexual feeling since the date had been set, and at night he dreamed that dignitaries of the Catholic Church were following him everywhere and that Pope Gregory XIII had ordered, "If he fails, he will bring down the deserved wrath of God and must confront the Inquisition," with Cardinal Borromeo shrieking, "He must burn at the stake!"

And then another terrifying thought engulfed him. Suppose the young virgin were told secretly that for the rest of her life she would be well provided for if she acted frigid, resisted him, and made it impossible for him to win on the field of honor. He felt as if he were in a dark dungeon with the walls closing in on him. He needed help desperately. *Who can assist me? My friend Dr. Tagliacozzi of Bologna, who healed me after that attack of erysipelas.* He insisted on permission for Gasparo to accompany him to Venice as companion.

At first, suspecting a ruse, the Grand Duke refused. He would not chance the Prince availing himself of the doctor's knowledge to procure from him an aphrodisiac to make him momentarily potent or to hand the virgin a love potion causing her to go sexually berserk and seduce the Prince into a championship in the art of lovemaking. Finally, the Grand Duke agreed that Dr. Tagliacozzi could accompany the Prince to Venice, provided he came without potions, drugs, or medication.

In Venice, Vincenzo Gonzaga insisted that Dr. Tagliacozzi examine the girl to ensure that she was a virgin, not a whore hired by his enemies to resist him.

Gasparo stepped diffidently into an enormous bedroom with exquisite decor, a perfect rendezvous for sex. On the bed was a gorgeous blond teen-age girl. Nervously, he asked her to undress. Smiling, proud of her body, she disrobed. Gasparo was overwhelmed by her beauty: the large blue eyes, the pink cheeks, the full red lips, the clean, natural fragrance of her body, the firm, voluptuous breasts.

The surgeon was at a loss. His erection embarrassed him, for he felt unprofessional. He took her pulse. It was beating fast but not as fast as his. She looked at him seductively and he winced, imagining that Lorenzo Desiri were in his place. Lorenzo would have attacked her instantly and the image aroused him the more. To suppress his ardor, he pictured Flaminio Vulpi in his place, outraged at such immorality, threatening to flog the girl and burn her at the stake. To his dismay, the image of Flaminio whipping the virgin excited his sexual appetite even more.

His hands were shaking as he examined her to make sure that anatomically she was virgin.

Then he said, "The Prince will feel ecstatic on seeing you and is anxious to make you happy. You will find him irresistible." The surgeon withdrew. *I thank the Lord,* he breathed, *that Giulia cannot read my mind.*

In the Prince's suite he beckoned Vincenzo Gonzaga. "She is a rare beauty, voluptuous; she will please you."

"But if I fail."

"Impossible."

"She may resist."

"Fantasy. She craves you. Have you ever failed?"

"Never, I swear it." Vincenzo was perspiring. "But I feel no lust."

"Have faith, my friend. Courage, and you will succeed in your endeavor."

"I do not know," whispered the Prince. "I do not know."

"This is a moment of great stress, my friend. You must fulfill yourself on the field of honor."

Vincenzo paced the floor slowly. He limped, as if crippled, and his skin was pale, almost green. "The Roman Church will watch me," he moaned. "It is inhuman."

"Think of your objective. Forget the bishops who will evaluate your performance and concentrate on the lovely virgin."

"Bishops," howled the Prince of Mantua. "Oh, my God!"

"You will be a winner," said Gasparo. "Pretend she is a courtesan and your victorious feeling will return."

"It is an undeserved humiliation."

"You are an individual of great worth. You are a man among men, a prince among princes. You are—"

"Shut up," bellowed Vincenzo Gonzaga, "for you, too, seem detestable. I hate the world, and above all I loathe the desires of the flesh. I will not fornicate before the Pope and his emissaries."

"Courage, my prince, confidence. Your insecurity betrays your mellow disposition, but your sense of worth, your virile prowess, will carry you through to victory."

"You think so?"

"Confidence rises within you. *You* are confidence. Care not what others may think, my prince. Your past boudoir performance will gain you honor!"

In the bedroom, the Prince turned, and there she was, the beautiful young virgin. She lay naked on the bed and he surveyed her milk-white thighs and soft slender belly and uptilted pink-nippled breasts. For a moment he felt desire, but then he remembered that hiding behind the curtains were eight of the most powerful officials of the mighty Roman Church. *Oh, my God,* he moaned, and collapsed wearily on the bed. *Oh.*

This will not do, he told himself, and rising on his elbows, he leaned toward the young beauty, embracing her with a great pretense of desire. *That fooled them,* he mused, *but then I must take my clothes off, and they will see that I am incapable.*

The girl stroked his hair gently and kissed him on the neck and on the lips. She nuzzled her nose against his neck and rubbed her soft belly against him. "Why do you not take your clothes off?" she whispered.

Dear God, the Prince murmured to himself, *what have I done to deserve this indignity?* But he dared not utter the words aloud, for the representatives of God were listening.

She kissed him again and again on the lips, breathing passionately, telling him how she desired him, pressing her thighs against his, but the Prince was thinking, *They are behind that curtain, eh? I will unsheathe my sword and pierce through all eight judges. And then I will go to Rome and butcher Pope Gregory. I will avenge myself on the entire human race.*

The girl was disappointed in his initial response but she was persistent. She began unbuttoning his blouse but he slapped her hand away.

"Have I offended you, my lord?" she whispered.

"No, no," murmured the miserable Vincenzo Gonzaga. "You may as well take my clothes off. It is *expected.*"

"You are handsome," she whispered when she had finished undressing him. "You have a fine body."

"Yes," said the Prince wearily, and stared angrily at his limp penis. *Avanti,* he commanded it, *arise.*

"Oh," she murmured, and started to caress his penis with warm gentle hands. "Oh."

But Vincenzo Gonzaga, Prince of Mantua, felt still more terrified. Up till now he had been obsessed only with the presence of the eight judges behind the curtain. Now a fresh fear assailed him: Duke Guglielmo, his father, would hear of his failure. *I could escape to Spain or even to America,* he reflected.

He heard a sucking noise then. *Cardinal Borromeo, behind the curtains, lighting his pipe?* he conjectured.

Then, turning around, he saw his lovely bed partner, leaning back, with her head on the pillow, sucking her thumb. "What are you doing?" he asked.

"I always suck my thumb when I feel deprived. You do not find me attractive, and this makes me very unhappy."

"No, you do not understand how—"

"Do not make excuses. I know that I am ugly and that your failure will ruin my life. Oh, I wish I were a baby again, feeding from my mother's breast." And, continuing to suck her thumb, she buried her head in the pillow; soon she was whimpering and then great wailing sounds emerged from her.

Covering his shriveled-up immobilized penis with the bedspread, the Prince of Mantua sat at the edge of the bed and gazed moodily at the carpeting. *I could give up my life of whoring and drinking and become a monk,* he moaned, but a new confusing thought crept into his mind. *The Church might show its disapproval of my performance by refusing to let me join.*

Gasparo, stationed with the eight religious judges behind the curtains, was hoping for the best. One of the bishops, too, was sympathetic and jockeyed for position. But all he saw was the Prince's drooping silhouette and, disappointed, the bishop fainted. Gasparo, not permitted to bring drugs, slapped him on the cheeks. His brethren, watching with anxiety, were quite relieved when he opened his eyes, but the bishop, on regaining consciousness, wept profusely.

Sitting on a chair in the unhappy Prince's reading room, Gasparo watched as Vincenzo paced endlessly back and forth, running his hands through his hair, clenching and unclenching his hands, murmuring oaths to himself, then pausing to gaze upward: *Lord, I have been an obedient son, an ardent lover, a scholar of merit. Why, my God? Why?*

Aloud, he said, "You are the only one I can trust."

"Oh, surely—"

"I am no longer on speaking terms with my father. My friends make jokes and I refuse to receive them in my home. I have stopped taking my daily walks because people in the street delight in increasing my misery. You, Gasparo, are my last hope. You must assist me."

"I will do anything in my power."

"Then you will help me train for this second encounter?"

"Yes."

"There are ten days between encounters. We must start today."

"I am at your service."

Restlessly, the Prince paced the floor. Usually immaculate, his clothing was disheveled and, untrimmed, his mustache was growing over his anguished lips. "Gasparo, this time I must prove myself. I cannot wait for the third encounter. If I fail this time, with everyone reminding me of my incapability, I will have no chance in the final encounter and this girl is too sensitive to survive another failure. It has injured her self-esteem, and then the cardinals and bishops— And my father despises me— Oh, my friend, I am the most miserable mortal on this earth."

Listening to Vincenzo's agonized, hysterical recital, the surgeon suppressed a smile. "My friend, do not despair. Perhaps we can find a strategy for dealing with this situation."

During their many conversations, Girolamo Cardano and Gasparo had talked about almost every conceivable subject. Cardano had postulated the hypothesis once that perhaps there was a connection between the workings of the mind and the functioning of the body. *Was Girolamo right?* mused the surgeon. *And, if he was, how can I help Vincenzo take his mind away from the people watching him from behind the curtain so he may behold this lovely girl and feel as he would in private?*

"Concentration," he said aloud. "He must learn to concentrate—and I must discover how to teach him this art. We will experiment with new techniques—ah, yes—in preparation for the second *encounter*. Oh, but they have phrased it exquisitely—encounter."

When he was a young boy, his father had instructed him in the art of playing chess and Giovanni Andrea had used this game to illustrate the necessity for focusing one's attention to the exclusion of all possible irrelevancies. When young Gasparo's mind would wander to the aroma of Isabetta's cooking or the gay singing of his sister in the next room, or to Lorenzo Desiri or Flaminio Vulpi outside the window clamoring for him to come out and play in the street Delle Lame, Giovanni Andrea would show him the error of his ways, taking advantage of the inevitable lapses to punch his pieces through to a quick checkmate.

And so the pair trained vigorously for the Prince of Mantua's second trial. They played chess to develop his powers of selection, and they exercised intensively to stimulate his athletic drives, taking long walks, indulging in calisthenics, dueling on horseback. Gasparo prescribed energy-building foods and watched carefully over the Prince's meals. And every night Vincenzo Gonzaga retired early to his bed.

The last did little good, Gasparo was willing to concede, for in bed the Prince could not sleep, tossing and turning, moaning about the indignity of his command performance before the Catholic Church. "It is the fault of my father," he would explode. "He is deformed, so he resents my physical superiority. He cares nothing about my sufferings."

"Perhaps, but do you not have to go through with it anyway?"

"Mother of God, yes, but, my friend, it is bizarre. How would you like to do such a thing with the Pope's personal representatives peeping at you from behind a curtain?"

"Not at all," said Gasparo, laughing. "You have my sympathies, I assure you."

"You can laugh. Everyone can laugh. I dare not show my face in public. Me, Vincenzo Gonzaga, the Prince of Mantua, famed for my exploits in the brothels, how can my potency be under question? To endure such an exhibition, it is grotesque."

Back to the chess matches. And more dueling, on foot and on horseback. Walking. Running. Resting.

"I feel physically fit," the Prince conceded, "even though I have not slept much. But what does that mean?"

"It means that you are prepared to give the premiere performance of your depraved lifetime."

"No—not before the public. My penis does not belong to the Italian people."

"You have been granted it by the will of God."

"But not by the will of the bishops and cardinals hiding—"

"There is your problem. To give a splendid performance, you must screen them from your mind."

"I could wear an amulet of theriac."

"No, you must do two things. First, pretend that these peepers behind the curtain do not exist. And, then, concentrate on this lovely young girl. She is beautiful, is she not?"

"Yes, but she sucks her thumb."

"A minor imperfection. Think, my friend, of her thighs. Are they shapely?"

"Oh, yes."

"And her breasts?"

"Magnificent."

"And her buttocks?"

"Round and firm."

"And now, Vincenzo, gather the fires of lust inside you into one compact force, and let your mind savor the animal joy of penetrating this proud virgin, and dwell on the excitement that she will feel in your handsome presence and—"

"My God," yelled the Prince of Mantua. "Gasparo, you are a magician! I have an erection. I listened to you, concentrating on each curve of her body, and— It is the first erection since this abominable affair started."

"I congratulate you."

"No," said the Prince, suddenly depressed. "These circumstances are nothing. But I am more hopeful. I will try to screen out of my mind everything but the loveliness of this sweet-fleshed damsel. And then I will drive through to victory."

"Good, but, Prince, do you remember how we jumped a fence running through the countryside?"

"It was simple."

"Yes, but it was more than a physical exercise. It was symbolic of what you must hurdle: the feelings of unworthiness that infest your mind like the plague."

"Perhaps I have found the cure."

"The cure, my friend, is that you must concentrate on your objective. Forget the bishops and the cardinals, my prince, and please yourself."

"I lash out with fire in my heart. The stars be willing, I shall penetrate her conclusively."

"A splendid goal, bravo. You will succeed—as in the past."

"I will make her swoon."

"I have faith that you will deliver."

"My erection throbs with a life of its own."

"This, my prince, is your true nature."

"I shall win, the virgin will be happy, the world will love me."

"Your virtues will shine forth."

"My penis will not waver."

"Are you a good fencer?"

"I am invincible."

"When you fence, Vincenzo, your mind overflows with your desire to pierce your opponent, to thrust with agility and grace, wounding your enemy on the field of battle. You prepare now to enter the field of honor but there is no opponent—only a cooperative virgin who longs for your thrust!"

"I will thrust like a champion," shouted the Prince of Mantua, exposing an erect penis.

"I applaud you. You are a noble prince."

The following day Vincenzo Gonzaga, Prince of Mantua, returned to the bedroom watched by all of Italy. The judges and Gasparo were behind the curtain but Vincenzo discarded this from his mind. He stared at the lovely naked virgin who was sucking her thumb. As the Prince undressed, he told himself that the virgin was dreaming of sucking his penis; by the time he was naked he boasted an undeniable erection. He attacked her hungrily and drove through to victory, as the girl ecstatically moaned and fainted. Two bishops, shaking with excitement, also fainted. The Prince of Mantua, redeeming his reputation, dressed and emerged from the fateful boudoir to enjoy the acclaim of the eight judges, though Cardinal Borromeo and a pious bishop gazed heavenward as if imploring God for forgiveness. The Prince turned to Gasparo, and both smiled impulsively as Vincenzo rushed to embrace him.

In the courtrooms of Florence and Mantua, Cavalier Belisario Vinta appeared in his most ornate tailored uniform to testify to the Prince's victory.

At the gates of Mantua, the guns of the fortress belched forth salvos to greet Vincenzo on his return. The bells in the cathedral tower rang out, and the public square, bedecked with banners, was crowded with people massed to salute their prince.

In Florence and Venice and Bologna and even Rome, the rejoicing overflowed into the streets and the cheering throngs shouted and sang and passed around wine bottles, though certain factions of the Church protested, with Flaminio Vulpi and the Dominicans in Bologna vowing that there would be punishment for the perpetrators of such blasphemous celebrating of a sinful exhibition.

Duke Guglielmo, intoxicated, chortling, threatening, greeted his triumphant son with open arms. "You have saved the family honor, my dear boy, leaving the accursed Farnesi to rot in their transparent lies."

The royal family of Mantua departed for Florence. People lined the streets along the route to shake the hand of their beloved prince, and halfway to Florence, the relieved, joyful, vindictive, generous, belligerent Guglielmo, drinking half a bottle of wine with each swallow, ordered the carriage to halt and clambered out to vomit copiously upon the countryside.

The City of Florence accorded the Prince another wild reception, showering him with confetti while cannons roared and firecrackers sizzled in the sky.

Finally, the wedding ceremony. Surveying his bride for the first time, Vincenzo sighed with relief. The eighteen-year-old Eleonora de' Medici was lovely—no, in her exquisitely embroidered pink gown topped by the Medici collar and string of pearls, her hair piled high, her lips full and sensual, she was beautiful.

The Prince of Mantua was once again elegant in appearance. His suit was of blue velvet, a richly embroidered sash pulling in his slender waist, white cuffs ballooning above his wrists, a gold chain encircling his neck and swooping down below his chest, his face framed by his close-cropped black hair and meticulously trimmed mustache and goatee. He stood by his bride during the ceremony—erect, poised, controlled. *Bless you, Gasparo,* he was thinking, and turned toward the surgeon and his elegantly dressed Giulia in the audience. *How can I ever repay you?* The crisis is over, and, thanks to you, I am victorious. Then another thought came to him and a smile curled over his lips. *Eleonora, my bride, you are marrying the only man in Italy whose sexual capacity has been certified by the Roman Church.*

There was a great feast, with huge roasted chickens and pheasants, enormous bowls of plump olives, green beans from the countryside, sweet-smelling freshly baked bread, honey cakes, tea, and dozens of choice wine bottles from the Medici cellar. Then waltzing in the ballroom.

After the ceremony, Giulia and Gasparo danced and danced. They had imbibed more wine than usual, and the surgeon imagined he was a prince and his wife a princess. Kissing her tenderly, he guided her up the winding stairway to their suite, or was she guiding him? *Oh, we will love each other,* thought Giulia, humming a melody as she undressed and climbed into bed. *Why is Gasparo still in the washroom? Why the delay?*

She could not know the strange fantasy gripping him. He imagined he was a prince about to prove his honor on the field of love. Twelve dignitaries of the Church—bishops and cardinals—were hiding behind the curtains in front of the window overlooking a garden. They conversed loudly, and he could hear every word.

"I am shortest. I should be in front."

"No. I am nearsighted."

"I will wager one hundred scudi that he will not gain entrance. A thousand scudi, my friend."

"Gentlemen, you represent the Pope."

"We are human beings, frail and of weak flesh. We wish our brother to succeed."

"He will fail! By the stars, I swear it."

"A thousand scudi that he will enter the virgin with honor."

"Gentlemen, stop quarreling and pushing, or you will pull the curtains down."

Suddenly, Gasparo fantasized, the curtains fell to the floor, and facing him were twelve prominent men of the Church. Embarrassed, they smiled at him and he smiled back. They noticed his enormous erection.

"The bet is off," a bishop yelled.

"You betray your word?"

"By your leave." *Vincenzo,* Gasparo smiled, musing, *your ordeal has overwhelmed my brain.* Undressing, he left the washroom and jumped into bed.

"Why so long, Gasparo, my darling?"

"I was contemplating our honeymoon in Florence, Giulia. And here we are again in Florence—another honeymoon."

"You look so young, my love, and so virile."

"It is your charms," he said, "you are lovely." And, to himself, *The Prince had to prove himself to a virgin. It was not love but sex. But with my beloved Giulia it is both—plus adoration. Oh, I will unleash my wildness. I will be savage and ardent.* Passionately, he kissed her neck, her bosom, her soft belly, her thighs, nuzzling her pubic hairs and licking hotly at her vagina.

"Gasparo," she moaned, "oh, Gasparo," and he leaped on top of her, his penis hard as steel plunging into her, knifing in and out with an intensity that fired her and, Greek gods singing a hymn to their mortal flesh, they strained into each other.

She was sleeping, and Gasparo returned to his fantasy. "Reverend signors," he whispered to the invisible audience of Church notables, "I, too, have proved myself on the field of honor. Could Lorenzo Desiri have acquitted himself more nobly? Come, gentlemen, admit my prowess."

And then he was sleeping. But he dreamed that the twelve church-men, crossing themselves and pulling out their amulets of theriac, had declared him an impostor. "He is heretical," Cardinal Borromeo insisted, "and he defies the will of God. To save our own souls, we must condemn him to die—brimstone around his neck, the flames rising to consume him."

Chapter 11

Life for Gasparo and Giulia was peaceful enough, but a rekindling of the feud between the militant clans was shaping. The spark was one Ghisella Minadoli, the most beautiful courtesan in all Bologna. One night when Count Prospero Castelli and Count Carlo Pepoli were attending separate parties the image of her voluptuous body took hold simultaneously in their wine-drenched minds and both departed early from the celebrations.

Count Carlo arrived first at Ghisella's house. The prostitute, teasing her small white fox terrier, answered his knock at the door. She looked ravishing in crimson velvet gown with puffed embroidered sleeves and a plunging neckline that exposed her full breasts. A rezzo of pearls encircled her neck, her golden hair was upswept and pinned, and her green eyes were mocking-cool crystals glistening out of her fiery rouged cheeks and thick painted lips.

Aroused, Carlo seized her and kissed her passionately, caressing her breasts, murmuring excitedly of his desire, when there was another knock at the door.

It was an inebriated Count Prospero Castelli, giggling in a silly fashion, stifling a hiccough. His anticipations of pleasure vanished at the sight of Pepoli. The thought that a Pepoli dared share a woman with a Castelli infuriated Prospero and the suspicion that Carlo had just finished ravishing Ghisella filled him with a blinding rage. He insulted Carlo, who retaliated, and quickly they were exchanging more insults. Prospero, out of control, struck Carlo on the chin, and

Carlo punched him back. Staggering away from each other, both young men groped for the hilts of their swords, while Ghisella shrieked at them to stop.

"I will leave," shouted Carlo Pepoli. "I would not darken your doorway with the stench of Castelli blood."

"I will take my revenge," bellowed Prospero Castelli. "You are a dishonorable swine, in the Pepoli tradition."

They reeled off in opposite directions, leaving Ghisella relieved at their going, but secretly elated that her beauty had caused resumption of the feud between Bologna's most famous families.

The following day the Castelli clan, with Count Alberto in the lead wearing the cross of Santo Stefano, marched to the public square to meet the Pepoli contingent.

"Shoot at the Pepoli chessboard," yelled Count Alberto Castelli. "Revenge."

"There they are," shouted Count Taddeo Pepoli. "We Pepoli will share no woman with the accursed Castellis."

The battle was joined and pedestrians ran for cover as arquebuses were fired and *bravi* from each side crossed swords. Castellano Castelli was killed and a few *bravi* were wounded but Captain Buoncampagna, whose army ruled Bologna for the Pope, had his soldiers ride in to disperse the combatants.

At dawn on the morrow the Castellis set out on horseback for Florence, after torturing a captured enemy and leaving him to die in their tower in retaliation for Castellano's death.

More drama a month later when Lorenzo Desiri and another Pepoli soldier, disguised as beggars, appeared before the Castelli palace in Florence. Lorenzo addressed a Castelli servant. "May we sleep in your stable? We came all the way from Perugia and are tired and hungry."

"Yes, but you must depart early in the morning before my master awakes. I will fetch you wine and bread."

"Thank you," cried out Lorenzo. "God bless you." But underneath his tattered rags he was gripping his sword.

In the morning, Alberto and Prospero Castelli ventured from the castle for a walk, but they did not get far. They were attacked near the stable, Lorenzo charging out with his sword to cut open Alberto's cheek, while his companion fired his pistol at Prospero, wounding him in the left arm. The assailants mounted horses, hidden behind a row of trees, and thundered away, while the wounded Castellis screamed for help.

"It was the bastard Pepolis," shouted a cousin of the Castellis, Alessandro Vestino, "was it not?"

"I could not tell," said Alberto weakly. "They were disguised."

A doctor applied compresses to the severe gash in Alberto's cheek. "Sire, you will need stitches."

"How many?"

"About a dozen."

"Secure me the best surgeon in Florence."

"I would prefer to recommend Doctor Gasparo Tagliacozzi of Bologna. He performed a splendid operation on my neighbor Tomasso Antinori."

"Tagliacozzi?" said Prospero. "He is an ally of the Pepolis."

"They are friendly because he extracted a bullet from the body of Taddeo after the Battle of Lepanto," said Alberto. "But *he* is not our enemy."

"Perhaps not, but he practices witchcraft. Fra Chiari and Flaminio Vulpi believe this."

"I need him. Send for him."

Twenty-four hours later, Gasparo was seated in a carriage rolling toward Florence. *This is the fourth time I travel over these roads,* he reflected. *On my first trip, as a child, I dreamed that someday I would be a great surgeon. The second time was on my honeymoon, and the third time was for the marriage ceremony of Vincenzo Gonzaga, Prince of Mantua. Now my dream comes true, and I am famous. The Pepolis and the Castellis seek me out and I am vouched for by Don Juan of Austria, the Prince of Mantua, and Tomasso Antinori.*

Then he grinned wryly. *I take myself too seriously, and Girolamo Cardano would not approve. He would say I was about to assume the posture of a pompous jackass. Touché, Girolamo, I will attempt to be more tolerable.*

At the Castelli palace, he examined the two patients. But it was not as in his dream.

"The bullet in your arm," he said to Prospero, "must be extracted, after which hot fomentations must be applied, consisting of a special decoction of lye, roots of althea, roots of wild watermelon, and half a head of chopped-up mutton."

"You sound like a magician," said Prospero, "stirring a witches' brew in your cauldron."

"What?"

"I will state my point plainly. I fear you will pollute me with your witchcraft."

"Witchcraft? If you think that, why did you send for me?"

"Count Alberto sent for you."

"Then I will *not* treat you."

"Calm down, my friend," said Count Alberto. "Pay no attention to what he says. You come highly recommended, but he resents your association with the Pepolis."

"I extracted a bullet from Taddeo's body and have attended a few large parties at their palace. That is the extent of my association with the Pepolis."

"You may treat me," said Count Alberto.

"Yes," said Gasparo, "but what of your friend? The bullet should be extracted or blood poisoning might set in."

"I want no witchcraft," said Prospero.

"As you wish. Alberto, have you confessed to a confessor?"

"This morning. Prospero witnessed it."

Gasparo opened his surgical kit and threaded his needles. "I will sew six stitches in your cheek to approximate the edges of the wound."

"It will be painful?"

"Somewhat, but it will last only a few minutes."

"You are using accredited methods and not supernatural powers?"

Gasparo snapped shut his surgical kit. "I am not a magician or a witch, but a surgeon. Good-bye, gentlemen."

Returning home, he seethed. *All for nothing. Is this the fulfillment of my dream? Girolamo, give me strength.*

A week later, Count Alessandro Vestino arrived at Gasparo's residence. "Prospero is sick with fever and Alberto looks like a monster with that gash in his cheek. They request your presence."

"And my witchcraft?"

"They repent their stupidity and wish your assistance because you are an expert surgeon."

Tagliacozzi agreed, telling Vestino that he would come with his new assistant, Dr. Cortesi, who was soon to move to Perugia, to set up his own surgical office.

At the Castelli palace he operated. Inserting his threaded straight needles in the puffed sleeve of Count Alberto Castelli's doublet, he used them to repair the patient's cheek. Driving the first needle through the opposing edges of the center of the wound, he tied the knot and pierced the flesh with his other needles. Six stitches and the ghastly-looking gap was reduced to a narrow line. Except for the thread, Alberto resembled his old self.

Prospero's arm was swollen, and while Gasparo probed for the bullet, Dr. Cortesi held the patient immobile. The wound was festering and Prospero was feverish but Gasparo, inserting a long pair of forceps into the wound, extracted the bullet—to the accompaniment of a hysterical howl from the agonized Castelli. Dr. Cortesi bandaged the wound and applied hot fomentations.

"You will remain in bed a week and drink fluids," said Gasparo. "Doctor Cortesi will instruct you on diet so that you move your bowels regularly."

There was no talk of sorcery from the patients, whose pain had been helped little by huge tumblers of wine. Moaning, but relieved, they were soon sleeping.

In a week, Gasparo removed the stitches from Count Alberto's face and applied hare's blood over the surgical line, which was invisible within a month.

There was great celebration at the Castelli palace. Alberto's cheek was as good as new, and Prospero's recuperation was total. In addition, carnival time had arrived.

It was a joyous occasion for the Bolognese. Men crowded the taverns, drinking and singing and boasting. The streets were alive with people and carriages. There were tournaments and chariot and horse racing, with cannon fired to signal the start and finish. Everyone would gamble on these sporting events, and in the streets, students would toss dice.

Overlooking the streets, the balconies of the houses were bedecked with tapestries and multicolored banners, while the sweet sound of flutes and piccolos and lutes showered down upon the costumed people in the streets—beautiful girls in gowns and men wearing Greek, Roman or Egyptian costumes, some with long red noses and enormous ludicrous eyeglasses over masks of demons and devils and grotesque animals.

Painted prostitutes were in flower-strewn carriages, horses decorated with flowing ribbons exhibiting colors of the rainbow, drivers wearing absurd double-faces or dressed like women with huge earrings and rings.

There was a brief threat to the festivities when *bravi* of the Castelli clan, in the robes of Roman emperors, pushed through the crowd at the race track and confronted Carlo Pepoli, with Lorenzo Desiri and other Pepoli *bravi*; the inevitable skirmish was soon over.

As the bright colors of tapestries and costumes began to fade in the sunset, lights appeared in the balconies and in carriages and in the hands of promenaders. Tapers, candles, torches—to bring light in darkness—plus bonfires and fireworks, rockets whizzing into the sky and fragmenting into many-colored stars that vanished in the night.

"Senza moccolo," people began shouting, trying to extinguish the lights, for the carnival was over. *"Senza moccolo."*

With the ringing of the Ave Maria, the crowd dispersed.

Gasparo's reputation was still increasing, and within a short period of time, he performed operations on the noses of four patients. Enrico Van Benesghem of Antwerp had lost most of his nose because of syphilitic infection. A pair of noblemen, Sigismondo Bariano of the Pepoli clan and Count Alessandro Vestino of the Castelli clan, were both from Piacenza and had severely damaged each other's noses while dueling. Finally, there was Ottavio Facino, a friend of Bariano's.

The operations were all successful and, indeed, Gasparo's major problem was protecting the Castelli and Pepoli from each other, since both were patients in adjoining bedrooms at the same time.

Knowing that a famed doctor, Girolamo Mercuriale, was authoring a book on surgery, Gasparo decided to write to inform him of his now proved methods.

To my dear Girolamo Mercuriale, Gasparo Tagliacozzi sends greetings!

The method of artificially fashioning noses, which you lately requested of me in your letter, I shall now gladly outline for you, but only briefly and in haste, for I cannot spend time in this task, since I am kept in the city occupied with professional duties, in addition to the imminent obligation of delivering lectures at the University. For this reason I shall only touch upon its main points and it will have to be an outline, since I have described in detail all those things that pertain to this skill in a comprehensive treatise which I am writing and which, unless some misgivings cast doubt on our undertaking, I shall soon turn over to be printed, so that it will be available to all people far and wide. I am the more eager to do this, because some of our illustrious colleagues, who have written superficially on the subject, attack my operation in a foolish way, like a book-bred sailor, to the detriment of the profession, the skill, and the patient . . .

My technique is simple—I use the skin of the arm, but only equal in size to the nose that is to be refashioned. I take this skin and join it to the nose by the same method of grafting which farmers and professors of agriculture use in tree grafting, just as I state in my treatise in a clearer and more illuminating way. But let us begin.

Thus, as soon as the patient has been received, have the temperature of the body noted at frequent intervals and in the best way possible, for every effort must be directed toward this as toward a goal and if the fluid humors in the body deviate from normal in their quality or quantity, they must be brought into balance; every bad fluid must be quickly removed with appropriate antidotes, and by a proper plan of diet one must guard against the possibility of some disturbance of the body fluids arising during the course of the surgical operation. Therefore, unnatural disturbances must all be conquered by counsel and artifice.

Sex urges above all must be entirely quiescent; anger, sorrow, and all worries of the mind must be removed. Nourishment is to be palatable and easily digestible, the intestines must be evacuated daily, or caused to do so artificially. Night air is bad, likewise rainy and hot weather. The patient is to be relaxed and sleep is to be moderate; for very much sleep causes the head to sweat. Thus the knitting of the wound is delayed by too great a flux of humors to the skin surface; and if the joined parts are aggravated by the conflux of humors they hinder a facile union of the seams and cause them to pucker. After these instructions for the preparation, conditioning, and toning of the body have been observed, have an incision made in the skin of either the right or left arm down to, but not including, the flesh of the muscles. This skin graft is separated from the underlying tissue, its size in length and breadth depending on the defect. Immediately this piece of skin itself ought to be suppurated, and thereupon dried, so that it be fit for union to the nasal stump. As soon as it is evident that the skin can be used to cover the defect, it becomes necessary to scarificate its edges and those of the nasal stump, so that the transplant can be properly attached to the face. However, in order that the joined parts be in no way torn apart or injured by the various movements of the body, have the arm tied and held to the head by appropriate apparatus and bandaged; the area of union of the stump and graft is to be treated with epulotic remedies. The knitting of the skin will indicate when the binding is to be removed; the time differs greatly in proportion to the various temperaments of bodies. But as soon as you have noticed a knitting of the wound, have the arm cut away from the face; then the loose end of the transplanted skin must be reduced to the proper size of a nose and must be fashioned with scalpels, into nostrils, columella, or shaft of the nose, and nasal tip. That this is not a difficult undertaking, almost all men have seemed to believe. For it is commonly said that there is a great deal of suffering and pain that goes with the satisfactory fashioning of a nose. But indeed the treatment is bearable by the patient . . . and there are more thorny and more difficult problems in the practice of surgery. But let us pursue the task we have undertaken. The new columella, fashioned by the scalpels, is joined to what is left of the old columella or else joined to the upper confine of the philtrum of the lip. A roll of linen is to be placed in the cavity of the nostrils according to their shape and size, later a reed of silver . . . Thus noses are refashioned by artificial means, so commendably, that at times nature is surpassed, and you may not in any way discern that a nose has been grafted, just as those can bear witness who have watched me rebuild noses this year . . . for there were a number, among them a noble, Sig. Sigismondo Bariano, another noble, Count Alessandro Vestino, both from Piacenza, who had had their noses amputated while fighting a duel with swords; also Ottavio Facino, friend of Bariano, and a man from Flanders, Sig. Enrico Van Benesghem of Antwerp. We restored noses to all of these gentlemen so naturally, so free from all demarcations, that they favored the restorations more than the former organs that nature gave them. And I should also like to state that the same technique is used to restore defects of the chin, ear, or cheek. I would have remained silent about these accomplishments, so as not to give people the opportunity to slander me, boasting as I seem to do, were it not for the fact that I was compelled to tell you the truth about my work. But I seem to have exceeded the scope of the letter; if I have not made it sufficiently clear in this, my dear Girolamo, I shall set it forth clearly in my treatise, which shall contain all the secrets and techniques of my skill. Although I have given my final approval to it, I am nevertheless constrained to delay the printing, since pictures and diagrams have been requested; these I shall plan to provide in the next summer months, and I shall publish them gladly for the common use of all people. For I am not the kind of scholar who wishes this skill to remain with me as it were in chains, but I am eager that it be spread abroad among the rest of the nations; for this same reason I offer an opportunity to all to be present when I perform an operation. But I have exceeded my pen. Therefore farewell, my eminent friend.

Affectionately yours,
GASPARO TAGLIACOZZI.

Bologna, on the 22nd day of February in the year of Our Lord 1586

My ideas are new, reflected Gasparo, rereading his letter. *Yes, they are original. But, Girolamo, and now I mean you, my dear friend Cardano, I will not wallow in my own conceit and fall before the power of arrogance and bombast. No, my cherished friend—and I hope with all my heart that you are comfortable in your old age—I will profit from your counsel and lose myself in the sweet flesh of my Giulia.* He recalled the passionate love he had made to Giulia in Florence after the Prince of Mantua's wedding. He was young and virile—then and now.

Chapter 12

As Gasparo's reputation continued to grow, patients traveled to Bologna from all parts of Italy to seek out his professional services.

For seven years he had been laboring on his first book, in which he was to elaborate the discoveries that would revolutionize the newborn field of plastic surgery. Working in his spare time, between operations, he was about finished.

He was at the desk in his consultation room organizing a chapter when Scipio Africanus Borzani entered. The black man was handsome and confident, and people no longer dared taunt him. He was an assistant to the surgeon and Gasparo felt fortified sometimes just to look at him, for this would renew his faith in the road he had followed, shaken every day by the hostility toward him in powerful university circles and among ignorant folk who, passing him in the street, would render the sign of the cross and finger their theriac amulets.

"A young man wishes to see you," said Scipio. "His name is Galileo."

"Galileo? Is he a patient?"

"I do not know, but his face seems normal."

Puzzled, Tagliacozzi nodded in affirmation and his assistant opened the door to the consultation room, ushering a young stranger, perhaps thirty years old, to a chair near the desk.

"Gasparo Tagliacozzi," said Galileo, "how pleasant to meet you."

"Galileo? When I was a small boy, a youth named Galileo befriended me."

"That was my father. He has talked of you so often that—" He stopped in mid-sentence. His forehead was creased and his face was pale. "I have left my home in Pisa."

"I see," said the surgeon. And turning to his assistant, he said, "Please, some sweet cakes and tea for Signor Galileo and myself, and you may join us if you wish, Scipio."

"My father has assured me that you can be trusted, so I shall tell you in confidence that I departed hastily from my home in terror."

"What were the circumstances?"

"You might say that I refused to heed the advice of my father and become a cloth merchant. Instead, I elected to study medicine and mathematics."

"I, too, defied my father, who wanted me to become a merchant of satins and damasks and fine silks. But tell me what happened, and how I can assist you."

"My studies led me to investigate the phenomena in my environment, and to think about them in experimental terms. One day, while attending Mass at the Cathedral of Pisa, my attention became focused on a chandelier swinging backward and forward over my head. Watching it carefully I timed its oscillations with my pulse, and thus I absorbed some general principles that enabled me to invent the pendulum."

"My congratulations."

"Perhaps," said Galileo, "but perhaps not. Because this led me to study further the relationship of time and weight. I spent months experimenting with weights dropped from the Leaning Tower of Pisa and this was instrumental in the evolvement of my theory of gravitation."

"A marvelous achievement."

"I thought so, I will admit, but everybody said I was a raving lunatic."

"The rewards of a true creator."

"My experiments with the pendulum inspired me with the notion that the earth with the moon moved around the sun, and my enemies, enraged by my growing reputation, spread rumors that I was a practitioner of witchcraft. The Jesuits opposed my new theories and condemned me for heresy. Then they prepared to hand me over to the Inquisition—but I escaped."

"And came here?"

"Yes. I searched my mind for someone I felt sure I could trust, and then I remembered how highly my father spoke of the Tagliacozzis of Bologna."

"I appreciate your confidence in me and assure you that I will not betray it. What are your plans, my friend?"

"I shall travel to the University of Padua. I require a place to sleep tonight and money—and perhaps food for my journey."

"They are yours, my comrade Galileo."

"I do not know." The lines on the scientist's forehead testified to the sufferings inflicted by the representatives of the Church. "They might come to arrest me, and if they should find me in your home, you, too, could be implicated."

"You are the son of a good friend," said the surgeon, "and I admire your courage. You will spend the night in my house."

"May God bless you."

"May He bless both of us—for we both seek to find truth in a universe eclipsed by ignorance and superstition. But, my dear colleague, although I revere God, I must ask myself what form does He take, that you and I share our convictions with the hierarchy of the Roman Church and the executioners of the Inquisition."

The door opened and Scipio entered, carrying a large silver tray with a pot of steaming tea and a platter of sweet cakes. The three men chatted while they ate, Galileo more relaxed now, and then the assistant left them to their conversation. For hours they exchanged opinions and experiences. Then, following dinner and wine, they talked far into the night, and not since the departure of Girolamo Cardano had Gasparo savored the delight of such intellectual stimulation.

In the morning, Galileo departed for Padua, and Gasparo, standing with Giulia outside his house, sadly waved good-bye to the young scientist and re-entered his home to breakfast and resume his work.

Lorenzo felt at the height of his powers. Taddeo Pepoli had decided upon a fencing tournament and, since he was now undisputed ruler of the Pepoli clan, all male members of the family and *bravi* participated.

But Desiri, confidence darting from his eyes, parrying his opponents' thrusts and charging forward inexorably at each rival, outfenced all entrants and outlasted Taddeo to reign as champion.

Married for years to the former Caledonia Bargillini, Lorenzo was a vigorous athletic stud in his late forties, and no inhibitions blocked his drive toward pleasure. He and Caledonia were a noisy, rollicking couple surviving endless stormy clashes of will to enjoy each other voluptuously in bed. There was little of the goddess Diana in Caledonia; she was more a temptress, a seductive beauty, a Cleopatra to lure a man to frenzy.

"Caledonia," muttered Lorenzo angrily. "How could she do this to me?"

For he craved a woman, he craved *his* woman, and where was she? In Rome, caring for her sick mother. This was not a satisfactory explanation for the captain of the Pepoli *bravi*. Why should he care if, in far-off Rome, his wife's mother was in agony? What mattered to Lorenzo was that Caledonia's passionate flesh was unavailable for his pleasure, that her ecstatic response to his aggression was not there to arouse him further, that she was ministering to someone else's needs—not to his.

"It is intolerable," grunted Lorenzo after a week of celibacy. "I am a man, not a monk."

Signora Rinaldi and her retinue had departed for Rome so he decided to call upon the beautiful courtesan Ghisella Minadoli.

The aftermath was tumultuous. The courtesan and the warrior were locked in fervent embrace shortly after his arrival, as he attacked hungrily, disrobing her and hurling her upon the bed; she was attracted to his vigor and they twisted together until he buried his hardness, every part of him, in her soft flesh and they exploded with desire.

Lorenzo dressed, paid the prostitute, and left, suddenly afraid that someone had seen him and would tell Caledonia.

And, in truth, someone *had* seen him.

A cousin of the Castellis, Enrico Gradenigo, mildly inebriated, had been staggering toward Ghisella's house at the same time as Lorenzo. He had heard often of the prowess of Desiri, so instead of challenging

Lorenzo, he returned to the neighborhood tavern. More drunk than ever, infuriated by the delay, he arrived at Ghisella's in time to see the Pepoli fighting man depart.

Gradenigo, still reluctant to fight his formidable rival, remained in the shadows and waited until Desiri had gone before knocking on the prostitute's door.

Ghisella's beauty overwhelmed him. She was wearing a flowing gown, the cleavage between her lovely breasts visible, her hair golden and swept up imperiously, an elegant silver bracelet on her wrist, her rouged cheeks accentuating the color in her face and the animal excitement still vibrating inside her.

"Ghisella, you look ravishing," he murmured. "Come here, you luscious whore, and I will—"

"Not tonight," she said. "It is that time of month ordained by the Devil. Return in a fortnight, my good Enrico, and I will welcome you into my arms."

The cousin of the Castellis allowed his rage to overwhelm him. "You lie," he cried out, weaving on unsteady feet. "You lie, treacherous harlot, and you fornicate with the accursed Pepolis."

"No."

"Yes," he stormed and, uncontrolled, lashed out to clout her savagely on the chin. "A Castelli will take second place to no Pepoli, evil bitch."

"No, I swear by—"

"You swear falsely," screamed Gradenigo, striking her again and again until he had sent her sprawling to the floor. "You lie."

Unconscious, the courtesan lay motionless but the Castelli was too drunk to notice, and pulling out his stiletto, he reached down and in his rage gouged from Ghisella's cheek a piece of flesh the size of a walnut, blood spurting from her to stain forever the exquisite patterned rug. Then he staggered to the front door and out into the street.

The maid was a witness to the stabbing. In a panic at the sight of her bleeding, unconscious mistress, she rushed from the house and ran all the way to the Tagliacozzi residence on the street Delle Lame.

"My mistress is dying," she shrieked. "She lies on the rug and does not move or speak and blood pours from her body."

Accompanied by the maid, Gasparo proceeded briskly to Ghisella's house, and while he was treating the bleeding wound, the courtesan regained consciousness. "I swear that I do not lie," she murmured. And sitting up, she suddenly screamed, "Please, Enrico, I would not lie to you."

"Enrico?"

"Oh," said Ghisella, seeing the surgeon for the first time. "You are Doctor Tagliacozzi?"

"Yes."

"Oh." And now she became conscious of the streams of blood flowing down her cheek and staining the rug. "What has happened to me?"

"Do you remember?"

"Yes—oh, yes, the pig—oh, yes, the filthy evil pig Enrico Gradenigo attacked me. We must get the military authorities to arrest him and bring him to trial. Bastard, he must hang for this; yes, he must hang. Oh, my God—what of my cheek?"

She rushed to an elaborate floor-to-ceiling mirror in her bedroom and, appalled at the sight of her mutilated cheek, sat down shakily on the bed. "Oh," she screeched, "bastard. I will strangle the filthy pig Enrico with my bare hands; I will tear his eyes out of their sockets. Oh, he has ruined my life. He has *ruined* me."

And sobbing, screaming curses, insulting the Castellis in Italian and French, bemoaning her fate, Ghisella Minadoli, the most beautiful courtesan in Bologna, walked on trembling legs around her exquisitely furnished house, in tears, her blood staining the carpeting while her despair rained upon the visiting Dr. Tagliacozzi. "I was beautiful a few hours ago," she raged. "Men desired me so ardently they could not live without me. And now—I am nothing. Nothing." And, as the truth of this blasted in upon her, she summoned up all the power of her imperious will and commenced to assert her frustration on her surroundings. She picked up pillows and hurled them against the wall, then tables and vases and lamps, and soon her house was pure chaos, the stained carpeting covered with glass fragments and wood splinters.

Gasparo tried to restrain her before she destroyed all the furniture in her heedless fury but she wrenched from his grasp and, kicking, clawing, punching, kept going at him until her energy was spent and, collapsing in a heap, she began to sob.

The surgeon felt sorry for her. Once she had begun to cry, she could not stop, and her wails were agonized, as with a baby helpless in a hostile world. Then a thought came to him. Of course. The situation had been so dramatic as to arrest his thinking processes. But Ghisella could board at his home for about a month, and during this period he would repair her cheek and restore to her the type of life that she adored. *Our Lord might frown on such a licentious life,* he considered, *but is Ghisella not a child of God, too?* And he said he could help her, explaining the procedure.

At first, the prostitute did not even hear him, for her screams of despair drowned out the sound of his voice. But then it registered and she turned to him. "This is not a joke?" she said. "You can repair my cheek?"

"Perfectly, so that you will be as beautiful as ever you were."

Suddenly, her tears gone, Ghisella was smiling and her exuberance was so overwhelming that she began to giggle and then to roar with laughter, then gratitude seized her and once more she was sobbing.

Then, impulsively, she packed her clothes and walked back with the surgeon to his house.

Giulia's initial reaction was predictable. "A prostitute staying in our house?" she whispered to her husband in the kitchen. "What will people say?"

But Gasparo prevailed on her to talk to Ghisella, seated sedately in the living room, and when his wife noted the hideous disfigurement she consented and, later on, sewed an apparatus to assist in her recovery from the operation.

And so the most beautiful courtesan in the City of Bologna resided with the surgeon Tagliacozzi.

Before he would operate, he insisted that she visit a confessor, as prescribed by Church ritual. She did so, and the stage was set for surgery.

The operation itself was the most ludicrous one Gasparo had ever undertaken. Lorenzo, assisting him, kept eying her breasts and flirting with her, and he would pinch her thigh now and then when he thought the doctor was not looking.

And still more incredible was Ghisella's solution for battling the searing pain of the surgical procedure. Where other patients, drugged with wine, were howling like mad, tortured animals, Ghisella, the courtesan, imbibed nothing but goat's milk, and when the pain grew intense, she would lash out, screaming, denouncing Enrico Gradenigo in the vilest language the surgeon had ever heard.

"I will cut Enrico's testicles off," the harlot would scream. "I will cut them off and hurl them in the garbage, where they belong. I will tie a tight cord around his penis and keep hauling it tighter and tighter until his cursed little thing turns black with gangrene and falls off—not that this would cause any woman despair. Ouch, oh, yes, I vow that I will get my revenge on this pig, this filthy bastard."

Lorenzo would pat her shoulder comfortingly, squeezing her breasts on occasion while Gasparo was peering intently at the wound on her cheek. Then the pain would pierce her through and Ghisella would ward off the agony.

"Is not Enrico Gradenigo a vile-sounding name to torture any tongue?" she would fulminate. "Is it not an abomination when a man of reputation, a nobleman from an honored family, attempts to gain entrance with a penis shriveled up, soft as a sow's belly, a vestigial organ that would inflict boredom upon an impassioned virgin?" Her answer carried the same sharp sting as did her question. "Sooner would I fornicate with a filthy, penniless beggar with loathsome breath and suffering from the French disease than grant the favor of a smile to the cowardly male impersonator Gradenigo."

The courtesan's presence in his house had repercussions, most of which the surgeon had anticipated when he decided to take her case.

Common people in the streets were even ruder to him than before, some stopping to stare contemptuously, and others scurrying away apprehensively, mumbling about the Evil Eye and the Devil's agent and pulling out amulets of theriac to ward off the danger of his presence.

His son, Giovanni Andrea, looked troubled. Giulia told him that Giovanni had been involved in a fistfight with a neighborhood bully and that other children had hurled stones, taunting him about the harlot living in his house. All this was unbearable to the boy.

The surgeon learned that the Censor of Books, Flaminio Vulpi, had declared publicly that Tagliacozzi was in league with the Devil and that this was additional evidence building for the eventual prosecution.

Other events further dramatized the whole affair. Enrico Gradenigo, leaving a tavern one evening, was killed by a masked man lunging from a darkened alley, stabbing him in the heart with a stiletto. This started more gossip. Most people believed the murderer was Lorenzo, trying to avenge Ghisella, but the warrior denied it—not that this stopped the rumors.

Ghisella's beauty was restored and, with the success of the operation and the increase in her fame, royalty from all the cities of Italy— Rome, Venice, Padua, Florence, Milan—journeyed to the University City to make her acquaintance and arrange for future rendezvous.

Meanwhile, at the university, the students were up in arms, demonstrating there and in the public square and parading around their professor's home, carrying placards and voicing their support for Tagliacozzi, and for Ghisella, the courtesan. Some of the more ardent students dispatched flowers for Giulia.

And Giulia? Now here was the most astonishing development of all.

The presence of Ghisella had a magical, almost mystic effect on the surgeon's wife. It was as if the courtesan's permissiveness (to phrase it delicately) in romantic affairs conferred upon Giulia a similar license. She started to wear an exotic Oriental perfume and, through her actions, it became obvious that she had identified with Ghisella and was play-acting the role of courtesan to Gasparo.

In bed, she was a tigress. She would saturate herself with such passion that she could barely wait for his embrace, and if he was unaggressive she would sneak up behind him—even in his consultation room where he was leafing through his manuscript pages—to fondle him and whisper provocatively in his ear and reach out to touch his penis and to stroke it until, aroused from his manuscript, he would seize her up in his arms and carry her ardently to their bedroom, where they would indulge themselves in an orgy of lovemaking that sometimes lasted through the night.

Giulia had shed all inhibitions. The surgeon would awake in the morning to find her sucking his penis and kissing his testicles and massaging his thighs tenderly with the tips of her fingers and then she would bury her head in his belly, her lovely red hair hanging down to tickle his rising organ, and the surgeon found that desire for sleep had fled his body—a vanishing ghost, an apparition—indeed, he felt immersed in such a state of insanity that he was compelled to ask himself if he was the respectable Dr. Tagliacozzi, eminent surgeon and professor at the University of Bologna, and he *knew* he was, but somehow this did not help him *feel* his professional identity.

Not that he failed to respond to his wife's demands. Every night that the now-famous courtesan resided in their household, the married couple was freed from all conventional restraints, soaring high in a labyrinth of fantasies that conveyed them into an exotic world of promiscuous carnal abandon. Savages inhabited their bedroom—almost strangers—and they wove a lush ecstasy compounded of imagination and reality.

"I am the depraved courtesan Giulia," she would whisper, half biting his earlobe, "of royal blood," and in her tone was delicate refinement conjoined with unabashed obscenity. They had already made love and he was snoring but she would press the wiles of her harlotry upon him until she had plucked him from sleep and tasted the fruits of his drowsy ardor.

On his part, the surgeon took to pretending he was Vincenzo Gonzaga, Prince of Mantua, proving his prowess to the assembled judges hiding hypocritically behind the curtain. His audience was enthralled, and one bishop could not restrain his expression of appreciation, whistling and calling out his congratulations in Latin or Greek. One night he revealed his fantasy to his wife.

"You have proved yourself, Prince," she murmured. "You are a champion of champions." And then, rubbing against him, wiggling her thighs ever so delicately, stroking the hair on his head, on his mustache, on his beard, caressing the hair on his chest and in his pubic area, she was licking his penis and kissing it with such heat that he could not control himself and, rolling over, landed urgently on top of her, breathing, "I cannot wait, Giulia, it is impossible," and thrusting himself inside her, he ejaculated instantly.

"The judges disqualified me," he said.

"No," she said. "They arranged a return engagement. For tomorrow."

And suddenly they were laughing, for was not sex a funny thing, its simple animalism mocking the pomposities and tensions of civilized manners.

"Underneath it all," she said wonderingly, "is that all we are—animals?"

"Perhaps," he said, "I am not certain—and if I were, I might be wrong."

"*You* are a nice animal."

"With an amulet of theriac, you could ward off my advances."

"But I am your whore," she said, snuggling against him, resting her head on his chest.

"Whore? The judges insist on a virgin."

"I will help you pass the test—tomorrow."

And this is my mother Isabetta's house, mused Gasparo. *Forgive me, Mama, for assuredly we are heathen.*

It had been an eventful year for the middle-aged Dr. Tagliacozzi. And now he was preparing to leave by carriage for Vienna to render medical services to Virginio Orsini, Duke of Bracciano, wounded in battle with the Turks in the outskirts of the Austrian city.

Guilio Riario, in the service of Ferdinando I, Grand Duke of Tuscany, had visited him. "Ferdinando is worried about Orsini, his nephew, and wishes you to leave immediately for Vienna to treat his wounds. A carriage awaits you, and your remuneration will be princely. Will you accept this commission?"

"I am most honored."

He rushed to Giulia. "My wife," he shouted excitedly, "I leave to treat Virginio Orsini, Duke of Bracciano, nephew of Ferdinando I, Grand Duke of Tuscany. Pack my instruments and medical supplies, plus a change of clothes and a huge basket of food and wine, for it is a long journey to Vienna."

"The Grand Duke of Tuscany?"

"Ferdinando, the most powerful nobleman in Italy. He succeeded to the title after the death of Francesco. Hurry, my darling, for there is little time."

Gasparo composed a short letter to the Grand Duke:

MOST NOBLE SIR:

I have been told of your wishes and after arranging some important matters I start now on the trip and as soon as physically possible I shall try to be in Vienna to serve the most excellent Signor Virginio Orsini, according to your wishes. May God permit that I reach him in time to be of service to him, which I desire with all my heart. I humbly kiss your hand and pray God to give you every happiness. Bologna, Oct. 17, 1594.

Your Highness's most humble servant,
GASPARO TAGLIACOZZI

Meanwhile, two additional letters were dispatched to Florence via courier.

Riario addressed the Grand Duke:

NOBLE SIR:

This morning your very kind letter of the fifteenth of this month reached me. When I learned from it that you were honoring me by requesting my services I immediately went to Signor Tagliacozzi. I arranged things so that early in the afternoon he left for Vienna. He went with all the diligence possible since I warmly recommended him to do so. I made arrangements so that he could be relieved of his duties at the university while away without any loss or inconvenience to him. I also had Buontempi pay him 300 scudi. I sincerely wish what your Divine Majesty desires for the most excellent Duke of Bracciano. I, as your most humble servant, feel deeply grieved for the occurrence and I humbly beg your Highness to order me again if you consider me worthy. I kiss your hand most humbly.

Your devoted servant,
GUILIO RIARIO

A certain Buontempi, in turn, drafted a letter to Belisaria Vinta, secretary to the Grand Duke of Tuscany.

MOST ILLUSTRIOUS SIR:

I received through Guilio Riario your letter of the fifteenth and I immediately carried out your instructions and gave three hundred scudi of the best gold I could find to Dr. Tagliacozzi. I have asked him for only one receipt which I am keeping and shall send to you if you request it. Will you please instruct Signor Napoleone, General Depository of Exchanges, to pay me for it. Begging you to order me again, I kiss your hand most affectionately. Bologna, October 17, 1594.

Signor Guilio has given you an account of the departure of Signor Tagliacozzi, who left as soon as possible. Again I remain,

Your affectionate servant,

FEBRITIO BUONTEMPI.

And so the ceremonials were concluded, protocol was satisfied, and Tagliacozzi was launched to the pinnacle of his career.

The leave-taking was more informal. Gasparo embraced his wife and his aged mother, pinched his son on the cheek, and climbed into the carriage destined for Vienna. His family, joined by Scipio, stood clustered together waving good-bye, and drawn by four high-spirited white stallions, the carriage bounced off down the street Delle Lame.

Soon the familiar church spires and towers of Bologna receded in the distance as the horses galloped along a road on the edge of a thickly foliaged forest. It was a cold day in autumn and the leaves of the deciduous trees, too, seemed to wave farewell, the wind almost pushing the carriage forward as the coachman yelled oaths at the horses, running in perfect formation.

Gasparo pondered the situation. No doubt about it, this was the most important case of his career. Would he arrive in time to save the life of Virginio Orsini? He felt optimistic. *If Virginio is not mortally wounded,* he mused, *Grand Duke Ferdinando will honor me if I restore him to health.*

But as the carriage had rattled through the streets of Bologna Gasparo had not noticed two Dominicans, in white robes and black hoods, standing in a doorway, crossing themselves and pulling out their amulets of theriac.

One had been Flaminio Vulpi, and Flaminio's lips had been compressed with rage. *I promise you this, Gasparo,* he had murmured to himself, *you shall not escape the Inquisition. As Chief Censor of the City of Bologna, I shall prosecute you.*

And yet he hated to see Gasparo depart; he feared that something would happen to him. Suddenly he realized that he missed the companion of his youth.

Flaminio longed for him and, later in his room, flagellated himself with a whip until his body was sore and bleeding. Then he sobbed, and burying his head in the pillow, he wept through the night.

Chapter 13

Exhausted by the three-hundred-mile journey, Gasparo, in the military camp on the outskirts of Vienna, was directed to a villa in which a bearded dirty group of soldiers was muttering obscenities.

Alberto and Prospero Castelli were huddled together, both glaring at a tired-looking Taddeo Pepoli, who was whispering to Lorenzo Desiri.

"Greetings, Lorenzo," shouted Gasparo, satchels in both hands. "I am happy to see you are well."

"Gasparo," yelled Lorenzo. "Taddeo, it is our fine friend Gasparo." He rushed to crunch the surgeon in an enthusiastic bear hug. "What brings you to Vienna, my friend?"

"I come to treat Virginio Orsini, at the request of Grand Duke Ferdinando. How is he?"

"I have not seen him today but yesterday he fainted for a spell, and they tell me he is throwing up the food he eats. I will take you to his bedroom."

Gasparo found Orsini in bed ablaze with fever. His left cheek was swollen, with a deep gash running through the left corner of his mouth. His tongue was dry and parched; his eyes were sunken and his face was yellowish; his body was pinched and thin and when he spoke his voice was almost inaudible.

"The pain is unbearable," he gasped, breathing with effort. "I cannot sleep by day or night."

Tagliacozzi located another deep lacerated wound directly above the left knee and tested it with a silver probe. Orsini's thigh was also swollen, as was his entire left leg. On his buttocks was an inflamed-looking bedsore nearly the size of the palm of his hand.

"With the assistance of God, you shall recover," said Gasparo, but he was thinking, *There is little hope for the Duke.*

In the garden outside the villa he conferred with a group of military physicians and surgeons.

"His thigh is full of pus," he said. "I cannot understand why no openings were made to release it. Also, there is a piece of necrotic bone in the aperture above the knee; why was this not removed? And the evil-smelling discharge over the wound, why was it not cleansed?"

"He would not allow us to come near him," one doctor answered. "For the last two weeks we have not changed the bed sheets. His pain has been so intense that we did not dare touch the coverlet."

"And what is your prognosis?"

"We are in agreement that his condition is hopeless."

"He is not dead yet," said Tagliacozzi, "and he is young. With God's help, I believe he has a slim chance."

The group of physicians was silent, the spokesman shaking his head in disbelief.

"We must work quickly," said Gasparo. "The bullet piercing his thigh above the joint has torn and lacerated vital tissues, producing pain, inflammation, abscess formation, and ulceration. We must make an incision near his groin to release the accumulated pus, remove the sequestered bone from the open wound, and cleanse the general area."

"Yes," said the spokesman for the group, "that is sensible procedure, but—"

"Now, the terrible bed sore on his buttocks. From lying on it so long without moving, there is excruciating inflammation and ulceration, causing considerable pain because of the sensitive nerves in this area. We must move him to another, softer bed, prop a soft pillow under his buttocks, and change his bedclothes and sheets. The excrements and foul vapors, retained too long in the bed, are drawn into his body, resulting in corruption of vital spirits. Do you gentlemen see it this way?"

The physicians exchanged looks without comment.

"I understand he has been unable to sleep?"

"That is correct, Tagliacozzi," said a second physician. "And he eats little."

"And what he eats he throws up," added another of the physicians attending the nephew of the Grand Duke of Tuscany.

"I assume," said the surgeon, "that we must attribute all this to his intense pain. To relieve the pain and fever, we must make an incision in the thigh to evacuate the retained pus. We must also remove the pus from the bed sore and extract the bullet. He looks emaciated and, my colleagues, I hear he has fainted?"

"Three times in the last five days," said the spokesman. "Plus one epileptic attack. And the Duke's heart beats feebly."

"Then all the more urgently must we remove the pus to diminish pain and fever so that he can sleep and recover his will to live," said Tagliacozzi. "Then we must apply hot fomentations constantly to his swollen thigh and leg. The decoction should contain—can one of you please write this down?—sage, thyme, lavender, flower of camomile, and melilot, red roses boiled in white wine, and a desiccant made of oak ashes, a pinch of vinegar, and half a handful of salt. This decoction will attenuate, resolve and dry up the thick viscous humor.

"We will treat the buttocks with a large plaster made of desiccative red ointment of letharge, bole armeniac, calamine and camphor and vegetable astringents of oak and chestnut bark, and myrtle. This will ease the pain and dry the ulcer.

"As for the deep gash through his mouth, we will cleanse it and apply astringents; we will repair it later, after he regains his strength.

"Meanwhile, to support the heart, we must apply over it a refrigerant medication consisting of oil of water lilies, ointment of roses, a bit of saffron dissolved in rose vinegar, and theriaca spread on a piece of scarlet cloth. Are there objections to my procedure, gentlemen?"

There was a brief silence and the physicians glanced at one another apprehensively. Finally, the doctor serving as spokesman addressed Gasparo. "Your procedures sound splendid, my dear Tagliacozzi. Please do not misinterpret our lack of enthusiasm because— Well, we feel the prognosis for the Duke is so poor that—your outline is—"

"I understand your point," said Gasparo sharply. "But the Duke is still alive and our duty is to keep him alive. Now, once he is able to retain food, we shall give him a wholesome diet: soft-boiled eggs, plums stewed in wine sugar, nourishing broths, and easily digestible meats, such as veal, kid, pigeons, and thrushes. Also, boiled herbs, such as sorrel, lettuce, parsley, chicory, and marigolds. And bread, which should be a day old—not too fresh, not too stale. Ideas, gentlemen?"

"The juice of the orange."

"The white meat of capons and the wings of partridges."

"Fine. And for his headaches we will cut his hair and run onto his head warm oxyrhodinum, and then we will leave a cloth soaked in this substance on his scalp, while to his forehead we apply a cloth soaked in oil of roses, water lilies, and poppies with a small amount of opium and rose vinegar, with a little camphor. He should smell flowers of lenbane and water lilies bruised with camphor and rose water and a pinch of camphor wrapped together in a handkerchief.

"At night he shall be given barley water with the juice of sorrel and water lilies, two ounces of each, with two grains of opium. To further induce sleep, if necessary, we can make water drip down from a high place into a cauldron so that, hearing the noise, he will think it is raining, for the sound of rain is restful."

Tagliacozzi looked at each in turn but no one objected. The message was clear. No one was courting the wrath of Ferdinando I, Grand Duke of Tuscany, and if the patient died, the other doctors could claim that it was Tagliacozzi's responsibility.

With his medical colleagues observing, Gasparo took immediate action, making an incision into the thigh; the patient cried out, while from the thigh pus began to ooze.

"Splendid," said the surgeon, "but hold him down."

Through the hole in Orsini's knee he probed for the bullet and the dead bone, extracting both. "Progress," he said, holding aloft the bullet. "Make him a fresh bed in a comfortable room."

The patient was given medication containing opium, and soon he drifted off into a deep sleep.

The next day he looked more rested and his breathing was somewhat regular. Gasparo injected into the depths of the cavities a solution of aegyptiacum dissolved in brandy. Then he treated the open wounds, covering them with a plaster of oil and letharge dissolved in wine. Finally, he carried out the remainder of his program, including institution of a light, nourishing diet with wine and water.

In three weeks Virginio Orsini, Duke of Bracciano, had regained the color of his cheeks and the flesh on his body. Then, supporting himself with a crutch, the nobleman crawled out of bed to hobble around the villa.

It was a big day for Tagliacozzi and, as Orsini greeted his comrades, a courier was dispatched to Florence to relay the good news to Grand Duke Ferdinando I.

Commanding the Turkish armies was the merciless Ulugh Ali, who had slipped away from the Christian conquerors during the Battle of Lepanto. Victorious in the Battle of Giavarino, where Virginio Orsini had been wounded, Ulugh Ali decided to continue westward and storm Austria.

With forty thousand Turks under his leadership, Ulugh Ali prepared to attack the thirty thousand Italians, Germans, and Hungarians. First, he bombarded the defenders with his battery of forty cannons. Austrian and Italian cannons responded, with the air filled with deafening thunder as both sides pressed the bombardment day and night, sparing no powder. Then the enemy prepared to establish a breach in the foe's lines.

Taddeo Pepoli, a section commander in the absence of the Duke of Bracciano, shouted to his men, "Pull down the nearest houses for ramparts."

The soldiers positioned posts and beams end to end and packed between them solid earth, bundles of wool, floor and ceiling beams, and bedposts. They hauled down scores of houses to use the structural wood and interior furniture for building defensive walls. From the city of Vienna trooped housewives with cauldrons, sacks, sheets, chairs, and chests of drawers—including family heirlooms—to augment the barricades and help their fighting men push back the Turkish hordes.

The Ottoman cannons roared, belching flame again and again, demolishing the wall, a breach eighty feet wide, allowing fifty foot soldiers to penetrate, but behind it was the homemade rampart, thicker and stronger than the original wall. A group of Italian soldiers attached live cats to the ends of their pikes, and launching them over the wall, they cried out with the cats, "Meow, meow, meow." The Turkish riflemen zeroed in, firing salvo after salvo at the screeching cats, then, enraged, halted their fire on realizing they were killing cats, not enemy soldiers.

The Pepolis and the Castellis and their *bravi* led the charge into the breach to hurl back the invaders. Prospero Castelli died instantly when struck with a cannon ball that blew his arm to one side and his body to the other. Lorenzo Desiri, aggressive as always, was struck with an arrow near his chest; fortunately, Gasparo nearby, removed the arrow and treated the minor wound. Alberto Castelli, suffering a broken leg from the direct hit of a cannon, wept in pain while the surgeon set the crooked leg and dressed it so skillfully that the pain disappeared and Alberto slept soundly through the night. Most seriously wounded of the Pepolis was Taddeo; a fragment of stone shot from a cannon clubbed him on the temple, fracturing his skull and propelling him to the ground, with blood spurting from his nose, ears, and mouth. Taddeo, vomiting hideously, writhed in convulsions, face swollen and livid. Trephined by Gasparo, he hovered between life and death for several days, but finally his youthful powers of recuperation prevailed.

A chaplain tried hurling a grenade at the Turks but set fire to it prematurely and it exploded, igniting a house near the breach in the wall, sending it up in flames. Soldiers used beer to extinguish the fire since water was in such short supply that it was necessary to strain the few drops left through napkins.

The Turks were inching forward through the breach in the wall but faltered at the ramparts. At this point, when momentum could have turned in either direction, Lorenzo, recovered from his wound, rallied a contingent of one hundred soldiers. "Forward," he yelled, waving his sword above his head, "forward," and his task force, armed with bucklers, cutlasses, pistols, arquebuses, halberds, and pikes, drove the enemy from the ramparts, back through the wall, and began slaughtering them in their trenches, fouling the atmosphere with cries of revenge and vile obscenities.

In the rear, behind the Turkish front lines, the alarm was given, drums beating out a call to arms and trumpets blaring out their summons as the infidel reserves came surging from their tents like ants, scrambling in all directions, to rush to the aid of their fallen comrades. Then, from one side, the Turkish cavalry descended upon the attackers, the dreaded Janissaries in white turbans, daggers clenched between their teeth, stampeding the counterattacking Italian troops.

Dozens fell dead and bleeding—stabbed, pistoled, and trampled by the fierce stallions—and an exhausted Lorenzo retreated with less than half his force, whipping through the breach in the wall and clambering hastily over the ramparts, Turkish horsemen and foot soldiers pursuing with menacing oaths.

No one could seem to win this bloody skirmish, and the onrushing Turkish soldiers were staggered by a deadly hail of artillery fire. Cannons belched gunpowder, stones, and iron, and the Ottoman charge was halted in a mass of dying bodies, horses and men intermingled in a fearsome pileup between wall and ramparts.

Back and forth raged the tide of battle during the next few days, with the casualties horrendous. Another Turkish sortie was stopped as a few hundred foot soldiers were surrounded. The Italian-German-Hungarian forces tightened the ring, then charged, hacking the bodies to pieces. Every prisoner was mutilated, there were no survivors.

Ulugh Ali cursed the brutality. "I will slit the throats of the Christians. If the noblemen of Italy and Austria do not pay heavily for their ransom, I will torture them to death and cut off their genitals."

On crutches, stumbling around the villa in Vienna, Virginio Orsini exhorted his divisional leaders. "We must defend Vienna to the last man and stain the battlefield crimson with the essence of the godless Turk."

Food rations were reduced as the battle raged on and on. Soldiers were warned not to eat fresh fish or venison, partridges, woodcocks, or larks, since they might have acquired pestilent air from the dead and would spread disease. This left only standard army rations: biscuit beef, salted cows, bacon, sausages, hams, mollusks, haddock, salmon, sardines, herrings, anchovies, and whale—great variety, but small quantities of each so that portions were slim. Peas, beans, rice, garlic, onions, prunes, cheese, and butter gave the fighting men a balanced diet, especially when added to the radishes and carrots pulled from the gardens of townspeople, but all were in short supply and the men were forced to prowl around in the forestland outside the Austrian capital city to kill boars and roast the substantial boar steaks over sizzling bonfires that licked hotly at the night sky, signaling their position to the always watchful Turks.

A spy reported that the enemy was massing for his most formidable thrust and, hobbling from his bed, Orsini thundered, "Each man must fight to the end. You know what will happen if you are captured. Our supply of food is almost gone. Biscuit beef and beans are all that remain—and not much of these. We must stand our ground even if we have to eat our asses and mules, or our horses. If we are pinned down and cannot send patrols out for food, we may have to eat our cats or even rats, and it is possible that we may have to fricassee and chew our leather boots. But we must not surrender to the barbarians."

Early the next morning, the Turkish cannons thundered. For a half hour, the big guns aimed at a new section of the wall, blasting the large stones into fragments and opening up a second breach in the wall. Now, through both breaches, the fierce bearded Turks charged, pouring through and turning to seize the defenders in a pincers movement. Drums and trumpets raged as, daggers clenched in their teeth, scimitars upraised, pistols at sides, the enemy rushed in to kill.

Lorenzo Desiri, a sectional commander now, yelled: "We are surrounded. Back. Over the ramparts. We must regroup so they cannot outflank us."

The soldiers hurdled the ramparts with the Turks on their heels. Bullets fired by the arquebusiers mowed down dozens of the enemy, but hundreds more closed in on the defenders, who hurled stones, melted lead, boiling water, and lighted torches at them. One stalwart bearded Janissary was set on fire; a torch struck his turbaned head, igniting the turban, then devouring his face with flame, his anguished howls rending the air until he died hideously. The survivors moved in for the slaughter, scimitars flashing, and behind the ramparts there were scores of life-and-death duels, the combatants lunging, cursing, bleeding, a reserve force of Austrians and Hungarians running to the aid of the beleaguered Italians, driving the Turks back across the ramparts and through the breaches in the wall, then returning to regroup. On the ground were piles of mutilated soldiers, Turkish and Italian men dying together, gasping for breath, imploring their gods to aid them in their distress.

The wounded soldiers—Italian, Hungarian, Austrian, and German—were carried to the rear on stretchers, crowded into an empty building and placed side by side on the wooden floor, heads cushioned by no soft pillows, battle cloaks the only substitute for blankets. It was a rude, comfortless hospital, and the moans of the crippled mingled with the frantic breathing of the dying as Tagliacozzi and the other surgeons labored mightily in a futile attempt to stem the pain and destruction, amputating legs and arms and stitching mutilated, bleeding parts to control fatalities through hemorrhage. In the distance, the deafening roar of the cannons; a few hundred yards away, the Turks were preparing to resume the offensive.

Instinctively, Desiri, in the absence of the Duke of Bracciano, had taken command of the Italians in the field. And, reflexively, the men turned to him for leadership.

"The infidels will attack again," he thundered. "We must hurl them back to Hell."

The troops were exhausted and their response was hardly enthusiastic.

"To Hell," yelled Lorenzo. "We shall dispatch the Turkish degenerates to Hell. They must not hurdle the ramparts. If they penetrate the first wall, we must counterattack. An arquebusier is stationed in every house on the perimeter to fire down on them and the Viennese women in the houses are instructed to hurl stones, tables, benches, and stools to harass them. Then we will plunge into the ranks of the Turkish pigs, cutting into them with the hard steel of our blades. We will send them to their accursed Muslim hell."

"We shall slaughter the Turkish heathen," shouted one soldier, whose head was bandaged.

"The fields will turn red with the blood of the godless pigs."

"They must not break through our defenses," roared Lorenzo. "If they do, we must retreat as planned, throwing all rings and jewelry into a blazing fire and putting all houses to the torch on the perimeter, breaking every vessel of wine in the cellars, and burying all surplus weapons and ammunition. No booty for the Turks!"

"We will not retreat."

"Death to the heathen."

"If the enemy overpowers us, they will overrun all of Europe; and in our homeland, they will come to rape our wives and daughters or capture them for the Sultan's harem." Lorenzo stood erect. "Will you tolerate this?"

"No." A harsh, accelerating chorus jarred the air. "Never."

"Then kill the brutal Turk. Plunge your blade of steel into his innards and kill him."

Toward sunset the Turks charged again through the breaches in the wall, but once more they were hurled back at the ramparts, suffering dreadful casualties.

The weather was cold and bleak, and soon torrents of rain lashed down, propelled by fierce winds; in a few minutes the battlefield was a sea of mud.

With the rain, the Turks retreated, disappearing from sight, and the artillery on both sides was silenced. For two weeks there were no massive attacks, but both sides sent patrols to reconnoiter and the wounded continued to filter into the improvised hospital. The overworked surgeons were able to rest now and then, with lulls in the action, but Gasparo was exhausted and noticed a sharp pain recurring in his chest and left arm.

What is this pain, he asked himself, *which feels like a knife piercing through me?*

But the stretcher-bearers would carry in another man wounded on patrol, and the surgeon would forget his pain as he slaved to make the man whole again.

Two weeks without a major Turkish onslaught. Virginio Orsini, Duke of Bracciano, wondered what new strategy Ulugh Ali was planning. But Tagliacozzi whispered in his ear, and Orsini suspected it was no strategy.

"The plague. The men die of the plague."

"Are you certain?"

"A dozen men have died before my eyes. They complained of headache and backache, of restlessness and weakness. At first I figured it was caused by the battles, but they collapsed suddenly with high fever, turned blue, and died. When I examined them, I found the glands in their groins were swollen."

"No wonder Ulugh Ali retreated," said Orsini. "If the Turks have departed, we shall break camp and leave at once."

A patrol confirmed the total withdrawal of the enemy, and Gasparo dispatched a letter to the Grand Duke of Tuscany.

MOST NOBLE PATRON,

We have broken camp and made plans for our departure, which we hope will be a happy one. There has been a constant improvement and, to speak frankly to your Highness, if your nephew, the most excellent Duke of Bracciano, were not of such a sensitive nature, he would be able to recover fully much sooner. I shall take him to Florence and further, if your Excellency wishes it. It is my only desire to serve your Highness, whom I greet very humbly and to whom I pray God to give every happiness and contentment.

Your Highness's most humble servant,
GASPARO TAGLIACOZZI.

Vienna, Austria, December 8, 1594

Virginio Orsini was placed in a coffer built specially for him, covered with pelts and sable and lynx. Eight men carried the coffer at the head of the procession of soldiers. Reaching the enemy's camp, they surveyed the thousands of Ottoman corpses, slaughtered by artillery, pistol, sword and dagger, cold, hunger, and the plague. For hundreds of yards the ground was blanketed with dead men's bodies and with the humming singsong of hundreds of thousands of flies buzzing around them. Trudging along the road, the Italian warriors came upon two living men groaning among the corpses.

"Can they be saved?" asked Lorenzo, leading one of the columns of march.

Gasparo examined them. "No."

Without anger, Lorenzo unsheathed his dagger and slit their throats.

The road turned left and soon they came upon a storehouse in which the Turks had held captured Italian and Austrian soldiers. The prisoners of war, all dead, were packed solidly like hay in a haystack, their throats mutilated, arquebus cords tied around their genitalia, and signs of the plague were unmistakable.

Chilled, the Italians turned away from the stench, proceeding to burn to the ground all houses in the area. Then they limped on to a nearby village, accompanied by the survivors of an Austrian battalion. The village was deserted, its inhabitants having fled to the mountains, but red crosses on the doors of many houses testified to the pervasiveness of the plague. Onward they struggled, and thirty miles from Vienna the Austrian soldiers detached themselves and veered off to report to their Emperor Rudolph II.

Now it was three hundred miles to Bologna, and through rain, sleet, and snow the weary troops plodded, two shifts of eight men alternating as stretcher-bearers for Orsini. They were a group of dirty, unshaven, evil-smelling men, the more robust carrying stretchers as well as weapons and knapsacks, since dozens of survivors were too crippled to walk. Grand Duke Ferdinando had dispatched two thousand healthy fighting men to wage battle; nine hundred returned, on stretchers or sore feet, with holes in their boots and bandages covering their wounds. At their head Lorenzo, laughing and singing and boasting of his exploits with the women, urged the men onward, the healing wound near his chest a minor irritation.

"Caledonia, my wife," yelled Lorenzo at the head of the column winding its way along the dusty road, "I return to set you afire with lust."

Hungry, cold, ragged, wincing with pain, the other soldiers could not match Lorenzo's spirit. Still, they marched on. Three weeks later the fighting men from Bologna arrived at the public square of their native city where some hurled themselves to their knees, kissing the ground and blessing the Lord for granting them a safe return.

The ensuing celebration involved the entire populace of Bologna. The courage of the warriors was saluted by orchestras and choruses, public officials delivered orations, and a splendid parade was topped by a huge banquet, with wine and dancing in the streets.

Gasparo came home to Giulia's embrace and saw his son for the first time in several months. Then, at the university he was feted by the majority of the students, but Cesare Aranzio, Ulisse Aldrovandi, and other faculty members refused to participate.

Virginio Orsini, Duke of Bracciano, stayed at the home of Cardinal Ottavio Bandini, the Vice-Legate, and Gasparo visited him. When he arrived, he felt apprehensive, for dignitaries of the Church were at the Duke's bedside, among them Fra Chiari and Flaminio Vulpi.

It was the first time that Gasparo and Flaminio had met in years and both were uneasy at the encounter, stealing nervous glances and attempting to look unconcerned.

"How are you, Flaminio?" said Gasparo, but he was thinking, *You are gray at the temples, my old friend, and your face is gaunt and pale and your eyes are bitter. I would pity you but I fear your power and vindictiveness.*

"I am well and hope you walk under the protection of Our Lord," said Flaminio politely, but the undercurrents were savage: *You are wicked, Gasparo, and you must repent or burn at the stake. You are a sorcerer, a practitioner of witchcraft, and it is my duty to prosecute you. I am building my case against you brick by brick, and when I have finished, representing the holy Inquisition, I will order your arrest and bring you to trial.*

"Pardon me, Flaminio, but I wish to examine the disfigurement on the Duke's cheek."

A few days later, Tagliacozzi operated. Orsini's health was completely restored except for the jagged gash on his left cheek that skirted the left corner of his mouth. The surgeon pared the edges of the wound as if repairing a harelip and then, with his assistants holding down the anguished patient, he sewed stitch after stitch in the flesh, closing the wound. A week later he removed the stitches. Overjoyed, Virginio looked at himself in the mirror, proclaiming his wish that Gasparo and his wife, with the Castellis and the Pepolis, Lorenzo Desiri, and a few other *bravi*, accompany him to meet Ferdinando I, Grand Duke of Tuscany.

So once again Gasparo, accompanied by his wife, was destined for the City of Florence. *At last,* he mused, *I will meet the Grand Duke and my dreams shall come true. I hope it is not egotistical of me, but am I not an accomplished surgeon and have I not brought joy into the lives of many people?*

When the procession of carriages reached Florence, the cannons of the new fortress of the Belvedere thundered in greeting and rockets propelled evanescent stars to the heavens, while crowds in the public square hurled confetti and shouted their admiration, houses in the background bedecked with banners and tapestries.

At the Medici palace, Ferdinando I sat on his throne attired in his most ornate ceremonial dress. In white doublet ornamented with stripes of velvet and satin, wearing over this the robe and red cross of the Grand Master of the Order of Santo Stefano, the Grand Duke sported a gold medallion bearing his image and name on one side, with his emblem, a swarm of bees and motto, on the reverse side. His crown was richly bejeweled with the Florentine lily, and under it his eyes, calm and sensible, appraised the visitors.

At his left, the Grand Duchess Christine was wearing a white silk gown that she had designed, with the lower part of the sleeves removable, fastened with large buttons to her cape. An elegant necklace of pearls encircled her neck, a crown was on her head, a gracious smile, courtly yet flirtatious, curled her lips, but it was tentative, awaiting the exigencies of protocol.

To the right of the Grand Duke, Virginio stood with his diminutive Donna Flavia, while nearby in red robe was Cardinal Scipione Gonzaga with Ferdinando's nieces, the beautiful blond Maria, in gown of gold and embroidered silver, and dark, vivacious Eleonora, in blue velvet sewn with gold fleur-de-lis. With Eleonora was her husband, Vincenzo Gonzaga, formerly Prince, now Duke, of Mantua.

The guest of honor, Gasparo Tagliacozzi, attired in flowing black velvet robe trimmed with sable, was trembling slightly as he approached the Grand Duke and his Duchess. *I am an idiot,* he mumbled to himself, *to feel such apprehension. I am a child. It is this elaborate ceremonial that I loathe. My dream disappears in a maze of court ritual and my surgical skills seem but the pomp and circumstance of a charlatan.*

But Ferdinando, in his regal costume, spoke simply. "I am grateful to you. You saved my nephew's life, and he is dear to my heart."

"You are generous."

"I have collected priceless works of Greek and Roman sculpture— the *Venus de' Medici, Niobe* and her children, the *Dancing Faun,* the *Wrestlers,* the *Knife-Whetter,* the *Appollino.* These statues—ah, the craftsmanship, the concentration of the artists, their superb talents—

And yet my art treasures are only stone, while you, my dear Tagliacozzi, exercise your art in the interests of humanity. I admire and honor you not only for your skill in saving the life of my nephew, but for your dedication in saving the lives of so many of my soldiers, rehabilitating their very souls."

"I thank you, sire."

"At one time your father served my father," continued the Grand Duke, "and I understand he was a supremely artistic weaver of cloth. I have been told that the dress my mother wears in Bronzino's portrait was fashioned from the material of your father. Is this so?"

"Yes." Gasparo was relaxing for, in spite of the ceremonial atmosphere, Ferdinando was a sincere man. "As a child, I saw this portrait. My father pointed it out to me."

"Your father was a splendid weaver of cloth, but you are an artistic weaver of flesh." Suddenly, Ferdinando smiled. "I, too, am a surgeon—but I rebuild *souls*. I have created the port of Leghorn, where Catholics, Protestants, and Jews may live together in peace. Thus, like you, I reshape the lives and souls of people—or so I hope."

"I have helped a few; you have rescued thousands. The Lord took a piece of rib from Adam to create Eve. Emulating this, I use a piece of skin to make a deformed face normal. But you, sire, have attempted to aid all of humanity, not merely a handful of unfortunates, and history will remember you for this."

"Years ago, Leonardo da Vinci drew up sketches of ships that fly in the air; it seems bizarre, but someday I believe this will be reality. But one must ask this question: Will these airships transport people and serve them, or will they wage war, destroying cities? Man's discoveries must find constructive applications. That is why I established the sanctuary of Leghorn—as a constructive lesson to a world torn by war and disease. And, Doctor Tagliacozzi, since your surgery serves humanity, I honor you with this gold necklace and reliquary and pray that Our Lord will bless you."

Gasparo, kneeling, received a necklace from Ferdinando, and then, after rising to his feet and bowing from the waist, he kissed the hands of the Grand Duke and the Grand Duchess and walked back to his adoring Giulia, exquisitely gowned, her eyes welling with tears as she watched Ferdinando honor her husband. *If only my father and mother were here, they would be so happy,* he reflected. *But perhaps this is too much to ask.*

Taddeo and Cesare Pepoli and Alberto Castelli, the latter supported by a *bravi*, stepped forward.

"I wish to express my gratitude," said Ferdinando. "Your families have honored me in battles on land and on sea. I regret to tell you, though, that while you were fighting at Vienna two men dressed as rogues shot and killed two friends of the Castellis. Seized, they confessed that they were hired by the Pepolis. At my orders, their hands were cut off and they were hanged and quartered.

"Gentlemen, I pardon the Pepolis for engineering the shooting, and I pardon the Castellis for attacking the Pepolis during carnival sometime ago. Your feud must terminate. This is not merely my request; it is my command."

The representatives of the rival clans embraced and assured the Grand Duke that they would make every effort to live in peace.

Then Ferdinando decorated Lorenzo Desiri, who had commanded so effectively during the convalescence of Virginio Orsini, praising him for distinguished service and for heroism under fire.

"You are one of my finest soldiers," said Ferdinando.

"That is true," said Lorenzo, unabashed, "and I will continue to offer my loyalty to your Excellency."

"I feel fortified by this evening," said the Grand Duke, "and hope that my reign will bring peace and justice and comfort to the people under my rule. Let us pray, gentlemen, that we will live long and that, more important, our lives will reflect a sophisticated wisdom, an acute creativity, and a tolerant kindness that will enrich the human spirit, so impoverished in so much of this perilous world."

That evening, alone in their suite, the surgeon and his wife waltzed together on the lush, thick carpeting, pretending that the orchestra was serenading them. Around and around they whirled, Giulia singing gaily. In their exuberance, they waltzed until dizzy and finally, laughing uncontrollably, toppled over onto the soft carpet.

They looked at each other and continued to laugh, but finally the surgeon, adoring his wife, removed the regal necklace and placed it around her neck.

Silently, they embraced and remained in each other's arms—and later they made love.

Chapter 14

With the support of Grand Duke Ferdinando, and numbering among his other benefactors the Duke of Bracciano, the Duke of Mantua, and Don Juan of Austria, Tagliacozzi's reputation was secure.

Still, his enemies were in positions of power—Flaminio Vulpi, Censor of Books for the Bologna arm of the Inquisition; Aurelio Morisini, wealthy nobleman, whose acquaintances reputedly included the Pope; and Cesare Aranzio, the renowned professor of anatomy, motivated by professional jealousy and backed by many faculty members at the University of Bologna.

From all over Italy, people flocked to Gasparo's door, seeking his medical counsel and surgical skill.

One of them was the candlemaker Duglioli.

Duglioli was a devout man who worked very hard at the business of making candles, which he had inherited from his father. As a young boy, he had been a member of the church choir, singing his praise of God in Heaven. Now, at thirty, he attended church regularly with his wife and, meeting Flaminio there, had come to admire Flaminio's announced intention of purging the city of heretics, sorcerers, and prostitutes.

Through Vulpi he had gained the commission to make candles for the Dominican monastery, and more devoted than ever to the censor, he became a secret informer for him, reporting anything of potential value to the Inquisition. Bigoted, also, he resented anyone who was not ultrareligious.

Thus, when he would walk past Gasparo—and this happened frequently, since he also made candles for the university—Duglioli would palm an amulet of theriac to ward off danger and, crossing himself, would turn away.

The candlemaker, married four years, had no children, but he and his wife wanted an offspring desperately and at church they would pray for one. And, as if by a miracle, the wife became pregnant. Had God heard their supplications? Duglioli was so overwhelmed that he did not allow his wife to do anything during her pregnancy, treating her like a princess; cooking, washing the dishes, sweeping up, and mopping the kitchen floor.

Duglioli and his wife were extremely superstitious. They would take measured walks in the late afternoon to avoid the sun, and when, on a warm summer evening, they planned to stroll along the streets near the church, Duglioli would check to see that no clouds were in the sky if the moon was shining. If there were clouds, the candlemaker would not let his wife out of the house, fearing that if she saw the moon with clouds hiding it from view she would give birth to a deformed child.

Poor Duglioli could not reason with his convictions, which perpetuated those of his parents when he was a small boy. Constantly, he warned his terrified wife, since they lived less than a quarter mile from Tagliacozzi's house, not to look at the doctor and to clutch firmly an amulet of theriac when he approached. Otherwise, he said, they might find themselves in league with the Devil, their child deformed, while God would condemn them to a lifetime of suffering, thwarted in their ambitions, for their boy (Duglioli had convinced himself that the child would be a boy), crippled, would not be eligible for the priesthood and could not realize his parents' ambition for him: to adopt a religious vocation and rise in the hierarchy of the Church.

Friends of the Dugliolis shared their feelings, supporting their delusion that Gasparo was a sorcerer and his wife a witch, and they, too, would avoid the couple as if they were carriers of the plague, taking every possible precaution—crossing themselves, fingering the omnipresent theriac, walking to the other end of the street to avoid contamination, and redoubling the fervency of their ritual observances.

Strolling from the street Delle Lame to the university or to the public square, the surgeon and his wife would note the furtiveness of the townspeople, and sometimes they joked about it. But it was, of course, no laughing matter. On the contrary, it was depressing, and Gasparo, disheartened, would contemplate the disappointments in store for his son, realizing that many children would not play with him and that they taunted him because of his father's occupation.

The boy would return home from school, bursting into tears, nose bloodied and clothes torn by a neighborhood bully, and Giulia would feel helpless to comfort him, since she knew it would happen again.

The enlightenment of the Renaissance, Tagliacozzi would ponder, *where does one find it in the minds of these ignorant, insanely deluded people?*

He recalled the story of Dr. Guglielmo Frascati, health officer for the City of Bologna one hundred years earlier when the city was in the grip of a terrible plague that killed hundreds of citizens. Dr. Frascati and his colleagues had struggled mightily to overcome the epidemic, but their efforts were futile and the contagious disease ran rampant through the populace.

Then, accompanying the physical disease was an even more deadly disease for which there were no known remedies: it was compounded of terror and suspicion and hysterical irrationality. *Surely,* reasoned the survivors, *this hideous epidemic cannot be explained by natural physical causes or it would have died out by now, like plagues of former years. No, this plague is more virulent than the others. Some evildoer among us, an agent of the Devil, must be secretly nurturing this holocaust.*

One morning Dr. Frascati, in his capacity as commissioner of health, embarked on a walking tour of the city to observe the condition of its inhabitants. Carrying a horn container full of ink, he ambled down the festering narrow streets, jotting down his appraisals. A number of times Frascati stained his fingers with ink, and he wiped them clean by rubbing them against the walls of a number of houses.

Crouched behind a doorway, an old woman saw him cleaning his fingers in this manner and called her neighbors as witnesses. They noted the black smears on the walls and recoiled in horror.

"Look," shouted one, "this agent of the Devil is spreading the plague."

"Yes," said another, "he has the Evil Eye."

Frascati's attempts to explain were howled down; the townspeople cursed him and hurled garbage in his face. The civil authorities arrested him in spite of his official position and he was forced to endure physical tortures that left him screaming in agony.

Finally, to escape the tortures, he lied. "Yes," he said. "I confess that I am responsible for spreading the plague. I am guilty."

Poor Guglielmo Frascati was burned at the stake.

Yes, said Gasparo to himself, *ignorance and superstition, hand in hand, court destruction. And Flaminio, was prosecuting Girolamo Cardano enough to satisfy his hatred for the forces that seek truth? Or does he wait for me to publish my book?*

Shortly, Signora Duglioli was scheduled to deliver her child and her doctor estimated that the baby would not arrive for about two weeks. He told her not to worry, that he was taking a week's holiday to go hunting, but that he would return well before the birth.

Two days later, at three in the morning, the labor pains began and within a few hours she was screaming with the intensity of the contractions. "I fear I shall die," she shrieked. "Fetch a physician, husband."

"It is five in the morning," said the candlemaker. "Everyone is sleeping and your doctor is hunting, may the Devil claim his soul. Where should I go?"

"I do not care. I need a doctor—any doctor—or I will die."

"Doctor Tagliacozzi is nearby. But I cannot summon such a physician, one who defies the will of Our Lord."

"Please fetch him. If you wish me to live, husband, knock on his door till your fist is raw and bleeding and bring him to my bedside even if you must drag him by the neck. Oh. Good-bye, husband, I think I am dying."

In a panic, hardly knowing where his legs were taking him, Duglioli careened down the street Delle Lame, skidding to a stop before Tagliacozzi's door. He smashed fiercely at the solid wood door in a staccato hammering motion that became a reflex action, repeating itself without conscious control.

"Who is it?" In nightgown and bathrobe, Gasparo had lighted a candle and bolted for the door. *"In nome di Dio,* who summons me in the middle of the night?"

"It is me, yes, me," yelled Duglioli, too hysterical to monitor the words into a coherent pattern. "Me. *I* am here."

"Oh," said Gasparo, peering warily through an aperture. "Duglioli."

"Duglioli the candlemaker. My wife is dying. She is with child."

"Yes." The surgeon opened the door. "Wait here. I will dress quickly and fetch my instruments."

A candle was flickering in the kitchen of the Duglioli household. They passed through into the bedroom, lighted by another candle. On the bed the young woman was moaning, tossing from side to side in her agony.

Duglioli threw himself to his knees near the bed, praying to God in a desperate, trembling voice, while his wife's hands pulled at his blouse and scratched him on the arm. Hands clasped in front of him, the artisan rocked back and forth, chanting paeans of praise to God and pleas for mercy due an upright and religious man who loved the Lord and strictly observed all the rituals of the Church.

"I will never touch you again," he groaned, thinking that his offspring was killing his wife. "I promise this on my sacred word of honor. Forgive me, wife."

Tagliacozzi attempted to lead the suffering husband away from the bedside, but it was hopeless. Duglioli seemed not to hear anything but the accusing voice of his conscience and desperately he clung to his wife's hand, whispering frantic words of endearment that could only have the effect of intensifying her terror.

The surgeon examined her under these difficult conditions. "You will be fine," he told the woman, wishing he was really certain of this. "Do not worry." Then he drew Duglioli away from the bed and into the kitchen. "There is a grave problem."

"But I have lived like an upright Christian," protested the candlemaker. "I have dedicated myself totally to Our Lord, and my wife has joined me in devotion."

"I am sorry, but the delivery does not progress normally. The baby is attempting to come forth feet first, and it is this which gives your wife such unbearable pain."

"Not normal? But how can this be?"

"I do not know, but to assist your wife I must keep manipulating the baby ever so gently until it shifts position and the head is aligned to come out first."

"Then do it," yelled the candlemaker, shaking with fright. "Do it quickly. I love my wife, and my baby is killing her."

"It may take a long time, my dear fellow."

For three hours, Gasparo, perspiring, worked patiently on the fetus, carefully maneuvering it toward a headfirst presentation. The conditions for the birth were abominable—the candlelight was inadequate, the woman was shrieking, and most wretched was the panic-stricken husband, patting his wife's hand excitedly, looking heavenward to God, urging the doctor to hurry.

Finally, as Tagliacozzi delivered the baby from the exhausted body of the mother, daylight poured through the windows.

The mother was utterly spent, but the father raised his clasped hands toward Gasparo, as if offering thanks to a priest. Then the surgeon slapped the little red bottom, the newborn screamed lustily, and in a spirit of thanksgiving the father threw himself to his knees to express his gratitude to God.

A moment later Gasparo blessed God too. When he turned the baby over and saw its face, he was grateful that the mother, snoring blissfully, was no longer conscious, so that she could not see its face.

"Visions of Hell," shouted the husband. "What is wrong with my child?"

The infant's tiny mouth was twisted and ugly, somewhat like a pig's, and the surgeon was horrified. Harelip—it was the first case of harelip he had ever delivered. The split in the upper lip was due to improper development of the lip buds in the embryo. This was how Scipio must have looked when he was born.

Duglioli could not bear to look at the countenance of his son. He turned away, suppressing a sob. "Why?" he stormed. "Why? I have been a devoted husband, a hardworking breadwinner, an obedient servant of Our Lord. Why?"

Tagliacozzi knew he had handled the case competently, but felt almost ashamed to bring forth this deformed baby into the world. Uneasily, he envisioned the mother waking up and crying out in agony at the sight of her first-born; what could he say to offer her comfort? *Still,* he thought, reflecting on Scipio, *I can operate and make the child whole.*

"I have not sinned," raged the father. "Why am I punished like this when I have not sinned?"

"I am truly sorry."

"How have I provoked the displeasure of God? *What* did I do? I have comported myself virtuously."

The mother, stirring, opened her eyes. "My baby," she murmured happily.

"A boy," said Gasparo nervously. "A big, strong boy who someday will become a fine, handsome man. But, Signora Duglioli, right now we have a problem."

"Problem? What do you hide from me? What is wrong with the baby?"

"Do not feel alarmed, for though he has a cut in his lip—"

"Cut in his lip?" howled Duglioli. "It is a monstrous deformity that could only have been inflicted by the Devil."

"Technically, it is known as a harelip, and although it looks hideous in a newborn baby, I can operate and give him a completely normal lip, so you need not worry."

"Need not worry? The Devil has accused us of sinning and violating the law of God, and you advise us not to worry. My son, an accursed cripple at birth, his lip an abomination beyond imagining, and you say it is nothing! We are God-fearing people who attend church regularly and render full obeisance to God, so why does He exact His vengeance upon us? It is not just, and I shall not accept it."

The Dugliolis had always enjoyed a compatible union. Husband and wife had shared a faith in God and Heaven and the Hereafter; dutifully, they had attended Mass together and their bed was a happy one for they felt a lovely passion for each other.

But now they began a series of interminable squabbles. One look at the infant's deformity was enough to ignite a fresh argument. For nine months they had anticipated the newborn's arrival with joy. The baby arrived and for the first time the couple was alienated.

The husband searched his mind for memory of an ancestor with evil inclinations. *No*, he mused, *there is no one. All were devout and obedient to the will of Our Lord. Clearly, the guilt must come from the family of my wife. Why did I not suspect this before?*

The mother was equally convinced that the bad blood came from the past—on her husband's side. She started to scrutinize him when she felt he would not notice. *Those eyes*, she said to herself, *yes, they are evil.*

At times the candlemaker was so enraged he would dwell on the sheer delight of strangling the wife whose bad seed was ruining his life. A rich variety of fantasies somersaulted through his mind. Perhaps it was not an ancestor, but his wife's own wicked actions. Had she committed adultery? *Yes, of course. With one of the town merchants— the apothecary or the grocer? Very possible. No, how could I be so blind—it was my best friend, Rico Matuso.* And an image exploded in his mind, Matuso kissing his wife, tearing off her robe, and—"Bastard," he yelled, yanking his dagger from its sheath, "I shall kill you, Rico, I shall slit your worthless throat."

Sheepishly, then, he would realize he had been daydreaming, but a glance at his baby revitalized his sense of outrage. In half a dozen swallows he emptied a large bottle of wine and, in a drunken stupor, staggered around the kitchen, bumping into a pile of dishes that splintered on the floor with a thunderous crash. This triggered off a fresh wave of anger, and for a moment he was terrified that he could not control the intense desire to murder the wife he had loved. But, thankfully, drowsiness washed over him, and reeling into the living room, he curled up on the sofa.

The fury returned in the morning. The couple had vetoed sexual relations, and husband and wife no longer talked to each other. Occasionally, Duglioli would ask himself why he had resorted to such a sorcerer as Tagliacozzi, but then he would forget about the doctor and return to hating his wife.

She kept wishing she could tear out her eyes since no longer did she wish to behold her husband, and she could not bear the sight of her baby son. She would nurse the infant, inserting her nipple into his loathsome mouth, and as soon as he started his greedy sucking, she would look away, unable to tolerate such an ugly organism possessing her proud firm breasts, which her husband had once desired.

Feeding the little fellow, her resentment overpowered her and she feared she could not master the dreadful impulse to suffocate him with a pillow. After this, she was tormented with guilt, and nourishing the baby became a traumatic ordeal; she mustered up all her self-discipline, acquired during years of religious schooling, and managed the task.

One day she placed a pillow for an instant over the offending mouth, shutting out the urgent cries for food. *What an ugly baby,* she thought, but then she remembered the loving beam in the little fellow's eyes as he surveyed the round, full breast and the nipple he craved, and suddenly she loved him, too, and throwing the pillow on the bed she swept her first-born child into her arms—ah, yes, he was beautiful, and thanks to the beneficence of God he had come forth from her body to breathe the air—and caressed him. *I am sorry, my little one,* she moaned. *Please forgive me.* And, lifting him in her arms, she began to weep and to sing him tender little songs, and through the night, weeping, she rocked him in her mother's arms. "I am sorry," she kept whispering. "Please forgive me."

Duglioli could endure it no longer. He hated his grotesque baby, detested his wife, and turned constantly to the wine bottle for comfort. In his misery the candlemaker went to see the Censor of Books.

Flaminio had been suffering from headache. A nightmare had disrupted his sleep the night before and he had paced the floor until daylight. Pale, haggard, trembling with fatigue, he tried to remember the dream but it seemed to dissolve into pieces that he could not put together. After enormous effort, he was able to recall two fragments only: his father, a cripple, was hobbling around the house on crutches, bringing him despair; and then he went to see Gasparo— they were both ten years old—to throw stones down at people from a tower with Fra Chiari (now what was *he* doing in this dream?). Gasparo showed him a new plaything, a pet snake, but the snake had lashed out and sunk its fangs into his leg and, terrified, Flaminio had catapulted out of bed to wake up abruptly and sigh with relief—it was but a dream.

And so Vulpi, shivering with fright and unable to go back to sleep, had paced all night. *Gasparo,* he mused, *it is sad to think of him because once we were so close. We used to exchange confidences and eat together and sleep at each other's houses and do insane things with Lorenzo.*

Flaminio's shoulders drooped. *It is sad to think of the disruption of our friendship, for Gasparo was warm and sensitive.* An image was struggling to break through into his mind. He and his companion had packed picnic lunches, riding their horses into the country, and then— Where had they gone? He could not recollect; it was hazy at the moment. Oh, yes, to the lake, spreading out on a blanket in the sun.

Of a sudden, Flaminio remembered how he had felt attracted by Gasparo's erect penis.

No, he thought defensively. "No," he said aloud, with increasing vehemence, "I did not commit sin with Gasparo. It was the Devil escaping from him forcing me to do his bidding. The Devil of Gasparo afflicted my spirit."

He recalled how Gasparo had hurled a rock at him, opening up a gash on his left eyebrow so that now he had what looked like two left eyebrows.

I shall take my revenge, he promised himself. *Tagliacozzi is an abomination in the eyes of Our Lord.*

In the morning he went to his office and there, waiting for him, was Duglioli, the candlemaker.

"You have heard my story," said Duglioli. "Please, Signor Vulpi, can you help me?"

Flaminio had controlled his feelings during the recital, soothing the distraught husband and leading his mind into channels that suited his own purposes. "Perhaps it was not the fault of your wife," he suggested slyly.

In an instant, the candlemaker was on his feet. "You dare accuse me?" he stormed.

"No, Signor Duglioli. I did not mean that, I assure you."

"Then what was your meaning?"

Flaminio arranged his face into a somber frown. "Perhaps the Devil had a hand in it."

"The Devil?"

"My son," said Flaminio carefully, "you have always been pious and honorable."

"Certainly. I have served God faithfully and cannot understand why He has inflicted this punishment upon me."

"Yes, but your good wife has also devoted herself to the will of Our Lord."

"Truly, sire, but then why?"

"Suppose," said Vulpi slowly, "that your regular doctor had delivered the baby?"

"This was impossible. The scoundrel was off somewhere hunting. He did not care"—and the candlemaker was sobbing, tears streaming from his eyes—"that my first-born child was a wretched abnormality."

"Yes, but suppose he *had* delivered the baby. Assume he had *not* departed on vacation. Would the results have been different?"

"This did not occur to me but—"

"Or," said Flaminio cagily, "did the impious Doctor Tagliacozzi breathe the Devil into the mouth of your child?"

The candlemaker, who had seated himself, exploded to his feet again. "Of course."

"It was Doctor Tagliacozzi who practiced witchcraft and, in shifting the position of the child inside the mother, brought into play the forces of the Devil."

"I see."

"You must understand, my dear Duglioli, that your wife and her ancestors are totally blameless in this catastrophe. You are somewhat guilty in that you called on this sorcerer instead of a God-loving, God-fearing medical man, but you must absolve yourself from this responsibility, as I absolve you. The agent of the Devil is clearly Tagliacozzi."

"I have been blind," said Duglioli, a happy smile flitting over his face for the first time since he had seen the baby's lip. "Now it is fit and proper for me to—"

"Yes," said the Censor of Books, "go to your wife, my son. But first let me caution you: Tagliacozzi will wish to operate on the lip of the child. Do you know why?"

"No."

"To cover his guilt, my son, so that he can use the instruments of the Devil to bury his transgression against the will of our beneficent Lord. Do not let him operate. Withhold your permission, Signor Duglioli, and come to see me. Together we will find a way to destroy this evil man for humanity, for the Church, and for the glory of God."

But, feeling a growing warmth for her baby, Signora Duglioli resisted the will of her husband, insisting that she wanted Gasparo to operate on the harelip. The candlemaker, furious, shouted that he would not allow it.

"I will unsheathe my sword and mutilate you and the baby if you defy the will of God and see this wicked Tagliacozzi again."

She said nothing but he sensed that she would sneak away with the child to visit the surgeon on the street Delle Lame.

And one morning, very early, while Duglioli was snoring noisily, she picked up the baby and tiptoed out the front door. But Duglioli had been play-acting; he waited until she had closed the door and then he sprang out of bed, fully dressed under the blankets. Then he followed her, staying a safe distance behind so he would not be detected.

His wife had left the outer door of the Tagliacozzi residence ajar and the candlemaker entered easily, walking into the physician's consultation room, well furnished now, with a heavy walnut desk flanked by solid straight-backed chairs. On the wall behind the desk was the surgeon's coat of arms, and nearby was a window looking out upon a garden in the rear of the house. Duglioli looked around him. A silver crucifix and a mirror were also hanging on the wall, rich, thick carpets covered the floor, and a plant in a Venetian vase was on the window sill. There it was, a door leading into the operating room, and the short-tempered husband yanked at the doorknob, but the door would not open and he banged on it with his fist. "Let me in."

Scipio, assisting Gasparo, opened the door a few inches but stood blocking the entrance. "The doctor is about to operate; you must wait in the consultation room until the procedure is finished."

"He is not a doctor but an agent of the Devil," shouted Duglioli. "And he exerts his malefic powers upon my baby."

"I am sorry, sir, but you will have to wait."

Once again, Duglioli found himself drowning in rage. "It is too much," he shrieked. "My son an abomination, my wife a traitor, and now this humiliation. Out of my way, black man, or I will kill you." He pulled his dagger out of its sheath and Scipio stepped aside.

His baby was on the operating table and his wife was talking to Tagliacozzi when the hysterical candlemaker rushed upon them. "I shall kill you if you touch my baby. *In nome di Dio,* I shall kill you, magician."

The sleeves of his doublet rolled up to the elbows, scalpel in one hand, compress in the other, the surgeon remained motionless. "I have already made a slight incision, Signor Duglioli. I must continue or the baby will bleed."

"No, sorcerer. I will not allow your witchcraft."

His wife pushed in between them. "You are a fool. The doctor wants to help us."

"*I* am your husband. You have disobeyed me."

"Only for the good of my son."

"Quiet, woman. I am the head of the household, and I forbid this blasphemy."

"Release the dagger." The husband whirled to confront Scipio, pistol in hand, and the black man repeated, "Release the dagger." Duglioli, feeling the steel hardness in Scipio's eyes, complied.

"Go," said Scipio. Reluctantly the candlemaker acceded, turning at the door to say, "The Inquisition will hear of this."

"Go."

"You will burn for this, Tagliacozzi," said the husband, and vanished.

Scipio locked the outer door and Gasparo resumed the operation. He pared the harelip, then used needle and thread in the same manner as on his first patient, Scipio, many years before. He induced the mother to stay with the child in his home to protect the baby from her husband until the lip had healed. Ten days later the mother squealed with delight to see her fine little son, his lip so perfect, his face so glorious.

It was an unhappy victory, however, for husband and wife quarreled interminably from this time on, and the beautiful little boy was to grow up torn with the dissension, hating his father and loving his mother. It was a painful experience for the surgeon, too, and once again he realized the power of the unenlightened forces opposing his efforts to help an ignorant humanity that seemed stubbornly determined to suffer.

And Gasparo was further saddened by the knowledge that his son, Giovanni Andrea, named for his grandfather and fourteen years old now, had witnessed the incident from the consultation room, clinging to Giulia's hand in terror as he saw Duglioli unsheathe his dagger and Scipio point his pistol at the outraged candlemaker. Giovanni Andrea pained the surgeon deeply.

Gasparo's mother, Isabetta, had died the year before, but while alive she had assisted Giulia, like a second mother, feeding her grandson, playing with him, helping Giulia bathe and dress him and administer toilet training when he was an infant.

Isabetta had been a devoted grandmother. Giovanni Andrea, named for her deceased husband, was the delight of her life, and when he was a little boy, she would sit him on her lap and relate anecdotes about his grandfather.

"He was a splendid weaver and a great man," she would say, eyes moist. "He was a marvelous artist, a weaver of incomparable talent, and always was he welcome in the courts of the Duke of Tuscany and other famed noblemen."

And Isabetta would chronicle, in glowing terms, the voyages of her husband throughout the land.

My son fears and hates me, the surgeon thought bitterly. *He avoids me.*

The fourteen-year-old Giovanni Andrea resented his father's work. Since infancy, he had shuddered at the screams of agony emanating from the operating room and, again and again, had shrunk from the deformed faces of the patients. Horrified, even more sensitive than his father, the frightened boy tended to withdraw into himself.

Walking down the street with his parents, he would note that people would cross themselves and scamper to the other side of the thoroughfare to maintain distance from them, praying to God for protection and yanking out amulets of theriac.

Giovanni Andrea loathed his father, tolerated his mother, and adored his grandmother. When Isabetta died, the lad was heartbroken; in his despair he blamed Gasparo for her death and his quiet anger intensified.

"What shall I do with Giovanni Andrea?" Giulia would sob to her husband. "He is so unhappy. He keeps to himself and has no friends. He refuses to play with the other children. I ask him what is the matter but he will not confide in me and, Gasparo, since Isabetta died— Last week Giovanni Andrea returned from school crying, his nose bleeding, his clothes torn. I asked him what had happened and he mumbled something about the other pupils saying his father was a sorcerer."

And now, mourned the surgeon, *my son is silent, hates me, and fears strange things. Helping humanity, I destroy my own child. Deep are his wounds, far deeper than the wounds of Scipio, and I know not how to operate on them or how to bridge the gulf that separates us. Oh, Girolamo, would that I could converse with you and benefit from your wise counsel! But then, my dear old friend, what could you tell me?*

The boy had grown even moodier after Isabetta's death, fantasizing that he would run away from home to attend weavers' school. In time, he dreamed, he would become a famous weaver of satins and silks, in the tradition of his grandfather. People had respected his grandfather. How many times had his grandmother told him this?

His resolve was strengthened after the affair Duglioli. Giovanni Andrea's nerves were shattered at the sight of Duglioli exploding into the house and brandishing his dagger, Scipio leveling the pistol at him. Finally, as a chilling climax, his father was slashing with his knife at a little baby, small, helpless, bleeding, another victim of Gasparo's wretched work. *Yes,* mused the boy, *I shall grow up to become a fine man like my grandfather.*

The surgeon was only too aware of the pattern of his son's thinking. *But,* he asked himself, *what can I do?*

Duglioli paid another visit to Flaminio Vulpi to tell him what had happened.

"You are an honorable man, Signor Duglioli," said the Censor of Books, smiling benignly. "This is one more prime piece of wood to kindle the fire that will consume the body of the magician Tagliacozzi."

"You are certain he is a sorcerer?"

Cannily, Flaminio smiled again, rubbing gently at his temples to ease the pain. "He may seem amiable, my friend. I knew him as a boy so I am aware that he can be charming if he so chooses. But he is a dangerous heretic, an agent of the Devil who defies the will of God and arrogantly prescribes his own brand of magic. The Church cannot allow this and, representing the Inquisition, I assure you that he will receive the punishment he deserves."

Chapter 15

———————————

Another long-time enemy was waiting in the wings. Aurelio Morisini had brooded for years, nurturing his resentment of Tagliacozzi until it had built to the proportions of a monstrous bomb perpetually on the verge of exploding.

The nobleman had felt miserable for so many years that life was almost meaningless to him. Almost. There was no more adventure—his days on the battlefield, his drinking and gambling and hunting, all in the past. In his fifties, Morisini was a recluse. He lived behind drawn shutters in his rambling, dark, gloomy mansion on the Via Castiglione, with a middle-aged manservant his sole companion. He owned another huge, elaborate dwelling on the outskirts of the city, and no other person had entered this residence for years. Never had he recovered from the sword wound his opponent had inflicted decades earlier. A gay blade in his youth, attractive to women, vain about his looks, Aurelio had been sought out by the parents of wealthy girls as escort and potential husband. He had frequented the brothels and dined in public with Bologna's most beautiful courtesans.

In the past. Gone. An illusion? One flicker of hope had lightened Aurelio's melancholy since the nasal deformity had crushed his spirit. That was when the surgeon Tagliacozzi had promised him a fine new nose.

Ah, the chill dancing up and down his spine when he heard this, and the glorious visions. He would again be the dashing ladies' man. As his heritage, he would claim in marriage a lovely young noble-woman and open up his mansions for parties that would ring out over the towers and spires of the great University City.

But what had *really* happened? Morisini's lips compressed with rage as he recalled the pain he had been forced to endure. And then the operation was a failure. He had suffered for nothing.

From that time, Aurelio had entrenched himself in his mansion on the Via Castiglione, imprisoning himself to escape a world whose fruits would forever elude him. He began to loathe his house. It was magnificently furnished, but he was bored by the exquisite drapes, soft carpeting, and the luxurious divans, chairs, tables, and dressers. His material possessions—priceless vases, golden goblets, intricate tapestries—depressed him and he longed to cast about with a stick and destroy everything in sight. As he secluded himself here, he began to notice everything detestable about it—the squeaking board on the living-room floor, the cracks on the kitchen ceiling, the frag-mented glass in a corner of the foyer mirror. Looking in the mirror, he could not tolerate his puny red nasal stump, and his image so enraged him that he feared he would destroy himself. He hated all women who did not love him—thus he hated all women. He resented even the manservant, a considerate, self-effacing middle-aged fellow who obeyed his orders at all times. Obsessed with punctuality, he would threaten to discharge his faithful manservant if a meal was served one minute late.

His hatred for the mansion on the Via Castiglione was so over-whelming that he could find relief only by repairing to his other property. Here, in the bedroom, he experienced his only feeling of belonging: on the walls were portraits of deceased members of his family: father, mother, uncles, cousins. Most had been great warriors, and he would converse with them as if they were still alive—indeed, they were his only boon companions.

He ventured forth from the mansion on the Via Castiglione for two purposes only: to visit the Censor of Books or to escape to his other property. When he did go outside, so overt was his fury that church-men and beggars and merchants and students and artisans and lords would veer to the side, dreading the approach of the grim, bearded, fierce-looking man, and in their fear they did not comprehend that he was a lost soul searching for someone who could love him when *he* felt he was grotesque.

And who is responsible for my plight? he would ask himself. *The sorcerer Tagliacozzi, who practices witchcraft yet has the unmitigated gall to pretend he is a surgeon.*

And, indeed, the desire to exact vengeance upon Tagliacozzi became Aurelio's only heartfelt objective, the one feeling still surging within him that differentiated him from the chair in which he sat day after day, obsessed with thoughts of the ludicrousness of his nose.

With the evangelical mission of retaliation a spark aflame in his mind, the deformed man had visited and revisited the Censor of Books. Flaminio had received him cordially, even eagerly, and more than once had gloated over the forthcoming prosecution of the doctor, but always there was an excuse to postpone seizing Tagliacozzi and bringing him to trial. Vulpi was rubbing his hands gleefully in anticipation, Morisini noted on his tenth visit to the Inquisition's headquarters—or was it the fifteenth?—but still he had initiated no action.

Finally, Aurelio remembered a powerful official in Rome who might be willing to help get him an audience with the Pope. With his manservant driving the horses, Morisini journeyed by carriage to Rome and entered into dialogue with the official, who escorted him to see a papal secretary, who shuttled him off to tell his story to a lowly clerk employed by the Inquisition, and the clerk jotted down his accusations verbatim in a black notebook, bowing him ceremoniously out of the cold stone palace housing the minor functionaries of the investigative body.

Another dead end, muttered Aurelio to himself in his inn in Rome, waiting for more important dignitaries of the Inquisition to summon him for further testimony. *No one will lift a hand to help me gain my just retribution against Tagliacozzi. It is a cruel, unfeeling world, and a man of character and honor must take action in his own behalf.*

For a week he lingered in Rome, but suspecting that the innkeeper wished to poison him, he refused his last meal and ordered his driver and carriage to return to Bologna. *The Inquisition will not assist me,* he reflected, *but I, Aurelio Morisini, swear that as a nobleman of fine blood, who has served his country with manliness on the battlefield, I will slash the broom-stick away from this sorcerer.*

It had been a difficult day for Gasparo. His son had roused him in the middle of the night, screaming and feverish, and Giulia, tumbling out of bed to rush to him, had jostled him further. The surgeon felt mounting anxiety when he thought of Giovanni Andrea.

In the morning, drowsy, he strolled to the University of Bologna to deliver his lecture on surgery. It was no propitious omen that the first person he encountered on campus was his inflexible enemy Professor Cesare Aranzio, his former mentor, an old man now, weary and stooped, but fires of steel still burning in his eyes. The two passed each other with no sign of recognition, not even a token phrase of greeting.

The customary morning rituals followed—Mass of the Holy Ghost at the Santa Maria de' Bulgari chapel and the ringing of the giant bell, *la scolara,* which shocked the students into scurrying to class.

Next, as always, the procession to the lecture halls, the richly at-tired beadles, maces on shoulders, preceding the professors up the spacious staircase. In full-length toga with sleeves ballooning over his arms, the traditional ermine mantle draped over his shoulders, Gas-paro inched up the stairs and here, too, was an unpleasant surprise, for the oily Professor Fracantiano, old-time adversary of Girolamo Cardano and now Aranzio's ally, paused to smirk and whisper hello with sly, almost malevolent, innuendo.

In the lecture hall the students rose to their feet at Tagliacozzi's entrance, standing silently as he trailed the beadle down the center aisle to the lecture chair, desk in front, canopy overhead—all el-evated above the student body, seated now on long rows of benches—the multicolored image of the Blessed Virgin overlooking the univer-sity scene.

It is unchanging, thought Gasparo, commencing his lecture, but then he noticed that the students seemed restless and inattentive.

Leaving for home to eat lunch, he understood the reason. In the courtyard, students were marching back and forth, fists clenched above their heads, striding out in two single files across the cold, hard pavement, leaders of the columns waving aloft placards and banners, their boots beating a fierce tattoo that rattled through the windows of the empty classrooms above.

"The Turks," screamed a tall, thin youth with warts on each cheek. *Is this Remoli,* wondered Gasparo, *from my Thursday lecture?* "Death to the Turks."

"Death befits them splendidly," yelled a canon law student in billowing yellow trousers with white blouse, raising high a banner with Latin words printed in bold capital letters. "They are barbarians, uncivilized and inhuman, and we must look upon them as we would upon a beast from the jungle or a mad slobbering dog. We must tear their skins from their bodies, as they did to our brave men, and hurl the torch of God to set afire their white turbans and black beards so that the infidel burn gloriously in the name of Our Lord."

Do we have no one to hate but the poor Turk? the surgeon asked himself, side-stepping the line of march. *Are there no hateful people in our own land? What of the candlemaker, Duglioli, who would ordain that his innocent little baby grow up smarting under the stigma of a monstrous deformity?*

"We will crush the Turkish murderers in a pincers movement that will cut off their supply of air and drive them gasping and retching to their knees to beg forgiveness of Our Lord."

Last week a demonstration against the Turks, moaned Gasparo. *Now, more incitement against this wretched people, eternal scapegoat for the splenetic tantrums of our populace. And these bloodthirsty cannibals are reputedly our most enlightened citizens, inheritors of the fountainhead of enlightenment that spurted out over our populace during our illustrious Renaissance. O Girolamo, what am I to think of the human condition? My dear friend, would that you were here to feed me the nourishing broth of your wisdom.*

The two columns marched belligerently around the courtyard, turning left and then left, forming a rectangle as they moved forward and around, their printed slogans bobbing above their heads, chanting and singing their threats.

And then, from the other direction, streaming from the streets of the University City into the courtyard, a still larger contingent of students, waving aloft *their* placards with slogans inscribed in Latin and Italian, calling for peace.

"The Turks are human beings," argued a medical student, in flowing white robe, crimson cape slung over his shoulder. "They are good and bad—both—as you and I. They fear us as we fear them. They have died at our hands as we have died at theirs. My comrades, the world needs peace and understanding."

The rival groups faced each other, and for a moment, Gasparo, about to exit the courtyard and turn into the street, feared there would be another outbreak of violence, a recurrence of the rioting of three weeks earlier, when factions of volatile students had clashed, shoving and wrestling each other to the ground until the military had arrived to halt the skirmish.

But the peace group tightened its formation, banding closer together as if for heightened solidarity, and began chanting somberly in Latin a martial-type song in which overtones of peace and conciliation prevailed. In deep-voiced chorus, their voices built to a humming that vibrated across the courtyard to the belligerent demonstrators confronting them, and the militants, sheepish-looking in the face of this, began to drift from their ranks to mill about with the peace students or to walk off campus into the city proper.

Perhaps I was correct to believe in human goodness, thought Tagliacozzi, encouraged, *for others, too, crave the blessings of peace.*

Arms linked, the students of peace raised their voices in a more lyrical song, the tenors arching their tones, as if in parabola, with the sound of the chorus seeming to launch out heavenward, held to the earth by the undertow of basses and baritones.

The surgeon recognized the melody. *Jacob the Pole was the composer.* He smiled wryly. *They say he was best when he was drunk.*

At home his discontent returned, a mass of gray clouds that would not disperse. His son was still feverish and Giulia looked haggard and dispirited. Giovanni Andrea, more timid than ever since the affair Duglioli, moaning with fever, turned away at his father's entrance; this saddened Gasparo and he feared his heart would break.

The surgeon left after bolting down lunch. Scheduled was the first day of annual preparation of the compound theriac, and he walked briskly toward the Archiginnasio to assist on this ceremonial occasion. With mixed feelings. For the irony of the situation struck him again:

that year after year he had presided at the making of the theriac used in amulets by the ignorant and superstitious to ward off the plague and the Evil Eye and that these pitiful souls, minds enslaved by the rigid Catholic ritual, would rely on the theriac to protect themselves against *him*, unaware of his role in its preparation. He believed in God, but did not the Roman Church speak for Him?

It is as you claimed, Girolamo, reflected Gasparo, passing an elderly couple, crossing themselves frantically when they recognized him, *a most curious world. A man of your wisdom, hounded by the Inquisition. The brilliant Galileo, hunted as if he were a fox. What an outrage! Ah, Girolamo, so naïve was I as a youth, imbued with idealism, aflame with a lust to save the world. But, then, I do cling to the last slim thread of my desire to lead a constructive life, to hunt out peace and inner contentment, to help shape a more humane civilization.*

At the courtyard of the Archiginnasio a crowd was assembling; doctors from the College of Medicine at the university, eminent pharmacists, and servants in green with gold ornamentation bustled around making ready for the afternoon's ceremonies. And ceremonies they were indeed. The Archiginnasio was resplendent: rich crimson damasks were draped over the balconies; two great pyramids were at one end of the courtyard, enshrined in damasks, with busts of the historic medical authorities Hippocrates and Galen, on top of which were two huge majolica vases for holding the theriac, while other pillars were stacked with beakers, filters, and additional apparatus for making the theriac; and enormous cauldrons were in the middle of the courtyard. Bustling and noisy, doctors from the College of Medicine were inspecting the ingredients and pharmacists were preparing to mix the drugs; all were elaborately dressed in splendid multicolored robes. In the upper loggia were noblemen and their wives and the spouses of those officiating at the rites, as well as *bravi* in suits of armor, white-robed, black-hooded Dominican priests, and prostitutes, faces rouged, blond hair dyed and embellished with artificial fibers, wearing gowns to display their seasoned breasts. A festive spirit filled the air, the laughter of the ladies mingling with staccato commands of the participants in the preparation of the theriac.

In the courtyard, Gasparo looked around. Professor Cesare Aranzio was present and yes, of course, Professor Fracantiano, and to the side, talking with one of the city's most noted pharmacists, was Professor Ulisse Aldrovandi. Not a group to bring delight to his soul. Ah, but looking up to the overhanging balcony, there was Lorenzo Desiri, now chief of the Pepoli *bravi*, decorated for bravery by Grand Duke Ferdinando, and Tagliacozzi waved to him, Lorenzo howling back a ribald greeting and pointing to his beautiful wife, the former Caledonia Bargillini, pinching her cheek and her shoulder, his fingers hovering near the firm swell of her bosom. Also in attendance was Ghisella Minadoli, wearing an amulet of theriac as protection against the French disease, conversing with a bachelor from Rome, a member of the Castelli clan, who was arranging a rendezvous for himself and his friends from the Papal City.

The surgeon turned away to assess the proceedings. The vipers had been dissected; he was sure of this, for he had executed a number of the dissections, and one viper had continued to thrash about for a while after severing of head and tail. Then the entrails had been thrown away, the body skinned, the fat removed, and the vipers had been cooked, as prescribed, over a red-hot fire of vine branches, with salt and sprigs of green dill. Cooking of the vipers had been perfect, the dignitary supervising had chortled. The viper flesh had been neatly separated from the backbone, and this boded well for the potency of the antidote. Then the cooked viper flesh had been crushed in a mortar, with well-cooked bread added, plus pure flour, and finally the mixture had been shaped into pellets, or troches. Following this, the viper troches had been put to dry in a southward-facing upper room, the rays of the sun penetrating into the room for most of the day but not allowed to strike the troches directly. For fifteen days the viper troches had been dried and then they had been oiled with opobalsam and stored in vessels of the finest gold until it was time for preparation of the theriac.

Making the compound required three days. On the first day Tagliacozzi and his colleagues from the College of Medicine would conduct their examination of the ingredients. Then the pharmacists, assisted by the *protomedici*, would undertake the mixing of the compound in the huge containers cradled on the harsh cement of the

Archiginnasio courtyard. After two days of mixing, pounding, and boiling, the theriac would be pronounced suitable and would be distributed to pharmacists of the city and surrounding hamlets. About five hundred pounds of theriac would be prepared, balm for the multitudes, its price fixed by the Gonfalonier and the Anziani at about twenty baiocchi (a copper coin worth a half penny) an ounce.

Gasparo fulfilled his ordained function but he felt weary, and underneath his surface calm a rage was bubbling. *What nonsense,* he thought, *and this is perhaps our most solemn ceremony.* He let his eyes wander over the mobbed courtyard—from the dignitaries thronging around the giant cauldrons and the majestic majolica vases (Flaminio Vulpi and Fra Chiari had arrived representing the Church) to the audience in the balconies (Taddeo Pepoli and Alberto Castelli, friends for the moment, had joined Lorenzo and his wife). The Governor of Bologna, looking grave to suit the occasion, was chatting with Cesare Aranzio. *It is insanity,* mused Gasparo, *sanctioned by our authorities and codified by law.*

For two years a stormy, virulent controversy had raged in the university over the theriac procedure, centering around Professor Ulisse Aldrovandi and exploding into a shooting war that had all but destroyed the colleges of medicine and philosophy of Bologna. Overwhelming animosity had been kindled in the lengthy dispute over the main issues: jurisdiction of *protomedici,* or pharmacists, over regulation, preparation, and distribution of the theriac and whether or not use of pregnant vipers was permissible.

The debate escalated into a conflagration and pharmacists opposed to Aldrovandi had announced that they would make their own theriac in the pharmacy Del Melone. Aldrovandi and colleagues had opposed this, but the colleges of medicine and philosophy had censured Aldrovandi and removed him from the faculty. Outraged, the famed professor had stormed from his house, pistol in hand, to avenge himself, but then, thinking better of this, he had laid his pistol aside and had appealed to the Bolognese Ugo Buoncompagni, now Pope Gregory XIII, in Rome. The Pope ordered Ulisse reinstated, and the controversy simmered down.

And what was this all about? the surgeon asked himself. *The most burning issue was whether or not the female vipers considered for use in the theriac were pregnant. And yet if I do not assist at this absurd ceremony, I will be denounced, punished, perhaps burned at the stake.*

Exhausted after the first day of the annual theriac ritual, Gasparo proceeded to a small tavern near the Archiginnasio for a glass of wine; he had taken to coming here now and then since Signora Rinaldi and her flock had left for Rome. But before he could lift the glass to his lips, the door crashed open and an agitated Scipio burst inside.

"My friend," said Gasparo, "what brings you here?"

"Your wife," yelled Scipio. "Kidnappers. They—"

"Kidnappers?" shouted Gasparo, springing to his feet.

"Your wife was attacked by two masked fiends. They burst into the kitchen, sire, to pounce upon your lady. I was resting in my room when I heard the commotion."

"Masked? You could not tell their identity?"

"I tried to wrench your lady free, but someone clubbed me on the head with a pistol and for a while I lost consciousness."

"You saw and heard nothing?"

"They seemed master and servant, sire, for one man directed the other. The master was dressed like a dandy, with thick black beard, but his face was masked. I rushed to your wife but—"

"Did he not say something?" Gasparo found himself screaming, and involuntarily he seized his assistant by the shoulders. "Tell me."

"He seemed a lunatic, sire, laughing in a most terrifying way."

"Cease your jabbering and give me some clue."

"He muttered to himself, sire; would that I might recall his exact words—"

"Scipio, what *did* you remember?"

"'Many years.' He laughed as if possessed by the Devil and kept saying 'Many years.' For many years, he said, he had waited to take his revenge. For many years."

"Splendidly dressed, thick beard, years waiting for revenge—could it be Aurelio Morisini? *Was it Morisini?* Scipio, did you see anything else?"

"Before I fell, sire, I believe I recall seeing a fine carriage outside your door, gilt-edged, made of the finest materials, with white stallions."

"It must be Morisini. He lives on the Via Castiglione. I must run home for my stiletto."

"Here you are, sire," said Scipio, pulling the sharp-bladed weapon from under his cloak and handing it to Tagliacozzi. "And I have a pistol."

"Let us go!"

Driving hurriedly away, the bearded kidnapper reined in the horses some distance from the Tagliacozzi residence, allowing his manservant to clamber from the carriage and walk to the mansion on the Via Castiglione. Then he whipped the steeds into motion and shortly they arrived at his isolated country estate, where he led the surgeon's wife, bound and gagged, into the house.

Morisini seated Giulia in a straight-backed leather chair in the elegant bedroom binding her into the chair with stout ropes and removing the gag from her mouth. The room was like an ancestral museum, portraits of the mutilated warrior's father and mother overlooking the enormous double bed and on the far wall the grim countenances of austere Morisini males: stern, tight-lipped grandfather Emilio and fierce, bombastic great-grandfather Riario and Uncle Alfredo, eyes seething with fury, who claimed he had butchered more than one hundred Turks with his sword. Immobilized, Giulia stared with horror at the man dancing back and forth in front of her, eyes rolling in their sockets, hands restless, clenching and unclenching, stroking his beard, massaging his ear. His appearance was frightening; even more alarming, he directed his conversation not to Giulia but to the portraits of his ancestors on the walls.

"Her husband, Emilio, is a practitioner of witchcraft," said Morisini, addressing the portrait of his stern grandfather. "He is a pernicious agent of the Devil, and God has ordered me to punish him. He is a sinner, so must he not pay for his sins?"

He is a madman, thought Giulia. *Oh, dear God.*

"At last, the sorcerer Tagliacozzi is helpless and I possess the power to consummate my revenge, and, Uncle Alfredo, this lovely lady is my instrument." Morisini was almost whispering, his feeling of omnipotence so strong that it required no strident assertion. "My revenge is sweet, ah, yes. For Tagliacozzi must learn his lesson and understand that no man can torture a Morisini and mutilate him and go unpunished. Certainly you must share my sentiments, Uncle Alfredo."

He turned from his ancestors to his victim. "Aurelio Morisini is a proud man, my lady, and once he was a brave warrior. Oh, yes, signora, Aurelio Morisini was one of the greatest warriors in the land."

Morisini walked agitatedly back and forth past Giulia, bound tightly in the chair; the surgeon's wife was pale, eyes huge with horror. "Oh, yes, my charming lady, you are gorgeous, and Aurelio Morisini, he—I—possessed many beautiful ladies before—" The rhythm of his stride sped up in tempo with the acceleration of his rage. "Once, signora, I was a brave warrior, adored by the ladies. But then I was on the battlefield, fighting the honorable fight, and my nose— I asked myself why this had happened to *me*. I served you faithfully, Lord. I slaughtered Turkish heathen in your blessed name, so why should I be so afflicted? I listened for the answer of Our Lord, but He would not deign to speak."

Giulia, paralyzed by panic, could not control the terror racing through her mind.

"And then hope, a ray of warm, bright sunshine, burned through to penetrate the clouds in my mind. A skilled surgeon could restore my nose—and with it my honor. Once again the beautiful ladies would desire me. Ah, signora, I thought my sufferings were over." During his recital, Morisini's face had been transformed: a beatific glow had filled it with sweetness. Now, slowly building, his rage mounted, his eyes two black balls of fire, until it overpowered him and he found himself screaming again. "Your *husband* was the surgeon who tortured me. He inflicted pain to kill any mortal. How I endured it eludes my comprehension. Had the Devil commanded him to kill me? And my nose—" The nobleman was sobbing, tears streaking down his cheeks to fall, fully absorbed, into the thick sponge of his beard.

Giulia, shocked into numbness, said nothing.

"All right, woman," howled Morisini, "why do you not speak? I charge your husband with infamy and you defend him not."

Trembling, Giulia could not utter a word.

"By the stars, I have sworn revenge. Yes, I, Aurelio Morisini, must take my revenge. Your husband, signora, is a sorcerer. *You* are my revenge against him."

She averted her head as he approached.

"I was deceived by your appearance—for you are beautiful, but in your soul lurks evil. In past generations, courtesans must have infested your family because I can feel the Devil's forces working inside me, setting me afire with unholy emotions."

Giulia's heart beat violently; she felt as if she were about to faint; she gasped for breath.

"I am a Morisini. We are one of the fine old families of Italy, but we are men first. My ancestors stare down at me from the walls, signora; my Uncle Alfredo pierced through in excess of one hundred Turkish barbarians with his sword, and I feel helpless to betray their good name or their faith in my powers."

Gasparo and Scipio had rushed to Morisini's house on the Via Castiglione but it was deserted except for the middle-aged manservant eating supper alone in the kitchen.

They cornered him, Tagliacozzi waving a stiletto and Scipio, pistol pressed against the man's throat, forcing him to admit that the insane nobleman owned a country estate and to write down directions to it on a piece of paper.

Then they whirled through the tight-packed streets, Scipio driving the carriage, whipping the horses mercilessly, while the surgeon, half crazed with anxiety, screamed oaths at him, prodding him to drive faster.

They rumbled past the public square, passing a beggar in tattered garments asking alms of a prosperous-looking merchant. They were engaged in a heated disputation.

"Certainly you could spare five centesimi for a hungry man?" pleaded the beggar.

"It is unthinkable to reward your lazy, shiftless ways."

"You are fortunate, sire, that I am not armed, or I swear I would dispatch you to Hell."

I have failed my beloved Giulia, Gasparo accused himself. *Her life is endangered because of my failure.*

Morisini untied Giulia and hurled her onto the bed. She squirmed away from his feverish embrace but Aurelio snatched her, ripped her gown from her body, and leaped on top of her, straddling her with his muscular legs. She tried to push him away.

"You find me repulsive. It is the horror of my abominable nose that drives you from me." Tearing off her chemise, he drooled with passion at the sight of her naked body. "Yes," he said, kissing her breasts and, excited, leaping to his feet to throw aside his clothing.

Instantly, she was on her feet, dashing for the door, but Morisini was alert. Encircling her with his arms, he dragged her back to the bed and, nude himself, launched himself on top of her. She kicked him but he was too strong for her.

"It is twenty years since I have tasted the sweetness of female flesh— Ah, but you are ravishing."

Morisini nuzzled her smooth white neck, planting his beard against her soft skin. But she bit his cheek and he reeled back, startled, as she pushed away. She tried to rise from the bed but he reacted instantly and drew her to him.

"A tigress," he chuckled indulgently and, attacking, buried his beard in her neck while she screamed and clawed him with her fingernails. He kissed the nipples on her breasts and caressed her soft buttocks, pressing his erect penis against her thighs, which she would not separate to grant him entrance.

Suddenly, she felt her fingernails scratching at his nasal stump, and he felt as if he were drowning in an ocean of fury. *"You* hate my nose," he raged. Lashing out, he began to pummel her, clouting her chin, temple, cheek, and shoulders with an abandon that he was helpless to check.

Giulia was unconscious and Morisini, trembling with desire, raped her.

Afterward, a fresh despair engulfed him. *She felt nothing,* he thought, *and her husband knows not what happened. Was it futile?*

Then a new thought came to him. "My revenge shall be complete," he shouted to the portraits of his ancestors. "I will do to you, lovely Lady, what your husband did to me. My servant informed me how Enrico Gradenigo slashed flesh from the cheek of the courtesan Ghisella and your husband repaired it. Thank you, Gradenigo, you bequeath me an excellent idea. I shall take my dagger from my dresser, and, lovely lady, when you wake up, you will see a disfigured face, a mass of mutilated flesh—*your* face—and your husband will be unable to repair it. Ah, yes, your beauty will be destroyed and that will be my revenge."

At this moment Gasparo and Scipio, breaking in through a ground-floor window and rushing up the staircase to the second floor, came running into the bedroom.

The surgeon stood there, stiletto in hand. His Giulia, naked in Morisini's bed, the deranged nobleman standing over her, naked, dagger raised high to slash her.

The blood pounded in his temples. "Turn around, Morisini," he snarled, and he felt that a stranger had taken possession of his body.

Immersed in blood lust, Morisini had not heard them and, startled, turned around, dagger raised, to confront Gasparo. Excitement, rage, and surprise battled for control of his face—but there was no fear.

"I shall kill him for you, sire," shouted Scipio, pistol leveled at the madman.

"No, he is mine."

Spittle oozed from Morisini's mouth. "You imagine that a sorcerer like you can outduel Aurelio Morisini?" He charged at the surgeon, but Gasparo leaped aside and lunged at his enemy with the stiletto, piercing him through the chest, then stabbing him in the abdomen.

Morisini died instantly, with his ancestors, stoical of countenance, witnessing it from their silent canvases on the bedroom wall.

Can this be real? Gasparo asked himself, *or do I dream this? My wife, kidnapped, naked in the bed of a madman, assaulted, terrorized. And I am a murderer. Always before have I used my knife for good.*

"Do not fear," said Scipio, "no harm can come to you from killing this man."

But Gasparo did not hear a word. Huddled on the bed, Giulia was weeping; never had he seen his wife so forlorn. He embraced her and she cried on his shoulder, while Scipio turned away so they could feel alone and offer consolation to each other.

"My poor darling," murmured the surgeon, but he was almost as distraught as she, "my poor darling."

Later, Scipio drove them back past the public square, empty now, to their home. Hysterical, Giulia went to their bedroom while Scipio helped the servant girl, Maria Boschetti, care for Giovanni Andrea.

As for Gasparo, he was unnerved by a searing pain in his left arm—it was the second time he had felt such a pain. His arm was heavy, like a lead weight, and the knifelike sensation slashed through him, then subsided.

It is punishment, he mourned. *God tells me that I sinned in grafting skin from the arms of my patients. My father was right. I have blasphemed against the will of God and the Lord chastises me for this. He has made the pain still more terrible because for the first time I have used my knife for evil.*

Chapter 16

Sleep would not come to Gasparo that night. His anxiety was so intense that he could not remain seated for more than a few minutes. Restless, he paced the floor till nearly dawn. The pain had gone from his left arm but he was exhausted and found it impossible to accept the nightmarish events.

I have betrayed my wife, he agonized, kneeling before the crucifix in his consultation room, *and now I have killed a man. It is a blessing that my parents are not alive to be humiliated by this disaster. My dreams, were they illusions? I am sorry, Father, and regret deeply that I have disgraced your good name.* Giovanni Andrea, the pious weaver of silks and satins, had bitterly opposed his desire to become a surgeon.

"These people must endure deformities," his father had proclaimed, "because God elected to punish them for the wickedness of their ancestors. Therefore, to correct these disfigurements through surgery is evil since it defies the will of God."

Had his father been right after all? After Giovanni Andrea's death, he had reconsidered, but then Isabetta had related her vision—with its symbolic pledge of her backing—and he had matriculated in the medical school at the renowned university in his city of birth, Bologna.

Thus, he had challenged the will of his father, supported by the authority of the Roman Church, and now for the first time in his life he had killed a man.

His mind, moreover, was filled with a conflicting twin image of

Aurelio Morisini: the grotesque, raw, irritated-looking nasal stump and the bearded, hairy male animal forcing himself upon his wife. The disparity between the images created confusion in his mind and he hated Morisini one moment with an intensity that made him almost nauseated, while the next moment he felt contrite.

Morisini deserved to die, he told himself, and then, *Forgive me, Aurelio, for failing you as your surgeon and making you lust for revenge.*

Finally, dizzy with sleeplessness, bewildered beyond endurance, he poured himself a tumblerful of wine, sipped it, and then, downing the remainder with a gulp, poured another tumblerful. It calmed his nerves, and soon he began to forget his terrible day, the image of Morisini fading away somewhat, but hovering on the periphery of his consciousness, the issue, if not the image, remaining his central concern.

To whom could he turn in his distress? His professor Girolamo Cardano had bolstered his faith in himself during his student days, and afterward, but where was Girolamo now? In Rome, an old man, living out his last years under the protection of the Pope.

His lovely wife had helped him build his strength when he was a young man, encouraging him to develop his aggressiveness and masculinity, and he had responded eagerly to the challenge—to what effect? That a madman had kidnapped her to revenge himself on her ignoble husband, who had blasphemed against the will of God. His feeling of guilt toward Giulia was so strong that he could not bear to think of her.

Striding the living room until dawn, he walked to the kitchen, opening the rear door as the sky began to lighten. Then, weaving slightly, intoxicated from the wine, he stepped into the garden.

His thoughts drifted to the university, and to a recent lecture he had delivered on anatomy. As always, he had enunciated it from his elevated platform at the far end of the classroom, a canopy above his head as he stood, hands on desk, shuffling his notes, the Blessed Virgin's image dominating the room, and after he had finished, ten or fifteen students sitting on the long rows of benches had jumped to their feet and rushed forward to the dais to ask questions and exchange pleasantries. He had been heartened to see once again that the young people liked him and were interested in his lectures.

This was especially important to Tagliacozzi since his fame had earned him the hatred of many professors. Members of the faculty during the ceremonial procession to the lecture halls, following the gaudily dressed beadles up the wide staircase, would gossip and joke with one another but many would turn their backs on him, pretending he was not there; wearing his long, dark robe trimmed with fur, he would observe the ritual, but he felt isolated.

Sometimes he considered moving to Padua, for clearly the University of Padua, also a reputable institution, would welcome him as a professor, perhaps even as head of the medical school or as professor emeritus. People would honor him there and his son could attend school and make friends without submersion under the stigma of his father's occupation.

I do not know, he muttered to himself. *This glorious image, is it reality or fantasy?*

He could not be sure. Perhaps in Padua, too, people, prisoner to the tenets of the Roman Church, would grab frantically for amulets of theriac at sight of him. Oh, yes, he mused, many vipers wear clothes and belong to the species *Homo sapiens.*

Sipping his wine, he continued to ponder the hostility of the ignorant and superstitious toward his attempts to make a contribution to human advancement. He recalled an incident a few months earlier that he had since banished from his mind. Walking from the university to his home at twilight—he had been preparing notes for a future lecture—down a darkening street, he had been staggered by a sharp blow on his back. Whirling, he had seen a masked man running in the other direction. He had not pursued—he had been tired from the day's work—but had stooped to retrieve an object on the street. It was a large rock, and Gasparo had blessed the fact that it was not pointed. As it was, his back had pained him for a half hour.

He had said nothing to Giulia, hoping to spare her worry. But how could he be certain it would not happen again, except that this time his persecutor would wield a stiletto and his lovely wife would find herself a widow.

In his garden, Gasparo, somewhat mellowed by the wine, seated himself in a chair under a tree. He surveyed his property: house, garden, white fence. A brown pigeon had alighted on the fence.

He sipped his wine and stared, fascinated, at the pigeon, balanced precariously on the slender top of the white fence—one half inch wide. Would not his friend young Galileo find arresting the question of the bird's equilibrium on such a narrow perch? Galileo, whose hypotheses, following from his honest observations, had brought down upon his shoulders the punitive wrath of the Roman Church. The pigeon maintained its balance in an awkward position that seemed untenable: facing south, it balanced itself on its left foot, hiding the other foot in its feathers. Most incredibly, it remained motionless in this position for almost half an hour, the surgeon watching it, enchanted, as he sipped his wine. There were spikes on the fence about three inches apart and in this constricted area the bird managed to turn around, and now it faced north on its right foot, the other foot tucked away beneath its feathers.

Remarkable, breathed Gasparo. *The pigeon seems comfortable in this ludicrous position.*

He poured himself another tumblerful of wine and continued to observe the pigeon with mounting benevolence.

Finally, he addressed the bird. "Signor Brown Pigeon, I congratulate you on achieving a most precarious adjustment to your pigeon world."

"Is this a compliment?"

"I do not know, Brown Pigeon, but your world seems no more secure than mine. Where have you come from?"

"From Rome."

"Rome? Ah, I understand. You represent the Roman Church."

"No," said the pigeon, "but Girolamo Cardano sends you his warmest greetings."

"Girolamo? My dear friend Girolamo? Brown Pigeon, you are his emissary?"

"Emissary?"

"What I mean is, Brown Pigeon, I have longed to talk to my dear friend Girolamo and now he has sent you to give me comfort. I bless you."

"It is nothing."

"I will tell you all my troubles. And, Brown Pigeon, they are many. But, friend, may I ask you a question?"

"You may. And, Doctor, if the stars are favorable, I will answer it."

"You sound like Duglioli or— Never mind. Signor Pigeon, do you not feel cramped and off balance perched so awkwardly on the fence?"

"It is my home."

"Yes, but you could move to my garden. It is ever so much more pleasant there."

"I am satisfied."

"Please be reasonable, Signor Brown Pigeon." The surgeon leaned forward in his chair. "Why stand so awkwardly on one foot if you can rest on two feet near the shrubbery in my delightful garden?"

"Doctor, discipline yourself. This is my jurisdiction, not yours. Unless you represent the forces of the Inquisition. Are you a bona fide member of the Church hierarchy with authority to ask such questions?"

"You are right. Please forgive me for intruding. I congratulate you for defending your position so strongly, though it is a ludicrous position."

As if affronted, the brown pigeon, on one foot on the narrow ledge on the fence, turned its nose skyward. "It is the will of Our Lord for birds," it recited.

Gasparo laughed. It was the first time he had laughed since seeing Morisini with his wife and this thought sobered him. He had drained his bottle of wine and plodded into the house to obtain another. *Pigeon-minded obstinacy,* he reflected, *but how is this pigeon different from the human beings who fear progress? How is it different from Duglioli, who shrinks from my approach, or from Flaminio, who cannot bear to face any truth, or from Cesare Aranzio, who cannot tolerate my fame, even though I feel no ill will toward him?*

The surgeon closed his eyes wearily, after reseating himself in the garden. *Is there meaning in life?* he asked himself. First, the trouble with Duglioli and now this catastrophe. His beloved Giulia was alone in their bed, miserable, frantic, and he was too depressed to offer her more than a token attempt at comfort.

He was also anxious about his son. The boy avoided and feared him and hated his work. He had asked his wife what was the matter and, tearfully, she had replied that the boy would cover both ears with his hands to shut out the patients' screams when his father was operating. " 'I hate Father's work,' " Giulia quoted Giovanni Andrea. " 'When I grow up, I will become a weaver of fine cloths, like my grandfather, after whom I was named.' " *Dear God,* Gasparo sighed, *what can I do?*

Opening his eyes, he inhaled lustily from his wineglass and looked around for the pigeon. It was not on the fence; even the pigeon had deserted him.

"Hello, my friend."

Gasparo looked down. There was Brown Pigeon, perched neatly on the grass in front of his chair. "Signor Brown Pigeon, what are you doing there?"

"On the grass? Well, I like it here."

"But what of your home on the fence?"

"Let us admit, Doctor, that I considered your advice and compared my one-legged discomfort on the fence to my two-legged mobility on your grass, and I concluded that you were correct." Brown Pigeon strutted imperiously on the grass, circling this way and that, darting an appraising glance at the surgeon.

"Magnificent," shouted Gasparo. "I am supremely impressed with your intelligence."

"Nothing. Really, nothing. I am, you know, a frequent visitor to your university."

"What?"

"I have long been aware of the controversies at the university, stimulated by your experiments in medical technique that have so outraged your colleagues. Naturally, I flew there to appraise the situation."

"Naturally?"

"Yes, naturally. If you believe that pigeons are stupid, that is what I must term people chauvinism. Anyway, I watched you through the windows, delivering your lectures, observing your rituals, and studying a mass of manuscripts in the library."

"This is remarkable," exclaimed Gasparo, lifting his wineglass again. "Incredible."

"Then I read many of those books myself."

"Really?"

"I swear it."

"And what did you read?"

"Greek philosophers like Plato and Aristotle, Roman poets, Pomponazzi—"

"You read Pomponazzi?"

"Yes."

"He was the idol of my adolescence," said the surgeon. "I admired his moderation, his constructive approach, temperate, responsible, and shrewd. But, Signor Brown Pigeon, how can *you* read books?"

"A singular gift. Shall I prove my veracity?"

"Please."

"Socrates said 'Know thyself.' "

"And Marcus Aurelius?"

" 'Be thyself.' "

"Splendid. But, Signor Brown Pigeon, are you familiar with the writings of the philosopher Epictetus?"

"He said something like this: 'What I made I lost; what I gave I have.' "

"I believe you," said Gasparo. "Indeed I do. And my sense of certainty increases; undoubtedly, my dear friend Girolamo Cardano sent you to offer me counsel during these trying days. Tell me, Brown Pigeon, how is Girolamo?"

"He is in good health and spirits, considering, of course, that he is an old man who has lost his desire for the flesh of women."

"A pity. A human tragedy that such a wonderful feeling should die before death."

"But what of your troubles?"

"It is as if Girolamo were here to console me and share his wisdom. And your adjustment to pigeon-type problems does build my faith in your judgment. But, alas, I flounder in an ocean of miseries, and no shore is in sight. My father was murdered by brigands, my mother died recently, my sister married and moved away, my closest childhood friend is my worst enemy, and Girolamo is old and will die soon."

"We are mere mortals, Doctor, and death comes to all of us. You know this."

"Certainly, but the sting remains. And this is not all. My son is disturbed by my lifework. My wife has been distressed by this, and now she has been terrorized by the fiend Morisini, who kidnapped and assaulted her to revenge himself upon me."

"But that was not your fault."

"She is a loving wife, and I have brought her horror and tragedy. Her sufferings are my responsibility, and I have been compelled to kill a man."

"But no harm can come to you—"

"I am not an idiot," yelled Gasparo. "Never have I killed a man before, Brown Pigeon. Never. Not in a war, not at any time. This outrages my moral scruples and makes me feel unclean."

"Life brutalizes all. We start out naïve and idealistic, but then we learn from the bitter experiences of living in a chaotic world."

"You comfort me, Brown Pigeon. You think sometimes as would Girolamo—wisely, tolerantly, with a seasoned benign wisdom."

"You destroy yourself with your guilt," said the brown pigeon, walking slowly on the grass, like an old man with hands clasped behind his back, "Let *me* help *you* now. I will ask you a question: Why do you walk on one leg?"

"I do not—"

"You will understand. For, as I did, you walk on one leg and in a narrow, cramped position. With your guilt you amputate your other leg. And you constrict yourself when you reject the memory of your constructive achievements."

"I have sinned," said the surgeon, drowsy, numbed with wine, hair disheveled, eyes bloodshot. "I betrayed my father and I have killed a man and my wife is distraught and my son is antagonized—and yesterday God sent his punishing fury into my left arm to cripple me for my audacity in challenging His will."

"Nonsense," said the pigeon. "Let me give you the benefit of my knowledge. Yes, *my* knowledge, for I have soared over half the world, my friend. I have seen terrible calamities devastating the human race. Feuds and wars and plagues and persecutions and natural disasters—earthquakes and floods and typhoons and periods of drought. I have encountered people beside whom the Turks might seem genteel; slaughtering, beheading, flaying, burning, cannibalizing. We pigeons are peaceful, you know, but we look down and see human beings massacring each other constantly."

"Yes, but what is your point, Brown Pigeon?"

"It is simple indeed. That you should commend yourself for your heroic efforts to ameliorate the trying human condition, for, Doctor, the Inquisition will otherwise have no need to bring you to trial and burn you at the stake—*you* will burn *yourself* to death with no assistance."

"Yes, you talk like Girolamo, my dear pigeon friend."

"And what would Girolamo tell you now?"

"I am not sure."

"He would say, 'Gasparo, my good fellow, life is hypocritical and deceptive and disillusioning, but there are a few values to cherish.' "

"Yes?"

" 'Your wife awaits you, alone and humiliated and frightened and despairing. Go to her, my friend.' Is that not what Girolamo would say?"

"Perhaps," said the surgeon slowly, "but, Signor Brown Pigeon, I have killed a man and cannot feel lust."

"Go to her," said the pigeon, hopping smartly upon the grass in the pale early-morning sun. "Comfort yourself and then give her comfort. The other will come in due time."

Gasparo went back into the house. In the bedroom Giulia was awake, still fully dressed, staring vacantly at the ceiling. He lay down beside her; cuddling in his arms, she began to sob and he stroked her head. For hours he embraced her tenderly while she continued to weep. Finally, she slept.

The surgeon returned to his chair in the garden. The effects of the wine had worn off; he yawned and stretched. *Have I been hallucinating?* he asked himself. *Have I held these lengthy conversations with a pigeon or have I imagined them?*

But it did not matter for he was saved. Into his mind flooded memories to ignite a resurgence of his spirit. He recalled how he had revitalized Scipio's life and had saved his friend Lorenzo from disintegration, and, in spite of the father's protests, he had created new possibilities for the Duglioli baby. With his determination he had breathed back life into the weakened frame of Virginio Orsini, earning the gratitude of Grand Duke Ferdinando.

I am sorry, Giulia, he thought, *for my failure with Morisini turned him into a mad beast who inflicted such horror upon you. Forgive me, my beloved, but remember that I love you and have tried to be a good husband.*

Arising from his chair, he trudged across the grass toward the house. *But father,* he reflected, *I was correct. It was my decision, my responsibility, and I exercised it wisely. I do my utmost to help suffering humanity. Should this not appear virtuous in the eyes of Our Lord? My faith in myself is restored, a tranquillity flows back into my bloodstream, and I will not waver in my purpose.*

The ignorant people here will render my life insufferable, but my spirit will not flag. There is Leghorn, an oasis in the midst of life's cruel desert. I am strong, and since my persecutors show me no mercy, I will repair to Leghorn, buy a cottage by the sea for my Giulia, and rebuild the soul of my son as I have rebuilt the faces of my patients. In Leghorn will we flourish and live in peace.

In the consultation room he knelt before the crucifix, meditating, offering a prayer to God.

He did not know that, from behind the kitchen curtains, the servant girl, Maria Boschetti, had listened to his conversation with the brown pigeon, and that she would render a complete report of this to Flaminio Vulpi, Censor of Books for the Bologna division of the Roman Church's Inquisition.

Chapter 17

Forty years before, in 1555, a trio of ten-year-old boys had climbed to the top of one of Bologna's steepest towers to launch pebbles upon people in the public square, a mischievous, boyish prank, spurred on by undercurrents of preadolescent rebellion. During those days the three friends engaged in a variety of such games, playing soldier and doctor and priest and teacher and merchant.

Now, at fifty, all had reached positions of eminence in their fields. Gasparo Tagliacozzi was one of Italy's most famous surgeons. Flaminio Vulpi had entrenched himself as Censor of Books for the Bologna wing of the Inquisition. Lorenzo Desiri was captain of the Pepoli *bravi,* and Grand Duke Ferdinando of Tuscany had publicly honored his heroism during the battle at Vienna.

In retrospect, one might ask how such an unlikely triumvirate had ever existed, for as adults they were so totally different from one another, and the seeds of their development had been planted during their childhood years.

Flaminio was the most powerful churchman in the City of Bologna, wielding absolute decision-making authority over each book submitted for his review. Was it heretical or not? Flaminio alone was designated to answer this question.

As always, a religious zealot, Vulpi worked night and day searching for passages that might be classified as anti-Catholic. His office was piled high with manuscripts and so were those of his assistants, and even his small bare room at the Dominican monastery was stacked with books, only his bed escaping the pervasive clutter.

Still, Flaminio had a secret. In one of his favorite books—by Thomas Aquinas—he had hidden a small mirror. He considered it a form of vanity and therefore a vice, concealing it in the Aquinas book; all this subterfuge possessed a magnetic appeal for him; he was attracted to the idea of pulling out the little mirror and looking at himself but resisted the impulse as much as he could, in the name of forbearance.

At last, after struggling with himself, he would open the book and take out the mirror. Staring back at him would be a rather tall, athletic-looking man with graying temples underneath his black hood, body encased in the flowing white robe of the Dominican Order.

When he looked into the mirror, he pictured himself picking up a pile of books and consigning them to the flames; this is what he saw, not a tall, good-looking man with a look of dissatisfaction marring his handsome features.

Flames crackled in his mirror and he could see them flaring and darting—and then Gasparo in the flames, Gasparo burning to death in the flames.

He could also see the fire within his soul, consuming him with vindictiveness, but he gave no thought to extinguishing the blaze, for he did not realize that he was destroying himself; instead, he envisioned the destruction as involving only enemies of the Roman Church and of the Holy Faith.

Flaminio had spent the greater part of his life restricting his outlook, confining his views to those espoused by his superiors in Rome, and his face reflected this rigidity, his mouth tight-lipped and grim, his eyes cold and calculating, his cheekbones and forehead gaunt and tight. Not that he saw these ascetic features in the mirror; what he saw was his righteous resentment of heretics and blasphemers and rebels against the will of God.

Studying his lean puritanical face, Flaminio failed to see the deprivation underneath. Instead, he would admire the determined sharpness of his chin and the cold fire in his eyes. *Oh, yes,* he would muse, *this is the face of the man who will purge this godless city of those lacking in faith and moral fiber. I will be as dedicated to the principles of Our Lord as was Savonarola before me. There shall be no more sin in Bologna: no evil books or prostitutes or gambling.*

In his little mirror, the Censor of Books noted the grimness of his lips, but he attributed this to his need to purge the Church of evil-doers; he noted the fury, but considered that this was a divine feeling, which he would use in the service of the Creator.

To him, his career was constructive. He could see himself in Heaven and Gasparo in Hell. The face in the mirror he regarded as lonely, but it was a conditional form of loneliness, in which he was separated from other people but not from God. He was God's instrument, His faithful servant. He would dedicate his life to serving the Lord.

At times, opening up the Aquinas book and removing the concealed looking-glass, Flaminio would feel so empty that he would have to strain to perceive his image and, indeed, it was almost as if he were invisible. In terms of his feelings, he had detached himself from his body, but it was a detachment, an *eviction,* that somehow left him bound closer than ever to God, and he reassured himself that he would receive his just reward in Heaven. Perhaps he would flourish in Heaven—a dignitary, commissioned in the name of God.

He understood that he was isolated from the common people but told himself that he belonged to God. Studying his sad brown eyes, he felt deeply his renunciation of worldly goals, but compensating him was his sense of fulfillment in the eyes of the Lord.

Finally, Flaminio would finish his reading and his self-analysis and go to bed. But sleep seldom came quickly. He had looked in the mirror, he told himself, and had captured the objective essence of himself. But had he? Or was he deluding himself with half-truths and rationalizations and superficialities?

The memories would then come crowding in on him. His mother, who had died when he was an infant, leaving him, an only child, with a father to care for him. He realized now, many years later, that his father had tried, but that the world had forced him to his knees too many times, crushing his spirit.

Almost in tears, Flaminio would recall how his father, humiliated by the degrading nature of his function as doctor for the Pepolis, overburdened as both mother and father to his son, would pace the floor night after night, unequipped to give the young boy a father's heartiness and laughter and aggressive manliness. *How I despised you when I was young,* Flaminio recalled. *You are dead now but forgive me, Father.*

His childhood chums had been Lorenzo and Gasparo. Finding himself unable to cope with the bullying Lorenzo, Flaminio had turned for solace to his friend Gasparo, who was more like himself, thoughtful and sensitive and somewhat introverted. Ah, the good times he and Gasparo had shared, their almost daily walks, confiding their plans and their dreams.

But then, later, Gasparo had met Giulia Carnali and since that moment their friendship had become less and less intense, dissolving completely for a while, until the final rupture that had left them sworn enemies, with Flaminio vowing to get revenge.

I cannot remember the precise moment when our friendship dissolved, thought Vulpi. *Is this not strange? Oh, well, the circumstance cannot be important.*

And then, as had happened only two or three times in the span of intervening years, the emotional impact of the scene crashed in on him: that day in the country, the horseback ride to the lake in the warm sun, lying naked in the sun on the blanket, drinking wine, until Gasparo fell asleep, and then his overwhelming lust for the flesh of his good friend.

"No," shrieked Flaminio aloud. "I did not commit that vile, obscene act; I was not responsible. I was under the control of the Devil; it was one of the evil machinations of Gasparo."

And, in a flash, the softness was gone from Vulpi's face—in its place, stone. *No,* he reasoned, *never again will the Devil take possession of me.*

Still, time and again, he would wish that somewhere in his world of pain he could find a companion to fill the aching void left in his life when Gasparo had recoiled from his advances and had flung the rock at him, disfiguring his left eyebrow.

Now there was room for only God. In his rage, he would seek out and punish the evildoers, and he did not perceive the fury as such; to him, it evidenced his determination to obliterate the heretics and blasphemers and to purify the world in the image of Our Lord.

He would allow himself no more softness, and when he felt anything that approached a sexual feeling, he would take a whip and beat himself with it, flagellating himself until he nearly lost consciousness.

One evening he put away the mirror and retired to bed but, as always, sleep would not come. He battled with himself for hours, the image of Gasparo in his mind, then he remembered the mirror. He had to see the mirror again; it was an irresistible compulsion. Was there not something else in the mirror, something that he did not wish to see? He said to himself, *I must sleep; I have much to do on the morrow and must be fresh in mind and spirit.* But the compulsion was too overpowering.

Climbing out of bed, naked, he looked at himself in the mirror, critically surveying his distorted eyebrow. Placing his finger over it, he saw himself whole again. Gasparo would operate on him, removing the scar, making the eyebrow normal, like his other eyebrow.

Gasparo was smiling and so was he. He saw himself thanking Gasparo—suddenly, in his mind, he felt he was kissing his hand—and wishing he could make love to his childhood friend. The truth was that he missed Gasparo and wanted him again. And then he saw the terrible guilt on his face, the revulsion of self. Standing naked in the darkness of his empty room, lonely, separate from the world of Gasparo and Lorenzo, separate from himself.

He went to his closet for a whip and turned it upon himself, flagellating himself until he was bleeding, but unable to purge from consciousness the love for his old companion. And, in his agony, Flaminio began to rally his defensive firepower into offensive action. Forever, he promised himself, would he serve God and persecute sinners. *Gasparo is wicked,* he mumbled to himself. *He must burn at the stake. It is the will of Our Lord.*

Finally, he found momentary peace and sleep.

Lorenzo Desiri, too, would appraise himself in a mirror—but in an open manner.

There was nothing furtive about it. The house of Lorenzo and Caledonia Desiri contained a number of huge mirrors, floor to ceiling, on the backs of closet doors, as well as several large bureau mirrors. The former Caledonia Bargillini was a beautiful woman who enjoyed admiring her features in a mirror, but the partner in this childless marriage who truly loved the sight of his reflection was Lorenzo.

At fifty, he was a strapping, swarthy man with bold black eyes and an erect, proud military bearing, his manner imperious but straightforward, and, surveying himself in shining suit of armor made specially for him by an artisan in Milan, he saw himself in the mirror as he was—no concealment or artifice. His attitude was bold and assured. "Here I am, the best fighting man in Italy," his face seemed to say, and he would stroke his mustache as he smiled approvingly at himself. He was inordinately fond of his mustache, and every day he trimmed it carefully.

Regularly, daily, Lorenzo would spend half an hour with his reflected image. Naked, he would flex his muscles and admire his rugged, powerful body. Seeing himself lifesize in one of the giant looking-glasses, he would practice deep-breathing exercises and push-ups and weight lifting, in the process renewing his admiration for his physique. He would sing and laugh and shout to his wife in an adjoining room, his conversation spiced with lewd jokes and sexual boasting.

Nude, sword in hand, he would practice fencing, thrusting and parrying, retreating and advancing. *I am not as young as I was,* he would reflect, *but I am still the best swordsman in Bologna. I can outduel any of the Pepoli or Castelli bravi. With the stiletto, too, I am a master. It was not for nothing that Grand Duke Ferdinando called me one of the bravest fighting men in his command. He was only speaking the truth.*

And he knew that he needed no weapons to demonstrate his prowess. At fifty, he could still outwrestle the champion *bravi* and surpass them in weight lifting and gymnastics. He was Aretino. He was Cellini. He was unequaled. "You are a fortunate woman, Caledonia," he would bellow to his wife in the next room. Appalled by his arrogance but attracted by his maleness, his wife would say nothing, but then, Lorenzo Desiri required no answer.

Sometimes the soldier would gaze at his penis and testicles, proud of his sexual potency. He and Caledonia had sex almost every night and, on the sly, he would also go to the brothels now and then.

And then, adoring his male organs, complacent, superior, he would suddenly feel a wave of agony pouring over him. For in his mind was the image of his father, naked, captive of the Turks, a string around his testicles, pulled by a sneering Ottoman soldier through the crowded streets, the spectators laughing—and then his father's head had been cut off by a huge bearded, turbaned Turk, one flash of the scimitar and his father, Luigi Rimini Desiri, was no more.

Spasms of anger filled him now and he saw again his vengeance at the Battle of Lepanto, leaping over the side of the enemy craft to plunge his steel blade into the body of every Turk he could reach. *I avenge you, Father.*

And then he recalled the piercing pain, an enemy sword slashing the flesh of his cheek. Never had he been so depressed, not even, in truth, by news of the mutilation of his father. For he was deformed, the women who adored him would find him repulsive, he would become a shadow of his former self.

But the deft fingers of Gasparo had healed his terrible wound, bringing him back to himself. Oh, the joy to see his face whole again; it was a miracle. From that moment on, his loyalty to his surgeon friend would never waver; no matter how numerous or powerful his enemies, Tagliacozzi knew he could always count on Lorenzo.

Then the land battle with the Turks in Austria. Virginio Orsini, their commander, disabled, the enemy mounting offensive after offensive, and Lorenzo Desiri, professional soldier unparalleled, assumed command, the multinational forces under his leadership repelling the mighty Turks. Honor upon honor was awarded him. He was decorated by the mighty Grand Duke of Tuscany, Ferdinando, and was named captain of *bravi* by Taddeo Pepoli on their return to Bologna. *Father,* he would think, *now we are truly united.* For his father, too, had been captain of *bravi* for the battling Pepoli clan.

Lorenzo was a simple, practical man. *The world is a jungle,* he would consider, in his rare reflective moments. *I fight for myself so that I may survive and take my pleasure.*

He did not concern himself with other people's feelings, and, indeed, was too insensitive, as a rule, to be aware of them. His psychological observations were either superficial or totally ignorant. He tended to view others as projections of himself, but not as strong or muscular or courageous, so that he was superior. Thus, to him, Flaminio was a fool for depriving himself of the fun of sex, but he saw none of the underlying forces in the churchman's personality. And, to him, Gasparo agonized too much, and he was aware of little beyond this in the surgeon's make-up.

Not that this last judgment tempered his admiration for Gasparo's surgical skill, his fame, his obvious intelligence. And, of course, his loyalty to his surgeon friend was unshakable.

Basically, Desiri, appraising himself, was honest. He was an expert gambler and could bluff his opponent, but he did not try to fool himself. *I am what I am,* he would admit. *I am not an angel, but I am a winner. I am a warrior, and death may strike me down at any time, so I worry about myself, not about others, and I take my pleasure where I can find it.*

And, turning from his reflection, he cupped his hands to shout to Caledonia in the next room, "Love of my life, my tigress, my courtesan, patience, for soon I come to you in your bed to set you afire."

Lorenzo was delighted with his marriage; they had no children but they were fun for each other. Caledonia was a wildcat, a scrapper who was able to stand up to her husband, and their relationship was a series of stormy quarrels, followed by passionate reconciliations and wild lovemaking. Lorenzo enjoyed ordering his wife around, bossing her, asserting his authority at every opportunity, and Caledonia would react by screaming oaths at him, vibrating with defiance, and hurling dishes and silverware in his general direction. Her tempestuousness would excite him and, scooping her up in his strong arms, he would throw her onto their bed, leap into an ecstatic embrace with her, and, while she scratched and clawed and attempted to bite him, he would lose himself in a fierce tenderness and they would then make love with primitive savageness.

Life is a gamble, murmured Lorenzo; *it is a mess. But I live it on my terms. Is that not the secret?*

Lorenzo was a pleasure-seeker, a taker, a potent animal; he was not complicated.

More subtle, Flaminio was too weak to take pleasure and, turning inward, directed his frustration at those more fortunate than he.

As for Gasparo, the fascination of his life was that he was not rigid, that his personality was many-sided, and that no feeling or mood was foreign to him; he was dedicated, loyal, idealistic, naïve, and responsible, and yet, in a curious intermingling, he was also questioning, cynical, and even iconoclastic.

In his consultation room was a mirror, a solid mirror nailed to the wall, with heavy wrought-iron frame, ornamented with nude figurines, enclosing the glass. When he was alone, writing his book at his desk, he would often stroll over to the mirror. Not as Flaminio, furtively and defensively. Not as Lorenzo, narcissistically and without sensitivity. For Gasparo, it was part of the scientist's eternal search for truth.

The surgeon was of medium height and slender build, and reflected back to him was the image of a handsomely dressed man, with ruffled white collar jutting out over his delicately woven jacket trimmed with fur, his thick, black, slightly curly hair topping a long, angular face. His chin was incisive, lending an air of determination to his ruddy face, and his carefully cultivated mustache and brief token beard were concessions to the conventional grooming of men during this period. His fingers were long and sensitive, and when not operating, he wore two rings on his right hand and one on his left hand, on the finger adjoining his thumb. The rings were of colored stones, gifts from nobility in appreciation of his services. Vincenzo Gonzaga, Prince of Mantua, had bestowed one of these rings upon him.

Still, one did not really see Gasparo until one looked at his eyes. They were piercing brown eyes, characterized by a type of kaleidoscopic complexity. Perhaps one quality projected consistently from his eyes: an intensity that lent weight to any of his moods.

What did Gasparo see when he studied himself in his office mirror? He was not sure. He was a fluid enough man with a keen enough intellect to perceive that truth encompassed many dimensions. Therefore, looking at himself, appraising himself, what he saw was too complicated to verbalize, or at least he granted that this might be objective.

He was a dedicated man of science, an ardent searcher after truth;

therefore, he wanted solid evidence before he would commit himself to a conclusion. This was one of the basic factors in his make-up. Perhaps it was because he had seen such irrationality in the world, but finding rationality was a passion with him, and certainly this predisposed him toward an inevitable clash with the Roman Church.

Or was it the influence of his parents? Even as a boy, Gasparo had not been close to his sister, Cassandra, who confided in her mother and her girl friends and then married and moved away from Bologna. But he was deeply devoted to his mother and his father and both were intense perfectionists, striving each in his way to live in terms of strict morality, trying to conduct themselves ethically in an unethical world, struggling to pave the road to an easier existence for their children. At home, Isabetta demonstrated this same passion for order that was later to characterize her son; her house was impeccably clean and she taught her boy to concentrate on his studies and to organize his thinking. Giovanni Andrea, the pious weaver of fine cloths, turned his drive into different channels, but in his business dealings he evidenced a doggedness, an indomitableness of the spirit, that was part of Gasparo later, but invested in the cause of science and truth.

Studying his reflection, Gasparo asked himself what he was seeking—in his work, in his dedication to science, in his relations with his loved ones, and with his responsibility. And the answer ricocheted back to him: self-respect.

He had read the philosophers—Plato, Aristotle, Thomas Aquinas, his favorite Pomponazzi, and so on. Socrates' message was Know thyself; Marcus Aurelius' was Be thyself. The essence of Jesus Christ's was Give thyself. But he was even more impressed by William Shakespeare's summation of the goals of life; the English playwright had stated that nothing was worthwhile without self-respect. Yet the answer had bounced back to him not from his reading of the philosophers, but from another breed of philosopher, Brown Pigeon.

And how would he earn this respect that must originate within himself?

By continuing to give his best to his patients and his community. The world was chaotic and violent—Pepolis murdered Castellis and Castellis retaliated against Pepolis—but he would press on, making his constructive contribution regardless of denunciation by his enemies. Like Girolamo, he would exercise prudence; if only for the sake of Giulia and his son, he would take no unnecessary risks.

Into his mind whirled images of all the violence he had seen and he struggled to accept these realities without going insane: the brave Michael Servetus burning in the flames, while the mob in Switzerland jeered; the numberless atrocities at the Battle of Lepanto, climaxed by the brutality of warriors in hurling scores of enemy corpses into the sea to clear the ship's decks; the piles of dead and dying bodies clustered en masse during the siege of Vienna. The memory of Servetus' terrible death especially haunted him because he had seen it at an impressionable age and it had shocked him awake to the potential horror of a world from which he had been protected. But he had been a man of peace all his life and never would he stray from this path. Never.

Now and then, the disaster with Morisini crept back into his mind and he would reproach himself for the horror he had caused his wife and reprimand himself for his inadequacy as a surgeon. But he would counter this with knowledge, for clearly he was one of the most skilled surgeons alive, and colleagues at the university used to tell him that such an operation as he performed on Morisini was so difficult that even the great Ambroise Paré could not have executed it properly. It could be done with his new techniques, he knew that now, but he realized that no surgeon alive could at that time have made Morisini whole again. And so he vowed that he would no longer reproach himself about the failure of his operation.

But, erasing his guilt over Morisini, cancelling out the nightmarish experience, he found himself back in the dungeon of despair recalling his father's violent death at the hands of robbers. He trembled with guilt, feeling once more that he had been responsible for Giovanni Andrea's death because he had insisted on becoming a doctor. The misery on his father's face before his death returned to haunt him and he wished he were still alive so that he could make amends. "Father," he would cry, "I shall become a weaver of the most beautiful cloths in all of Italy."

But it was another unpleasant reality that his father would never live again. And this was one of a multitude of disturbing facts. These included the imprisonment of Girolamo Cardano, the persecution of Galileo, his alienation from Flaminio Vulpi, the disturbed state of his son, and the intense hostility directed at his humane work by a formidable triumvirate: the Roman Catholic Church, a powerful clique at the university headed by Cesare Aranzio, and the common people, who, like Duglioli, relied on superstition and violated every concept of reason.

As a rule, he tended to shrug off Flaminio's vindictiveness, which always hovered in the background, by characterizing Vulpi as a puritanical, frustrated bigot, which he was. But then he would recall the young Flaminio, friendly, earnest, sensitive, fun-loving, and a sadness would envelop him like a shroud. *Poor Flaminio,* he grieved, *how has life brutalized you? Where did you lose your way?*

And he recalled what his old chum had done on the blanket while he was sleeping that day in the country, decades ago, but with a new poignancy. For, previously, when he recollected the incident, it was with revulsion. Now, at the age of fifty, he saw in his mind the impassioned, eager, adolescent Flaminio murmuring, "I love you, Gasparo," as he made his clumsy homosexual advances and how he had jumped to his feet and hurled a rock at the young Vulpi, inflicting a gash on his eyebrow, while he cursed him as decadent. Then, he remembered, Flaminio had announced his desire for vengeance.

"Nome di Dio," he exclaimed aloud, "what harm did I do to Flaminio?"

And, even more agonizing, *Is that where Flaminio lost his way? I could have rejected his overtures, but in a more acceptable fashion. Once again am I guilty. Not for throwing the rock; that is not the main concern. But for the withdrawal of my friendship. Is that what embittered Flaminio? I have been blind for so many years.*

He recognized that nothing he could say would reach his old friend now, that he was helpless to remove this scar from the past or to do anything but immerse himself in guilt.

Reality was a bed of shifting quicksand, dragging its guileless victims to their doom. Cardano had told him this in different words and, as usual, Girolamo was right. The adult world was an endless series of problems.

Would Flaminio convict him or would his enemies at the university be first to slip the noose around his neck? Gasparo looked at himself in the mirror, dressed handsomely, skin healthy, but what he saw was an emaciated prisoner, condemned by the Inquisition, living on bread and water in the Garisenda Tower, tortured, isolated, cockroaches and water his only companions. And then the Roman Church would burn him at the stake. As with poor Servetus, a wreath of straw and green twigs covered with brimstone would be placed around his head and Duglioli and his friends would hurl stones and twigs at him. Then the executioner would apply the torch.

I am in flames, agonized the surgeon, *I am dying.* He felt like screaming for help but suddenly it dawned on him that a fantasy had swept him away. *I am safe, but for how long?*

He wished he were ten years old again, protected by his parents, sheltered from brutality. He could relax then, and no one would hate him. He could retire from the university and forget his troubled son; who would hold a young boy responsible?

But this would constitute a betrayal of himself, a renunciation of his obligations, and he could never trick himself with such self-deception.

I am fifty years old. I am a surgeon with responsibility for my patients, a husband with a wife dependent upon me, a father who must fulfill his duties toward his son.

And, no matter how difficult, I shall battle my enemies and problems and insecurities and I shall struggle to do my best in an insane world. And, that I am able to do this, herein lies my self-respect.

"I am a human being," cried out Tagliacozzi, not caring for the moment who might hear him. "I am a weakling and a coward and a fool but I make myself the finest human being that is within my potential and I try to deal humanely with other people and I wish not to evade the truth or to hide from myself. Certainly, I have earned the right to respect myself."

My battleground is not against the Turks, he mused, *but within me. The hostility of my enemies will not cause me to retreat from my convictions. Inside me the strength grows.*

In spite of his powerful enemies, Gasparo continued to practice surgery and to lecture at the university. One afternoon he was walking home and was assaulted in a narrow street by a fanatical student, an informer for Vulpi. The masked student was about to drive his stiletto into Gasparo when the surgeon kicked him in the groin. Howling in pain, his attacker fell backward onto the cobblestone street and Gasparo started running.

Out of breath, he opened the door of his home and went to his consultation room, where he sat down to rest. When his tension had subsided, he walked to the mirror and looked at himself: *Gasparo, what is it that you see?*

Many things, Image, he reflected. *When I was ten, standing on top of the tower, I saw the Apennines in the distance and wondered what was beyond these mountains. But tell me, Image, what view do I see beyond my face? And how does one measure the value of the life of a man? Is not self-respect an accurate scale? Would that I could make this world inside me secure, regardless of uncontrollable destructive forces outside. Self-respect may I build for myself in my mind as I would build a new face.*

Like Cardano, my teacher, I desire to do good and yearn to find the best in myself. Why should I concern myself with enemies at the university? Is the battle outside with others, like the student who attacked me? To a degree, but basically it is an internal battle I must win—and now. Yes, the time is now!

Image, I see many complications but, like an archaeologist, I must dig under the debris to uncover for myself the source of inner peace.

When I visited Girolamo in prison, the cold prison walls encircled me. But tell me, Image, are there not prison walls within the soul? And are these not more terrifying than cold stone?

I see Flaminio standing over me in the torture chamber as assistants put the screws on my fingers. I see the crowds jeering me as soldiers escort me to the hill of execution and tie me to the stake. Then the flames—Oh, Image, I hear my scream of anguish.

No, Image, I am a good Catholic, and confess regularly. Have I defied the papal decree? Have I treated a patient without ascertaining that he has made fresh confession? The penalty for operating on a non-Catholic is burning at the stake! Assist me, Lord, show me the way.

But, Image, the clouds are lifting for I know what I must do. I must leave Bologna at once and journey to Leghorn, where people of all faiths are welcome and there is a spirit of brotherly love. I understand my needs and the needs of my wife and son. I will move to Leghorn, protected by my friends Grand Duke Ferdinando of Tuscany and Vincenzo Gonzaga.

And then the surgeon saw Signor Brown Pigeon in the mirror. "Stay, Gasparo, and fight for your beliefs."

"No, Brown Pigeon," he said softly. "Your wisdom is indisputable, but in Leghorn will I find my sanctuary."

And so, in the years following the great humanistic explosion known as the Renaissance, the childhood friends traveled separate roads to adulthood.

And, in a sense, they came to represent the three prime influences of their time—the cross, the sword, and the scalpel.

Flaminio, the cross, embodying the asceticism and vindictiveness characterizing the Church for hundreds of years, dipping back into the Middle Ages and involving dogmatic pronouncements that would brook no interference by those interested in experimentation and advance.

Lorenzo, the sword, embodying the direct, virile warrior who reacted in terms of blatant selfishness and physical strength, as had brave soldiers since the beginnings of recorded history.

Gasparo, the scalpel, his application of medical techniques and his search for more effective methods of treatment embodying the idealistic thrust of the Renaissance, a period of intense vitality and creativity coexisting with and in some ways rising above the violence and political chicanery of the times.

Chapter 18

"Is this the house of Signor Tagliacozzi?" asked the man, who was wearing a flowing black robe with a hood encircling his face, in the manner of a mendicant friar.

"Yes, Father," said Giulia, "but my husband is at the university. I expect him shortly; would you honor me by coming in to await his return?"

"Thank you."

"You look fatigued, Father."

"I have traveled from Ferrara, my good lady—on foot."

Giulia looked apprehensively at the stranger. There was a wild look in his eyes and since her terrifying ordeal with Morisini her anxieties were easily aroused. *Still, he is a religious man,* she thought, *and will not harm me.* And, aloud, "Would you like some refreshment?"

"Yes, a glass of wine."

"But the prohibitions of your order—"

"I must admit that my clothes deceive you. I am not a mendicant brother, my good lady, but a boyhood friend of your husband's. My name is Torquato Tasso."

"The poet?"

"That is my calling."

"You are the poet laureate," said Giulia suspiciously, "and you come from Ferrara—on foot?"

"It sounds unlikely," said Tasso, "but it is true. I swear it, my good lady."

It was over thirty years since their last meeting, and Gasparo was shocked at sight of Tasso. Where was the tall, slender youth with the large blue eyes and the light-brown hair? This old man, gray-haired and slightly stooped, with bloodshot eyes and an artery throbbing spasmodically in his left temple, could this be the friend who had filled so great a void in his life after the murder of his father? Tears in his eyes, the surgeon rushed to embrace his former soul mate. "You look tired, Torquato, but I rejoice to see you."

The poet spoke softly. "So many years have passed and so much has transpired since we walked and confided our life plans."

"Yes."

"I recall vaguely that we would stroll to a fountain in the center of Bologna, with jets of water streaming from it, and a huge statue."

"It was the statue of Neptune."

"Ah, it comes back to me—yes. My memory, my dear old friend, leaves something to be desired. I am forgetful and often negligent."

"Still, Torquato, you have realized your dream. Today you are the greatest poet in Italy."

"Yes." For a moment Tasso's eyes glowed with pride, but then he hung his head as if ashamed, and the artery was throbbing in his temple, symbol of the unease consuming him from within. "Yes," he repeated dully. And, then with a great effort, he said, "You, Gasparo, I hear that you are our greatest surgeon."

"Perhaps." Gasparo was too conscious of the poet's pain to respond at any length. "What ails you, Torquato?"

The words, spoken gently, moved Tasso almost to tears. "I don't know, and I doubt that I will find the proper words."

"You, Torquato?"

"My mind is not as nimble as once it was. I am puzzled—and I dread many things."

"Like what?"

"I don't know. And therein lies my trouble—that I feel enveloped in darkness."

The surgeon felt sadness creeping through him like an infiltrating cloud. Aloud, he said, "You have never married?"

"What? Oh, no."

"An unhappy love affair?"

"No. Oh, my dear Gasparo, I have won the heart of many ladies—but—terror stalks me."

"What do you fear?" Gasparo felt alarmed at the incoherence of the poet's thinking processes. "What, Torquato?"

Tasso said nothing. His eyes were glazed and his forehead was wrinkled. "I do not understand, Gasparo," he said finally. "Some weight crushes my spirit, but what is this weight?"

"Is it your writings, my dear friend?"

"I cannot recall. No—yes, my epic poem."

"Have you offended the Church?"

"Yes, this is what tears me asunder, yes. I thank you, Gasparo, for reminding me of my offense."

"But have you written something that the Church has denounced? Has the Inquisition condemned you?"

"No," said the poet, eyes mirroring his tension, "but I received intelligence that the Inquisitor of Bologna was proceeding to Ferrara to interrogate me."

"And the nature of your offense?"

"On Cardinal Gonzaga's advice, I dispatched my epic poem *Jerusalem Delivered* to Rome, but the critics made merry at my expense. Antoniani suggested deletion of all the love passages, which would have emasculated the work—and my main purpose was to glorify the First Crusade."

"Your literary confreres try to destroy you out of envy for never could they create poetry as lyrical as yours, Torquato. Laugh at them."

"My understanding is that the censors relayed my manuscript to Flaminio Vulpi, head of the Index in Bologna. Oh, but I cringe at the heat of his wrath."

"He did not send for you?"

"Not specifically, but this is of no import, for he would pursue me anyway— But, tell me, is this the companion of your youth, this Vulpi?"

"Yes, he has great power now; he is a religious fanatic who dedicates his life to combating heresy."

"I am lost. He will prosecute me; his intention is to annihilate me."

"You worry needlessly, my friend, for you complied with Church procedure. You forwarded your manuscript for review, did you not say that?"

"Yes."

"Then your fears are groundless, Torquato; drive them from your mind."

"No." The poet's eyes were feverish and the artery in his left temple continued to throb. "I must confess to Vulpi. I suspect the couriers from Rome have delivered deletions to him; I must defend myself against my accusers."

"Nonsense. Your imagination betrays you. I, too, have written a book in hopes that I may help surgeons throughout the world to heal the afflicted. People hate me for my aspirations and condemn me as a practitioner of witchcraft. But this will not crush my spirit. I will publish my book because I will not allow the Inquisition to trample the fires of truth."

"The fires, ah, yes, the fires."

"Courage, Torquato, have courage. Your terrors are not real."

"Yes, I imagine this is so. But Gasparo, these images penetrate into my mind and horror surges through me like a frenzied river overflowing. I cannot abide these images."

"What images, Torquato?"

"Red-hot fires, the flames reaching up to lick the sky with a passionate avenging tongue, flames that devour, and the Devil, cackling hideously, allied with a witch who rides in the night air."

"But the Inquisition may not burn you at the stake—"

"Sometimes I feel the sting of the Devil's hatred. For I have lived licentiously. I have sinned against the will of Our Lord. I have delighted in affairs with ladies of the court and have fornicated in brothels and— You would not understand, Gasparo, for you have savored the ripe fruits of virtue."

Relieved for the first time, Tagliacozzi laughed. "Is this what haunts your conscience? Of course I understand, and before I married, I would go to the brothels—Lorenzo and I."

"The flames are red-hot," said the poet, as if from far away, and Gasparo's mood turned to dismay. "In the flames resides the Devil, but his flesh will not burn and his laughter is hideous. Oh, they will pursue and torture me."

The surgeon bowed his head, too sad at heart to utter a word. *My poor Torquato,* he said to himself, *once you were so animated, but in your middle age you are an old man in spirit.*

"I have been imprisoned in the hospital at Santa Anna," said Tasso, "for seven years of insufferable misery. Duke Alfonso resented my relations with the Medici, my correspondence with Princess Leonora, and perhaps my writings, too. He was responsible for my confinement. I must examine my food carefully before eating, for they would delight in poisoning me. Then they would not have to burn me at the stake."

Poor Torquato, he endures hopeless darkness; is this because his parents were so hounded when he was a child?

"While in the hospital, I corresponded with my friend Scipione Gonzaga, and his nephew Vincenzo Gonzaga, Prince of Mantua, arranged my discharge. Elated, naturally I left in haste, but regrettably, I did not wait on Duke Alfonso to kiss his hand. Then Vincenzo became Duke of Mantua and no longer had time for me so I journeyed to Rome to reside with Scipione Gonzaga, the cardinal. And then—I cannot remember but, truly, my beloved friend, I have traversed the length and breadth of Italy in my restlessness. Ah, yes, I tried to recover my mother's fortune but failed."

Gasparo recalled conversing with Scipione Gonzaga while he was ministering to the beleaguered Prince of Mantua. "I am always ready to welcome Tasso to my hearth and heart," Scipione had said, "but his humors render him mistrustful of mankind. In my palace are rooms and beds always available for his use, and servants to wait on him hand and foot. Yet—and I swear this by the stars—he mistrusts me and runs from me. It is a sad misfortune that this age should be deprived of its greatest poetic genius. But what wise man ever spoke out in prose or verse more fluently than this sweet, gentle madman?"

"I visited Florence," continued Tasso, "but the Medici did not welcome me. *Nobody* wants me. Only the Grand Duke's nephew Virginio Orsini was kind to me. A courageous soldier and a gifted writer, he admired my poetry and insisted on helping me with funds in Rome and in Florence. When he married the beautiful Flavia Peretti, I penned a poem in her praise. Orsini prevailed upon Duke Ferdinando to place me in his service, but for political reasons the Duke did nothing, though he showered me with gifts. Melancholy at this rebuff, my fears of the Inquisition increased in intensity, and I came to Bologna to confess to Flaminio Vulpi."

This sounded more lucid and, heartened, Gasparo resumed the conversation. "But, my friend, you are safe."

"Yes, but the flames sizzle and crackle in my mind and the Devil taunts me with his wicked laugh and in the forest the wolves and mad dogs snarl and launch their poisonous spittle upon the quick-sands that wrench even the stoutest trees down into a pit of deadly vipers."

Gasparo's hope vanished in an instant. Aloud, he said, "Return to Ferrara, as befits the poet laureate of the court. You may stay in my home as long as you wish, Torquato, but this is the most considered advice I can give you. Confess nothing to Flaminio Vulpi. When you have recuperated from your tiresome journey—in two or three fort-nights, perchance—return to Ferrara."

Torquato retired to a guest room, and the surgeon felt drowned in despair. His former soul mate—how enriching those exchanges of confidence so many years before—was dying internally. What infes-tation had taken root in his mind? Gasparo was aware that the poet had inherited a sensitive, melancholy disposition from his parents and that his unhappy childhood had been traumatized by awareness that the Inquisition had proclaimed his banished father a heretic. Then he had come under the influence of Jesuit dogmatism. Had this crushed his will, depriving him of the capacity to think freely or act independently?

Torquato's unfortunate life had encompassed a series of convulsive attempts to elude reality through the overpowering richness of his verbal talents, but never could he escape the weakness of his charac-ter. Traveling from city to city, restless, apprehensive, volatile, never at peace with himself, he could project his internal disturbance into towering lyrical flights of the imagination whose fire and magic en-chanted a generation. He was cautious, screening out of his poetry any phrases that could conceivably irritate the Church authorities; but, irrationally, he dreaded the Inquisition after he had skirted any conceivable offense.

And now, thought Gasparo, *Torquato is insane. He has surrendered to the Roman Church—and his will is lost. More fortunate is Galileo, who has dared to battle for his right to seek truth; yes, even persecuted and fleeing, he is luckier. And I, too, like Galileo, the son of a cloth merchant, will assert myself, weaving the truth as I see it.*

He was seated at the desk in his consultation room submerged in depression when he felt Giulia's fingers caressing his shoulders and her lips brushing his cheeks.

"Poor Torquato," he whispered. "He has lost his soul."

The surgeon had begun to formulate his plan to move to Leghorn during his long talks with Brown Pigeon, for he realized that the cloud of superstition hanging over Bologna was oppressive and could not be dissipated, no matter how hearty his good will, and that his well-entrenched antagonists would never relent. But, aware of Giulia's reluctance to move from the city of her birth, he delayed telling her. This postponement had intensified his depression and sharpened his nerve ends, heightening his fears of the Inquisition, for, he fretted, what would he do if his wife opposed his wishes?

Now, broaching the plan to Giulia and fortified by her acquiescence, Gasparo fed the flames of his exuberance. "In Leghorn we shall tie together the tensile threads of our family and weave together patterns of enrichment and harmony. For the first time will I find it possible to be a father to my son. We shall take long walks by the sea and go fishing together in our little boat.

But his son's reaction startled him. Summoned downstairs and jubilantly told of the planned move, the boy remained silent, staring morosely at the floor.

"What is the matter?" said Gasparo. "Surely you approve of my plans?"

"No, Father," said Giovanni Andrea. "I do not want to go there."

"But your acquaintances will not jeer at you there."

"I wish to stay in Bologna."

"But why?"

Giovanni Andrea said that he wanted to become a weaver of satins and silks, like the grandfather for whom he was named, and it was his desire to study the craft in Bologna. On many occasions, he revealed defiantly, he had watched the old men weaving in the public square and they remembered his grandfather with affection. "They liked my grandfather and honor me because I am his grandson," stormed the boy, "but they detest you because you are a sorcerer, and I know they tell the truth because I see the ugly people who come to your office and I hear their terrible screams when you torture them."

Gasparo felt an intense rage building inside him until he feared he would explode. "You are my son," he whispered, "and *you* call me a sorcerer?"

"I will become a famous weaver like my grandfather," said the boy. "I will own a splended carriage and travel all over Europe. The homes of the wealthiest noblemen will be open to me when I arrive with my satins and silks and I will marry a lady from a noble family."

"I torture people?" The surgeon could not contain his rising staccato shout. "You said I torture people?"

"I cannot stand it anymore. Harlots in my home. You operate on harlots. The children at school make jokes about that every day, and they laugh at how you torture your patients."

"How many times have I explained to you that your father is a good man?" rasped Giulia. "Can you not understand—?"

"I will handle this," said Gasparo. "Please leave the room, Giulia."

Giulia closed the door behind her and Gasparo turned to face his son. He felt so enraged that he feared he would lash out and strike the boy. "My own son against me. I can tolerate Cesare Aranzio and live with the threat of Flaminio, but my own son! You are fourteen years old, and yet you are too young and too foolish to comprehend what I try to do for people with my surgery? How dare you call me a sorcerer and tell me that I, your father, torture people!"

"I am sorry that I called you a bad name, Father, but I hate your work, and it is wrong to harbor a prostitute in one's home. I will stay in Bologna and study weaving, like my grandfather. You cannot force me to go with you."

"You heed my words," shouted Gasparo, and the extent of his rage alarmed him. "I am the head of this family, and I have made the decision to move to Leghorn. Shortly, I will journey there to buy a cottage. As soon as possible, we will sell our house, pack our belongings, and depart for Leghorn. That is the end of our discussion, and I *am* commanding you to accompany us. Go to your room. Instantly. For I do not wish to see your face."

Angrily, Giovanni Andrea turned on his heels and rushed upstairs to his room, slamming the door.

Gasparo stood rigid for a moment, hands clenched tightly at his sides, then began to relax. The anger was draining out of him, his tension relieved by the outburst.

Of a sudden, he recalled his arguments with *his* father when he was slightly older than his son. *It is uncanny,* he mused, *but it is as if the temper of my father came surging up out of some untapped well inside me spouting forth like a geyser.*

But he was different from his father, too. After a while, he smiled inwardly, eager to forgive his son, and admiring him for possessing the courage to stand up and fight for his rights at such a tender age. *I feel better, Giovanni Andrea,* he whispered to himself. *You have bestowed a gift on me, unwittingly. I feel for the first time that you are a fighter, and that you will survive in this tempest-tossed world.*

Chapter 19

A week later, the renowned surgeon was seated at the desk in his consultation room. The sun poured in through a casement window. At his right, on the wall behind his desk, hung a coat of arms, a white font in the center of a light-blue background. From the font protruded a plant, and on each side, two branches of a tree, above four fleurs-de-lis in gold and a red alembic on dark-blue background. He was inordinately fond of the blazon for its branches symbolized his lifework; it was his awareness of tree grafting that had led him to formulate new techniques in grafting skin crucial to the progress of plastic surgery.

The room was furnished comfortably. To his left was a couch alive with vivid Florentine tapestries. Somber black-leather upright Italian chairs were at each end of the room and near the desk a more elaborate chair from Cordova, Spain. On the floor was thick multicolored carpeting from the looms of Smyrna. On the window sill of another spacious casement window was a large plant in a Venetian vase. A silver crucifix and a mirror were hanging on one wall, and nearby was a painting by Pessellmo portraying Saint Cosmas and Saint Damian grafting a leg from one man to another. This consultation room led through a door to the operating room and beyond to bedrooms for patients.

Attired in black cap and gown, Gasparo was leafing the pages of his manuscript with long, sensitive fingers. The sapphire ring near his right thumb and the selenite ring on his left hand glistened brightly. He was reading the finished manuscript on which he had labored for many years; his eyes were afire with pride and yet he was agitated. Restlessly, he stroked his mustache and pointed beard. *I will publish my book,* he breathed to himself, but the resolve stirred up unease, and he rose from the desk to pace from the consultation room to the adjoining room and back, pausing to utter a short prayer before the silver crucifix. *I do believe in God,* he mused, *but to the Roman Church I am a sinful heretic.*

The door to the consultation room opened and a black man in his late forties, athletic and handsome, hurried to him. "Sire," he said, "in the streets I was followed by a swordsman in black."

"What is that, Scipio? A swordsman in black? Did you see his face?"

"Yes, sire, I turned the corner near the cathedral and observed that he was following me, so I tried to discern who it was, and never have I seen this man before, I swear it in the name of Our Lord."

"The Inquisition," whispered Gasparo, and a wave of dizziness washed over him. "It must be the Inquisition."

There was a knock on the outer door and, apprehensively, the surgeon motioned for his assistant to answer it. Crossing himself, Scipio walked through the open consultation room door to the anteroom and unlatched the outer door leading into the house. Gripping the desk for support, the surgeon held himself upright and listened to the approach of footsteps.

Scipio re-entered the room with a tall, stately-looking soldier attired in a doublet of black damask thinly edged with fine sable and girdled by a jet-black sword belt with solid-gold buckle and sword. His hose were black, and so were his stout boots of soft cordovan leather laced at the sides and turned back at the knee. His feathered bonnet was also black and, indeed, it seemed as if the soldier had come for a sinister purpose—or so Gasparo feared.

"Is this the house of the eminent Professor Gasparo Tagliacozzi?" asked the soldier.

"Yes."

"And you are Professor Tagliacozzi?"

"Yes."

"You are the surgeon who repairs noses?"

"Certainly."

"I am the Chevalier Etienne de Saint Thoan," announced the soldier, sweeping the feathered bonnet from his head with a courtly motion. "I have journeyed from Paris to seek your medical advice and I cannot tell you how delighted I am to meet a surgeon so illustrious as you are, sir."

Gasparo sighed with relief and the blood seemed to resume its circulation around his body. "I am honored by your presence. Would you care for some refreshment? My wife—"

"May I come directly to the point?" St. Thoan seated himself in one of the straight-backed chairs as Scipio walked quietly from the room. "I will remove my artificial nose."

"How long have you had this contraption?"

"Many years. For many years, signor, I have not known the meaning of comfort. This artificial nose has tormented me and caused me mental torture beyond my powers of description."

"I extend to you my profound sympathy, Chevalier. But kindly let me examine your nose. Would you please step over here near the window, signor? Ah, that is fine." The surgeon peered closely at the defective nose. The lower half was missing, including most of the nostril area. He probed the tissues gently with his fingers, then holding the warrior's head back slightly surveyed the nasal cavity. "Splendid."

"Can you assist me?" asked the swordsman in black. *Mon Dieu. You cannot refuse me.*"

"I will not. I feel confident that I can give you a handsome new nose."

"You are my savior."

"No, I am your *doctor*. But let us discuss arrangements, Chevalier." *How could I refuse to operate on this courteous noble warrior, who has journeyed from Paris to see me?* mumbled Gasparo to himself. *This will not delay our departure for Leghorn since I have committed myself to operate on Count Carlo Torticelli shortly. But then we leave, and nothing will sway me after this.*

"First, Chevalier, may I ask if your lodgings are comfortable?" The surgeon beckoned Giulia to enter with a pot of tea and a tray of sweet cakes. She put them down on a small table near the desk and, after a quick appraisal of St. Thoan, exited unobtrusively. "Would you like some tea?"

"Yes, thank you—that is, I will have tea. I do not really understand—"

"The relation between your lodgings and your nose?" finished Gasparo. "Let us indicate merely that your occupancy of your lodgings will encompass a period of two or three fortnights, so that I must concern myself with your comfort."

"Then this surgical procedure—"

"Procedures, my Chevalier. For a number of incisions will be necessary."

"How many?"

"Let me see your arm, my friend."

The swordsman in black rolled up a sleeve of his doublet and the surgeon studied the flesh intently. "Admirable. Your skin is of sturdy texture."

"You will use my arm? You will fashion me a new nose from the flesh of my arm? Is it conceivable that this is your meaning, Doctor Tagliacozzi?"

"It is more than conceivable, my Chevalier."

"And my nose will be normal?"

"It will function quite as well as your original organ, as God intended it to function. And, my good fellow, once again you will look splendid; the ladies beholding your countenance will sigh with desire."

St. Thoan cupped his face in his hands, his body heaved ever so gently, and when he removed them his palms were wet. "I must apologize, signor, for behaving in the manner of a woman, but I feel deeply affected. For more than twenty years have I garbed myself in black, in mourning for the loss of my nose. The only lady I ever loved found me disgusting after my tragedy and mocked me, and for twenty years I have waged a desperate battle against my urge to drive a dagger through my heart."

"You have worn this artificial nose for twenty years?"

"Ten years, signor, with this silver monstrosity. Before that, an additional ten years of horror, with citizens who had once bowed at my very presence staring at me insolently, as if I were a freak."

"And who fashioned this organ of silver?"

"I consulted the renowned surgeon Ambroise Paré, and he dispatched me to see a silversmith."

"Ambroise Paré, physician to His Majesty Charles IX, King of France?"

"It is he."

"I have imbibed priceless wisdom from his courageous book on surgical technique. He was unable to assist you?"

"The most eminent war surgeon in France required the assistance of a silversmith."

"I am appalled," said Gasparo and, to himself, *I must publish my book, for I realize more than ever that I could not in good conscience suppress it.* Rising from his seat behind the desk, he strode briskly to the consultation room door and called for Scipio. "Chevalier, would you be so kind as to examine my assistant's face? Come here, Scipio, to the window."

"But you must be jesting," said St. Thoan, after scrutinizing the black man's face. "I see nothing."

"Separate your mustache, Scipio, please."

"Is that a tiny scar? It is so faint that I can barely discern it."

"Ah," said the surgeon, delighted, "many years ago I operated on this splendid man's harelip. You see, my friend, he was born with a wretched hole in his lip."

"It is unbelievable."

"I was the only medical man in the City of Bologna who could help him."

"And I," said Scipio, "am eternally grateful."

"Grazie," said Gasparo, "but, my noble friend, you reward me every day, for beholding your handsome visage, my heart feels renewed and my sense of purpose returns. Scipio, I wished to use you to demonstrate to the Chevalier what is possible, and now I must converse with him again privately."

"Magnificent," said St. Thoan as Scipio exited, "my spirits soar."

"And you, Chevalier, must be a living example of the healing powers of my art. When you journey back to your native land of France, you must pay your respects to the surgeon Paré and convey to him the nature of my surgical discoveries, exhibiting the classic contours of your new nose, with my acknowledgment of my debt to him and my hope that he will learn from me as I have learned from him, and that he will be able to utilize my innovations to serve the deformed without persecution or intimidation."

"You have had difficulties with the authorities?"

"There are edicts and papal bulls that prevent me from exercising my surgical skills freely. The Roman Church and its Inquisition— My dear Chevalier, ignorance and superstition ride roughshod over the truth and we live immersed in a quagmire of prohibitions so dispiriting that in my weaker moments I would like nothing better than to shrivel up into a fetus and find sanctuary in the nourishing warmth of my mother's womb. One papal decree binds me, my friend, not to render treatment to a patient for any period in excess of three days without ascertaining that he has made fresh confession to a dignitary of the Roman Church."

"You are not permitted to operate on any but a confessed Catholic?"

"The papacy has issued a bull forbidding physicians to treat heretics on penalty of death."

"Then you would allow a human being to die in the street, like a homeless dog, just because he was a Turk or a Jew or a Huguenot?"

"I do not make the laws, my friend, but if I violate them, I am liable to prosecution as a heretic. The Inquisition is ardent in its thirst for victims."

"Yes," said the swordsman in black, and a sadness had crept into his eyes. "I *do* understand."

"But let us get back to your case, Chevalier, for you are an honorable man and I want to restore your lost nose and speed your return to France as a living example to Paré. Let us finalize the details. We will begin the incisions early tomorrow morning—after Mass."

"It will take a lengthy period of time. Why?"

"The procedure is complex," said Gasparo. "The preliminary step is to prepare the skin on your arm with a special clamp I invented for this purpose. This clamp contains the ribbon of skin needed while I make two parallel incisions in the skin and separate it from the underlying tissues. This ribbon of skin, freed from underneath, is attached to the arm above and below and continues to receive bodily nourishment."

"And then?" asked St. Thoan, but his manner was gloomy.

"After two weeks, when this skin flap has grown strong, I will sever it from the arm above but leave it attached to the arm below so that it continues to absorb nourishment from the body. At this point, Chevalier, after two weeks, the peninsula of skin, fortified, must be lifted to the nose; still attached to the arm, the skin flap must be sewed into the deformity of the nose, so that while it is growing into the nose it will ingest more nourishment from the arm."

"How long would I have to keep my arm pinned against my nose?"

"Two weeks."

"It is impossible," said the Frenchman wearily. "What human being is capable of remaining motionless for a fortnight?"

"Ah, but I have created a head-and-chest apparatus to immobilize the arm and allow the skin flap to grow into the defect and take root as a new nose."

"And that is the complete procedure?"

"After two weeks, I will remove the head-and-chest apparatus, detach the skin flap from your arm, and bring your arm back to its normal position. Later, I will shape the undersurface of the nose and the nostrils from the end piece of the skin graft. This involves several operations, but I have perfected my technique with experience, my friend, and you need not worry about the result."

"It is a miracle," said St. Thoan, "and I salute your genius. But I must leave Bologna in three days."

"Three days?"

"I would be eternally grateful if you could complete the surgical procedure within that time."

"It is impossible," said Gasparo. And then, thoughtfully, "Three days?"

"I am afraid this must be the limit of my stay, Professor, so I will attach my artificial nose and take leave of you."

"I do not know," said the surgeon warily, "but tell me, Chevalier, how did you suffer this dreadful misfortune?"

The soldier hesitated, and his scrutiny of the surgeon was tinged with apprehension. "It was," he said finally, "at the Massacre on Saint Bartholomew's Eve."

"Will you tell me about it?"

"Well—I will. Yes, I shall trust you, Professor. France was torn by religious civil wars between the Huguenots and the Catholics—you surely recall hearing of them—and Henry of Navarre traveled to Paris to marry Marguerite de Valois, sister of His Highness Charles IX of France, at the same time that Henry's mother was poisoned by Catherine de Médicis. Henry swore vengeance and led his Huguenot force to the gates of Paris to link up with Admiral Coligny, but the Duke de Guise, leader of the Catholics, was plotting to annihilate the Huguenots. De Guise was determined to slay Coligny to avenge his father's death, and in the aftermath of Henry and Marguerite's wedding, he appealed to Charles IX and Catherine de Médicis for permission to attack the Huguenot contingent and, alas, it was granted. A guard in the service of the King, Henry of Navarre, I was assigned to defend the person of Admiral Coligny, but I was helpless to protect him from one of De Guise's hirelings, who shot him with his hand pistol. And so, with the Admiral abed and the surgeon Ambroise Paré in attendance, I stood guard outside the bedroom door. And then they invaded, De Guise's men rushing into Coligny's house to murder him. The surgeon Paré escaped by jumping out of the bedroom window and so did I—but not intact—for I was forced from my post into the bedroom and then this too proved untenable."

"Your nose?"

"Crossing swords with a Captain Attin before leaping from the window, I plunged steel into his heart, killing him, but first he slashed the end of my nose—and, Professor, I was at the time a callow youth."

"And a Huguenot?"

"One of the survivors, for that day the Catholics slaughtered thousands of my brethren."

"Again abomination in the name of humanity," cried out the surgeon. "The City of Bologna celebrated this barbarity with bonfires and fireworks, and in Rome a *Te Deum* was ordered by Pope Pius V to rejoice over the Devil's demise."

"The Massacre of Saint Bartholomew did not terminate the civil war in France."

"You are a Frenchman," said Gasparo, "and in your country two human beings destroy each other, stoop to petty intrigue and, still more tragic, fail to comprehend the sacredness of life."

"When Henry III ascended the throne of France, there was a period of peace. We Protestants were permitted to practice our religion and families of victims of the Massacre of Saint Bartholomew were exempted from taxation. But then— Oh, signor, would that peace might have tightened its hold on the hearts of the leaders of France. But the Catholics, under the leadership of De Guise, formed the League of the Holy Trinity for the avowed purpose of drenching the soil of our proud nation with Huguenot blood. Oh, oft the world seems a dungeon to me, for where, my dear Professor, is the land where the sun shines and the birds sing?"

In Leghorn, the surgeon whispered to himself, *in Leghorn.* And, aloud, "And what then, Chevalier?"

"Today our ruler is the degenerate Henry III, who concerns himself solely with his debaucheries. He cares nothing for human life, but curls the end of his hair with a hot iron and designs new ruffs for his prodigious retinue of dogs. His court reeks with the smell of perfumed dandies and powdered harlots and the nobles eye one another warily, wearing armored breastplates under their tunics and concealing daggers and handguns on their persons."

"I extend my sympathies. For, truly, my heart goes out to your countrymen."

The swordsman in black was on his feet, eyes blazing. "I come to you for assistance," he thundered, "and you relate that you Bolognese celebrated the Massacre of Saint Bartholomew with a display of fireworks."

"You misunderstand me, Chevalier. You do not know the good will I feel toward you."

St. Thoan's demeanor did not change. "Your protestations fall on deaf ears, Doctor Tagliacozzi, for your gentle phrases will not ease my pain or will your sanctimonious feelings heal the deformity that has caused me such wretchedness."

"My dear fellow, I offered to operate upon your nose and I have not retracted my offer."

"And now that you are aware that I am a Huguenot? Will you give me back the nose that Our Lord bestowed upon me at the time of my birth?"

"It would be my delight and my privilege. But if the Roman Church learns that I treated a Huguenot, it would condemn me to burn at the stake."

"Then your answer *is* no?"

"Chevalier, I am a family man who loves his wife and his son and feels a sense of responsibility to them."

"You are a hypocrite."

"I will be most pleased to perform the operation if you fulfill one condition."

"State it, then."

"My country is Catholic and your very presence here places you in grave danger. Your peril mounts ever more when you pass through the portals of my residence, for my enemies are powerful and one, Flaminio Vulpi, is Censor of Books for the City of Bologna; as head of the Inquisition, he would not hesitate to order your arrest if he knew your identity and whereabouts—a possibility, for Vulpi employs informers."

"You are telling me to leave?"

"No, Chevalier, I am suggesting that you convert to Catholicism and then confess. If you do this, I will operate and, in the name of God, I swear that I will give you a handsome nose."

Rage burned from St. Thoan's eyes to lash out at the surgeon. "My nose mutilated, my brothers slaughtered like animals—by Catholics. And you, sir, you have the audacity to ask me to convert to this blasphemous religion?"

"I concern myself not with influencing your faith or swaying your convictions; I attempt solely to ensure your safety, and mine, and that of my family."

"Nothing, not my nose, not my life, could induce me to join the Roman Church. My decision is final—torture would not compel me to change my mind."

Gasparo sighed. "How can I serve you then?"

"You will not," said St. Thoan brusquely. "I will depart instantly and bring relief to your coward's soul. Is not this what you wish?"

"No, it would make me wretched." Tagliacozzi sat behind his desk, in black cap and gown, the rings on his fingers glistening. His surgeon's fingers betrayed his state of agitation, picking up a manuscript page and depositing it on the pile, rumpling his thick black hair, tugging at a portion of his white ruffled collar, straying to his mustache, dropping in despair to the pile of manuscript pages on the desk. "It is a difficult matter, Chevalier."

"You took an oath," said St. Thoan. "As a physician, you were required to swear that you would honor your moral responsibility to the sacredness of human life. Papal decree or no papal decree, you, Doctor Tagliacozzi, possess the power to breathe life back into my soul, disintegrating from the brutality inflicted upon me; you can repair the wound administered to me by a Catholic. You, signor, can bind up the piercing scars on my face and in my bloodstream. The gift, the talent, the capacity, bequeathed to you by God—would you, so blessed by the Lord, deny me in my need? Your power is awesome but unexercised it is nothing, and you have betrayed the Ruler of the Universe, who gives us all the most splendid inheritance—the fluids and tissues of life, and the moral courage to use this life in the service of the common man."

"Your words are eloquent, my dear friend. The priesthood should have been your calling."

" 'Let there be no strife between thee and me for we be brethren.' "

"From Genesis, is it not?"

"Its meaning is profound and penetrates to the heart of the precepts underlying ethical life—let there not be war between a man and his image—for you and I, each is one, and our images shine forth from God's image, like the sun shining through your window to warm the heart of your exquisite carpeting, which, alas, lacks the awareness to savor its gift or feel gratitude toward its benefactor."

"Your words ring out like cannon, Chevalier, and their hot steel singes my flesh."

"It is not my intent to destroy, signor, but to—"

"This do I understand," said Gasparo. "Your demeanor, your character, the elegance of speech that flows from you like wine, these qualities plus your grasp of ethical imperatives stagger the imagination. You epitomize the human qualities that the Roman Church was established to exemplify—and which it so sadly lacks. *You* should be a great religious leader, but if it were so would you not be corrupted and callous to the suffering of humanity?"

"Your sensitivity, too, impresses me, signor, and I hasten to retract the insulting remarks I have made and to render you a heartfelt apology. I pray that your verdict is favorable, but let me convey this: I will regard you as a dear friend if you tell me nay, for you may be assured that I shall grasp the consequences that weigh in the balance in your mind, and I shall have faith that your motives spring from your virtue."

The surgeon stared at the sapphire ring on his finger; his examination appeared to be minute and yet he did not see the ring at all. Finally, he raised his eyes, bright with excitement but dulled with fatigue, to confront the gallant, lyrical swordsman in black, who had traveled from faraway France to seek out his services. "My lovely wife will serve you more refreshments in my living room," he said finally. "You must give me an hour to arrange my thoughts. Then I will give you a definite answer."

The surgeon ambled through the consultation room, from the coat of arms on the wall near the desk to the spartan Italian chair at the other end of the room. His boots pressed down into the thick gaily-colored Smyrna carpeting as his hands moved about restlessly, massaging the firm chin beneath the pointed beard, smoothing back the shock of black hair, toying with the lobe of his ear, rubbing his slightly bloodshot eyes. *Would that you were here, Girolamo,* he mused, *for my mind seethes with conflicting disputation and I know not what to do.*

After deciding to move to Leghorn and initiating negotiations for a cottage by the sea, Gasparo returned to work on his manuscript for a short period before publication and to terminate his association with the university while consulting with a handful of patients in the interim on minor matters. Aside from one case he had scheduled, that of Count Carlo Torticelli, he had determined to do no more surgery until he was safe in Leghorn, and his resolve had held firm until the appearance of the swordsman in black with the courtly manner and the spiritual preoccupations. Impulsively, instinctively, he had accepted the case of St. Thoan, heartened by the thought that the Chevalier, returning to France with a handsome face, would relay his knowledge to the surgeon Ambroise Paré, so that if his own fate were sealed by Flaminio and his book burned with his body, his discoveries would not be lost to humanity.

And then to listen to the revelation that St. Thoan was a Huguenot— It was terrifying. His adversaries had awaited the opportunity to destroy his reputation and even his life. While the prostitute Ghisella was staying at his residence, they had heaped abuse upon his good name and encouraged the populace to ostracize his wife and son. *Heaven protect me,* he thought, *if Flaminio ever found out that I operated on a Huguenot and gave him lodgings. But Heaven could not grant me succor, for I would be ashes.* And once again, in his mind, the image of Michael Servetus, stoned and cursed, the executioner applying the torch, the brimstone afire, and Servetus, in flames, screaming. *Oh, will I ever forget the horror of his hideous death? Can I chance a similar fate, with my wife disconsolate and my son fatherless, abandoned to cope prematurely with a brutal pseudocivilization?*

No, he decided, *I could never sacrifice the welfare of my family for a stranger. After Torticelli, we depart for Leghorn.*

In the consultation room, fatigued by the torment of his deliberations, he lay down on his couch and closed his eyes but he could not rest. Thoughts and images charged whirling and spinning into his mind, like Lorenzo Desiri hurling himself into battle against the Turks. He felt pride come surging into his consciousness as he saw again the deformed lip of Scipio, the black youth, timid, morbidly sensitive, enduring the insults of his peers, and then the full impact of the man's changed personality crashed in upon him, for the new Scipio was fearless and loyal. And this he had done, this miraculous reshaping of the image and the soul of a fellow human being. *I was right, Father,* he cried out silently, *and I did not mean to make you unhappy.*

Gasparo asked himself if it was coincidental that his father's image had swept into his mind. *I feel tortured by the thought of refusing to treat this fine gentleman,* he mused, *and I can no more easily turn him out into the street than I could have become a weaver to please my father.* He had saved the soul of his friend Lorenzo by healing the terrible gash in his cheek, and he had brought Virginio Orsini, Duke of Bracciano, back to life after colleagues had declared the case hopeless. At the battles of Lepanto and Vienna, he had ministered tirelessly to the wounded, doing without sleep when necessary to make his positive contribution to embattled humanity. Returning to Bologna, he had pressed forward his personal crusade to do good in a world bent on self-destruction.

The image of Galileo was alive in his consciousness, fleeing, hunted, spirit undaunted, and he contrasted him with the poet Tasso, placating, accepting humiliation to avoid censure, beyond reproach, his soul eaten up by the cancer of cowardice. *It is too much,* he agonized. *I vacillate and tie my own hands. What would Girolamo advise, or Signor Brown Pigeon?*

This was hopeless speculation. Girolamo had gone long ago. As for Brown Pigeon, it had not come back to the Tagliacozzi garden. He would have to provide his own counsel.

It was late afternoon now, and the sun no longer propelled its bright rays into the room. He glanced unseeingly at the painting of the two saints grafting a limb from one man to another. And then he thought of St. Thoan. *A man of spirit and substance, but is he free as a human being? Can the Chevalier tolerate the inferiority of status and resignation attendant upon his physical deformity? Can he endure the feeling that he is inevitably separated from the world of normal people? Can he bear the reality of crawling on his knees with a mutilated face that God did not give him at birth? Is his spiritual strength so sustaining that he can accept the darkness, or will he walk away from life toward the Black Angel of Destruction? Is he a man in a ship without sails, floundering in the stormy seas, unable to reach port? Can he abide the darkness within him, the clouds in his mind that block off the sun?*

The surgeon understood that his facial deformity had imprisoned the Frenchman in an internal dungeon within his mind. Without assistance he would suffer paralysis of the spirit, forever lost, forever unfulfilled. He had committed no crime, but there were no keys to release him from his blackness.

But this is not so, reflected Gasparo, *for I possess the keys to his freedom. I can give him a face as inspiring as the face Michelangelo bequeathed to David and as powerful as the one he shaped for Moses. My surgical skills can be his salvation. I can help him navigate in calm waters in a ship with sails, hastening his arrival at a wonderful port—a land of tranquillity. I can assist him in tearing down the walls of his affliction, uncovering the self-respect underlying the debris of his disfigurement, mobilizing him to escape the darkness and move toward the sun.*

And yet I hesitate? Gasparo asked himself. *If I refuse him, who will be the prisoner? Clearly, I will not find peace in Leghorn if I betray my own nature.*

He had found the answer. His family came first, the Frenchman second; but, if he sent St. Thoan away to a life of bleakness, he would be consigning himself to a dungeon from which he could never extricate himself, festering inside his soul, incarcerating it with a power the Inquisition did not possess. And then, he realized, he could never again love Giulia fully or ever hope to be a good father to his son. Not even in Leghorn, sanctuary for refugees fleeing persecution, for he would never feel capable of fleeing the persecution of his conscience, reproaching him until death for dereliction of duty toward such a fine human being as the Chevalier de St. Thoan. Resolved to stay in Bologna and treat those who needed him, he knelt before the silver crucifix and prayed to God for guidance.

"My answer is yes," he said to the courtly swordsman in black. "You shall have your new nose."

"I know," said St. Thoan softly. "You did not have to utter a word. Conversing at length with your lovely, virtuous lady, after she related some events dear to her heart, I commenced to understand more than ever that you are a truly honorable gentleman and that in my passion I have grievously wronged your character."

"You are gracious, Chevalier," said the surgeon, "but we must make arrangements instantly. You will lodge in my household until the operations are over and your physical condition is irreversible."

"Gladly."

"You traveled with no servants?"

"Merely *your* humble servant."

"Excellent. You will not leave my house until your departure from Bologna, and you will not hover near doors or windows. We will draw the curtains before you enter any room of this house. I must minimize the risks attendant upon your presence, my dear friend, or my family and I will be exposed to needless jeopardy."

"Agreed."

"Your religion must be in strict confidence; the word 'Huguenot' must never cross your lips. And hold no converse with the poet laureate Torquato Tasso, who resides in my guest room. Remember that if you do not keep your religion a secret we are all *in extremis.*"

"I am deeply appreciative of your kindness, and bless you for bringing me light to chase away the darkness. I pray reverently for the safety of you and your family, Doctor Tagliacozzi, and give you my sacred word that I will honor your instructions."

"We will start tomorrow." Gasparo regarded the Frenchman curiously. "Tell me, what is that horn hanging from your neck?"

"It is a ram's horn," said the Chevalier de St. Thoan. "Used in time of war to notify my people, my fellow Huguenots, of danger ahead. Often have I prayed that the time would come when I could blow this horn for peace and brotherhood."

"The time is now," said the surgeon. "Blow it!"

Chapter 20

Alone in his room, the Chevalier de St. Thoan considered his situation: in an alien city in a foreign country, with his life in danger, and his presence a threat to the surgeon's life.

What will be the outcome? he mused. *Will the operation succeed? Before the catastrophe, I was carefree and laughed happily on beholding my image in the mirror. Will I find again the laughter and the song? Will I move out of the shadows to bathe once more in the glorious sun? Lord, will I regain my desire to live in sanctity—with myself, and with my brothers and sisters? At last, will my good fortune enable me to conquer the heartaches of yesterday? Tell me, O Lord, will I fulfill my true destiny as a child of God and your humble servant? Tell me, O Lord, will Doctor Tagliacozzi create this miracle with your guidance and your blessing, permitting me to reclaim the human dignity that rightfully belongs to me?*

He had taken a Holy Bible on his journey. Meditating, praying to God, he opened the Bible and turned to Psalm 13, A Psalm of David:

> How long wilt thou forget me, O Lord? Forever? How long wilt thou hide thy face from me?
>
> How long shall I take counsel in my soul, having sorrow in my heart daily? How long shall my enemy be exalted over me?
>
> Consider and hear me, O Lord my God; lighten mine eyes, lest I sleep the sleep of death;
>
> Lest mine enemy say, I have prevailed against him; and those that trouble me rejoice when I am moved.

But I have trusted in thy mercy; my heart shall rejoice in thy salvation.

I will sing unto the Lord, because he hath dealt bountifully with me.

Outside his window was the garden, and running his eyes over it, he asked himself if he would find again the cool garden in his mind—refreshing, growing.

I shall, he told himself, *for this I crave, and God has kindly directed me to the house of this fine surgeon.*

He reread the psalm and felt more relaxed. He could smell the flowers in the garden and hear the chirping of the birds.

Later, he lay down and breathed deep in the soothing womb of sleep.

The morning of the operation, two distinguished gentlemen arrived at the surgeon's residence: Lorenzo Desiri, who with Scipio would assist the surgeon, and Dr. Girolamo Mercuriale, professor of medicine at the University of Padua.

Professor Mercuriale was an eminent-looking man of about sixty, dressed in cap and gown of black velvet trimmed with sable. His appearance was deceptive. He was muscular and lithe in his movements, with deep-set eyes that reflected a strong-willed, autocratic personality. His physical presence seemed to symbolize authority, and a stranger, anticipating harshness, would be startled by the soft gentleness of his speech.

Born of good family, he had studied medicine in Bologna and Padua. His brilliant scholastic record won him recognition, and at thirty-two he served on an important mission to Rome. There, Cardinal Farnese, impressed, took him under his protection and Mercuriale stayed for eight years, analyzing ancient documents on the art of gymnastics. Later, he treated the ill Maximilian II, Emperor of Germany, Bohemia, Hungary, and Austria; his royal patient's condition improved and he was knighted. His fame was assured and his medical practice prospered.

His specialty was improvement of the body through exercise, and following his eight years' research in Rome, he wrote the most comprehensive book of that time on gymnastics, dedicating it to Emperor Maximilian II. The book contained a wide variety of exercises for sick and healthy, young and old; his reputation greater than ever after publication, he was named personal physician to Pope Gregory XIII.

Visiting the University of Bologna in his ceaseless search for knowledge, he met Gasparo, who had written to him about his surgery, and they exchanged views on many subjects. The professors found they had much in common, and the surgeon invited Mercuriale to observe the process of reconstructing St. Thoan's nose, without, of course, betraying the secret of the Frenchman's religion.

"Will you pass your water?" asked Gasparo, handing the patient a urinal, and then, examining the specimen, "It is fine. Now, Chevalier, please remove your doublet and sit down."

The half-naked patient followed instructions, and Gasparo took off his own robe and rolled up the sleeves of his doublet, a precaution to avoid soiling his garments. "Bring the wine, Scipio," he ordered.

The French soldier swallowed a tumblerful in an instant and steadied himself in his chair. Tagliacozzi, peering closely at the nasal defect, measured the extent of lost tissue and examined the anterior aspect of St. Thoan's left arm. He massaged and pinched the skin to speed up circulation. Raising the arm to the nasal defect, he mapped out on the arm the area of skin required to form the new nose.

Then, lowering the arm, he explained the procedure to the Chevalier. "I will use the smooth surface of your arm so that hair will not grow on your nose, my dear friend. Your left arm so that while I shape your new nose you will have full use of your right arm. If you will, Scipio, stand to my left and hold firmly the right hand and shoulder. You, Lorenzo, if you would stand to my right and firmly pin down his left hand. Excellent."

The surgeon, again pinching the skin of the left arm, imprisoned between the blades of the clamp he had invented a strip of skin more than two inches wide, an area one-fourth wider than necessary to cover the defect and allow shrinkage of the graft.

At this time, participants in surgery were not accustomed to use soap and scrub their arms up to the elbow in warm water, nor did they wash their hands in alcohol or don sterile gowns or rubber gloves handed them by a nurse in a sterilized uniform. To them, cleanliness meant removing their robes and rolling up the sleeves of their doublets to avoid contamination from the patient. But Gasparo was different. Though he did not use soap, he washed his hands before the operation.

He then took his instruments from his kit and, knife in hand, cut deftly into the imprisoned skin, making two parallel incisions about four inches long. Writhing in pain, St. Thoan managed to suppress the impulse to scream. He had downed two huge tumblerfuls of wine, but the knife ripped him right out of his insensibility and his nerve ends were quivering as Scipio braced his knee on the Frenchman's right thigh, holding his arm as rigid as in a vise.

"Courage," yelled Gasparo. "Courage, my Chevalier."

"I do not understand the meaning of fear," said St. Thoan, his face pale, "for I have faith."

Quickly, precisely, the surgeon separated the bridge of skin from the underlying tissue without touching the muscle underneath. Perspiration dribbled down the patient's face, flushed with his effort to endure the pain, but he would not cry out.

Swiftly, Gasparo completed the separation of skin from the tissue underneath as finally St. Thoan could no longer bear the pain and howled with outrage. The separated tissue was still attached to the arm above and below in a fashion reminiscent of the handle of a valise.

"The operation is proceeding splendidly, Chevalier," the surgeon said to the Frenchman, but the latter was screaming too loudly to hear him, as Scipio and Lorenzo pinned him into the chair.

Tagliacozzi paused a moment. *What a blessing it would be if one could induce patients to sleep while operating so they could escape the dreadful pain. Ah, but I dream. Reality is that I have attempted to induce sleep with the juices of mandrake root, hemlock, and poppy, but these drugs are dangerous when efficacious and impotent when free from danger. If a patient is rendered so benumbed by these drugs that he loses his sense of pain during the operation, he may expire from use of the drug. And a semi-conscious patient cannot withstand an operation as well as one who is fully conscious.* He shook his head and sighed. "My dear friend," he said, "I regret that I must proceed."

Gasparo tied the open bleeding area with stitches, as advocated by Ambroise Paré. "Hot sponges," he ordered, and Scipio applied them to the ribbon of skin to increase its circulation, as Lorenzo fastened his muscular arms around the contorted patient and made futile his struggles to bolt from the chair. "Good." Then the surgeon inserted a linen gauze dressing, dipped in olive oil and turpentine, between the graft and the arm to keep them separated, bandaging the area.

"Wine," shrieked St. Thoan. "Give me wine."

"I have finished," shouted Gasparo. "You may imbibe all the wine your heart desires, Chevalier."

"Wine. *Mon ami,* you *must* give me wine."

"You are a brave man, sir. Lorenzo, give him a large tumbler. I bequeath it to you for your superb display of courage."

"I am a coward," said St. Thoan, gulping the wine. "I scream out like a baby. I strained to flee the operation I have desired so ardently for so many gloomy years. How can I apologize for my infantile conduct?"

"You are an honorable gentleman," said Lorenzo, speaking with surprising gentleness. "I tender you my admiration and will gladly toast your health, my Chevalier, and the restoration of your nose, with which you will capture the hearts of all the ladies of this fair land," adding, with a twinkle in his eyes, "except, of course, my wife, Caledonia."

The surgeon, after washing his soiled hands and mopping his perspiring face, drank a glass of goat's milk and, accompanied by Girolamo Mercuriale, walked to his consultation room and seated himself at his desk, as the professor from Padua eased himself into the ornate Spanish chair.

"You are an artist," said Mercuriale. "I congratulate you on your superb technique. My dear Gasparo, I have seen other surgeons operate and your touch is both delicate and deft; you are an incomparable craftsman."

"*Grazie,* you are kind, but it chills me that my patients must endure such suffering, and I long for some medication that will spare them such agony and allow them to sleep through the operation."

"He was a marvelous patient and struggled mightily to ignore the pain."

"Yes, but it was terrifying. Would that I could give him his new nose without exposing him to this awful ordeal."

"He sleeps now, and it is his good fortune that he journeyed to consult the premier surgeon of Italy."

Gasparo's conversation with Mercuriale was comforting. *Is it not curious,* reflected the Bolognese doctor, *that this eminent man who gives me reassurance and understanding is also named Girolamo?*

But later, at dinner, his son was morose and uncommunicative. He ate rapidly, brooding, refusing to respond to his father's efforts to talk to him.

"What is the matter?" asked Gasparo, feeling rage building inside him. "You hate me as if I were a criminal."

"You tortured that man," Giovanni Andrea blurted. "You are a sorcerer, and never will I forgive you for challenging the will of Our Lord."

"You spout nonsense, my son," said Giulia. "Your father is a wonderful man, who loves you and wishes to help other people."

"He is an agent of the Devil. The children at school tell me this every day."

"Your father works to advance truth and human progress. You should feel very proud of him and tell the children to feel ashamed and to fear the wrath of Our Lord—for they tell falsehoods."

"I wish to be like my grandfather," yelled Giovanni Andrea, jumping up from the dinner table. "Princes and dukes respected him, and he traveled everywhere with his fine silks and satins. I will become a weaver, Mama, and people will admire me and say I am a good man like my grandfather."

The surgeon sat hunched over, feeling helpless, as his son stormed from the room. His fury was so intense he could not trust himself to speak. *Could it be possible that the Devil has won my soul?* he asked himself. *Nonsense, I am thinking like Flaminio.*

But this, too, was a sobering thought, and he found his pride over the operation on St. Thoan vanishing.

On the fourth day after the operation, the surgeon removed St. Thoan's bandage and, though there was mild irritation in the area, he was elated to find the skin flap strong and healthy. Shrinking from side to side, the skin was now of a width sufficient to cover the nasal defect.

The dressings were changed daily to keep the area clean and to hasten healing of the undersurface of the skin bridge. Fourteen days after the surgery, the skin graft boasted good circulation, and the time had arrived for the second operation.

Once more St. Thoan was seated in the patient's chair, and Gasparo deftly separated the skin bridge, severing it from the arm on the side nearest the armpit, the procedure requiring only one minute.

"Hot fomentations, quick," ordered Tagliacozzi, placing them on the graft, which had turned slightly bluish, contracting like a rubber band under suddenly cut tension. But he had outlined the graft longer than was necessary, to allow for shrinkage. Soon the transplant was again pink—though soft, toneless, and wet. Applying olive-oil-and-turpentine dressings to the area and around the graft, he prevented it from attaching itself to the healing wound of the arm.

Professor Mercuriale was once more a fascinated observer, and Gasparo addressed him. "At this stage, all flaps turn blue when severed but, as you have seen, application of hot fomentations can restore proper circulation. Before we attach the skin flap to the nose, it must pass through several stages comparable to the aging process in human beings. The graft, soft and wet, is now in its puberty stage; it is not very strong since it receives food from one side only, so we must watch it carefully. It may become inflamed, ulcerate, or die, but I guard against this by attentive supervision plus daily changes of dressing. A few days more and the graft is fully adolescent, becoming dry and firm, while its borders and underside commence to heal. Later, the graft grows tough and hardy; it has arrived at the stage of adulthood and is ready for transplantation onto the stump of the nose."

"A splendid explanation," said Mercuriale, "lucid and sensible. But, my dear Professor Tagliacozzi, you neglected the question most relevant to me. When is the next operation?"

"In about a fortnight. Not much longer than that, for otherwise the graft will continue to shrink, and if it becomes too hard and scarred near its root, nourishment may not reach it. If this happens, the whole process will fail because the graft will not possess sufficient strength to grow into the stump of the nose."

Two weeks after the second surgical procedure, St. Thoan was prepared for the third operation. On its eve, his head and face were shaved clean to impede motion of the cap on his head and to ensure firmer approximation of arm to face. The patient was attired in a leather jacket and then downed two enormous tumblers of wine. Gasparo was ready, with his assistants, Scipio and Lorenzo, and the trio stripped to the waist. The surgical instruments were spread out on a table—sharp knives, scissors, forceps, along with needles, thread, and linen bandages. The doctor wound a bandage around the patient's forehead, inserting several threaded needles in the bandage so that they would be instantly available.

Positioning a piece of paper over the nasal defect, Gasparo cut out a pattern of the size and shape of skin needed to cover the defect. Then, with his knife, the surgeon started to pare and freshen the scarred edges of the nasal stump. It was almost as if he were tapping a tree, but St. Thoan, battling to retain his composure, moved restlessly in his chair until the assistants grasped him more firmly.

"This process is crucial," said Gasparo earnestly, and his eyes were alive with his excitement, "but you must hold still for a few minutes."

"I will do my best," groaned St. Thoan and, watching, Professor Mercuriale heaved an empathetic sigh.

At this juncture, Gasparo placed the paper pattern over the skin flap and cut away excess from the flap, making sure that the graft was somewhat larger than the pattern to allow for shrinkage, as the French soldier, recoiling at the sharpness of the pain, began to howl. *Yes,* mused the surgeon, *the shape of the rim of the graft will fit snugly into the shape of the rim of the nasal defect.* As always, the shrieks of the patient disturbed him, but he did not permit this to affect his skillful functioning. "Raise his hand and forearm over his head, Lorenzo, and try to hold his head steady. And you, Scipio, pin his arm close to the nasal stump so that I may sew the graft in place without pulling on it."

His assistants followed instructions and Gasparo, plucking a threaded needle from the bandage on the patient's forehead, sewed a stitch through the center of the graft and through the center of the nasal stump. He inserted the stitches at equal distances from each other but did not tie them.

With nimble fingers, he tied the laces uniting jacket, cap, and arm sling to prevent motion of arm or head. Attaching the arm sling at the shoulder to the back of the jacket, he tied the sling at the wrist to the front part of the cap, which immobilized the wrist but allowed the patient's fingers to rest comfortably over the back of his head. Then he laced a halter running from the sling at the elbow to the cap near the right temple, finally lacing the last halter, from sling at elbow downward to the chest. The graft was now totally immobilized: neither arm nor head could move in any direction.

At this point the surgeon tied the stitches connecting nose with skin flap, applying a gelatinous medication to the area and dressing it. After bolting down four tumblers of wine, and with some lessening of the pain, the patient was drowsy, and Lorenzo and Scipio lifted him carefully from the chair and carried him to his bed.

"Well?" said Gasparo, turning to Mercuriale. "Any observations?"

"You are the world's most brilliant surgeon."

Tagliacozzi wiped his perspiring body with a towel and poured himself a tumbler of wine. "For *my* pain," he said, smiling wryly. "A surgeon has pains too."

Professor Mercuriale eyed him with some surprise. "I paid you the ultimate compliment, and you do not react. Is it possible that you are free of the egotism that afflicts the rest of mankind? I have observed Ambroise Paré at work, and you are his superior."

"You are a fine man, Professor, and I do appreciate the generosity of your feelings toward me. Oh, I am vain, but I have perspective, too. And, my dear friend, what you say rings pleasantly in my ears, but I crave not the applause of the multitudes, or even of connoisseurs of knowledge like yourself. And I court not acclaim, but the sense of utilizing my productive capacities and of channeling them toward assisting people to find some form of oasis in this harsh desert."

"I honor you for your wisdom. But let us return to your surgical procedure, for it fascinates me. For one thing, my colleague, how long will you keep the stitches in?"

"In the nature of a week, for after a period of this length they may commence to irritate the skin. If proud flesh develops, I shall treat it with aqua fortis. The line scar of union between the nasal stump and the graft will gradually disappear after daily treatment with hare's blood."

"And how long will he wear your contraption?"

"About two weeks, Professor. By that time, with careful application and with assistance from Our Lord, the graft should prosper and the concluding stages of this procedure will be routine." A hopeful statement but the surgeon's thinking was more pessimistic. *Please, Lord,* he prayed. *Let it not inflame and perish, as with Morisini, or my work is futile. And let not Flaminio hear of this, or learn that the Chevalier is a Huguenot, or I will find myself in prison—or in ashes.*

Daily, he loosened the halter extending from elbow to right temple, changed the nasal dressing, dabbed astringent on the stitches to ward off irritation, and laced up the halter. After danger of inflammation of the graft had passed, he took St. Thoan off a fluid diet and prescribed a rich soft diet that included eggs and gruels, attacking his bowels with laxatives.

The French soldier became restless and six days after the most recent operation he began complaining about the pain in his shoulder. *"Mon Dieu,"* he moaned, "I feel that a mad butcher has seized on the possibility that my shoulder is a fine steak and that he stabs me constantly in this sore, throbbing area with daggers and stilettos and Turkish scimitars."

"The pain comes from your raised arm, which throws your shoulder out of position. When I remove the apparatus, I will massage the irritated area and apply medications, Chevalier, and your shoulder will cease to pain you."

"When will you remove it?"

"In somewhat less than a week, my dear friend. You must understand that if I removed it now the condition of the skin graft would be precarious and if it died you would have endured all this terrible suffering for nothing."

St. Thoan complained also of a pain in his wrist, and the doctor positioned a wad of cotton under the wrist, between this member and the cap. "When can I get out of bed and move around?" the French soldier asked.

"Soon."

"Perhaps, some wine?"

"In a few days, my Chevalier. For now you must content yourself with goat's milk and hold some melon in your mouth."

"It is inhuman, but my faith in you is strong, and faith is the pivot around which human existence revolves."

"Your courage will earn its reward, and you will bask in the glow of your striking handsomeness. Your nose will not be silver or gold— but real."

The following day St. Thoan was allowed to leave his bed and for the next ten days strolled about the house, arm raised to his face, face lowered to arm imprisoned in this ludicrous contraption that was so totally rational and creative. Fortunate he was that, in this apparatus, he was not required to walk the streets of Bologna, for he would have been accused of harboring the Devil.

Lorenzo came every day to visit the patient, praising his bravery under the knife and entertaining him with tales of escapades with women and adventures during the battles of Lepanto and Vienna. The Chevalier would respond, speaking gingerly, out of the corner of his mouth, to avoid damaging the graft. The conversations with Lorenzo soothed his spirit, for he was able to forget the pain in his shoulder. He, too, related his adventures, talking about the first swordsmen of France—Pardaillon and DePiles—who had lost their lives during the Massacre of St. Bartholomew.

"You would have relished drawing swords in practice with Pardaillon or DePiles," said the Frenchman. "Their adroitness would have stimulated you. Their natures were spirited, and they would have challenged your agility." Then, aware of his imprudence in mentioning the massacre, he fell silent.

"I will fence with you," blurted Lorenzo insensitively, "when your bandages are removed and your recuperation is complete."

"Oh, no. It was in a sword duel that my nose—"

"Accept my apologies, Chevalier, and pretend that I said nothing. For truly I meant you no harm."

"I wish peace," said St. Thoan, "and faith."

Two weeks after the most recent operation, the Chevalier was once more in the operating chair. "Hold his head firmly, Scipio," ordered the surgeon. "Chevalier, you must not move, for this is the crucial part of the operation. Pinion his right arm, Lorenzo, so that it cannot move. And, Professor, will you keep his left arm rigid, pressed against his face?"

With his two assistants and Mercuriale immobilizing the patient, Gasparo cut the graft at its root on the arm. As always, St. Thoan, struggling to control his emotions, suppressed a sob.

When the graft was completely detached from the arm, the surgeon untied the laces and removed the cap and arm sling. "Now," he commanded, "lower the arm gently, Professor. Gently. Lorenzo, hot compresses."

St. Thoan began to scream as Mercuriale carefully lowered the arm. When the member was halfway down to his side, the French soldier was howling, and if the Professor released it for an instant, it tended to ride back toward his face. Finally, with patience and cautious manipulation, the arm was brought down to the side.

Gasparo was applying hot compresses to the nose. "The graft begins to look better, Mercuriale. Ah, yes, this is splendid to behold. It was cold and pale because of its abrupt separation from the arm from which it received nourishment. Now it derives nutrition from the nose. After application of compresses, it is warm and pink in color. Oh, this is heartening. Chevalier, this day is shining with promise for you."

The Frenchman was in too much pain to hear. He writhed and groaned, fighting to wrench free from his captors, but they pinned him into the chair and only his legs, thrashing wildly, were able to elude their control.

"The graft is a trifle too long," said the surgeon, cutting away the excess tissue, then covering the transplant with an astringent salve and bandaging the nose. "We will shape the nostrils in about two weeks."

The patient was carried to bed and Gasparo then dressed the arm wound, which was supported by a pillow. While St. Thoan howled, Gasparo massaged the sore shoulder and continued application of hot compresses to the nose.

Then he prepared another solution. Taking thirty pounds of lye, some roots of althea, and roots of wild watermelon, mixing six parts of each with half a head of mutton, sliced, he made a compound of these substances, boiling them until a third of the lye had evaporated. Adding beton, then camomile, two parts of each, he boiled the solution and applied hot compresses to the shoulder area. After fifteen minutes of this treatment, the Chevalier stopped shrieking, and the doctor washed the shoulder with warm wine, drying it with a special ointment and then protecting it with a bandage.

Each day, for two weeks, Dr. Tagliacozzi treated the inner surface of the nasal graft with desiccating salves to hasten scar formation, later cleansing it with wine.

Often, Mercuriale would accompany him to the bedside.

"Tomorrow we will perform the cosmetic operation," Gasparo announced one day after they had left the patient and strolled back to the consultation room. "We will reconstruct the nostrils and the columella."

"The columella?"

"Yes, the piece of skin between the nostrils on the undersurface of the nose where it connects with the lip."

The surgeon, drawing the shape of the new nostrils and columella with ink on the graft, peered intently to ascertain that both nostrils were symmetrical and that the rear pieces were properly incorporated. Then he started paring the edges of the pieces of natural nostrils, and once again St. Thoan, manfully, was waging his battle to retain his poise in the face of unendurable pain.

"Wine," he cried out finally. "Wine."

Lorenzo poured him a tumbler full to the rim, and the doctor waited for the patient to swallow the wine and then began to prepare the septum by making incisions into the graft obliquely inward, which joined the septum at the tip of the nose.

Gasparo sewed each new nostril and joined each to the old member with four stitches. Then he inserted a quill into each nostril. Forty minutes of delicate surgery and the tip of a new nose with two nostrils was formed.

"You see, Mercuriale," he whispered, "I use the pieces of old nostril to create the new ones. I make the incisions obliquely inward so as not to weaken the septum and to permit the borders of the nostril to be covered with natural epidermis. The quills are inserted to support the septum and prevent the nostrils from contracting."

Daily for a while the surgeon dressed and bandaged the nose, treating the wild flesh of the nostrils with aqua fortis.

"It develops magnificently," he whispered to Mercuriale at the patient's bedside. "But say nothing to the Chevalier. In due time he will see for himself. My revered colleague, the operation is an unqualified success—no doubt remains."

Excited, he related the patient's progress to Giulia. "His nose is handsome," he exulted, seizing her by the waist and spinning her around.

The Chevalier de St. Thoan's face radiated happiness as he looked in the mirror. For an interval he said nothing and then, finally, on the verge of tears, he murmured, "I will always cling to my faith in human nature, Doctor Tagliacozzi, because you risked your life and your wife's and your son's to minister to my needs. You may rest assured that I am your faithful friend forever; ask anything of me, sir, for never will I fail you."

Professor Mercuriale was present at the unveiling, as was the Gonfalonier, Jacopo Buoncampagna, Captain General of the Church of St. Angelo and military commander of the City of Bologna, who had also witnessed the cosmetic operation. Buoncampagna, a heavy-set man in his mid-fifties, was a loyal friend of long duration, and though Gasparo would not trust him with the information that St. Thoan was a Huguenot (only Giulia was aware of this), he invited him to view the surgical outcome.

"Your skill is unparalleled," said Buoncampagna, "worthy of admiration."

"*Grazie,*" responded the surgeon and, turning to the patient, "Chevalier, you are handsome enough to arouse the envy of any rival."

St. Thoan wondered if he could rely upon such good fortune. "Doctor—in hot weather?"

"Your nose will not melt."

"And when frost chills the air?"

"Your nose will function as famously as the one with which you were blessed at birth."

"When may I drink?"

"Anytime, my Chevalier, but in moderation. How is your sense of smell?"

"Splendid," said the French soldier buoyantly. And then, relapsing into doubt, "But what if I sneeze?"

"Your nose will not fall off," said the surgeon, handing him a snuffbox. "Take some snuff."

"I have fear."

"Take a pinch."

St. Thoan applied the snuff to his nose gingerly, then waited. "Doctor, I fear I will sneeze." He lifted his hands under his nose, as if to catch it, then, terrified, submitted to a nasal explosion that rocked his whole body.

"You see, your nose will bear up under the winds of misfortune. Now, say *M.*"

"*M,*" said the Chevalier. "*M . . . M . . . M . . .*"

"Say *N.*"

"*N . . . N . . . N . . . N . . .*"

"Your pronunciation of these nasal letters is perfection, further proof that everything is in order."

"I can sing again," said St. Thoan, jubilant, no lingering doubts obscuring his joy. "And in my heart a chorus of angels harmonizes."

"I offer you my most fervent congratulations," said Buoncampagna, "and, Chevalier, I wish you long life and good health."

"You are generous. And I wish you all an inner contentment, a divine peace, a shining faith."

"You talk not like a soldier, but as befits a man of the spirit," Buoncampagna smiled.

"My nose exalts me," said the Frenchman quickly. "A spiritual wave washes over me when I recall my past humiliations. This silver nose."

"A remembrance," said Mercuriale.

"No, Doctor. I leave it here," said St. Thoan, drawing it from his doublet. Then turning to the surgeon, he asked, "And you, my benefactor, how do you feel?"

"Reborn again. God has made it possible."

"Forever am I your friend," said the Chevalier, embracing the surgeon, kissing him on both cheeks.

Gasparo smiled on beholding the Frenchman, for once again he was tall and dignified-looking in black damask doublet, girdled by gold-buckled black sword belt, hose and leather boots also black, atop his head the black feathered bonnet. The swordsman in black had resumed his military posture, as formerly, but his face was new. Not just the nose, but an aliveness in his eyes, the set of his chin, and the smoothness of his now-unwrinkled forehead betokened an individual revitalized, in whom hope had vanquished despair.

"I, too," said the surgeon softly, "am forever your friend."

Giulia entered the room. She was overwhelmed by the Chevalier's handsome appearance. Gallantly, he bowed, asking her to dance. She curtsied and they whirled gaily round and round.

"Gentlemen, tea is ready," announced Giulia.

The surgeon, who had been glancing out the window, turned to Mercuriale and Buoncampagna. "Tea?" he suggested. "My wife bakes delicious cakes."

Mercuriale and Buoncampagna followed Giulia from the room, the military commander closing the door behind them.

As soon as they were gone, Gasparo rushed back to the window, allowing his feelings of dread to show. "Soldiers are stationed around the house," he whispered to St. Thoan. "They are everywhere. I saw Flaminio Vulpi directing one of them, handing him a long sheet of paper. You must leave at once." From his desk drawer he pulled the robe of a Dominican monk. "Change into this instantly—and hurry—we are both in danger."

"How shall I escape? They will apprehend me."

"Through a secret door. Make haste, my friend."

The Frenchman had donned the Dominican robe and Gasparo ushered him to the silver crucifix. It was a handle that opened a secret door, and pulling it toward him, away from the wall, the doctor exposed the opening. "No one knows about this secret door. It leads down a narrow flight of stairs to an underground passage that opens quite a way from this house in fields that we own. The exit is covered over with leaves and branches."

"My dearest friend—"

"Go now—"

"How can I thank—"

"Hurry. A torch is hanging on the wall. And remember to pull the hood of the robe over your head before you emerge from the passage."

St. Thoan disappeared and Gasparo pushed the door closed. "Good-bye, Chevalier," he murmured, and rejoined the others.

A staccato pounding on the front door drove terror like a stiletto into the surgeon's heart. Another rapping noise, a harsh tattoo, and Giulia ran to answer the summons.

Chapter 21

In a vestibule branching off at a right angle from the front door, the surgeon, with his friends Buoncampagna and Mercuriale, listened. A gruff voice barked out a staccato demand, and Giulia was bravely disputing the point. Then a cold, resonant voice boomed out. "I am sure he will be happy to see me, even though he should be occupied."

Flaminio Vulpi, followed by Giulia, walked briskly into the house. Tall, with classic features and distinguished-looking gray hair, Flaminio would have been handsome except for the ugly scar on his left eyebrow and a sinister quality underlying the controlled manner of his speech.

"Flaminio Vulpi," said Gasparo.

"Your former companion," said the Censor of Books coldly. "We meet again, Doctor Tagliacozzi, and I find you in most exalted company. Is this not the Pope's cousin, accompanied by His Holiness's personal physician?"

"The company is the more exalted by the presence of the head of the Index in Bologna," said the surgeon carefully, steeling himself not to betray his real feelings.

"But, Gasparo, you have nothing to fear."

"Fear?"

Giulia's face was pale. "The living room would be more comfortable. Perhaps we could repair there, gentlemen."

But Flaminio suggested the surgeon's consultation room, and sitting in the Spanish chair, he resumed the dialogue.

"What I mean is, you may depend upon the military to protect your civil rights, the physician to safeguard your body, and the Church to stand watch over your soul."

"I am most fortunate," said the surgeon, weighing each phrase of Vulpi's and tasting each word before allowing it to issue from his mouth. "Indeed."

"And which of the three conditions stand in most urgent need?"

"My civil rights—my body—or my soul?"

The Censor of Books nodded, mouth tight, eyes vigilant, but said nothing.

"I was not aware that I *was* in dire need, either physically or spiritually."

"You may be right, my old friend, but perhaps I am the more acute judge of the condition of your soul."

Gasparo considered this, detecting the underlying menace beneath the surface banality. "I have no wish to appear overrighteous," he responded, "but I am not afraid to meet my Maker."

"If it were necessary for you to die today, would you say that? Would you so blaspheme? Would you condemn your soul to Purgatory?"

"There is no fear in my heart." It was a falsehood, but the surgeon felt it was the proper retort. "I fear not, Flaminio."

"But," said the Censor of Books, and a spark of hatred appeared briefly in his eyes, "is it not reckless to forfeit your hopes of living eternally by dying with an unclean conscience?"

Giulia could no longer control her feelings. "My husband is a fine human being and a good Catholic," she said.

Vulpi turned toward her, studied amusement replacing rage. "Are you sure? Pray tell me, what is a good Catholic?"

"A man who reveres God," said Giulia, and then, more assertively, "a person who adheres to the teachings of our beloved Lord Jesus and—"

"There is no more than that to being a devout Catholic?" Flaminio's glance was contemptuous. "Should he not appear before God in His Church regularly?"

"Yes."

"And confess his sins regularly?"

"Yes."

"And do you confess *regularly?*"

"Yes."

"Even you," interjected the surgeon, "cannot doubt *her* piety and devotion."

"*Her* devotion, yes. But you, Doctor Tagliacozzi, do you worship in God's Church and visit your confessor regularly?"

"Yes, I worship regularly and confess frequently."

"Ah, frequently," said the Censor of Books. "How frequently?"

"You must understand that it is not always possible to visit on the same day at the identical hour. My work—I must serve those who need me at their convenience."

"It is sinful to pander to the worldly vanities of others and neglect the welfare of your own soul."

"In serving the afflicted, I serve God. In fact, it is my purest way of expressing my love and my belief in the teachings of Christ."

"And yet you profess no faith in the teachings of the Church? Can they not guide you? Help you avoid the pitfalls and machinations of evil?"

"Of course."

"But you do not always follow them?"

"I do to the best of my ability, but life would lose its meaning if I could not use my talents to benefit those who come to me."

"There are members of the faculty at the University of Bologna, your own colleagues, who strongly disapprove this misuse of your knowledge of medicine, gained only through the generosity of Mother Church. Some stigmatize it with an exceedingly ugly name."

"They do not understand."

"Ignorant?"

"No," said the surgeon warily, "I would not say ignorant. Let us say that they have deliberately closed their minds to the value of my work."

"For what reason? Would you say jealousy, or because they find it unnecessary to tamper with the established order of things? Perhaps they prefer to avoid such notoriety."

"I do not seek notoriety."

"Oh, you have been most successful of late, I hear."

"My success depends upon the number of people I am allowed to help."

"Your reputation is spreading among certain people," said Flaminio, smiling coldly, and an angry volcano seethed beneath his suave tones. "I hear they travel vast distances to see you. In fact, you harbor in your house at this very moment a stranger to Bologna, whom I believe you are, by some unnatural means known only to yourself, providing with a new face."

The surgeon was silent, fear whipping through him like a fierce, chilling wind, and then he gathered his resolve. "Yes," he said firmly, "there is a stranger here whom I am treating."

"His name?"

"Count Carlo Torticelli."

"From?"

"The City of Florence."

"One of the Castellis. He should be a good Catholic."

"I am sure he is," said Giulia, managing to state this with conviction, though underlying it was visible apprehension. "My husband would not treat him otherwise."

"I should like to see him if you have no objection."

Gasparo nodded his head and his wife walked quickly from the room. Warily, the doctor studied the lean, ascetic face of the Church official.

The Censor of Books glanced at Gasparo's desk piled high with papers. "A manuscript?"

"A record of my surgical investigations."

"No doubt it will make interesting reading," said Flaminio, eyes gleaming with fresh pleasure, "when you submit it to the Index for criticism." The Censor of Books, openly malevolent now, leafed a few pages, halting to study an illustration. "What, may I ask, is this noxious contrivance?"

"It is an arm appliance. I invented it to prevent undue movement, which might cause my—"

"Your victim?"

Pausing to control his anger, Gasparo strolled away from the Church official and turned to face him again. "Which might cause my patient unnecessary pain. For the success of my treatment depends upon the appliance's efficiency."

Hearing a door open, Flaminio whirled, a look of astonishment building on his face, for the man walking into the room was wearing a duplicate of the arm appliance depicted in the manuscript. Giulia trailed after the patient.

In a rage, the man rushed to the doctor. *"In nome di Dio,* what is this, Tagliacozzi?"

"A monster," said Flaminio, crossing himself. "From all powers of darkness, dear Lord, preserve me."

"Signor, I beg of you—" started Gasparo.

"I am brought from my room by a woman like a fractious child," snarled the intruder. "Am I to be publicly admonished?"

"An abortion of evil," murmured Flaminio, lifting his eyes heavenward, as if in supplication to God.

"What is this?" said the patient, suddenly contrite, noticing the Church official for the first time. "Please forgive my bad temper, Father, but I did not see you."

"I understand, my son, but I was merely alluding to the pernicious device you are wearing. I presume you regret yielding to the sinister persuasions of Doctor Tagliacozzi?"

The man's eyes swept over the room. For the first time he seemed aware of the assemblage of dignitaries, and Buoncampagna nodded his head in greeting. Abruptly, the patient became conscious of his ludicrous appearance—in dressing robe, arm inclined at a severe angle to his nose, immobilized by the apparatus—and of his rude, tactless entrance.

"I have no quarrel with the physician," he muttered, lowering his eyes, "as long as he fulfills his promise and makes me whole again."

"You have faith in him?" snapped Flaminio.

"Heaven may prepare to receive him if he should falter in his service to me."

"How come you by this misfortune?"

"An unlucky blow in a duel."

"Did it take place in Bologna?"

"No, Father, on the outskirts of Florence, my city of residence. I am Count Carlo Torticelli."

"I recognize you, Count Carlo, and indeed I have enjoyed cordial relations with numerous members of the Castelli family on many occasions. You are a loyal son of the Church, I trust. When did you last confess?"

"Before leaving Florence, Father."

"And how long have you been in the City of Bologna, Count Carlo?"

"Two fortnights, perhaps."

"So brief a period, and already the iniquitous atmosphere of this house has caused you to neglect your religious duties?"

"His physical condition made it impossible for him to leave the house," interjected the surgeon. "I forbade him, as his physician."

"You have seen fit to neglect me," complained Count Carlo Torticelli. "As my physician you neglect me when I have most need of you. I am suffering considerable discomfort."

"If you will retire now, I will follow as soon as my guests have departed."

"I await your presence. Good-bye, Father. Signor."

"One moment," said Flaminio. "When your discomfort has subsided, Count Carlo, I shall be most happy to provide you with a confessor."

"*Grazie,* Father."

"You will find me at the Castello San Angelo, the Chamber of the Index." The Censor of Books turned to the surgeon, as the patient, bowing stiffly and with absurd difficulty, departed. "We are seriously disturbed, Doctor Tagliacozzi, for you have renounced the oath you pronounced when, after completing your studies, you were granted a medical degree."

"Always am I aware of this vow."

"The souls of your puppets should be in your safekeeping but, in truth, you have ignored your sacred responsibility to the Church of Our Lord."

Jacopo Buoncampagna, seated beside Professor Mercuriale, had said nothing while the Church official proceeded from suave civilities to sarcastic taunts to curt reprimands. Now, with Vulpi advancing to direct accusation, he decided he could no longer remain silent. "That is a gross exaggeration," he trumpeted.

Flaminio ignored the military commander's remark. "And, Doctor Tagliacozzi, this sin of omission is mild in comparison to the hideous crimes you have committed under the guise of practicing medicine."

"Absurd," rejoined Buoncampagna. "Why, the doctor—"

"He helps his fellow man," said Girolamo Mercuriale, "to the fullest extent of his knowledge and ability. Such a man should not be subjected to such humiliation."

"You would have me think he is a public benefactor?"

"Indeed he is," said Mercuriale. "Certainly he is not the criminal you claim he is."

The Censor of Books massaged his forehead slowly. "He poisons the minds of his victims."

"That is malicious," said Buoncampagna, "and outrageously unjust."

"This misguided partiality in both of you is quite reprehensible considering the closeness of your association with the Holy See."

"This is beyond endurance—" started Buoncampagna, but subsided in favor of Girolamo Mercuriale, professor from the University of Padua, personal physician to Pope Gregory XIII.

"Are you accusing me—?" said Mercuriale, pausing to measure his words. Slim and athletic, in superb condition for a man of about sixty, Mercuriale was wearing a skullcap and his full beard extended down over the top of his flowing black professor's robe. "Rest assured, Fra Vulpi," he said with precision, "I am willing that our illustrious Pontiff should sit in judgment on my conduct and, additionally, on the conduct of my esteemed colleague, Doctor Tagliacozzi."

"Whose barbaric, inhuman indulgences transform men into beasts?" asked Flaminio, and rage poured freely from his eyes now. "This is sorcery. It reeks of magic and, Professor Mercuriale, it cannot be tolerated."

"*You* speak of toleration?" snarled Buoncampagna.

"My friends, I beg of you," said Gasparo, "*I* must assume full responsibility for my actions, and, indeed, there is no reason why I should not do so. For, gentlemen, I feel no fear."

At this moment, fortified by the support of his staunch friends, the surgeon felt boldness in his heart, but a pale, trembling, slightly stooped old man entered the room, his large blue eyes bloodshot, on his left temple an artery throbbing in rhythm with his terror. It was the poet Torquato Tasso, elderly in middle age, apprehensive at sight of the number of people present.

"I beg your pardon," he said, seeming to apologize for his existence, "I wondered what the turmoil was about."

"Torquato Tasso," said Flaminio. "What is the poet laureate of the court of Ferrara doing in Bologna?"

"Flaminio?" breathed the poet, eyes filling with fright. "You are Flaminio Vulpi, who—"

"Indeed."

"Oh," said Tasso, and his eyes flitted swiftly around the room, as if he were seeking out a protector. "I was even now leaving for Ferrara."

"Ah, but I must tell you that I have been reading your book with the greatest of interest."

"Oh. You—you like it?"

"I trust you will not leave Bologna without honoring me with a visit," said the Inquisition official, "for I desire so much to discuss it with you."

"*Visit* you?" The poet's face was a study in horror and his attempts to convey pleasure were disastrously obvious; on his left temple, the undisciplined artery throbbed wildly, a fist clenching and unclenching. "Call on you? Delighted—yes. Discuss my book? Visit you? Yes, yes, of course. I shall visit you. Of course. Yes, I WILL." And, shrieking the last words, face pale, body shaking as if from the plague, the poet stumbled blindly from the room.

In the ensuing silence, Gasparo felt his courage vanishing.

Vulpi was smiling now, for the appearance of the servile poet had fed his sense of power. As if by magic, his headache had disappeared, and he felt monstrously tall, like the Pepoli tower or the lordly structure of the Castellis. "I have warned you constantly," he said to the surgeon, and smugness made his tone more menacing than ever. "I warn you again. If you persist in your noxious practices, corrupting the ethics of your honorable profession, defiling the sacred teachings of the Church, not only will you jeopardize your career as a physician but you will endanger your life and the lives of those who are dear to you."

He turned as if to go, taking one step toward the consultation room door, which led to the vestibule and front door of the Tagliacozzi residence. But then, from the direction of the operating room, the sound of a man singing a folk song floated in to them through the closed door, and Vulpi, halting, turned.

"What room is that?"

"My surgery."

"I should like to see it," said the Church official, striding briskly to the door.

The singing stopped and a man said softly, "Maria, I am singing to you. Stop working and appreciate the melody, for it is very beautiful."

As the man resumed singing, Flaminio flung the door open and entered, exasperated by the romantic overtones. He came upon Maria Boschetti, the pretty, young servant girl, and, startled, the maid uttered a cry of dismay. There was a dustcloth in her hand and, recognizing Vulpi, she dropped to her knees.

"Forgive me, Father, I could not help listening. I did not want to. Oh, forgive me."

The man was not in the room. Dressed in work clothes, he was standing just outside the window, his elbows on the window sill as he serenaded the young girl.

"Forgive you, Maria? Was my singing so horrible?" Then he sighted the Censor of Books. "Ah, Father, it is of you she seeks forgiveness, but she does herself an injustice. You see, Father, I was singing to her out of joy. Not long ago, an ugly sword gash disfigured my cheek, and the doctor brought me back to normal."

Flaminio shot a withering look at him, then turned to Maria, one of his informers, whispering, "Is this the stranger of whom you spoke?"

"No, Father. He helps with the chores."

Flaminio turned back to the consultation room, slamming the door irritably, and then, a maliciousness sparking from his eyes, turned to the surgeon. "Where is the Chevalier de Saint Thoan?" he demanded.

Gasparo said nothing. His eyes met Giulia's and he could feel her apprehension. Agonized, he faced his childhood friend, uttering not a syllable.

The Censor of Books smiled but his eyes were cold. "The Chevalier cannot go beyond the walls of the city, for soldiers are stationed at the gates." Proceeding to the window, he signaled someone outside.

Buoncampagna, lounging by the window, reacted instantly. "Why do you call my escort of soldiers?"

"As the military arm of the Church," announced Flaminio, "I wish you, Captain General Buoncampagna, to conduct Doctor Tagliacozzi to the Chamber of the Inquisition."

"You are placing him under arrest?" asked Mercuriale.

"You have not the right," said Buoncampagna.

A sob escaped Giulia and she rushed to her husband's side, burying her head in his neck and pressing herself against him while she moaned in disbelief.

"We have reason to believe the Chevalier de Saint Thoan to be a heretic," said Vulpi, and at sight of Giulia's grief, he pursed his lips sternly as envy surged through him, and the thought assailed him, *You cannot have Gasparo, he is mine,* and then he hated himself for his desire and vowed once more to exterminate the surgeon.

"A heretic—dear God," screamed Giulia, throwing back her head to glare furiously at Flaminio, but of a sudden she felt dizzy and, her knees about to buckle, clutched at Gasparo and sobbed wretchedly.

Two soldiers in suits of armor, armed with dagger and pistol, entered and looked questioningly at Flaminio.

"Search the premises," he commanded, and after a challenging glance at Buoncampagna, the churchman accompanied them.

The military leader turned to Professor Mercuriale. "Our only hope is Rome."

"I will attend to the matter," responded the Professor. "Rest assured, my friend, that the Pontiff will not allow such high-handed procedures."

The surgeon looked around the room but his eyes seemed blinded by the film of despair clouding his spirit, and inside him the blood seemed to have surrendered its power of mobility, deserting his arteries and veins and flowing instead into an unknown tributary that would nourish neither body nor soul. Helplessly, he embraced Giulia and struggled to comfort her, but what consolation could he offer when he could not console himself?

"I cannot leave her like this," he beseeched his friends, but their faces were pools of sorrow, and drowning in their despair, he glanced away and clutched grimly at his wife, whose sobbing would not be suppressed and, heartrending though it was, its rhythm was the rhythm of life unvanquished, her will uncrushed, her self-expression not distorted or warped, her grief pure in its intensity, and it was as if she were saying, *This will not happen, for I will never accept it; my love will not be taken from me, no, never,* and her fierce and anguished cries symbolized her refusal to humble herself before the forces of death-in-life.

"I will take good care of her," muttered Mercuriale almost inaudibly.

Jacopo Buoncampagna, Captain General of the Church of St. Angelo, commander of the military forces of Bologna, strolled awkwardly to the surgeon. "Come, my friend," he said gently. "With the deepest regret, I must ask that you accompany me to the Chamber of the Inquisition."

"Gasparo," cried out his wife, "Gasparo." But he had wrenched free from her and he and Buoncampagna departed.

"He has gone," said Mercuriale.

"What will they do to him?"

"Buoncampagna will assist him."

Giulia had stopped crying and she tried to find comfort in the professor's words, but she could not delude herself. Her husband was in grave danger; Vulpi would revenge himself upon the doctor. "Mother in Heaven, protect him," she shouted, "for he does not deserve—"

"He depends upon our help," soothed Mercuriale, "yours most of all. Do not despair."

"I will be strong," said Giulia, throwing back her head in an imperious gesture, her lovely red hair flowing austerely beneath her shoulders. "I will be strong for both of us."

"I must leave for the Vatican before nightfall. If you have sufficiently recovered—"

"Do you think—"

"Speculation is a luxury that we cannot afford, but we shall hope."

"My prayers go with you," said Giulia, eyes burning with pride and determination. *"Adio."*

"Adio, my lady," said the professor from Padua, and then he too was gone.

Alone, Giulia went to the *prie-dieu* and knelt in prayer. *Dear God,* she pleaded, deep in her soul, *help us,* but hearing approaching footsteps, she rose to her feet.

It was Vulpi, accompanied by another Dominican friar, and they walked briskly to the consultation room desk. The friar, lips pursed, pulled open each drawer, examined each paper, banged each drawer shut with a staccato motion, while the Censor of Books, hefting Gasparo's manuscript, handed it to him with whispered instructions. Then the friar departed.

Flaminio strolled quietly over to Giulia and, of a sudden, he felt drawn toward her. *The Devil had invaded my being,* he told himself, but it was pleasurable and harmless enough, so he held out his hand to her in sympathy for her bereavement, but she shrank from him in horror.

The Church official ignored this and quietly, his tone reverent and kindly, said, "We will both pray for him, my child."

In fear and rage, Giulia confronted him, but she thought of her husband's ordeal and of Flaminio's power over their destiny. *I must exercise caution and temperate wisdom,* she mused. *I must not oppose this madman who wears the cloth of the sacred Church.*

Kneeling, she turned to the crucifix and clasped her hands before her in supplication. Vulpi knelt alongside her and prayed aloud, chanting softly, in Latin, phrases of piety and goodness. And so the two prayed together. *It is insanity,* thought Giulia. *I pray for the safety of my husband with his avowed persecutor. Oh, would that I might speak my mind, but I dare not.*

For the first time during his lifetime of service, Gasparo left his home a prisoner. With Buoncampagna at his side, he strolled listlessly through the streets of Bologna, flanked by eight soldiers representing the secular arm of the Church.

As they escorted him toward the Garisenda Tower, half a mile distant, his spirits rose somewhat and he held himself erect, drawing shoulders back sternly, as if announcing to the world, *You cannot crush me.*

The column of men proceeded down the street Delle Lame and

veered off toward the public square, and Gasparo recalled the quackery of Professor Bartoli and the Great Van Zandt. They passed the tower Gasparo had climbed as a boy and the majestic Fountain of Neptune, its ninety jets spurting water into the air. So many years he had traversed these streets, and suddenly a wave of love for them swirled through his bloodstream, warming and chilling and cleansing with a mystic fervor. *Am I losing my mind?* he asked himself, but he felt that these sights were beloved, a part of his soul, and he could never bear to leave Bologna for Leghorn, no, not if the Inquisition judges found him innocent. His senses vibrated to the sounds of horses' hooves and carriages pounding on cobblestones, to the smell of fresh fish in the market, to the sight of the elderly wine vendor pushing his cart before him.

But this splendid feeling vanished for, inevitably, the townspeople were crowding the streets to savor his torment and to deluge him with the spleen of their frustrations and the weirdness of their superstitions. The more frightened were crossing themselves and clinging to amulets of theriac. The bolder were jeering and snarling their contempt, among them, making obscene gestures, Duglioli, the candlemaker.

And how could he stave off the recurring memory that assailed him? For this mob reminded him of the mob that had taunted Servetus in Geneva, anticipating with eagerness the burning at the stake. Yes, he recalled Servetus as if his death had taken place that very day.

And will mine? he pondered, envisioning his own death. Horrified, he heard a soldier scream at him, "Confess," and his rejoinder, "I have *nothing* to confess," with the soldier mocking him and the crowd flinging stones at his head. At the hill of execution, he was tied to a stake, twigs encircling him, the mob insulting him, and then the executioner applied torch to twigs and the twigs ignited and the fire leaped toward his oh, so human flesh.

"What ails you, Doctor?" yelled Jacopo Buoncampagna. "Why do you scream in such fashion?"

"You must forgive my outburst," said Gasparo. "I was—reminiscing, and the memory, my dear friend, was impossible of endurance."

Duglioli was not so charitable. "That unearthly wailing," he bellowed, "proves he is a witch. His craft is sorcery, and he must burn."

From the university street, then, the students advanced, six abreast, arms linked, singing and shouting, their leaders in the front column waving placards: WE LOVE GASPARO; DOWN WITH VULPI; FORWARD—FREEDOM. In the ranks, they waved stout sticks and challenged the mob of townspeople to face them in battle.

At their head was Count Lorenzo Desiri, accompanied by his toughest *bravi* and Scipio. Lorenzo had received his title but recently and it had not changed him, for arrogance came naturally to him and he feared nothing. He was wearing his finest suit of Milanese armor, made by one of the most famous artisans in that city, with bold letters engraved just above his chest, *LD*. His initials also were emblazoned on the handle of his dagger, of black steel tapering to a razor-sharp point, and he raised it above his head as he bounced forward exuberantly, black eyes piercing, chin a fortress of solid bone, muscular legs driving forward irrepressibly.

"We will save you, Gasparo," thundered the captain of the Pepoli *bravi*. Cupping hands over his mouth and carefully trimmed mustache, he shouted, "We will liberate you. Never will we desert you, and this is the promise of a man who has killed dozens of the godless Turks."

The soldiers on each side of the prisoner braced themselves for a violent confrontation as the mob of townspeople and the columns of students led by Lorenzo, advancing at right angles to each other, converged. But the students halted, letting the townspeople pass, swinging around then to follow in the line of march.

At the rear of the mob was Flaminio, ambling along with one of his assistants. Lorenzo, after the linking of the two groups, found himself just behind the Censor of Books.

"Listen to me, Flaminio," he roared. "We wish peace; did we not avoid a collision? But if any harm comes to Gasparo, we will mutilate every Dominican friar."

Flaminio, praying aloud as he walked, said nothing, and this enraged Lorenzo.

"I warn you, Flaminio," he said harshly. "Do not ignore my threat. If you do, it will be at your peril, and the streets of Bologna will flow red with the blood of the Roman Church."

Striding along, Desiri felt the blood filling his body with lust. *Ah, Caledonia,* he mused, *tonight we will surrender to our little games. You will resist me, my tigress, I demand it, so that I can tear off your lovely little garments and take you by force. You will claw me with your fingernails and bite me with your teeth and you will tell me "No, I do not like you," but I will have my way with you. I will mount you, my love, while your soft white thighs wriggle to entice me onward, and then, ah,* glorioso, *I will thrust myself into your pink deliciousness, my penis exploding like a cannon firing a salvo at the Turks. Ah, Caledonia.*

The procession moved onward and Lorenzo, returning to ponder upon the plight of his friend, resumed his onslaught upon the Censor of Books. "You stand warned. If you harm Gasparo, we will burn down your church buildings and destroy the university."

But Vulpi, reciting his prayers in a monotone, would not respond.

Gasparo smiled wanly as they neared the Garisenda Tower, where he was to be imprisoned. He was depressed that such a humiliation could befall him and he worried about the agonies of his wife and son. But his fears were under control. In a sense, a quiet revolution was taking place inside him, for he was challenging his anxieties and bolstering his resolve. *I shall fight Flaminio and the bigots of the Roman Church,* he promised himself. *And I shall win, with God's protection, knowing that my desire is to do good for humanity.*

To the rear, Flaminio exulted in his feeling of power. He had finished reciting his ritual prayers—Lorenzo's threats had not stopped him from this—and now, en route to the Inquisition prison, he savored the heady taste of authority. Was he not the most important figure in Bologna? As the Church's leading official, was he not more powerful than the Senators who ruled Bologna, or the Governor, or the chieftains of the Pepoli and Castelli clans?

No longer did he suffer from headache, and his mind was freed from the bleak gray memory of his father. Gone also was the memory of that fateful day in the country with Gasparo.

He was the law; no one dared oppose him—and he would humiliate Gasparo. At the trial, he would prosecute him with a brilliance that would bring acclaim from the Pontiff in Rome; like Savonarola, he relished the opportunity to serve the Church and to cleanse his native city of sin.

And so Flaminio felt a new spring to his step, an unaccustomed smile hovering about his lips, and his fingers tingled with excitement. The students' shouts did not ruffle him, nor did Lorenzo's taunts. To him, the sky looked bluer, the flowers smelled sweeter, and the chirping of the birds was more beautiful than ever. *Are they birds,* he asked himself, *or are they messengers of the Lord, singing to me?*

Peering far ahead, craning his neck, Flaminio could barely make out the figure of Gasparo at the head of the line of march. His childhood companion was striding forward vigorously, head high, shoulders thrown back.

But the surgeon felt once more the scorching heat of the flames, and the last time he saw Bologna the sky was gray, the birds had flown away, and his nostrils flinched from the suffocating, nauseating stench of fire.

Chapter 22

In the Garisenda Tower, the soldiers escorted Gasparo along a bleak, narrow corridor to a staircase, and their boots clomped heavily on each step as they led him down to a dark, cold-looking basement with banks of cells on one side, and, on the other, a solitary cell, apart from the others.

A guard saluted the soldiers and authorized their departure. He pointed to the solitary cell, and when the surgeon did not leap to adopt his suggestion, he grabbed him by the arm and hurled him through the open door.

"Take your clothes off," ordered the guard. He was stocky, almost to the point of obesity, and his lips were petulant, almost pouting, as if perpetually he felt cheated and would wreak his frustration on anyone unfortunate enough to come under his command. "You will find a robe on the cot."

The cell door clanged shut, and Gasparo, naked, sank wearily upon the cot. He was alone in the semidarkness of the tiny cell, and a fresh wave of terror galloped through him. *They could leave me here to die,* he thought, horrified, *and then they would not have to take me to trial.*

He slipped the drab gray cotton robe over his head and looked around him. In the dim light he could discern the harsh stone walls of the cell; like Cardano's cell, it was little larger than a closet. Through the apertures on the bars girdling the steel door, he could see the guard camped on a stool outside the cell. This was not a cheering sight. The fellow looked mean and spiteful, as if for a purse of gold coins he might be bribed to enter the cell while he was sleeping and strangle him.

His thoughts alarmed him and, morosely, Gasparo stared at the damp, cold cement floor. But this, too, was unnerving, for some creature crawled by him and slithered toward the cell door—was it a huge bug or a small mouse? The surgeon was not sure, and his investigations were merely underlining the nastiness of the dungeon prison, so wearily he closed his eyes and threw himself face down on the cot, burying his head in a grimy pillow that smelled abominably.

For a while he rested, and with his eyes blinded to the coldness of his surroundings, the images in his mind assumed a rosier hue. His friends would rush to his defense, he assured himself, men of power like Lorenzo and Buoncampagna and Mercuriale and Virginio Orsini and Grand Duke Ferdinando of Tuscany. And, of course, Vincenzo Gonzaga, Duke of Mantua. But what could they do to stay the power of the Roman Church?

He raised himself to sit up on the cot and, as he did, thunderous reverberations from the corridor outside the cell assaulted his eardrums. He leaped to his feet to squint through the bars of the cell door, but all he could see was an empty wooden stool, vague in the poorly lighted basement. Listening, he identified the tramping of many boots and someone moaning piteously and then thought he heard a key opening a cell and a heavy metal door banging shut with a resounding crash. Was someone shouting? It was impossible to tell in the gloom of the Inquisition fortress, for the heavy stone walls muffled all sounds. Was someone dying? One would never know; one could merely formulate hypotheses. *And then,* mused the surgeon, *you can ask yourself if your speculations are rational or whether your thinking processes have degenerated into a state of lunacy.*

He was still standing by the door peering through the apertures between the bars and now the mean-looking guard plodded back into his line of vision, his more-than-ample buttocks settling down onto the stool.

Gasparo turned around to pace the tomblike stone floor of his rectangular cubicle but this, too, was dispiriting, for there was no room. He was locked in a cage, like a dumb animal, and of a sudden an impulse seized him: he would scream to the world that he was innocent, that he had wanted only to help people, and he would keep on screaming until his jailers listened to his defense and released him to return to his family and his work.

I am going mad, he agonized, but then a more encouraging thought: *I did not really scream. I had the impulse but, in my sanity, I suppressed it.*

And he realized, as he had in the past, that his struggle was not solely with the Roman Church and the Inquisition but, in a substantial sense, it was a battle to reach the stronger part of his complex personality. There was a confrontation in his soul between two clashing forces: his belief in himself and the fears that threatened to undermine this belief. *For we are strangers,* he whispered to himself, *in that we do not know each other. And, more frightening still, we do not know ourselves. In my nature is a fortifying faith and a self-destructive disbelief. I wish to survive and I wish to perish. My spirit is fragile, and yet it endures.*

Was there not an English poem "My Mind to Me a Kingdom Is"? Yes, it came from the pen of an Elizabethan bard. *I reside in a dungeon, true, but inside me must I maintain a palace, with no shadows, for God has bestowed upon me a gift to help the afflicted, and I shall not fail Him.*

He contemplated the dimensions of courage. It was required on the battlefield as valorous men faced the naked steel blades of the Turkish hordes. *But,* he asked himself, *is not courage in its most sublime form the victory of man over his inner negations, an exquisite affirmation that at heart one loves virtue and keeps faith with God and himself?*

Submitting meekly to his deprivations would be a simple matter; his sufferings would evoke sympathy from well-wishers. *And yet,* he reflected, *my imprisonment offers me an opportunity, morbid and deadening but real and live, to escape the confinements of my body and render nourishment to the roots of my soul. For no evil have I committed and, I swear this on my honor, my efforts have been directed toward enrichment of the human spirit, as initiated by the creators of our illustrious Renaissance. Never will I reprimand myself for my operation upon the Chevalier de St. Thoan.*

Feeling more tranquil, he collapsed on the cot, succumbing to spiritual exhaustion as sleep, blessed sleep, washed over him and the waves swept him into unconsciousness.

He was awakened by the muffled clatter of boots outside his cell door and rushed to the bars but, again, he could see little more than the empty wooden stool of the guard and then he thought he heard a key inserted in a lock, an iron door smashed shut, and the moan of another unfortunate wretch, crying out to a god who would not acknowledge the existence of so intolerable a place as this dark, damp, filthy, evil-smelling, lonely, shut-in, cold dungeon in which human beings were brutalized and deprived of any capacity to exercise the essence of their humanity.

Gasparo seated himself slowly on the cot and, refreshed by his sleep, thought not of himself but of his wife and son. *Are they safe and well?* he wondered, and he missed Giulia. He mulled over the whereabouts of the gallant Frenchman, the Chevalier de St. Thoan. He grew more worried then and the doubts began to multiply in his mind, for these circumstances were totally out of his control.

And so he returned to the surroundings in the Garisenda prison, but this only intensified his feelings of malaise. The quiet was maddening, and the odors invading his nostrils were repulsive. He realized suddenly that he had to move his bowels and rushed to the cell door to shout to the guard through the bars.

The latter, without comment, opened the door and handed him a wooden bucket, relocking the cell with a shattering crash. The surgeon felt humiliated and his outrage swelled; the bucket smelled as if every man, woman, and child in Italy had defecated in it. But there was nothing he could do but empty himself into it and yell for the guard to remove it from the cell.

The stool outside was unoccupied, and it seemed an eternity before the guard, screwing together his lips in distaste, collected the bucket and banged the door shut with a metallic clang that penetrated the marrow of his bones.

Gasparo felt so furious that he feared his skull would explode and that his blood would erupt from it like lava pouring from a volcano, searing and tarnishing the cold stone floor. Squatting on the dingy cot, all his senses blurred and paralyzed, he felt once more like screaming, but even more terrifying, a sense of emptiness was devouring his soul, destroying his mind.

The office of the Censor of Books, Bologna, was rectangular; it was a monument to austerity. The walls, ceilings, and floors converged at right angles, unsoftened by carpeting, paintings, or paraphernalia to break up the sharp, stark lines. Only a crucifix was on the wall, and in front of it Flaminio Vulpi would kneel to pray. Otherwise, the room was furnished with straight-backed chairs, severe desks and tables, and candles. Not even books were visible in this ordered, controlled cubicle, for Flaminio had filed them all neatly into the desk drawers, and the overflow was consigned to the rooms of his assistants.

One manuscript was on his desk now, a dissertation by a student at the university, but Flaminio had not leafed a single page. Why should he? It held no interest for him. Gasparo was his prisoner now, under his power; at last the time for his revenge was at hand.

No longer did he suffer from headache or battle demoniac forces before he could sleep. The memories haunting him had vanished, and instead he felt sensations of gratitude.

Reverently, he assumed a humble posture before the crucifix, knees on the bare floor, hands clasped in front, eyes gazing heavenward. "My heart goes out to you, dear God," he murmured, "and in your name will I administer fitting retribution to the heretical Doctor Tagliacozzi."

Was the evidence conclusive enough to condemn Gasparo to execution? Doubtless it was, but Flaminio would leave nothing to chance. His informer Maria Boschetti, the surgeon's servant girl, had told him of the Chevalier de St. Thoan, and of her suspicions that he was a heretic. Had St. Thoan escaped the Church soldiers stationed at strategic positions encircling the City? Or was he still in Bologna, in concealment?

We must find St. Thoan, mused Vulpi.

Under his direction, search parties were organized, while the soldiers on lookout remained at their stations.

Church mercenaries ransacked the house of the distinguished surgeon, while Giulia screamed abuse that might have come from the lips of the courtesan Ghisella. They discovered no trace of the Frenchman, nor did they learn about the secret door and tunnel.

"Perchance his friends or colleagues conceal the heretic," said the Censor of Books, and search parties were dispatched to the homes of

Scipio, Lorenzo, Buoncampagna, and people at the university—professors, students, rectors—who had ever expressed agreement with Gasparo's ideas. Again, the searches were fruitless. The only revelation was that Lorenzo and Caledonia were naked in their bedroom, and, as Lorenzo groped in a dresser drawer for his pistol, bellowing murderous threats, the soldiers of the Church ran for their lives. The soldiers never gained entrance to Buoncampagna's house, for the military commander of Bologna, forewarned, blocked the doorway, and since he was their superior officer, they stumbled away cursing Vulpi's instructions.

Count Taddeo Pepoli had once made complimentary remarks about the surgeon in Flaminio's presence, so the next destination of the leaderless Church soldiers (Buoncampagna would not participate but had no authority to countermand the censor's orders) was the Pepoli palace. Here the searchers were indeed fortunate to escape without casualties; Count Lorenzo Desiri, captain of the Pepoli *bravi*, had alerted his warriors and, seething with outrage at the recent violation of his privacy, ordered his men to shoot to kill. Thus, the troops of the Church, marching in routine formation toward the Pepoli palace, were greeted by a volley of pistol fire that sent them scrambling for cover, clutching amulets of theriac and beseeching God to assist them in this crisis.

They retreated in panic and regrouped, the more rebellious whispering of mutiny if they should receive instructions to search the Castelli palace.

But these orders were not forthcoming. Flaminio recalled Ghisella's lengthy stay at the Tagliacozzi household and proclaimed her brothel as next on the searchers' agenda. The soldiers' morale improved instantly.

But Ghisella was now an entrepreneur; after the operation of her cheek, her fame had spread throughout Italy and she had employed five other harlots to help with her expanding clientele, reserving her own attentions for noblemen of repute and for favorite customers. As a madame, she viewed with jaundiced eyes the entrance of the search party on her premises. A senator from Venice was in one chamber, a merchant from Florence in another, and a trio of professors from the University of Bologna were other visitors. "My house will not be invaded," she stormed. "My establishment is reputable and my clients insist on privacy. Your presence is as welcome as an epidemic of the French disease."

The soldiers did not answer. Most of them were too busy admiring the full breasts swelling out from above her low-cut gown.

"Oh," said the courtesan, noting the direction of their gaze, and her painted lips parted in a smile of invitation, while her mascaraed eyes mirrored her gratification. "My apologies, gentlemen; I have been hasty. For all I knew you might have been comrades of the late gloriously departed bastard Enrico Gradenigo, who died of a disease falsely attributed to Vincenzo Gonzaga. I am confident that you gentlemen do not suffer from this insufficiency, so abhorrent to the woman who craves pleasure."

The soldiers of the Church stayed, reporting later to Flaminio that they *had* conducted a search. And, in a manner of speaking, they had indeed.

Flaminio accepted the negative reports gracefully. After all, the tribunal would assuredly support his prosecution of Gasparo and sanction his execution; he did not really need the Frenchman.

Still, he would conduct one more search operation, for he suspected that the surgeon's accomplices had taken the French heretic to the Tagliacozzi country home. And this time *he* would supervise the procedure.

It was a long journey and the Censor of Books, in his fine carriage, was followed by six soldiers of the Church on horseback. They found nothing on the premises. Then Flaminio said they might eat lunch while he, borrowing a splendid white horse, galloped to the nearby lake, where so many years ago he had attempted to make love to Gasparo.

Why do I do this? he wondered. *What demon inside me compels me to return to this infamous area?*

But he urged the horse on, and at the lake, alone, he inspected the area. *It is mad,* he admitted to himself. *What is it that I hope to find?*

Predictably, the Chevalier de St. Thoan was not there. What Flaminio did discover was the memory of the last truly human feeling of his lifetime.

But it was an agony to him, an insufferable burden that his conscience could not tolerate. His headache had come back, and he was so dizzy he feared he would faint.

And so, in the carriage rumbling back to Bologna, he discarded the memory and concentrated on mulling over the evidence against his sworn enemy. He felt sanguine over the prospects. He would not have to use the Frenchman at the trial; the proof was strong without him.

As for St. Thoan, he emerged from the tunnel into a field some distance from the Tagliacozzi house in Bologna. He dared not rest, but walked quickly across the field, glanced in all directions to ascertain that no carriages were near and then strode vigorously down a cobblestone street, eventually turning off onto a dirt road and proceeding to one of the gates of the city.

Sentries were on duty here, two of them, armed with pistols, but St. Thoan, in his clerical garb, assumed what he thought was an appropriate posture for a member of the Dominican Order and it worked.

Outside the gates, the Frenchman breathed in relief, but he could not allow himself to relax his vigilance. Briskly, he continued on the road toward Florence, walking on the side of the road, warily watching for anyone approaching on horseback or in a carriage, darting off into the bushes to crouch low every time someone did thunder past.

At nightfall he stopped at an inn but he was penniless, forced to ask for alms. The innkeeper, a simple soul, granted him a meal of freshly baked rolls, cheese, and goat's milk with honey cake, and then offered to let him sleep in the barn.

Gratefully, the Chevalier sank into a soft bed of sweet-smelling hay, conversing with his sole companion, the servant of a merchant and wife en route to Rome who were lodging at the inn for the night. The servant had tied his horse to the side of the barn, and after giving the animal food and drink and eating his own supper, he proved a jolly fellow. He and the French soldier wearing religious habit swapped harmless stories for hours, and lulled by the fresh country air and the wine (the servant had shared the bottle pulled from his knapsack—"I know you are a man of the cloth, my Lord, but God will forgive this indiscretion"), both drifted off into sleep.

Beforehand, St. Thoan had disciplined his mind to awake at first sign of dawn; he had developed this capacity over many years. He had slept fully dressed in Dominican garb and, on arising, had merely to brush the hay from his costume. Then, tiptoeing so as not to rouse the snoring servant, he stole silently out of the open barn door.

He scanned the area, but no one seemed to be observing him. *Lord, he murmured to himself, I have always tried to honor your commandments, but of late this has been impossible. I have lied, and now I deeply regret that I must steal, and from a sweet, generous man whose behavior toward me has been exemplary. But no other choice is open to me and, Lord, I beg your understanding for what I am compelled to do.*

St. Thoan unfastened the rope tying the horse to a post protruding from the side of the barn. Then he swiftly mounted the animal, and galloped off down the main road branching into the City of Florence.

Finally, he reached Leghorn, the seaport under the jurisdiction of Ferdinando, Grand Duke of Tuscany.

He eased the horse into a gentle trot, whispering soothing words into the animal's ears, for it looked fatigued and he wondered guiltily if the change in masters had upset the dumb beast. At a house fronting a beach on the Mediterranean he hauled in the reins.

It was his house. Escaping from the religious persecutions in Paris, the Chevalier had sought refuge in Leghorn. Purchasing the property, he had contemplated life with a fresh perspective. But, still, there was his nose, and thus the journey to Bologna. He had mixed truth and fantasy in relating his life story to Dr. Tagliacozzi. Not that he enjoyed deception; on the contrary, it violated all of his stern, proud religious principles. But he feared that if his story was not dramatic enough the surgeon might refuse to perform the operation, and he would spend the remainder of his lifetime loathing his uncomfortable, ugly, artificial nose of silver.

I feel contrite, Lord, he mused, that I have engaged in such evasion, for verily I feel a transgressor, but I intended no harm and, indeed, my motives are beyond reproach. You cannot gainsay that, so forgive me, O Lord.

After giving the horse food and drink, the Chevalier de St. Thoan lunched frugally and strolled to the beach, where the waters of the Mediterranean washed in upon the shore. Then, removing his boots, he walked barefoot on the wet sand. The sun was beating down hotly and there, preceding him, was his shadow moving forward as he advanced. *This shadow,* he thought, *represents a human being fortunate enough to be reborn in a world where so many never receive a second chance. Ah, yes, praise be to God, I have been twice blessed.*

He recalled how pleasure had radiated from his face when, after removing the dressings, the surgeon had handed him a mirror. For his nose was handsome, and once more he could love a woman without dreading rejection.

Since his arrival in the seaport, declared a haven for freedom of religion by Grand Duke Ferdinando, he had remained in seclusion, obsessed with the thought of his ludicrous nose. His period of isolation had lasted several months.

But no longer would he hide behind the shutters of his house. With his splendid new nose, he felt a resurgence of his old confidence in himself, and it was as if the sunshine warming him from above were inside him as well, fortifying his spirit. *For now,* he thought, *I am mercifully enabled to emancipate myself from the dread memory that haunts me, the recollection of the mutilation that has desecrated my life, and give my energies to realizing my lifelong ideals. I will meditate upon the values that always I have cherished: the brotherhood of man, the exercise of humanitarian concerns, the enhancement of productive creative capacity.*

Not that meditation would suffice. St. Thoan understood the need to give a splendid performance for the glory of God. And he was aware that translation of thinking power into action was basic.

Verily, may I listen to reason, exulted the Frenchman, *and this is no mean achievement, for reason operates minimally in this insane world.*

He told himself that the misfortunes of others would be his misfortunes. Once more, he would feel for all human beings, as his religious convictions had taught him. Reprieved from his obsession with his nose, he would reclaim a view of life embracing perspective and wisdom and sanctity of purpose.

"Blessed art thou, O Lord," he cried out suddenly, stretching out his arms to clasp to his bosom the heavens.

As a very young man, good-looking and from a fine family, he had taken for granted that life would be a bounteous banquet table, rich and fulfilling. So that, after such a drought of suffering, the return of his good feelings brought him back to familiar ground. And yet it was unfamiliar, for the fervency of his appreciation was alien to the days of his youth, and cake from the same grain tasted so much sweeter.

Alone, he walked barefoot on the sand washed by the sea, his footprints starkly outlined, then erased by the waves that marched forward and receded. "It is good to be alive," he shouted. "Blessed art thou, O Lord, Ruler of the Universe."

The Frenchman vowed that he would take action on the words of the Greek philosopher Epictetus, "Lead the good life and habit will make it pleasant."

But he would do more; pleasure for himself was not sufficient. His religious teachings schooled him to give as well as to receive and, yes, he would aspire to live in a spirit of brotherliness, involved with the affairs of others, too, breathing compassion for all of humanity, dedicated to enriching the spirit of the human race with deeds as well as thoughts.

"Truly," cried out the Chevalier de St. Thoan, "existence itself is the most sacred blessing."

Bathed in the glow of his sweet feelings, he recalled the surgeon who had created them. His personal savior, Doctor Tagliacozzi.

He castigated himself for his insensitivity, that he could applaud his rediscovered self-esteem and fill in the rosy image of his future while his benefactor was—where?

Shamelessly, he had run away while soldiers of the Church encircled Tagliacozzi's house. And where was his comrade-in-arms? In prison, awaiting prosecution by the Inquisition?

Of a sudden, St. Thoan hated himself. *Do I believe in my wonderful human values,* he reflected, *or am I a hypocrite? My study of the Bible, of the great philosophers of ages past—is it all a sham? I breathe the fresh air of the sea and, feeling free and whole, I exult and my spirit takes wings. But how can I accept the joys of my freedom if the man who liberated me suffocates beneath the pressure of the Roman Church? I am an abominable ingrate.*

He could not, the Frenchman decided, keep faith with himself if he could not help the surgeon in his time of trouble.

He could not indulge himself in pleasure while his benefactor was oppressed.

He could not desert a dear brother in his hour of need—and he would not.

And yet, if he were to return to Bologna, he would not be helping his brother; instead, he would be hammering the nail in Gasparo's coffin.

It was late afternoon and the sun was setting. It was a small orange ball now, and soon it would be gone. The waters of the Mediterranean were placid and the Chevalier was magnetized by the natural beauty that enchanted his eyes.

Barefoot, he prayed to God for guidance.

In his house was the Holy Bible, which he read often. He turned to Proverbs 4:5-7 and digested again the wise counsel of King Solomon:

> Get wisdom, get understanding: . . . and with all thy getting get understanding. . . .
> Extol her, and she will exalt thee; she will bring thee to honor, when thou dost embrace her.

But, Lord I do understand, mused St. Thoan, *I understand that I cannot respect myself when I flee in terror, leaving my noble brother to suffer in solitude.*
He leafed through the Bible to Psalm 70 and read:

> Make haste, O God, to deliver me; make haste to help me, O Lord.
> Let them be ashamed and confounded that seek after my soul; let them be turned backward, and put to confusion, that desire my hurt. . . .
> Let all those that seek thee rejoice and be glad in thee: and let such as love thy salvation say continually, Let God be magnified.
> But I am poor and needy: make haste unto me, O God: thou art my help and my deliverer; O Lord, make no tarrying.

Gasparo, your peace of mind is my peace of mind. But how can I go to you? It would mean death for both of us.

Chapter 23

The Censor of Books was in an expansive mood. The symptom of headache had not afflicted him since his visit to the Tagliacozzi country home. He smiled easily and exchanged gibes with other Church officials. With or without St. Thoan, he felt that his prosecution of his childhood companion could not fail. His witnesses awaited their cues; his evidence was substantial. The day of the trial approached, and he savored the imminent triumph.

Flaminio had systematically crushed the will of the prisoner, or so he conjectured. Isolated from the other prisoners, on a diet barely sufficient to sustain life, Gasparo was denied visitors by order of Vulpi; even his wife was not permitted to see him.

Daily, the fat, petulant guard reported to his superior on the prisoner's condition. When he told him about Gasparo's screaming and banging on the walls, Flaminio beamed. When the guard said that he found the surgeon unconscious on the cold stone floor, Vulpi, deducing that the time was ripe, instructed his subordinate to take Gasparo from the cell and escort him to a special room in the Garisenda Tower of the Castello San Angelo, used on occasion by officers of the Inquisition.

Gasparo found himself seated on a chair in the semidarkness, the chamber illuminated by a single shaft of light shooting through a windowlike aperture located high up near the ceiling, the concentrated light causing him to blink rapidly, for many days in his cell had accustomed his eyes to almost no light at all and this shaft was aimed directly at him.

"I am sorry," said Flaminio blandly, "that we meet again under such distressing circumstances."

"Your deep concern overwhelms me," said Gasparo, and the Inquisition official was disturbed to note the hearty ring in his voice.

"The situation, however, can change for the better."

"I hope so," said Gasparo carefully.

"Remember the days of our youth? You returned with your father from Geneva, Switzerland, and related a story about a man who was burned at the stake."

"A brilliant scientist. A man who discovers something new in medicine should be honored."

Flaminio frowned; he had anticipated humiliating an already crushed man. "Not if he is against the Church."

"Helping mankind is sacred to the Church."

"Under certain circumstances."

"Ah, but there should be no conditions attached to helping the sick. You should know this, for your father was a doctor."

"And a dear friend of *your* father's," said Flaminio, puzzled, putting on a show of cordiality to hide his confusion.

"They respected each other."

"They went to church regularly."

"And what did they pray for?"

"For their souls."

"They prayed for love and compassion," said Gasparo, who had devoted himself to meditation during his lonely, miserable days in prison. "We live in an age of renaissance. When Michelangelo painted the ceiling of the Sistine Chapel, he portrayed love and compassion. When he saw a huge block of stone in a quarry he said he saw Moses there. He chipped away pieces of stone for days—weeks— months—two years, and, finally, he gave us *Moses*. Love and compassion created this work of art."

"For the glory of the Mother Church."

The surgeon glowed with pride, the blanket of fear and depression falling away from him. He was passing the test; solitary confinement had weakened his body somewhat, but his spirit had not been conquered. "For the glory of the divine spirit in man to live creatively and achieve fulfillment. And when he reaches this plateau of fulfillment, without destructiveness or violence, he expresses the godlike quality within him."

"Your philosophy is radical."

"There is nothing radical in compassion."

"We must protect those who stray."

"And Leonardo da Vinci was straying when he gave us the flying machine?"

"It will never come to pass."

"I believe it will, for man's greatest quality is his imagination. In this glorious era of human achievement, some men are creative; but others are destructive, instigating violence, hatred, wars, mutilations—destructive forces of evil. It is our duty to alert mind and soul to resist these evil forces and to search ardently for our nobility of spirit." The words were pouring from Gasparo now, and he marveled at the flow; even to himself, had he ever articulated his ideas with such clarity?

Flaminio paced the room. Imprisonment had not softened the fibers of his adversary's convictions; the shaft of light, blinding, and powerful, had not intimidated him.

"Those sound like the heretical words of Pomponazzi."

"He wrote of man and the world as he found them, not as they ought to be. There is goodness in this world despite the violence and other forms of evil, and religion is useful to society only insofar as it achieves a measure of goodness. Am I in the house of my brother? Am I in the house of evil? Am I in God's house of peace or am I in a dungeon of hatred with thumbscrews waiting for me?"

"I do my job as a servant of the Inquisition."

"And I do my physician's job as a servant of God."

"Blasphemy. You have thwarted authority, scoffed at the papal decree. Confess!"

"I have nothing to confess. I repair the wounds of war—wars that should never exist—wounds that one Christian inflicts upon another—making man whole again and through it removing the cleft in his heart and soul, giving him back his spirit, his image, his image in God's image."

"I prefer to call it conceit."

"If helping a mutilated human being who has lost his wings is conceit, then I am conceited. If helping others, not destroying them, is conceit, then I am conceited. And what have you here?" The surgeon pointed to the shaft of light and to a chair with thick ropes. "A torture chamber. For whom? For me? No. For yourself. When you torture me, you torture yourself."

"I uphold the teachings of the Church."

"Thinking you are a Savonarola? He was a mad fanatic, who burned at the stake. The Church eliminated Savonarola."

Flaminio ambled past a crucifix hanging over a wooden bench. "This will not happen to me, I assure you."

"But to me?"

"I hope not. If you confess—"

"There is nothing to confess."

"We have the soldier from Paris in our custody," lied Flaminio. "You operated on him."

"Then why bother with me?"

"I can save you."

"Only to destroy me."

"No," said the Censor of Books evasively. "Remember, our families were devoted to each other."

"And once you had the character of your father," said Gasparo. He had anticipated imprisonment and questioning by the Inquisition for so long—and with such terror—that he was astonished to grasp how well he was surviving the ordeal, and as Flaminio lunged, he would parry and counterattack. "He was an honored doctor until he came under the control of Abizio Pepoli. He wanted you to follow in his footsteps. You would have been an illustrious physician."

"I hated his profession—and his books."

"But he used his agile fingers for good, until Pepoli forced him to compromise his principles."

"Like your father, who wanted you to be a weaver. You, too, could have saved your soul."

The surgeon stared in wonderment; never would he comprehend fully the complexity of human beings. Flaminio, cold, vindictive, inhumanly suave, distorted, this was the Censor of Books; but there was the other side of Flaminio, the side he had enjoyed as a youth. The sadistic Inquisition official prosecuting him was also sincere and companionable; it was unnerving, and somehow it was very very sad.

"I preferred surgery," Gasparo mumbled. "You see, Flaminio, we are both headstrong."

"Yes, of course. But you fancy yourself a giant, while I am a midget," said Vulpi, lapsing into sarcasm. But, of a sudden, he was back in childhood, reminiscing, an excited gleam in his eyes. "Remember the time—that enormous crowd gathered in the public square near the Fountain of Neptune? We were ten years old."

"Ladies in their gay silks and white ruffs, beggars, merchants, priests, prostitutes with painted faces. You were standing next to two Dominican friars."

"And you were near Count Abizio Pepoli, who had lost his nose in a duel; he was seated on a fine white stallion. What was the name of that barber quack?"

"Bartoli."

"Ah, yes—gaudy robe, a rusty dagger in its filthy sheath. His words come back to me: 'Ladies and gentlemen . . . I am the famous Professor Bartoli, who repairs noses with remarkable skill . . . noses lost in the war and from the French disease. I make new noses better than the old ones. I am known to all you higher and lower persons. I have cured one emperor, two kings, four dukes, and seven princes, as well as the brother of the Turkish emperor. Those who need my services step forward and I shall help you.' He said something like that."

"He spotted a beggar without a nose. The poor fellow tried to run, but Pepoli ordered one of his *bravi* to stop him and take him to the quack. He was figuring that if Bartoli could help the beggar he could help *him*. Wretched beggar!"

"Two acrobats pinned him down. The charlatan removed rusty dagger from sheath and made an incision with his knife. The beggar screamed as if he were dying. Bartoli struck his victim on the head with a pistol, knocking him unconscious."

"Then he proceeded with the operation," said Gasparo. "He cut a cylindrical piece of skin from the arm and attached it to the stump of the nose with stitches, claiming that in two weeks the bandage would be removed and the beggar would have a new nose. But the procedure was wrong."

It was as if they had resumed their childhood friendship; with animation, with teamwork, companionably, they brought back jointly an adventurous spectacle that had thrilled them, and with it the warmth that had once cemented their relationship. But this was for merely a fleeting moment, and the fun they had shared made their enmity all the more tragic.

"Of course," snapped Flaminio, "Bartoli was an enemy of the Church. He was a sorcerer and should have been burned at the stake for witchcraft."

"He had no skill and didn't perform the operation correctly. No skin graft could live completely detached from the arm."

"He was a charlatan and received just punishment. He worked against the will of Our Lord, a sorcerer in league with the Devil."

"And you would like to see *me* punished?"

"I come as a friend."

"With malice and hatred."

"With compassion and love."

"You mouth words," said the surgeon, "but what do you know about compassion and love? Did you forget our first fight when we were young?"

"I shall never forget."

"And you will never forgive. We were singing songs as the carriage careened over the bumpy road leading to the country. Giulia was there, and Scipio. A wheel passed over a rock, throwing Scipio against you. You struck him and shouted, 'How dare you come near me, you creature of the Devil!' I punched you in the face. We fought and I warned you not to strike him again."

Restless at the discomfiting memory, Flaminio moved about the darkened room, bypassing the blinding shaft of light, trudging heavily past the crucifix and a lighted candle, swinging around the straight-backed chair with heavy ropes coiled on the seat. "He was possessed by the Devil," he said finally.

"He was born with that hole in his lip. He didn't ask to look that way."

"He was suffering from the sins committed by his ancestors."

"It could happen to a king, a prince, a beggar. You hated him because he was black."

"He and his family represent the Black Angel of Destruction."

"That is bigoted. His parents came, in truth, from noble Moorish ancestry."

"Driven from Spain, the infidels."

"They were devout Christians and attended church regularly. Giulia's parents, desiring to protect them, took them into their home as servants."

"Misguided people."

Gasparo's eyes were closed, but the blinding light outlined the firmness of his chin beneath the sharp-pointed beard. "It was as if a hole had been bored in the center of Scipio's lip. Through it his front teeth were visible."

"He looked like a dog."

"A human being overcome with loneliness and despair. It must have been an ordeal for him to see his reflection in a mirror. How many times he must have dreamed that he looked like other children, not stuttering and hissing, no need to cover his mouth with his hand. Still, his parents loved him all the more. And you, a pillar of the Church, what were your thoughts?"

"I believed there were black witches and sorcerers in his family, and that the affliction was punishment for their heinous sins. Beyond question, I was correct in my opinion. Is this not transparently clear?"

"Ridiculous. Scipio is a man now—a splendid human being—and you still think he is bewitched?"

"That is my considered opinion," said the Censor of Books, but his thinking was not so confident. *Why*, he mused, *do I again suffer from headache?*

At this moment, a furor raged at the university. Dissatisfied by the incarceration of their professor, grumbling at the futility of their peaceful demonstration on the day he was escorted to his basement dungeon, the students were now up in arms, ignited by a recent development.

They had discovered that one of their number, a religious zealot, was an informer for the Censor of Books, the intermediary a Dominican friar residing at the monastery. At this, the leader of the main body of students seized the law in his own hands. Hiding in the shadow of the monastery at nightfall, he waited patiently. The suspect approached and the friar, slipping out the door, engaged him in conversation. The leader heard them plotting how to obtain perjured testimony against the surgeon and, enraged, leaped out from ambush to stab them with his stiletto, killing them both instantly.

"It will be a warning to the Church," said the leader to his cohorts, back on campus, "that we will not tolerate the continued persecution of Doctor Tagliacozzi."

The other students were aghast at the double killing, but more determined than ever to effect the release of their professor. The leader fled to escape punishment, but Count Lorenzo Desiri, who had won acclaim for his role during the peaceful demonstration, took charge.

"We will butcher the arrogant officialdom of the Church," roared Lorenzo. "If they do not release Gasparo, we will separate these fellows from their heads."

Once again, the students set out for the Castello San Angelo, but this time they were a mob, carrying sticks and torches in their hands and loaded down with bricks and daggers and stilettos.

Waving his pistol, ringed by his most trusted *bravi*, Lorenzo urged them forward. "We will demand the release of Gasparo," he thundered. "Let us hope they exercise wisdom."

From the Garisenda Tower, Flaminio peered through an oblong aperture at the disorderly mob. "Your loving students of the university," he said. "They have erred—like you."

The chants of the students wafted up to the Chamber of the Inquisition.

"Free Tagliacozzi."

"This outrage must be rectified, and we question the authority of the Church for perpetrating it. Does this reflect the will of God?"

Gasparo smiled. "They do not fight for me, but for truth and self-respect—for mine, even for yours."

"Many will be hurt needlessly."

"But they are willing to die for freedom of expression."

Far below, the infuriated students marched and countermarched, singing and shouting threats, waving sticks and daggers and bricks.

"They will not gain entrance," said Flaminio. "Our portals are too stout and soldiers of the Church stand guard, heavily armed."

But, below, near the fortress, flames were leaping high, sizzling, crackling.

"Idiots," barked Flaminio. "They are idiots to start a fire. It will avail them nothing."

"We will burn down the Inquisition fortress," shouted one student. "We will murder the officials of the Church."

But one hour later the fire had died down and the mob had dispersed.

Gasparo tried to open his eyes but the shaft of light was too powerful. Closing them, he sat in the chair and addressed Vulpi. "*You* have erred. *You* have walked away from the reality of the world into dark tunnels in your mind. *You* have walked away from God toward the Black Angel of Destruction. I was forced into a dungeon of torture but *you*, of your own free will, have walked into a black dungeon in your mind and in your heart. Who speaks for God—you or me?"

"That we shall find out shortly," said Flaminio. "When *you* are brought to trial and prosecuted, as you merit. All your assertions now, they mean nothing."

"You lived a solitary existence for years," continued Gasparo, paying no heed. "You were seized with attacks of melancholia. We found out about them, and about how, shrieking and wailing, you went mad."

"Fantasy."

"Reality. You saw yourself in a vision, screaming, as you stood before a blazing bonfire directing the burning of all pomps and vanities, encompassing the destruction of all heretical books and pamphlets."

"I admit having these visions."

"Fra Chiari helped you through your illness. He designated you as Inquisitor, with authority to scrutinize all books and to approve them or ban them."

"I am the head of the Inquisition in Bologna; as such, I owe a debt of gratitude to Fra Chiari."

"Seeking revenge."

"Perhaps," said Flaminio. "But, since you refuse to confess to me, I will confess to you. I have carried a secret within me for many years—my scar." He pointed to his eyebrow and, voice muted, continued. "It has turned me into another human being, isolating me from the rest of humanity. I do not feel whole, but like Scipio did before your operation."

"And you tell me this in a dungeon of torture?"

"How could I tell you about it before now? Gasparo, can you repair it?"

"Yes, but why do *you* want it done?"

"That is my secret. I was not sure what occupation to pursue when my father urged me to become a physician. But after this, I decided to enter the ranks of the Church."

"I am astonished."

"This will amaze you more. Before receiving this scar, I was in love with Giulia, and I carried this love with me into the Dominican monastery. Images of Giulia's beauty would invade my senses. In repentance, I would beat myself in an agony of flagellation."

"Operating on you, how would this help?"

"It would bring me back to what I was. But, on second thought, I would not have the courage."

The surgeon was shaking his head in bewilderment, for the contradictions in his old companion's statements left him grasping in futility for the real essence of the man. His complexities, his swift turnabouts, the range of his evasions; what could he believe?

"You play cat and mouse," he said finally. "Why do you not be truthful? You did not love Giulia. But you still love me, do you not?"

"Yes, I do love you, even now. And I hate myself for it. Oh, I flagellate myself, but there is no possible release for me except—"

"To do away with me?"

Flaminio's face hardened. "I must do my job. Moreover, you have sinned."

"You have."

"Only you know the secret."

"And so I am expendable."

"There is no other way."

"Hiding behind the Church to destroy me."

"No alternative is open to me."

"You are evil," said Gasparo, eyes open, squinting as the torrent of light battered his face. "God will punish *you*—not me."

"I have the power," said Flaminio, and once again his eyes were as cold as ice.

"The scar on your eyebrow is superficial. Deep inside of you—in your mind, in your heart—lies the scar that mutilates you and shrinks the substance in your soul. But your scheme will not work."

"Ah, but it will."

"You will never be able to face yourself. Your despair will drive you mad." Suddenly, Gasparo overrode his outrage and said craftily, "Release me, for you will be free only when I am free."

Flaminio's manner was now tinged with self-pity. "Either way I will never be free. For, in any case, I loathe myself for not destroying my feeling for you."

"*You* are the Black Angel of Destruction."

"My love, my hate—they are the only purposes I can reach."

"You want revenge because you are lonely."

"You oversimplify," said Flaminio, but he was thoughtful. "Perhaps I envy you. Fulfilling yourself by helping people, you have somewhere to go. But what of me?"

"Go back to yourself, to the warmhearted, understanding youth who was my best childhood friend. In a world seething with violence, your responsibility in your calling is to overcome this in yourself. And the Church teaches that compassion is the basis of all morality."

"Do you not think that I am in a better position than you to know what the Church teaches?"

"I wonder." Gasparo's eyes were once more closed to the penetrating push of light and he spoke softly, as if to himself. "Flaminio, why not be your own surgeon? Use not a knife but the healing power of compassion to remove the evil inside you. Redeem yourself; cut out this disease from the depths of your soul. I speak to you as the young boy who, years back in childhood, was your devoted friend."

"My power, I rely on this alone."

"Remember what your father told us when we were children?

About the preferability of a modest understanding over a great misunderstanding?"

"I know all that, but I am what I am—it is my fate. And now, my dear old friend, before it is too late, you must purge yourself of this evil, of this black heresy, operating against the decrees of the Papacy. Confess that you operated on a heretic. Confess and discharge your conscience. For it is *you* who are guilty. Confess."

"You must—not me!"

Restlessly the Censor of Books walked past the crucifix and the lighted candle, and turning around to face the surgeon, agitation spurting from his eyes, hands shaking in excitement, the words came pouring out of him. "I confess now that you had the qualities I never had—confidence, courage, and the persistence to do something new. I hated you for it. Yes, I confess this. Never was I anything, but now I am the most powerful official in the City of Bologna, and I wish to remind you of this at this moment."

He clapped his hands and, at the signal, two uniformed guards entered and awaited his instructions. Flaminio nodded his head and the soldiers of the Church seized the prisoner, dragging him from the chair in the light to the chair with the heavy ropes. They tied him rigidly into it, pulling back fiercely on the ropes so that arms and legs were immobilized. Then, upon another abrupt nod from their superior, they began attaching mechanisms to the thumbs of both of Gasparo's hands. These instruments of torture, thumbscrews, were employed by the Inquisition to elicit confessions from prisoners.

Flaminio nodded his head again, and at his signal the guards began tightening the screws. Unable to watch, the Censor of Books turned away, walking to the crucifix, where he began to pray.

The surgeon paled and, as sporadically during his internment in the prison cell, doubts of his capacity to survive assailed him. "Flaminio," he said urgently, brown eyes bulging with fear, "where is the respect you felt for yourself when you were very young and oblivious to the meaning of hate? You know in your heart that I am innocent. Do you not see that when you hate me you hate yourself? Do you not understand that in losing respect for my rights, you surrender—nay, discard—your respect for yourself? Do you not remember that once you agreed with your father, when he was an observant and righteous man and an illustrious physician? A true Christian believes that faith and reason can walk happily together to the glory of God and the majesty of the Holy Mother Church."

But at the crucifix Vulpi was kneeling, lost in prayer.

"Flaminio," pleaded Gasparo. "Once we were like brothers, Flaminio."

But compression of his thumbs was firing his nerve ends with pains that he could not endure. Finally, he began moaning and struggling to burst his bonds and then, as the pressure intensified, he was screaming, unleashing his agony to take by storm the ears of his persecutor.

Flaminio did not hear. Kneeling in front of the crucifix, clasping his hands in front of him, a beatific glow illuminating his eyes, he prayed aloud, in resonant tones. "I do my duty, O Lord," he said in Latin. "In your name do I demand punishment for this blaspheming sinner."

Gasparo was unconscious, head slumped forward on his chest, and Flaminio asked the two guards to leave.

Of a sudden, a wave of repentance cascaded over him. *My poor old friend,* he thought, and quickly he loosened the ropes binding him to the chair, hurling them onto the stark wooden bench at the far end of the torture chamber. Then he drew a drape across the windowlike aperture, shutting out the blinding light, plunging the room into almost total darkness, only the sputtering candle providing a flicker of light.

He felt pure, cleansed of hate, and glancing at the surgeon, he thought only of the good times they had shared as small boys and of how they had confided their most precious secrets.

Disturbingly, an unpleasant memory intruded: his father, forlorn and dispirited, compelled to forsake his professional ideals by the ruthless Abizio Pepoli, moving around the living room late at night, plagued with insomnia, drowning in guilt, inadequate to cope with the responsibilities of fatherhood.

And then an even more alarming image: his mother, looking at him with shining eyes and—vanishing. Where had she gone? Why had she deserted him? In truth, she had died when Flaminio was a very young child, but to Flaminio's child's eyes it had been an act of desertion, and never would he forgive her. But, then, he had buried his image of her so deep in his mind that almost never did it emerge.

Again, I suffer from this infernal headache, Vulpi thought, and he cursed the ailment and the accompanying dizziness and nausea.

Suddenly, he felt an overwhelming affection for Gasparo. He wanted to come close to him and touch his flesh. Impulsively, he reached out to stroke his forehead and then to smooth back his hair. "You *are* my brother," he murmured, "and Our Lord approves of your goodness."

Bending over the unconscious prisoner, he kissed his forehead lightly and—he did not know why—this aroused him and he could no longer control himself.

Flaminio rushed to lock and bolt the door and then swept back to the unconscious man in the chair. He lifted Gasparo's gray cotton prison robe and stared, fascinated, at his penis. He touched it fleetingly and caressed it more slowly, lovingly.

Flaminio felt the blood catapulting wildly through his body as gently he massaged the thighs of his childhood friend, stroking his testicles and his penis, swelling and hardening with his touch. He threw himself on his knees so that he could kiss the erect penis and suck it, and in his ardor, he felt the stirrings in his own loins, the vibrations filling him with a desperate ecstasy that excited him so much that he feared he was going mad. Finally, Gasparo exploded and at that instant Flaminio felt the wild rhythm of his own orgasm.

Unsteadily he rose to his feet a few moments later and now only anguish surfaced in his consciousness. *What have I done?* he asked himself. *What insanity came over me?*

But then he wiped Gasparo's penis dry with a cloth, pulled down the prison robe, and examined his own costume to make sure no stain was visible.

Afterward, he dispatched a messenger to fetch the fat, sulky guard and one of the specialists at torture. The pair lifted up the prisoner and carried him back to his cell in the isolated sector of the basement.

In his own office, the Church official seated himself at his desk and initiated examination of a fresh manuscript, a dissertation speculating upon the potency of theriac made of vipers caught in late spring and, still more unorthodox and heretical, arguing that theriac had not been proved effective in preventing plague during an epidemic.

But Flaminio could not concentrate on the subject matter. Instead, he found himself battling to overcome his self-loathing. *I am nothing but an animal,* he scolded himself. *How can I forgive myself for my sin?*

He stuffed the manuscript in a desk drawer and leaned back in the chair. *Still,* he reasoned, *I have always lived virtuously. My life has been distinguished by propriety and devotion to Our Lord. Only Gasparo has excited such disgusting propensities in me.*

Relief flooded the harsh contours of his face, and the grim, tight lines of his lips softened. *Yes, the Devil is in him, and so long as he lives his presence will embroil me in danger. He will not confess and renounce his sorcery so, in your name, Lord, I must effectuate his punishment. Goodness must prevail and, dear God, I swear that I will do my duty. Once I have exterminated the Devil from his body, no more will I be contaminated by such unholy desires.*

Chapter 24

The Tagliacozzi trial was conducted in a long, rectangular stone hall in the crypt of the Castello San Angelo, employed frequently as a chamber for Inquisition proceedings. It was a spacious auditorium, regal and substantial, with ceilings towering to a height of perhaps thirty or forty feet, massive pink pillars on each side, four to the left, four to the right, engraved and topped by white stone arches with bright-red borders. The walls were painted an austere white, relieved by the pillared arches and by sputtering torches in ornamental sconces. Dozens of torches were required to illuminate the huge courtroom; they were scattered throughout the hall, but concentrated at the front, near the rostrum for key officials of the Inquisition.

Flaminio Vulpi, promoter at the trial, was seated at a long table in this area, reading a document. "Hand me the remainder of this accusation," he said, not looking up, to a Dominican friar serving as notary.

"It has not arrived yet."

"What?" The Censor of Books raised his head to stare at the theologian sitting next to him. "How can this be?"

"Brother Nicholas has not yet finished his transcription."

"What detains him? I should have had these papers yesterday."

"He has been working on them all night, Father," said the notary. "The Inquisitor General did not return the accusation until late yesterday."

Nearby was an hourglass, a double-compartmented glass vessel, and Flaminio turned to study it. "The court will be in session by noon. Send for Brother Nicholas at once; he can finish his transcription here. I must see how many more of these charges have been eliminated."

The notary whispered to a boy serving as page, and the boy hurried off while the Censor of Books continued to peruse the document. Finally, jumping up from his chair, he hurled the paper onto the table in disgust.

"They will finish by offering him an apology," he snarled. "Are the confiscated belongings of the accused here for exhibition?"

Another pageboy, arms full of books and scrolls, approached the table.

"Ah, they are just arriving," said the notary. "On the table, please, my boy."

"Find the book," said Flaminio, "in which he describes and illustrates the ingenious way he has of torturing his victims."

The notary leafed through the assortment of documents on the table. The courtroom was filling, teen-aged messengers bustling among the Inquisition officials, soldiers of the Church taking their stations at key positions throughout the room, a babble of voices humming in the air as townspeople arrived to view the proceedings.

At the table for Church officials representing the prosecution, Flaminio turned as another member of the Dominican Order entered with some documents. "Brother Nicholas," he said, "at last! You have been an unconscionable time."

"I am sorry, Father," said Brother Nicholas. "The heat. I kept falling asleep."

"Let me have them now."

"Yes," said Brother Nicholas, and he delivered the papers to the Censor of Books.

"Is this all you have?"

"Why, yes, Father."

"But this is impossible."

"I did notice that the weight of the document was somewhat reduced when it came back from the Inquisitor General."

"Imbecile!"

"Sorry, Father."

"Get on with the transcription," snapped Flaminio, his lips tight with rage, pacing back and forth past his assistants at the table.

"Yes, Father," said Brother Nicholas, "immediately." He was perspiring and kept pausing in his work to mop his face with a napkin tucked away in a pocket of his flowing robe.

"It is warm," said the notary, also seated at the table, "is it not, Brother Nicholas?"

"Very sultry, even for this season of the year."

"Thunder," said the notary, looking upward toward the ceiling high above, as if to see the rumbling, crackling noise registering on his ears. "Thunder."

"I am sure I felt a mild quake this morning."

"In your sleep, Brother Nicholas?"

Brother Nicholas focused his attention on his transcription duties, while the notary, apprehensive as he observed Vulpi striding back and forth muttering oaths under his breath, remained silent.

The Inquisitor General arrived, striding past the assistants to confront the scowling Censor of Books. "Good morning, Fra Vulpi. You seem worried. Is there anything troubling you?"

Curtly, Flaminio handed him the sheaf of documents. "What is the meaning of this?"

"Excuse me a moment," said the Inquisitor General, calling for a messenger. "Here, boy."

"Yes, Inquisitor General?" said the page.

"Put these vellums in order for the Fiscal Promoter and arrange them on his desk."

"Certainly, Inquisitor General," said the messenger, walking to a nearby table ringed by other Church officials.

"Now, Fra Vulpi," said the dignitary, "how can I help you?"

Flaminio stood rigid, hands clenched at his sides. "I compiled an accusation for the Fiscal to present to this Holy Office and sent it to you for approval. On its return to me, I find that nearly half of the articles have been removed."

"Yes, that is true," said the Inquisitor General. "We decided to confine the accusation to charges of heresy, repudiation of his medical oath, and contempt for and obstruction of the Holy Office of the Inquisition, and, of course, perjury."

"Perjury?" whispered Flaminio, and rage poured hot and naked from his eyes. "The man is a sorcerer. Why, the main part of my case depends upon his being convicted of sorcery. He is guilty, and he must burn."

"You must not let your zeal carry you away, my brother."

"I have been guided solely by a desire to defend the Church for the glory of God, and to discharge my duty as a good Christian and an officer of the Inquisition."

"Yes, I know. But, Fra Vulpi, we must be quite sure of our facts."

"I can prove my accusations to the satisfaction of this court."

"If he is a sorcerer he will burn, rest assured of that. But we must be careful to *prove* that he is a sorcerer. And, by the way, have you arranged for an advocate to defend him?"

"He prefers to speak in his own defense, though why he should be allowed to do so is beyond my understanding."

"What more could you ask, my brother?" said the Inquisitor General. "A man who holds such radical views of medicine and philosophy as does Gasparo Tagliacozzi cannot help but incriminate himself. You will be grateful to him, I am convinced."

"Grossly irregular," snapped Flaminio, his teeth hard and sharp against his gums. "The whole proceeding. This was to have been a closed trial. I heard only this morning that it is thrown open, and the accused is to be confronted with witnesses."

"Cardinal Bandini is undoubtedly in a far better position to relieve your mind on those points than I am."

"Is Bandini coming here?"

"He has sent word that he will preside."

"Why this unseemly interest? He has not been present at a trial of faith for more than a year. This is monstrous—this interference. He is deliberately tying my hands."

"Patience," counseled the Inquisitor General, "have patience. It would be foolish to bring the wrath of Rome upon our heads when your case is so strong as it now stands. The justice of the Church is not a travesty."

"My case was doubly strong before you deleted half the articles of accusation. I have spent years gathering incriminating evidence, and with one stroke of the pen it is practically destroyed. Justice! How can you expect me to bring him to justice if I am not permitted the foolproof charge of sorcery and to advance these books, these diagrams, these—"

The Censor of Books felt a mounting frustration. There was a bitter taste in his mouth, his stomach felt acid, his chest muscles were as rigid as a rope pulled taut, and, once again, he suffered from headache. Abruptly, he turned to Brother Nicholas. "Where are the instruments?"

But he received no answer and, indeed, a hush enveloped the assemblage congregated in the Inquisition's chamber of justice. The papal Vice-Legate, Cardinal Bandini, had arrived.

Bandini was a commanding figure. His stride was brisk and his posture was almost military as, accompanied by an entourage of subordinates, he made a dramatic entrance. An indomitable will surged forth from his face—piercing brown eyes; high, firm cheekbones; sturdy, outthrust chin—and yet, as if in contradiction, a smile hovered about his lips, softening the impact of his personality. The respectful stillness greeting his appearance had been punctuated only by Flaminio's angry outburst and, taking his place on the rostrum, he directed his initial remarks to the Censor of Books.

"Pray continue," he said. "I seem to have arrived at an opportune moment. Did I hear you mention sorcery, Fra Vulpi?"

Flaminio bowed and carefully moderated his tone. "Can you tell me, Lord Cardinal, why the charge of sorcery was eliminated from the accusation?"

Cardinal Bandini leaned forward in his seat. He was dressed simply, wearing no ornamentation, in a long, flowing white robe overlaid with a dark-red fold over chest and shoulders, a red skullcap trimmed with white perched almost jauntily on his head.

"How pale you look this morning, Fra Vulpi," he said, and his manner was benign. "Did you not sleep well last night? Or is this a recurrence of your miseries with headache? Can I recommend to you my personal physician?"

"I am feeling perfectly well," said Flaminio, uncomfortable, "thank you, my Lord Cardinal."

"Extraordinary how pale you are. It must be the heat."

"May we confine ourselves to the case in point?"

"Why, certainly. Oh, but I remember, you do not like physicians, do you?"

Unsuccessfully, Flaminio struggled to control his irritation. "I do not like sorcerers," he said finally.

"Neither do I, Fra Vulpi," said the Cardinal, his forehead creased with wrinkles, his eyes stern, and it was as if he had said, *I have had my little joke. Now let us transact the business of the Mother Church.* He asked for the documents and examined them minutely. "The evidence in most of the articles of accusation seems fairly conclusive."

"It is absolutely."

"Have you examined the evidence, Inquisitor General?"

"I have, my Lord," said this dignitary. "It was unnecessary to depend upon the usual two hearsay witnesses."

"We dispensed with hearsay witnesses," said Flaminio sulkily, "using only eye or ear witnesses; in some instances we have the double testimony of both."

"I congratulate you, Fra Vulpi," said Bandini. "You must have spent considerable time on this case."

"Nearly all my life."

"And you have known Gasparo Tagliacozzi personally?"

"We were at school together."

"Of course, it is superfluous to ask if personal feelings have influenced you in these matters?"

"I bear no malice toward the prisoner. My only purpose is to save his soul from perdition."

"Very commendable of you," said Bandini, and his eyes reflected a sophistication and emotional balance uncommon in many of his rank. "The evidence of heresy is overwhelming and it should prove simple to bring him to justice or confession. Yet I must caution you that your task is not easy. You are dealing with a brilliant man."

"Who used his talents for evil. It would have been much easier to bring him to justice if this had been a closed ecclesiastical tribunal instead of an open court."

"There I disagree with you, my friend. It is necessary that the people of Bologna realize there can be no trafficking in the justice of the Church. They must believe in the absolute sincerity of our condemnation. Now, I understand there was an attempt to rescue the accused recently from the Castello San Angelo?"

"There was."

"I do not say this critically," said the Cardinal, and his tone was measured, his manner both probing and respectful, "but our worthy Pontiff does not like to hear that the students of his favorite university are rioting over the so-called persecution of their beloved tutor."

"A handful of undeveloped youths bewitched by Tagliacozzi's new-hatched radical theories," scoffed Flaminio. "They were readily dispersed."

"True, but driven underground, they could gradually become dangerous, a malignant uncontrollable growth. They could then make a show of strength by seceding from the university."

"The City of Bologna would be well rid of such subversive heretical elements."

"I would gladly echo your sentiment, my friend, but this would not solve our problem. It is not quite so simple, and Papa Gregory would not like that at all."

"Might I respectfully inquire why periodically my authority as Promoter in Bologna is undermined? What is this interference that comes from Rome?"

"Not interference, Fra Vulpi—interest!"

The dialogue pressed forward, a disputation of basic principles between the Censor of Books and the papal Vice-Legate. Or was it more meaningful than an articulate skirmish of conflicting egos? Was it the eternal struggle between fanaticism and moderation? Was it the time-honored clash between suppression and revelation, of that invisible, yet oh-so-precious element, unrecognized, unsung, destroyed: truth?

"No matter how much you honey the pill, my Lord," said Flaminio, "it is bitter to realize that all my industry, my devotion, is distrusted and unappreciated."

"No one has ever doubted your sincerity," responded Bandini, "or failed to wonder at the infinite capacity of your burning zeal, which has brought so much honor to you and glory to the Holy Office. Albeit we may find it necessary occasionally to guide, shall I say, the footsteps of our most trustworthy sons."

"The nobles of the Inquisition are not schoolboys to be monitored by Rome."

"Please do not misunderstand. This is not a question of infringement of rights, but just the natural pride and interest of Papa Gregory in Bologna. After all, he was born here, and his pride is, I think, quite normal and justifiable. The university has of late become the most important seat of medicine in Italy, has it not?"

"It has, if that is important."

"It is to Gregory XIII, and should be to you, my friend, considering your sufferings from headache."

"Perhaps you might overlook my complaints of headache in view of the fact that I acquired them in the process of purging this great city of heretics."

"But we must be sure they *are* all heretics, Fra Vulpi. Padua would welcome with open arms any students seceding from this university, and that would be disastrous to His Holiness and to the people of Bologna."

"Remove the master heretic, this sorcerer Tagliacozzi, and you remove the incentive to secede."

"Only if they are convinced of his guilt."

"Have you any doubt, my Lord?"

"Of his heresy, none whatever. As for this sorcery you keep harping on, frankly, this makes me uneasy, for we must not confuse sorcery with medical progress."

"Would that be possible?"

"Perhaps not. Yet why run the risk when another simpler and nonetheless effective way lies open to us?"

"I fear that my dull wits cannot cope with the brilliance of your imagination, my Lord Cardinal."

Cardinal Bandini, representing the Pope, paused to weigh his words. For a moment he closed his eyes, and when he opened them, he seemed to glance slightly upward, over the heads of the people in the courtroom, and perhaps the direction of his gaze was symbolic of his desire to rise above the petty prejudices and violent passions of his time.

"I shall be very direct in my explanation. Science itself, not the Church, is the most formidable opponent of medical progress. Physicians are, as a rule, quite ready to argue against any new theory propounded. It is not because they are deliberately opposed to scientific progress, but that they cannot readily welcome drastic change, or so I assume, for to do so would constitute a tacit admission that they themselves are lacking in perspicacity and powers of observation. Therefore, any acceptable change must be gradual and along accepted lines. The fact that often a young man, who has not yet acquired full knowledge of the great body of science sanctioned by older, established individuals, gives birth to an idea merely adds to the readiness with which his seniors are apt to consider the new proposition absurd. Ecclesiastics have done this also, but not nearly as frequently as scientists would have us believe. If they accuse us of prejudice, verily, they should first take stock of themselves. For instance, there was a teacher of anatomy in Padua some years ago. The name, I think, was Fallopio." Again, closing his eyes, forehead wrinkling, the Cardinal paused to reflect. "Yes, Fallopio. He it was who put forward some very interesting theories regarding childbirth. His colleagues ridiculed him, made his life miserable, unendurable, and he died of a broken heart, or so I have been informed. Tragically, we have recently come to the conclusion that he knew much, indeed, about his subject."

"Fascinating, my Lord Cardinal," said Flaminio, "and you suggest that we—"

"Leave him to his fellows!" thundered the Inquisitor General, who had remained silent during the lengthy dialogue.

"And confront him with his accusers," snapped Flaminio. "Ah, gross irregularity! I *can* prove the charge of sorcery to the satisfaction of this court."

Sighing resignedly, Bandini fanned himself with his hand, the conclusion of his meditations visibly relaxing the muscles of his face. "It is too hot."

"I agree, my Lord," said the Inquisitor General. "Much too oppressive to spend more time than we need to in this stuffy courtroom. Might I respectfully suggest we have the prisoner in." He picked up the hourglass and examined it closely. "According to this, we should have been sitting a half hour since."

"Bring in the accused," said Bandini. "Swear in his accusers. Let us proceed."

"Bring in the accused," bellowed the First Inquisitor. "Gasparo Tagliacozzi."

"Gasparo Tagliacozzi," echoed the sergeant at arms.

Silence filled the courtroom. Anticipating the prisoner's arrival, hundreds of townspeople comprising the audience froze into immobility, statues seated on wooden benches, in red and white and black and yellow and purple costumes, wearing skullcaps and turbans and hoods, some bareheaded, and women with shawls draped over their flowing hair. Sprinkled strategically around the crypt, flasks of vinegar and incense were burning. These were considered preventives of plague but many of the common people, distrusting their efficacy, clutched amulets of theriac.

For the moment, the officials, too, were gripped in a paralytic vise. At the head of the auditorium, in the center, Cardinal Bandini was seated in a chair on an elevated rostrum, a mounted platform commanding a view of the entire assemblage, above him a huge mural with bright-orange background, a Madonna in black robe and hood holding a naked baby, other children at either side.

Below the papal Vice-Legate were the Inquisitor General and the Fiscal, and below them, on the lowest level of the three-tiered rostrum, were two long tables with chairs and here were seated Flaminio Vulpi, Censor of Books, his assistants, and other Church officials. To their right, on the same level, near a massive pillar, was a chair for witnesses giving evidence. To the left of this was a chair for the prisoner. Both chairs were empty but benches in an archway at the left were jammed with witnesses, professors of the University of Bologna, Dominican friars, and other university officials. Spreading out in front of the Pope's representatives were rows upon rows of benches crowded with agitated townspeople and infuriated students. *This hearing must weather many storms,* mused Bandini, and his eyes were reflective and somewhat stern, and yet there remained a benignancy about the set of his lips.

There was not a sound as the accused, hands bandaged, was escorted into the hall by two soldiers of the Church and their leader, Captain General Buoncampagna. The surgeon was marched to his chair and stood in front of it while the soldiers and their commander stationed themselves at the side of the lowest level platform. Trailing them, Giulia, accompanied by Caledonia, Lorenzo, and Scipio, moved to the overcrowded benches in the archway. Giulia and Caledonia managed to find room to sit down, but Lorenzo and Scipio, standing erect, focused their attention on the proceedings.

"What is your name?" asked the First Inquisitor, his voice booming out over the assemblage.

"Gasparo Tagliacozzi." The surgeon, pale, spoke softly, but his carriage was proud and his eyes burned fire.

"How old are you?" thundered the First Inquisitor.

"I am in my fifty-second year."

"Where were you born?"

"In the City of Bologna."

"What is your occupation?"

"Physician and surgeon."

"What is your father's name?"

"Giovanni Andrea."

"His occupation?"

"Weaver of satins and fabrics."

"And," continued the First Inquisitor, "how long since you were arrested?"

"Two weeks."

"Two weeks?" said the First Notary. He turned to look at the Inquisitor General; they talked in hushed tones and then, joined by the Censor of Books, engaged in a more whispered consultation.

"That is quite all right. I believe it was Fra Vulpi who arranged for an immediate trial." Cardinal Bandini said this blandly, but added, "Highly irregular."

"The formal accusation will be read to you," resumed the First Inquisitor, addressing Gasparo. "This is not your first appearance for examination?"

"No."

"You remember the oath you took before the examining tribunal?"

"I do."

"If you wish to change or to add anything to the statements you made on that occasion, you should do so now, according to the oath that you have taken."

Standing erect before the prisoner's chair, shoulders thrown back fiercely, Gasparo stared directly into the eyes of the First Inquisitor. "Everything I have deposed is strictly true. I know nothing more than I have already declared."

The First Inquisitor turned, nodded briefly to the Fiscal, seated on the middle level of the rostrum, and sat down at the table for the Censor of Books and his associates.

Rising, the Fiscal, document in hand, proceeded to read the text of the formal accusation. "The accused, Gasparo Tagliacozzi, being a Christian baptized and confirmed, disregarding the fear of the justice of God and of the Holy Inquisition, with great contempt for religion, scandal of the people, and condemnation of his own soul, has been and is a heretic, an unrepentant, perjured, negative and feigned confessor. He is a blasphemer! He has resisted the officers of the Holy Inquisition and has impeded its jurisdiction. He is a perjurer in that he has persistently refused to confess to these accusations even after taking a solemn oath at his interrogation. He received, one, the Chevalier de Saint Thoan, Huguenot and heretic. He protected him, provided him with lodging, treated him with kindness, and visited him in the course of his profession as a physician.

"He is a heretic himself in that he has expressed himself in a manner unbecoming to a professor of the University of the Papal City of Bologna, and has been found to be neglectful in his devotional duties as a good Catholic.

"I pray to have the accused found guilty of the crimes recited, and wish him condemned to confiscation and his person relaxed to the secular arm to be executed with all rigor, as to serve as a punishment to him and an example to others, and may God have mercy on his soul."

His facial features controlled, expressionless, the surgeon seated himself and folded his bandaged hands across his chest.

But, seated on a bench in the archway to the left of the three-tiered rostrum, Giulia was unable to stifle a sob, and, at her side, Count Lorenzo Desiri, in full-dress armor, seized the handle of his sheathed dagger, as yet another rumble of thunder burst explosively from the heavens, causing townspeople in the audience to cross themselves as they fumbled for their amulets of theriac.

As the Fiscal took his seat, the First Inquisitor, on his feet, assaulted the throng with his stentorian tones. "Gasparo Tagliacozzi, you have heard the accusation. Do you wish to confess before you are confronted with your accusers?"

"I have nothing to confess."

From the upper level of the rostrum, Cardinal Bandini leaned forward to appeal to the prisoner. "Doctor Tagliacozzi, do you not believe in the spiritual comfort and relief that accompanies confession?"

"My conduct has not always conformed to the religion that I profess; nevertheless, I am most passionately attached to the faith of my ancestors."

This statement aroused the wrath of the white-robed, black-hooded Dominicans clustered with the other groups to the left of the rostrum.

"Confess," shouted one friar.

"Clear your heart."

"Purge your soul."

And, in unison the Dominicans chanted, "Confess. Confess."

Flaminio had kept silent for as long as he could. The chorus of voices seemed to fortify his resolve and he asserted stridently, "I demand that he be tortured as long and as often as it might be necessary in order to force him to confess the truth."

"Have you not already resorted to this form of argument?" asked Cardinal Bandini blandly.

"Mildly. To some extent."

"With what result?"

"Negative."

"Torture is not always a sure means of discovering the truth," said Bandini. "Weak men, at the first twinge, confess crimes of which they are not guilty; others support the most exquisite torments. The tortures should not be repeated."

"No, my Lord Cardinal," debated Flaminio, "but they might be continued to some advantage. To continue tortures is much more merciful than to repeat them."

"You have a very pretty wit, Fra Vulpi. The tortures shall not be repeated." The Cardinal's tone was precise; he turned to the accused. "We would be your friends and help you. Will you not confess?"

"No, for I do not feel myself guilty to these charges."

"I see," said Bandini. "But, Doctor Tagliacozzi, why have you refused the services of an advocate so generously offered?"

"I would not place any human being in such a position, where an accidental overzealousness in my defense might bring him under a charge of heresy."

Again, the group of Dominicans exploded, leaping to their feet, enraged, shouting, "Heresy! Blasphemy!"

"Gentlemen," said Bandini, "control yourselves. Consider the dignity of this court."

The temperateness of the papal Vice-Legate was irritating the Censor of Books. "Do you accuse the Church of partiality and double-dealing?" he asked Gasparo, afraid to express his resentment at Bandini.

"Oh, no, I have supreme confidence in the impartiality of the Church."

"I am happy to hear this," said Flaminio sarcastically, mopping perspiration from his forehead. "Call Duglioli, the candlemaker."

"What is your name?" asked the First Inquisitor.

"Simone Duglioli."

"You are a native of Bologna?"

"I was born here."

"And what is your occupation?"

The first witness at the trial was patently uncomfortable. He squirmed miserably in the witness chair. The First Inquisitor's booming voice seemed to unsettle him and his eyes, like those of a hunted animal, rolled around in their sockets as if seeking an escape route.

Flaminio interceded, trying to soothe the witness. "My friend, how do you earn your livelihood?"

"But you know, my Father," said the candlemaker. "We have conversed often."

The response aggravated Flaminio. "Answer the question," he said curtly.

"Yes, Father. I make candles for your monastery. I have sold you many hundreds—"

"Answer the questions simply and directly," interposed the Fiscal.

"Yes, Father," said Duglioli. "I am a candlemaker."

"You are married?" boomed out the First Inquisitor.

"Yes."

"Have you any children?"

"A boy, six months old today."

"Do you know or suspect or surmise the cause of your being summoned to these chambers?" asked Flaminio.

"Well—I did not wish him to touch my child. He did it against my will."

"Please listen carefully and answer directly," said the Inquisitor General.

"I am listening."

"Do you know why you were brought to this court?" asked the Fiscal.

"To tell you about *him*," said Duglioli, and with his finger he pointed to Tagliacozzi.

Menacingly, the First Inquisitor marched over to the witness, seizing his hand and placing it on a Bible opened on a nearby table. Alarmed, the candlemaker pulled his hand away but the First Inquisitor was equal to the situation and forced it back onto the pages of the Bible.

"Do you swear to tell the truth," boomed out the official, a lion roaring in the jungle, "as to anything that may be asked of you to the full extent of your knowledge and to disclose whatever you may have heard said to the offense of God, Our Savior, and against our Holy Catholic faith, as well as against the just and free exercise of the power of the Holy Office, without concealing anything or giving false evidence?"

"What?" said Duglioli, and his eyes were scrambling here and there; clearly, he wished he were not in the witness chair. "What?"

Of a sudden, Flaminio felt like screaming. *Bandini is insufferable,* he complained to himself, *and now Duglioli is making a mockery of my case.* Pacing back and forth in front of the terrified witness, he did not speak until he had gained control of his rage. Then, whispering, "Do you know what happens to those who lie to the Inquisition?"

"Yes." The candlemaker's eyes were wide with horror. "Yes, but I swear I do not lie."

"Then what have you to tell us?" said Flaminio mildly.

"It concerns the Evil Eye," said Duglioli. "He put the Evil Eye on my child from the moment it was born."

"What had he to do with the birth of your son?"

"The midwife was sick. There was no one to help. Tagliacozzi is my neighbor, nearby on the street Delle Lame. My doctor was out of town and the midwife was sick. My wife was dying, so I ran to fetch him."

"You mean he delivered your child?"

"Yes, and he breathed the Devil into him."

"Why do you say that?"

"The child was born with a hole in his lip and Tagliacozzi was responsible."

"Why do you believe Tagliacozzi bewitched your child?" asked Cardinal Bandini. "May it not be suffering from the sins of your ancestors?"

"I did believe it was a curse on me at first."

"What made you change your mind?" asked Flaminio.

"His conscience must have been biting him; he never stopped begging me to let him have the child."

"And why did he want the infant?"

"He swore he could heal the lip. But then I commenced to feel he was trying to hide the wickedness of his deeds."

"So you refused to let him have the child?" asked Bandini.

"Yes, but that did not satisfy the sorcerer Tagliacozzi. He put a spell on my wife." Duglioli was so infuriated by the memory that his fears dissolved in an avalanche of words. "He sought her behind my back and got her to take the child to his house of evil. But I was aware of her evil intentions. Filled with disgust when I saw her leave with the baby, while I pretended I slept, dreading the possibility that I should be too late, I ran after her to Tagliacozzi's house. But my efforts were futile. His black assistant kept me at bay with his pistol, and the Devil's agent kept my little boy while I was compelled to flee. My child has been seduced and bewitched forever."

"Apart from what you feel about Professor Tagliacozzi," asked Bandini, "did you at any time see anything to justify the suspicion of sorcery?"

"Yes," added Flaminio, "did you see anything unusual—anything peculiar?"

"Yes," said Duglioli. "Before he proceeded to deliver the child, I saw him wash his hands."

This statement evoked a mixed reaction. Flaminio evinced satisfaction and the members of his order of Dominicans murmured gravely among themselves, but Cardinal Bandini looked puzzled, as did the prisoner's friends, and Gasparo, listening, was bewildered that his personal cleanliness was being used as evidence against him. In the audience of townspeople were many acquaintances of the superstitious candlemaker, and they were seen to cross themselves, looking heavenward beseechingly, praying to God for mercy, and some of the extremely devout turned in the direction of the burning flasks of vinegar and incense to inhale the fumes and thus prevent the plague from descending upon them.

Flaminio Vulpi, Censor of Books, turned to Duglioli. "You may retire, my good man, but do not leave the vicinity of the court."

The candlemaker's exit was as ludicrous as his entrance. Relieved at hearing these words, he bolted out of his chair, almost tripping over his own feet, giggling nervously, and rushing to the edge of the platform. Then he realized that he had not genuflected to Cardinal Bandini, and hurrying back, he bowed awkwardly, straightened up, and made a quick getaway on unsteady legs.

There was laughter in the audience at this but Gasparo was incensed by the testimony. "The whole thing is ridiculous, your Honor, Lord Cardinal. I suggest that it is Fra Vulpi who has bewitched Signor Duglioli."

"Where is your evidence," asked Bandini, "to prove this assertion?"

"His wife came to seek my help, with his consent, and when Fra Vulpi heard of this he must have poisoned the candlemaker's mind against me. Perhaps he threatened that the monastery would stop buying candles from him."

"Preposterous!" sneered Flaminio.

"And I am sure he will say the same thing about my assistant, Scipio. Would you step forward, Scipio."

Standing next to Lorenzo in the archway to the left of the rostrum,

Scipio Africanus Borzani, erect, handsome, regal in his bearing, took one stride forward and halted.

"Lord Cardinal, do you think he is a human being?"

"Of course I do," said Bandini somberly. "He appears to be a man of honor and substance."

"Fra Vulpi does not think so," said the surgeon. "Scipio was born with a harelip and I made him whole again. Does he look bewitched? Fra Vulpi insists that he is, that he suffers from the sins of his ancestors, that, indeed, all black people are in league with the Devil."

"I never made such a statement," shouted Flaminio. "I could not—as a member of the Church. Lord Cardinal, he is merely trying to evade the issue. In the name of Our Lord, I swear this."

Tactfully, Cardinal Bandini addressed the accused. "You see, Doctor Tagliacozzi, unfortunately there is no conclusive evidence in either instance." Turning then, with equal solicitude, he addressed the Censor of Books. "Proceed."

"Call Torquato Tasso," ordered Flaminio.

"Torquato Tasso," bellowed the sergeant at arms.

"Torquato Tasso," echoed the soldiers of the Church.

In the prisoner's chair, Gasparo sat calmly, his bandaged hands folded in his lap. *I do not despair,* he mused. *Two weeks' confinement. Torture. They have weakened my body but not subdued my spirit. Have hope, my beloved Giulia, for my thinking is rational and my will is not crushed, and I will return to your arms. Ah, Girolamo, the Inquisition has imprisoned my body but my soul is unchained. Oh, I do not despair; no, my resolve grows stronger. But a festering doubt, alas, begins to assault my mind and pierce it through, and, shrieking inwardly, shaking as with the plague, I dread being compelled to witness the humiliation of my dear old friend, the greatest living Italian poet. Take courage, Torquato. Take courage.*

But sight of the poet confirmed his worst fears. In his robes, Torquato shuffled in, a walking dead man. His face was white as chalk, his forehead severely indented by lines of worry, while in his left temple an artery pulsed in and out, superficial testimony to the agonized disrepair of his spirit. His eyes, large and blue and ardent in his youth, were now blank slates upon which any persecutor could write. They seemed hammered into his face—like nail ends into the cold wood of an executioner's scaffold—by an indifferent artisan who cared for nothing but his petty fee. The lyrical fire in the man, which had made his reputation as Italy's most renowned poet, had it been severed from him completely? Chilling it was, and mysterious, for the lust of life that had characterized the sensitive, melancholy, but vibrant young Tasso had departed—an itinerant wanderer swallowed up in the shadows of the night.

"Your name?" boomed out the First Inquisitor when the poet had eased his stooped, trembling body into the witness chair.

"Torquato Tasso."

"What is your age?"

"Fifty-two."

"Where were you born?"

"On the island of Sorrento."

"Do you remember," asked the First Inquisitor, "having deposed before an examining tribunal against any person or persons with relation to matters of faith?"

"I do," said Tasso slowly, hanging his head as if the recollection overwhelmed him.

"Do you remember the oath you took?"

"I do."

"You are ordered if you have anything to alter, to add to, or retrench from your previous deposition to do so now, so as to state the entire truth, to affirm and to ratify it, for upon what you are about to say depends the opinion of the Holy Court."

"I do not recollect anything beyond that which I have already disclosed," said the poet uneasily. "I do not know why I was brought to this court."

"To repeat the substance of your evidence," said the First Inquisitor.

"But everything I said was perfectly true and according to my oath."

"Then you have nothing to fear."

"No—no—of course not."

The First Inquisitor seated himself at the prosecution table and the Censor of Books rose to question the witness.

"How long have you known the accused?"

"I met him as a student at the University of Bologna."

"You have remained on friendly terms with him ever since?"

"I have—yes. I have a great love for him."

"And how will this great love of yours conflict with your obligations to your faith?"

"I am guided only by the desire to discharge my duties as a good Christian and Catholic."

"Then I am satisfied. By profession you are a poet, I believe?"

"I have the honor," said Tasso, as if reciting from rote something he could not fathom, "of being poet laureate to—to the court of Ferrara."

"Ferrara? Do you visit Bologna frequently?"

"Seldom."

"I see. How long have you stayed here on this occasion?"

"For many weeks."

"Had you any special reason for coming?" asked Flaminio. And noting the intensified fright on the poet's countenance, he said, "Have you not recently written an epic poem about the wars in the Holy Land?"

"Yes," said Tasso feverishly, the artery throbbing in his temple. "Yes, yes. I admit this fact, but you must understand that I sent it to the Index for approval."

"That was dutiful of you, and we are considering it at the moment. But, pray tell, where are you residing during your present stay in our fair city?"

"At the Albergo del Sole d'Oro."

"Have you been there the entire time?"

"Well—no."

"Answer the question directly," ordered Flaminio, and for the first time he assumed a sharp, stinging tone with Tasso, as if in rebuke.

The poet flinched as if struck. "Why," he stammered, dismayed, "why— That is, I stayed at the residence of the—of Doctor—Gasparo Tagliacozzi."

"Did you visit the City of Bologna at Doctor Tagliacozzi's invitation?"

"No."

"When were you last in our great city?"

"A very long time ago—nearly twenty years."

"Then this was a visit of some import?"

"Well—yes."

"Was it for your pleasure? Perhaps for your health?"

Tasso did not answer immediately. He cowered in the witness chair and thought but he was unable to frame a reply.

"Maybe you were just curious?" prodded Flaminio.

"Curious?"

"As to how your book was being received?"

"My book," burst out the poet, the words seeming to explode from him without control. "I did not mean harm. I did not mean to offend the Tribunal. I swear this to you, signor, I mean Reverend Sir. It was done in ignorance. You must believe me when I state that I did not know."

"That you have behaved or expressed yourself in ignorance does not exempt you from punishment by the Inquisition," said Flaminio coldly.

"I will tell you anything," moaned Tasso, almost crying in his anguish, "but please, you are a merciful gentleman, please do not torture me. Please."

"It was about your book, then, that you came to the City of Bologna?"

"Yes."

"Why did you not proceed directly to the Council of the Index?"

"I intended to. Why, I wanted to, but—"

"I see," said Flaminio frostily. "Well, we will return to that later. Now, while you were staying in the house of the accused, were you alone?"

"Alone?"

"Were there other guests?"

"A number of individuals receiving medical treatment came and went."

"Did none of them stay in the house?"

"There were two."

"And, my friend, were his patients all Italians?"

"There was one Frenchman—the Chevalier de Saint Thoan."

"I see. And how long did you stay in Gasparo Tagliacozzi's house?"

"About six or seven weeks."

"Did you visit a confessor?"

"No. That is, I—"

"Were you in ill health?"

"Yes—no. I mean, no."

"Perhaps a confessor visited the house?"

"I do not know. I—"

"What do you mean, you do not know?" stormed Flaminio.

"Answer the question," ordered the Inquisitor General. "Did a confessor visit you at the house?"

"Oh, Heaven forgive me," wailed the poet laureate.

"Why did you neglect your religious duties for such a lengthy period?" pursued the Inquisitor General. "For I presume that your answer is no."

"It was difficult—you might say that I was in hiding."

"In Tagliacozzi's house?" asked Flaminio.

"Yes."

"At his suggestion?"

"He helped me."

"Why were you hiding?"

"I wanted no one to know— That is, my presence in Bologna was not—"

"Then you really intended to leave Bologna without visiting the Index."

"Yes. I mean, no. I intended to—"

"Then why did you not come?" said Flaminio harshly.

"I was—advised against it."

"By whom?" The Censor of Books waited impatiently, but Tasso, trembling, remained silent. "By whom?" The poet, face pale, almost green, could say nothing. "Do you realize that if you perjure your soul, the least possible punishment would be excommunication?"

"Have mercy on me. I am not a heretic. I am a devout Catholic. In the name of the blessed Saint Dominic, please do not harm me."

"Who advised you not to visit the Index?" interposed the Inquisitor General.

"We are waiting," said Flaminio, lips tight and hard. "We have exercised patience with you, but we will wait no longer."

The poet, as in a cataleptic trance, stared at the floor near his boots, but he gave no sign that he had heard.

"Take him away," ordered Flaminio and armed soldiers of the Church converged on Tasso.

"No," cried Torquato, bursting out from within himself. "Do not touch me. I will tell you."

Flaminio, with a wave of his hand, directed the soldiers to stop. "Well?"

Torquato Tasso, poet laureate of the court of Ferrara, whose lyrical, rhapsodic verses had captured the hearts of a generation of his countrymen, slumped in the witness chair. Though middle-aged, his back was stooped, his hair was grayish-white, and his face was a mask of death. He loathed himself for what he was about to reveal but feared his persecutors too fervently to suppress it. "Gasparo Tagliacozzi," he whispered finally, and never would he forgive himself, for Gasparo had been his friend.

"Have you any further declarations to make?" asked Flaminio Vulpi, Censor of Books. "Any that are within the competence of this Holy Office to receive?"

Ashamed, Tasso began shaking his head, but then, from up above, another rumble of thunder descended upon the packed courtroom, and this time its reverberations whiplashed through the sultry, heavy air, cannon assaulting the eardrums of each individual. In the heat, with superstitious townspeople in the audience beseeching God for mercy, inhaling incense and vinegar and clutching the precious theriac, crossing themselves and muttering prayers, staccato explosions penetrated the walls of the stout building, crashing down from a darkening sky to terrify the multitudes. In the witness chair, Torquato squirmed wretchedly at the first burst of thunder, and as crescendo after crescendo detonated menacingly, his shattered nerves gave way completely and his guilt escalated into a hysterical panic.

"I will tell you anything," he screamed. "I will give all my property to the Church. If you say I am a heretic, I will perform any penance, go anywhere— Please have mercy upon me, for I am a devout Catholic. Please, do not torture me. Reverend signors, do not harm me."

The thunder had stopped but the poet continued to rave, and at a signal from Flaminio, two soldiers of the Church, assisted by their commanding officer, Captain Buoncampagna, plucked him from the witness chair, heaving him onto their shoulders and carrying him, writhing and shrieking, from the courtroom.

"Oh, Mother of God," cried out Torquato, and these were his final words, "what have I done? I did not mean to, Gasparo, I swear that. Oh, my God, what have I done?"

Chapter 25

For the first time during his trial, Gasparo Tagliacozzi felt the oppressiveness of the heat hanging over the courtroom. He did not feel betrayed by Tasso, for the emotional instability of his old soul mate had long been obvious to him. Instead, he seemed to be drowning in despair, and for an instant he wished he could return to his bare cell in the dungeon and sleep on the dingy cot.

Is it not too much to bear, he mused, *that my closest childhood friend prosecutes me from envy and love and that Torquato endures insufferable humiliations in the name of safety? Is it not intolerable that an ignorant candlemaker fails to appreciate the service I rendered his baby and testifies that I am a sorcerer who bewitched the child I saved? O Giulia, I behold your sorrowful face and torpor wears down my soul, for I ask myself if sufficient strength remains to me so that potently I may combat my adversaries.*

Then, from his position on the upper level of the rostrum, Cardinal Bandini called for the next witness.

"Call Maria Boschetti," said Flaminio Vulpi.

"Maria Boschetti," echoed the sergeant at arms.

"Maria Boschetti," repeated the soldiers of the Church.

It was another unpleasant surprise for the surgeon, for he had been unaware that the servant girl in his employ was a spy for the Inquisition. Coming on the heels of his apprehension stemming from the damaging testimony of Tasso, the near-certainty that this was so all but crushed the courage that remained in his heart.

Maria walked sedately to the witness chair, pausing only to genuflect to the Cardinal. Her manner was crisp and almost businesslike, and, shortly, it became obvious that she was thoroughly familiar with court procedure.

"You are Maria Boschetti?" asked the First Notary.

"I am."

"What is your occupation?" queried the First Notary.

"I am a serving maid."

"Where were you last employed?"

"At the house of Professor Gasparo Tagliacozzi."

"Do you know or suspect or surmise the reason for your being summoned before this court, the Holy Office?"

"I believe," said Maria calmly, "that it is to give information on a matter of faith."

"Do you remember the oath you took before the examining tribunal?"

"I do."

The First Notary seated himself at the long table, and Flaminio rose to begin his interrogation. "You are giving this information as a dutiful Catholic? You have not been coerced to come before us?"

"I come here of my own free will."

"How long have you been serving maid in the Tagliacozzi household?"

"Nearly two years, Father."

"Can you remember if, during this period, a father confessor visited the house?"

"Yes, Father, quite frequently. He was sent for at least once a week. That is, up until some months ago."

"Then what happened?"

"He stopped coming."

"Do you know, or can you give any reason, why in your opinion the invitations ceased?"

"I think I can place the time when they stopped—exactly."

"How?"

"It was on a particular day on which two unusual events took place."

"What were they?"

"In the midmorning, during my master's absence, Tasso, the poet, arrived from Ferrara in the garb of a mendicant friar."

"And the other?"

"Later in the morning a Frenchman arrived, travel-stained, all the way from Paris."

"How did you know he was a Frenchman?"

"I overheard him announcing it. He said he was the Chevalier de Saint Thoan."

"Is that all you noticed about him?"

"No, Father; he had a silver nose."

"And you say that from the day these gentlemen arrived, from this moment onward, you never observed the father confessor entering the house?"

"That is true."

"Of the two, whose presence do you think was responsible for this regrettable circumstance?"

"Both were, but I surmise one more than the other."

"Why did you come to this conclusion?"

"Because of what I heard the signor say to them. He advised Tasso, the poet, not to call on you, Father, and said that he feared only God Himself and not the Inquisition."

At this, the Dominicans in the left archway exploded once more. Leaping to their feet in unison, they shouted abuse at the prisoner and demanded his death.

Depressed by the denunciations of the servant girl, Gasparo glanced almost indifferently at the outraged friars. *Are they demented?* he asked himself. *But it matters not. For all is futile, and insanity rules the world.* In this section, on benches, were seated professors from the University of Bologna, his fellow faculty members, but his eyes skipped over them to focus on his wife. *O unhappy day,* he mourned, *for my love is so sad, despair etched into every line of her face. And I sit, helpless, tyrannized by informers and sycophants, dancing to the tune of Flaminio Vulpi, who must destroy me to save himself.*

"Heretic," shouted one friar. "He must burn."

"He practices witchcraft," yelled another. "If he is pardoned, the Mother Church will perish."

"Gentlemen," said Bandini. "You must control your indignation, however righteous."

The Censor of Books turned back to the questioning of his informer. "And in the case of the Frenchman?"

"He told the Chevalier that he denied the right of the Church to interfere with his practice as a physician, that he should be allowed to treat whoever came to him, no matter what his race, color, or creed."

The papal Vice-Legate silenced another incipient outburst among the Dominicans, and Flaminio continued his questioning. "Was the accused sober when he so expressed himself? Or was he intoxicated or were his words the outcome of madness?"

"I did not think him mad," said Maria Boschetti precisely, "and he was never overcome by wine at such a time—at least, not to my knowledge."

"Then why did he utter such vile heresies?"

"Because of something the Frenchman said."

"What was that?"

"He was bemoaning his ill fortune because he had journeyed all the way from France to acquire a new nose and yet the Professor refused to treat him."

"But surely, my child," interposed Bandini, "he did operate upon the Chevalier?"

"Oh, yes, my Lord Cardinal, but that was after he was sworn to secrecy."

"Tagliacozzi swore the Frenchman to secrecy?" pursued Flaminio. "Is this your statement?"

"Yes, Father."

"Why?"

"The Frenchman called himself a peculiar name." Maria Boschetti was a consummate performer, when the occasion demanded, and, craftily, she built dramatic interest in the audience as she reached the climactic revelation in her testimony. "He was—what he called—a Huguenot."

Bandini's attempt to maintain order was a token gesture, for on hearing the word "Huguenot," the Dominicans leaped to their feet screaming threats and many townspeople in the audience joined in heaping curses upon the prisoner. The outburst continued in intensity, unrestrained, until Bandini signaled Captain Buoncampagna and the military commander dispatched soldiers to restore quiet.

"Need we go further, my Lord Cardinal?" exulted Flaminio, who had bellowed as loudly as anyone during the demonstration. "I demand a conviction forthwith. He shall burn, my brethren, he shall burn."

"I appreciate your enthusiasm, Fra Vulpi," said Bandini temperately, "but do you not think we should at least hear the accused in his own defense?"

Muttering angrily to himself, the Censor of Books seated himself at the prosecution table, offering no reply.

The Cardinal turned to address the witness. "Can you tell us anything more, my child, that is important for the Holy Office to hear?"

Unperturbed as always, Maria was counting her beads. "I think that is all."

And indeed it was, as far as Giulia was concerned. She was sobbing and moaning, and more than once, Lorenzo, standing by her side, prevented her from rushing from her bench, whether to go to Gasparo or to claw the traitorous servant girl, no one could tell.

"Did you at any time," continued Bandini, "see the Professor wash his hands before treating a patient?"

"He always seemed to be washing his hands."

"I do not doubt your honesty, my child, but is there anything you wish to add or to retract from your statements? You must realize that a man's life hangs upon the truth of what you have told us."

"My only wish is to assist the Inquisition and to express my love for Mother Church."

"You may go," said the papal Vice-Legate.

Maria got to her feet, genuflected gracefully to the Cardinal, and began to walk away from the witness chair.

"Not yet, if it please your Excellency," said the Censor of Books, "for, with your permission, I should like her to testify shortly on another matter."

With this, the next witness was ushered into the courtroom, causing another noisy eruption from the spectators, for indeed this was a sensational development.

In the prisoner's chair, Gasparo had slouched morosely, barely listening to the informer's recital. The emotional mutilation of Tasso had filled him with sorrow; then the revelation that his servant girl had been an Inquisition spy enraged him beyond endurance. Finally, with the word "Huguenot" ringing in his ears, a sense of hopelessness infested every particle of his being. He felt not only deserted and persecuted but, to his terror, felt that he was losing himself. Determination had fled from him, a ghost slipping away in the darkness. Courage had eluded him, too, and, as for compassion, empathy for his wife, sobbing uncontrollably, had overwhelmed him, and unable to tolerate the extent of her misery, he closed his ears and hardened his heart and was relieved to discover that no longer did the sounds of her grief pierce him through. But this comfort did not last long; for shortly, revolted at the transformation taking place inside himself, he felt the first stirrings of a cancerous growth *taking root*—for perhaps the first time in his life he really hated himself.

And then his eyes bulged with amazement as he observed the progress of the next witness for the Inquisition: Brown Pigeon.

The Censor of Books led the witness to a position on the lower level of the rostrum near the chair occupied by Maria Boschetti, who had, upon Flaminio's request, remained for further testimony. He was accompanied by the sergeant at arms, who marched the pigeon, a long string tied around its neck, to the rostrum.

It was all so unexpected and seemed so ludicrous that people who had been screaming for the prisoner's blood a moment before were laughing at sight of the proud, strutting little bird, nudging their neighbors, asking one another how such a creature could bolster the Inquisition's case against the surgeon.

On the top level of the rostrum, Cardinal Bandini, perched on his elevated chair, waited until the laughter had subsided. Then he addressed the Censor of Books. "What have we here, Fra Vulpi? This is a witness?"

"If it please your excellency."

Unsuccessfully, Bandini struggled to suppress a smile. "The witness speaks our native tongue?"

"I indulge your patience, my Lord Cardinal, and assure you of the soundness of this procedure."

"Proceed," said Bandini.

In his long robe, the bottom folds brushing the floor, the Censor of Books interrogated the little bird. "Do you speak our native tongue?" he asked, but there was no answer. "Have you conversed with human beings?" he demanded. Silence. "Is it not true that you held long dialogues with the accused, Gasparo Tagliacozzi?" No answer. "Do you deny these conversations?" No response. "Are you aware that another witness swears to observing these secret meetings?" The brown pigeon opened its beak and the townspeople gasped but no sound emerged.

"Your line of questioning," suggested Bandini wryly, "is producing no evidence against the accused."

"Your Excellency," said Flaminio angrily, "this is why I requested that Maria Boschetti remain in the witness chair."

"Proceed."

"Tell me, my dear child, did you at any time overhear a conversation between Tagliacozzi and the brown pigeon?"

"On two different occasions, Fra Vulpi."

"Did they converse at length?"

"Yes, Father. Their blasphemous dialogue covered a wide range of subject matter."

"Would you elaborate on this statement?"

"It is my privilege," said Maria Boschetti primly, "to aid the Mother Church in exposing the enemies of Our Lord. Signor Tagliacozzi conversed with the pigeon on diverse topics. They discussed controversies at the university, various philosophical issues, and ethical questions as well. They dissected the ideas of Pomponazzi and Aristotle and Plato. The Professor expressed admiration for the freethinker Girolamo Cardano. And he stated his view that there was evil in the Roman Church."

The mention of Cardano aroused the ire of the Dominican contingent, but at the mention of evil in the Church, once more they surged to their feet howling for the surgeon's death.

Triumphant, now, the Censor of Books turned from his informer to confront the brown pigeon, but it was an absurd-looking challenge, the tall, broad-shouldered Inquisition official, lips tight and hard, eyes flashing malevolence, a jagged gash disfiguring one eyebrow, staring down at the tiny bird, bearing its imprisonment with dignity, beak high in the air, feathers in place, feet on the floor. "Do you deny now, Bird of Hell, that you have conspired with the Devil's agent Tagliacozzi? Do you dare refute this charge before the Lord Cardinal? Do you not admit bearing intelligence from this sorcerer to other practitioners of the malefic arts?"

But the little pigeon remained mute and, further enraged, Flaminio was about to press his cross-examination even more forcefully when the bird defecated near his boots, almost soiling his official robe. In his frustration, Vulpi turned back to Maria Boschetti. "Please tell his Lord Cardinal the circumstances of the pigeon's capture."

"Yes, Father. You advised me to watch the Professor's accomplice and to report the nature of the dialogues. Finally, you asked me to bring the Devil's agent to you so that you might further investigate the witchcraft. For it has long been clear that this bird is evil and that it conspires against the teachings of the Mother Church and of Our Lord."

"You have earned my gratitude. You may go, my child."

Genuflecting to the papal Vice-Legate, Maria made her departure with impeccable efficiency and, abruptly, the Censor of Books faced the prisoner. "Do you deny holding conversations with your accomplice, the pigeon?" he stormed.

Gasparo said nothing. *So, Flaminio,* he mused, *this accounts for the disappearance of Brown Pigeon. You apprehended even this gentle, harmless bird to help you destroy your love for me.*

The brown pigeon recognized his friend at this moment, and, Flaminio having released his hold on the string circling its neck, it flew to Gasparo, alighting on his shoulder, leaning over and pecking him near the ear.

Excitedly, Flaminio turned to Cardinal Bandini. "You see, my Lord, how they communicate with each other? Why, it is their sorcerers' language."

Bandini's eyes were solemn, but the suspicion of a smile continued to play about his lips. "This is an interesting hypothesis, Fra Vulpi, but I cannot grant that the evidence is conclusive."

The surgeon contemplated this latest excursion into fantasy, but, in spite of the absurdity of the situation, he felt a resurgence of his spirit, sitting in his chair, the pigeon still nestling on his shoulder. *Are you with me still, Girolamo, lending me courage in time of adversity?* he mused. *Or is this, too, nonsense?* No matter. In some strange mystical sense, the pigeon's confidence in him had initiated a renewal of his own self-esteem. Cardinal Bandini seemed a fair-minded man; he would reason with him.

"I was deeply disturbed by a personal tragedy, my Lord," he said, "and, suffering from insomnia, turned for relief to the wine bottle. At dawn, I repaired to the garden in back of my house and you might say that I addressed the brown pigeon, but, in reality, sir, I engaged in disputation with my conscience. It was not sorcery, Cardinal, but the troubled musings of a man trying to resolve the intricate complexities of the human condition."

The surgeon sighed with relief on finishing his statement, for it constituted a heartening return to self. But, though Bandini listened attentively, it fell on Flaminio's deaf ears. The dispute raged on between the prisoner and the Censor of Books, with the latter fulminating against disciples of evil.

"This pigeon is a winged messenger of the forces of Satan," Flaminio said, while the bird, still perched on Gasparo's shoulder, pecked again at its companion's ear.

Bandini, the Pope's representative, declared the evidence inconclusive and ordered the immediate release of the bird. On its two feet, Brown Pigeon strutted proudly from the courtroom before launching itself into its home in the skies.

"Next witness," barked the Cardinal.

"Call Giulio Cesare Aranzio," said Flaminio Vulpi.

"Giulio Cesare Aranzio," trumpeted the sergeant at arms.

"Giulio Cesare Aranzio," echoed the soldiers of the Church.

Cesare Aranzio was ushered in with pomp and ceremony, Cardinal Bandini greeting him formally upon his entrance, for he was renowned as one of Italy's foremost scholars.

"What is your name?" the Inquisitor General asked, initiating the interrogation along the prescribed lines.

"Giulio Cesare Aranzio."

"Where were you born?"

"In the City of Bologna."

"You are a professor at the University of Bologna?"

"Professor of anatomy."

"That is a very important position, is it not?" asked Bandini.

"It is considered so," said Aranzio, his pretensions of modesty belied by the pompous airs he affected.

"I had that impression. Your work has done much to enhance the reputation of your noble university—this is my understanding."

"You are being very kind."

"Not at all. As the founder of this new chair of anatomy, you deserve the respect of the community and the high commendation of our glorious city."

"Oh, my Lord Cardinal, you overwhelm me."

The Inquisitor General and the Censor of Books had exchanged looks of disgust while the Pontiff's representative handled the Professor with as much diplomacy as one might lavish upon the head of a royal family.

Finally the Inquisitor General rose to his feet. "With your kind permission, my Lord Cardinal," he said sarcastically, "might I be allowed to administer the oath?"

"By all means."

"Have you ever deposed before an examining tribunal in regard to matters of faith?" asked the Inquisitor General of Aranzio.

"I have."

"And do you remember the oath you took on that occasion?"

"I do, quite well."

"Thank you, that is all."

The official seated himself on the middle level of the rostrum, and Flaminio initiated the interrogation proper.

"How long have you known Gasparo Tagliacozzi?"

"More than twenty-five years. To be exact, since he became a medical student at the University of Bologna."

"Did you enter into personal contact with him?"

"He attended my lectures in anatomy."

"Was he satisfactory as a pupil?" Bandini interjected the question.

"In what way, my Lord?"

"Was he diligent in pursuit of his studies? Was he conscientious in application of principles?"

"Exceptionally so, your Excellency. He became very skillful in the art of surgery."

"Gratifying for you, no doubt," said Bandini.

"I made him my assistant," responded Aranzio but his eyes were cold.

"How long did he remain your assistant?" resumed Flaminio.

"For many years—until we had certain differences of opinion."

"Were you dissatisfied with his work?"

"No, but his attitude became ever more arrogant."

Again, Bandini assumed an active role in the cross-examination. "Do you mean he insinuated you had nothing more to teach him?"

"No one could teach him anything," said Aranzio angrily, "not then or since."

"And so you appointed another assistant?"

"Yes, I did, my Lord."

"I see." The Pope's representative paused and, weighing his words carefully, resumed. "Am I mistaken or was there not some incident between you a few years ago, when the Rector of the university, at the request of the medical students, granted Tagliacozzi permission to do a public dissection?"

"An entirely erroneous decision, my Lord Cardinal."

"My dear Professor," said Flaminio, "this was merely a minor incident, was it not, in comparison with what had gone before?"

"Almost from the moment of his appointment he became a source of annoyance and irritation."

"In what way?"

"He was continually disregarding our usual methods at the university—the established order of things."

"A radical?"

"Emphatically, in every sense and construction of the word. He ridiculed our routine procedures of treatment, calling them old-fashioned. There was one particular case in point—an eye condition. The diagnosis was cataract."

"You disagreed," interjected Bandini, "on the diagnosis?"

"Oh no, my Lord. We agreed it was cataract, but Tagliacozzi insisted on performing an immediate operation."

"Why should he not have done so?" pressed Bandini.

"The sun had just entered Aries. It is unethical to perform such an operation at that period of the year; the danger of insanity is enormous."

"He ignored the astrological authority?" asked Flaminio.

"He ridiculed it."

"In the light of your extensive knowledge and experience," said Flaminio, "what can you tell us of other strange practices indulged in by the accused?"

"Reconstructive surgery of the face is against all canons and teachings of the university."

"You do not believe in it?"

"Meddling with the handiwork of God—definitely no." Cesare Aranzio sat almost primly in the witness chair, hands folded precisely in his lap, an elderly man, with white hair, who held his head high, chin at an angle jutting upward, as if to emphasize his assumed superiority to other humans.

"Have you any idea where the accused obtained his iniquitous ability and power?"

"Certainly not at the University of Bologna."

"No other physician or surgeon attempted such procedures?"

"No one."

"Are there any known manuscripts on the subject?"

"Nowhere in Italy that I know of, nor in all the world, for that matter."

"Then there is nothing to show how the accused acquired the power to do this work?"

"Nothing."

"You say he was a source of irritation to you in the early days of your association?"

"Yes, I found him aloof and unapproachable in many ways."

"Can you be more explicit?"

"He had some very annoying habits."

"What were they?"

"I am myself a firm believer in cleanliness of the body as well as of the spirit." The Professor paused to establish this point. "But Tagliacozzi was forever immersing his hands in water. I would send for him to assist me in a post-mortem and would find him washing himself. It seems to be a part of a ritual with him."

"Part of a ritual? Were there other indications?"

"He would frequently wander off into the garden of the university. One day I followed him to the orchard, he was standing there muttering to himself while staring through the branches to the heavens above."

This statement aroused the wrath of the Dominicans once more, and with cries of "Sorcerer" filling the air, with robed and hooded friars screaming for his blood, with his long-time adversary at the university destroying his good name with innuendos and subjective opinions while the townspeople crossed themselves and whispered gravely about phenomena outside their scope of knowledge, the prisoner, silent since Aranzio had begun his testimony, leaped to his feet to defend himself.

"These statements are absurd," he said. "They are fictions not worthy of presentation in this courtroom."

"These were your malefic formulas," charged Flaminio, "for invoking evil spirits."

"Ridiculous," stormed the surgeon. "That was how I acquired my knowledge."

"Then you admit it?"

"Of course I admit it."

"That you acquired your knowledge standing in an orchard muttering to the heavens?" The question was from Bandini.

"No, my Lord Cardinal. I was watching the trees."

"The trees!"

"Yes, my Lord Cardinal. I came to believe that if the branch of one tree could be grafted to the stem of another, then the flesh of the human arm could be safely used to repair mutilated faces."

In the oppressive heat of the courtroom, murmurs of the superstitious intensified, a humming, vibrating sound hanging steadily in the sultry air. Then, another crackling rumble of thunder from above, like firecrackers bursting or horses' hooves clomping metallically upon cobblestones, and this time the thunder echoed and re-echoed, snarling and belching and roaring, followed by a brief shaking of the ground underfoot.

"The earth shakes," a woman screamed. "The earth shakes under our feet."

"The day of judgment is at hand," shouted a friar. "We are in jeopardy."

"Remain calm," commanded Bandini as townspeople began stampeding from their benches. "It was a mild earth tremor, perhaps stemming from the Apennines, and it has passed. Return to your seats, gentlefolk. Calm yourselves, and we will proceed."

"It is a direct indication that this man's evil influence must be destroyed," said Flaminio. But, inflammatory as this statement was, the panic had subsided, and after a hostile glance at the Censor of Books, Cardinal Bandini turned to the witness.

"Professor Aranzio, as a renowned student of anatomy, are there medical grounds for this amazing assertion of Gasparo Tagliacozzi?"

"None whatever!"

"You are not perchance suggesting magic?" asked Flaminio.

"I have nothing to prove it is not so," said Aranzio complacently.

"You dare not accuse me of sorcery on the word of a jealous colleague," raged Gasparo, and at this the Dominicans once more released their fury at the accused.

"Gentlemen, gentlemen, have respect for this court," said Bandini, impatient, and to Flaminio, "If you insist on proceeding with this line of argument, Fra Vulpi, you must be very sure of your facts."

"The facts will be self-evident, my Lord, if you will permit me to continue."

"Proceed."

Addressing the prisoner, Flaminio said, "Do you persist in your denial that you are aided in these disgustingly morbid practices of yours by the power of darkness?"

"Knowing I am in danger of burning for my opinions—" the surgeon began.

"Since you realize the seriousness of your position, Doctor Tagliacozzi, might I suggest you think carefully before continuing?" said Bandini.

"I stand on my oath and deny such a monstrous and ridiculous suggestion."

"Perhaps," leered Flaminio, "you would deny entirely the existence of witchcraft and sorcery."

"If you prove to me that they exist, I am quite willing to believe they do."

"That is blasphemy! Of course they exist. The laws enacted against them and the punishments provided are useless if they do not."

"I agree. They are useless."

The Censor of Books curbed his annoyance at this rejoinder and resumed the interrogation. "Professor Aranzio, in the course of your association with the accused, have you ever noticed anything in his behavior to conform with this suggestion of sorcery?"

"His obstinate defense of Cardano."

"Do you mean," asked Bandini, "Professor Girolamo Cardano, who was deprived of his chair at the university some years ago?"

"The same, my Lord Cardinal. Tagliacozzi considers him unjustly treated."

"There is no question of this," said Gasparo hotly. "Girolamo was persecuted by the superstition and blind ignorance of his fellows."

"You have the insolence and gall to defend him publicly?"

"You, most of all, were the cause of his despair and isolation."

"Gentlemen," expostulated Bandini, "what are the main points of disagreement on the relative merits of Professor Cardano?"

"A magician," snarled Aranzio.

"He was a public benefactor," said Gasparo. "He helped the maimed, the dumb, and the blind."

"By magic he helped the dumb to speak and the blind to see."

"They were simple hand signs that an innocent child could understand."

"Invented by your master, the Devil," raged Flaminio.

"What a demon may be, I know not," said Gasparo. "These things I neither recognize nor love; I worship one God and Him alone I serve. All my life I have respected the Church, and of a truth I know of no evil spirit or even a guardian angel that attends me, but should one come to me even in my dreams—if it should be given to me by God, I will still revere God alone—to Him alone will I give thanks for any benefits that may befall me as the bountiful source and principle of all good."

"Enough of this sacrilege," said Flaminio. "There is more than ample proof that you have no respect for religion."

Bandini addressed the accused. "You are very firm in your belief that Cardano was a great man."

"His knowledge was profound and his ability remarkable. He was full of gentility and courage; but for him I would not have had the confidence to go on with my work."

The Censor of Books returned to interrogating the witness, Aranzio. "Did Cardano encourage the accused in his vicious practices?"

"He was the only member of our faculty who did so."

"And he was accused of sorcery?"

"He was."

"What say you to that?" said Flaminio challengingly, to the surgeon.

"I know full well that God has given me, for my good reason, patience in trouble and a high disregard of indignities; I am now using these gifts to the utmost."

"What say you to that, Fra Vulpi?" said Bandini, and a half smile hovered about his lips.

"We have a very fine example of what the exercising of his gifts will lead to. Will the Count Carlo Torticelli of the Castelli clan be good enough to rise."

Thus far, Cardinal Bandini, presiding at the trial, had managed to quell fierce confrontations before they accelerated into overt violence. But the arrival on the scene of Torticelli precipitated the stormiest of these controversies.

Count Carlo's nose was bandaged, and the Censor of Books went directly to the point. "Why are you wearing that bandage, Signor Torticelli?"

"Because of treatment begun by the accused, Doctor Gasparo Ta- gliacozzi."

"Were the treatments successful?"

"No, the disfigurement is much worse than it was before."

"Did you seek the advice of the accused voluntarily?"

"Yes, I did."

"For what reason?"

"I have seen splendid results."

"To what do you attribute the failure in your own particular case?"

"To the fact that Tagliacozzi was arrested and not allowed to complete the treatment."

Count Carlo had delivered his testimony from the archway to the left of the rostrum. The Censor of Books granted him permission to resume his seat and then turned back to question the distinguished professor of anatomy.

"Professor Aranzio, did you attempt to complete the surgical treat- ment of Signor Torticelli begun by the accused?"

"At your request."

"You have observed the effect of Tagliacozzi's surgery on other men?"

"I have."

"But you were unable to achieve the same result with Count Carlo Torticelli?"

"Had I the desire, I had no knowledge of this peculiar method."

"When you first visited him, in what condition did you find the Count?"

"He was raving, in high fever. There were signs of gangrene."

"His life was in danger?"

"Very much so, Father."

"To what do you attribute your success in saving him?"

"I immediately severed the head from the arm and after treatment the fever subsided."

Gasparo joined the discussion, and now the pace escalated. "Why did you not sever the *arm* from the *head* instead of the *head* from the *arm?*"

"What do you mean?"

Manfully, the surgeon curbed his temper and spoke softly. "Without the knowledge of the details of my treatment, your surgical skill should have told you that once the graft had grown into the face an excellent result was assured."

"There were signs of gangrene," snarled Aranzio. "Emergency measures were indicated."

"My Lord Cardinal, might I be permitted to examine Count Torticelli's arm?"

"It is unnecessary," insisted Flaminio, "for the result is obvious.".

"My Lord, I beg you—"

"Will you come forward, Count Torticelli? And will you bare your arm, please?"

Torticelli followed Bandini's instructions. A livid but healthy-looking scar was plainly visible on his arm.

"My Lord," said Gasparo, "the graft is healthy and intact. There could have been no signs of gangrene. He should have waited another ten days to give the graft a chance to grow in its new place." His tone was exultant, but turning to Aranzio, he lashed out, "And after that, had you severed the *arm* from the *head* you could have obtained an excellent result."

"I have not your surgical skill," said Aranzio sarcastically.

Gasparo feared he would be unable to restrain the impulse to spring from his chair to fasten his hands around the neck of his enemy. "You deliberately disfigured Count Carlo for the purpose of destroying my work."

"You are mad," howled Aranzio. And then, to Bandini, he said, "I protest, my Lord, that all my ability and experience as a surgeon could not equal his supernatural devilish power."

This aroused the Dominicans again, but near them a new voice boomed out.

"Silence. I have heard enough from you. The blade of my sword has pierced into the innards of Turkish heathen who were better men than any of you rabble. And I warn you, friars, that the next man who raises his voice against my comrade Gasparo Tagliacozzi will rest peaceful in his grave."

The voice belonged to Count Lorenzo Desiri.

"I have heard lies," bellowed Lorenzo. "I have held my tongue while false accusations have been made against my friend, but no longer will I remain silent. This fine man has no advocate; I will represent him before this tribunal. I will speak the truth, I swear this in the name of my father, a warrior before me, also chief of *bravi* for the noble Pepolis, beheaded by the barbarous Turks, who paraded him naked through the streets, spitting upon his noble skin, then butchering him in cold blood.

"Hear this, my good Lord Cardinal. I respect you and I honor your good name, but no authority will compel me to tolerate this debasement of a great man. If an unjust punishment shall befall him, I will avenge him, as I avenged the humiliation and desecration of my father. And, Reverend Sir, I, Lorenzo Desiri, mouth no words that I will not back with the steel of my blade."

Lorenzo stepped forward from the left archway, away from Caledonia, Scipio, and Giulia, and stood at attention, in his most splendid suit of Milanese armor, dagger sheathed at his side, above the armor a chin that brooked no surrender, delicately trimmed mustache, and black eyes that knew no fear. He stood there, magnificently arrogant, shoulders squared, muscles bulging from his arms, and looked directly at Cardinal Bandini.

"You are a splendid man, my Lord Cardinal," he trumpeted, "but the case against this eminent surgeon is a fraud and I demand his acquittal."

He faced the Censor of Books. "You are a coward, Flaminio," he shouted, "and you were a coward when you were ten years old. Your accusations are vile and disgraceful and I will not honor them with any further comment."

Then, to the witness, he said, "Aranzio, I had a deep sword wound right to my mouth. I am whole again, owing to the skill of Doctor Tagliacozzi. You call this witchcraft? Well, let me tell you this, if anything happens to this illustrious doctor, something will indeed happen to you."

"Enough of these threats," said Bandini, but his tone was surprisingly mild.

The soldier turned to face the Pope's representative. "The students know of Aranzio's hatred for Doctor Tagliacozzi. If he is crucified, they will destroy Aranzio—and they will burn down the university. And I will aid them, I swear this on the virtue and loveliness of my wife, Caledonia. Yes, my Lord Cardinal, I will join them in burning the university to ashes."

A large group of students, seated on benches with the townspeople, jumped up to cheer Lorenzo, who acknowledged the applause with a courtly bow.

"I insist that you have respect for the dignity of this court," said Bandini. "Otherwise you will be forced to leave. I cannot respond to your threats of violence, but I will ignore them and advise you that this is a tribunal of justice in fact as well as in name."

At this Lorenzo retreated to his former position alongside Caledonia, after genuflecting to the Cardinal; the trial was ready to continue.

But first the body of students sent volleys of cheers into the air, saluting Lorenzo and vowing loyalty to their dear Professor Gasparo Tagliacozzi. "Free Tagliacozzi," they yelled. "We demand his release. His only crime is the ardor with which he pursues the truth."

The demonstration did not waver in intensity, and Bandini called a brief recess.

When the trial resumed, a fresh reinforcement arrived to do battle on behalf of the surgeon.

Ghisella, the courtesan, whose fame had encompassed the continent of Europe, made a remarkable entrance into the courtroom.

In the cafés of Paris, the bordellos of Venice, members of royal families would regale listeners with tales of her fabulous charms, and always they would return to marvel at her soft, smooth rouged cheek, gouged hideously by Enrico Gradenigo and restored to its pristine splendor by the surgical genius Tagliacozzi.

Her house was a treasure trove, for admirers from all over Europe showered her with *objets d'art* and with gifts of perfume, rare wines from vintage years, and exotic spices and jewels from the Orient.

Ghisella had enlisted the charms of five additional prostitutes, but the commercial opportunities multiplied geometrically, and she added to this voluptuous staff an opera singer from Milan, a belly dancer from Beirut, and a black girl with orange hair from Morocco. Each day the madame would deposit purses crammed with gold coins in a metal safe in her bedroom closet.

Daily, Ghisella would bless the surgeon. He had saved her beauty and had rescued her from a life of degradation and poverty. She had installed a crucifix near her bed, and before retiring each night, she would thank God for her prosperity and would add a fervent benediction in honor of Gasparo.

Then came the sad news of his imprisonment in the Garisenda Tower. In her lacy pink chemise, Ghisella had raged around the house like a tornado, wreaking devastation on anything—animate or inanimate—unfortunate enough to cross her path. Tripping over a footstool in her living room, she had cursed it eloquently and, picking it up, had hurled it out the window, the object sailing past the bald head of a duke from Cremona, who had suffered from impotence and had regained his genital capacity under the tutelage of the opera singer from Milan.

"What are you doing?" shouted the Duke, who had been catnapping on the sofa. "You are mad."

"And you," screamed Ghisella, "can take that puny little vestigial organ that hangs around uselessly inside your trousers—it is smaller than the magnified clitoris of Enrico Gradenigo, who died of malformation of the testicles—and you can—"

In a huff, the Duke stormed from her house, howling back that he would never return, and Ghisella, still more frustrated, barged into the bedroom of the opera singer from Milan, bullied her in petticoat into the street to retrieve the furious Duke, then, repentant toward both, ushered the reunited couple into her own bedroom, closing the door after them, so that, beneath the crucifix, they could execute the will of God.

I must help the savior of my ravishing beauty, Ghisella moaned to herself later. *I must express my gratitude.*

And, as the trial resumed after Lorenzo's outburst and the student demonstration, Ghisella asserted her presence.

She entered the courtroom on her knees, covered by a ragged old dress made perhaps of burlap, a black veil shrouding her face, a dustcloth used as a kerchief to cover her lovely hair. "I have sinned," she cried out, on her knees, "but I will try to reform and I ask God for mercy."

And with this dramatic announcement a fresh wave of excitement circulated through the auditorium, but it was a rather neutral cross-current reflecting mostly astonishment.

"Who is this woman?" whispered Cardinal Bandini from the top level of the rostrum, beckoning to the Censor of Books.

"She is an abomination, my Lord Cardinal, a courtesan lascivious beyond possibility of redemption," snarled Flaminio. "By rights, she should burn at the stake."

What next? mused Bandini, leaning back in his elevated chair, sighing. *Oh, Papa Gregory has handed me a choice assignment.*

"I have decided to mend my evil ways," proclaimed Ghisella, waddling toward the rostrum on her knees, hands raised high in supplication to God. "No longer will I practice my malefic art."

"You *should* practice it," said Flaminio, "in Hell."

Accompanied by Captain Buoncampagna, the courtesan inched forward on her knees, and finally she arrived at the rostrum where she remained, still kneeling. "I repent," she wailed, "and throw myself on the mercy of this noble court."

"My Lord Cardinal, I protest this transparent fraud," said Flaminio. "It is a deceitful performance that impugns the honor of this distinguished tribunal, casting aspersions upon the authority of the Mother Church, invoking the wrath of Our Lord, and pouring oil upon the troubled waters of the judicial process."

"I dispute that, my Lord," said Jacopo Buoncampagna, the military commander. "I talked to this lady in the morning and, though her occupation is disreputable, I am convinced that she sincerely wishes to disavow it and to lead a life of virtue. Please, your Excellency, allow her to plead her cause."

"And this cause," asked Bandini, "is relevant to the case under consideration?"

"Yes."

"Proceed," said Bandini, motioning Ghisella to take the witness chair, vacated by Professor Aranzio during the recess, but she asked permission to testify kneeling and it was granted.

"I have sinned," began Ghisella, sobbing and rocking back and forth on her knees.

"Most assuredly *this* is true," said Flaminio.

"I have been a courtesan," admitted Ghisella, and no one disputed her veracity. "The accursed Enrico Gradenigo, whose shriveled-up—" She collected herself. "My apologies, my Lord Cardinal, I repent my evil ways and wish to do penance."

"The woman lies," said Flaminio.

"If it pleases the court, when Gradenigo gouged my cheek, I despaired, but the honorable Gasparo Tagliacozzi healed my wounds and—"

"For what purpose? To carry on your sinful, wicked depredations?"

"No, I have changed. I wish to be a good woman."

"An abortion of evil."

"No, my Lord Cardinal. Please hear my plea. I am sincere, I swear it. I was born beautiful, my Lord, but my depraved father raped me when I was a child, and I vowed to take my revenge on all men. So I adopted my vocation as courtesan. And then the vile pig Enrico Gr—I am sorry, my Lord, he was a pitiful man—gouged out my cheek and I was ugly. I was desperate. I prayed. O, my Lord Cardinal, I was saved from suicide by the skill and the goodness of Doctor Tagliacozzi. He restored my beauty and my soul. But then, after his imprisonment, I began to realize that I, too, was a prisoner—a prisoner of the flesh. 'Is it too late to repent?' I asked myself. 'Is it too late to mend my evil ways? My face is normal now; can it be too late?' I began to pray."

"May the Lord forgive you."

"And then I realized the truth," cried out Ghisella, "that inside I was more depraved than my beauty could hide; my face was restored to perfection but inside my soul was evil. I prayed to Our Lord for forgiveness and asked Him for the opportunity to redeem myself and to return to myself, as the Mother Church teaches. I beg forgiveness and swear that I will devote the remainder of the years left to me to the glory of Mother Church."

"Blasphemy."

"No, my Lord Cardinal, grant me forgiveness. I swear that I will journey to a faraway city and commence leading a life of virtue, as befits a good woman." Still kneeling, she ripped off the veil and the populace caught a glimpse of her beautiful cheek, down which tears streamed as she sobbed. "My Lord, see what the surgeon Tagliacozzi, a man of inestimable virtue, did for me, and ask yourself, my Lord Cardinal, how can such a man be punished for the glory of his work?"

Her exit was a virtuoso achievement. On her knees, she moved slowly toward the door, face shrouded once more in the veil, hands clasped together in front of her beatific face, as in supplication. She was accompanied by Buoncampagna, and she turned to address the audience at the door. "God bless you all and may your lives radiate seemly satisfactions to please Our Lord and sanctify the Mother Church." And she was gone.

"A bizarre episode," derided Flaminio. "It constitutes undeniable proof that, operating on the whore, Tagliacozzi was in league with the Devil."

A hushed silence had prevailed during the courtesan's appearance, but at this moment murmuring was heard in every corner of the packed hall, with ripples of laughter and noisy debates. The noise swelled in volume, and Bandini, sensing it was irrepressible, announced another brief recess.

Flaminio suffered from headache. He felt dizzy and nauseated and his rage was so great that, especially in the sultry, humid courtroom, he feared he would faint. The trial had been a nightmare. The deletion of the articles of accusation had riled him and then the neutral attitude of Cardinal Bandini had been unsettling. With the unorthodox use of the pigeon ineffectual, with Gasparo surprisingly formidable for a man enduring two weeks of solitary confinement, and with

Lorenzo asserting himself so stridently, his feeling of power was waning—and then Ghisella, the courtesan. *Disgusting,* mused Flaminio, *sordid and debauched; still, I will not retreat. I must destroy Gasparo; there is no choice.*

He turned to the prisoner. "Do you admit that the Frenchman you treated was a heretic?"

"I feel I should be allowed to treat any or every one who comes to me for help irrespective of color, race, or creed."

"My Lord, I demand that the accused be excommunicated and turned over to the secular arm. I demand that we purge the Church of God of such infection and cut off from it so rotten a member because he is a sorcerer and a magician on the word of Duglioli in that he bewitched his wife into allowing her child to be used as an offering to the Devil; and on the word of Professor Aranzio that no doctor has ever been able to accomplish this uncanny metamorphosis of the human face; because he is a heretic in that he prevented Tasso from visiting the Index and so interfered with the function of the Holy Inquisition; because, on the word of Maria Boschetti, he treated a heretic and broke his oath as a physician not to attend to patients without confession; because he is a heretic himself in that he denies the right of the Church to so make these laws." Taking the surgeon's manuscript in one hand, the Censor of Books grasped his instruments in the other hand. "I therefore demand that he be taken to the place of execution and there be burned at the stake," raising both hands over his head, "together with his manuscript and instruments."

A mighty crash resounded from the heavens, and once more the earth vibrated underfoot, a furious growling splitting the air as the first bolt of lightning knifed diagonally through the darkening sky to pierce into the terrified hearts of the onlookers.

"Brethren," shouted Flaminio, "the Lord speaks to you again; it is another warning that His wrath will rise to the full if we do not rid the City of Bologna of this heretic."

Cardinal Bandini confronted the accused. "Have you anything to say before the sentence of this Holy Court is pronounced?"

Gasparo rose. Passively, he had witnessed Lorenzo's bravura exhibition in his behalf, followed by the extraordinary appearance of Ghisella, but they had warmed his blood and fortified his resolve. He stood erect, proud, and self-doubt had vanished. "I fear that through excess of suffering may I prove faithless. I desire the glory of God. All my life I have respected the Church. I love God and the spirit of good, and when I am by myself I let my thoughts dwell on these, their immeasurable beneficence; the eternal wisdom, the source and origin of clearest light, that true joy within us which never fears that God will forsake us; that groundwork of truth; that willing love; and the Maker of us all, who is blessed in Himself, and likewise the desire and safeguard of all the blessed. Ah, what depth and what height of righteousness, mindful of the dead and not forgetting the living. He is the spirit who protects me by His commands, my good and merciful counselor, my helper and consoler in misfortune."

From above, another staccato explosion, a rumbling echoing and re-echoing in the stale, hot air, punctuated by a lean sliver of lightning that slashed down through the black sky toward a populace trembling with fear.

"The Lord speaks again," said the surgeon, "against the evil in the Church."

"What does that mean?" asked Bandini.

"I would prefer you ask Fra Vulpi, my Lord Cardinal."

"I am asking you."

"He knows the reason for this trial."

"Are you implying that personal motives are influencing Fra Vulpi?"

"He should answer. Please."

"What statement will you adduce, Fra Vulpi?"

"Of course not," said Flaminio.

"He does not speak the truth," said Gasparo.

"Where is your evidence?" asked Bandini.

"His scar."

"His scar? Of what import can this be?"

"My Lord Cardinal, would you please ask him how he acquired this disfigurement of his eyebrow?"

"An accident in my youth, Lord Cardinal," said Flaminio. "I tripped and fell on a rock."

"I threw the rock," said Gasparo.

"Why?" asked Bandini.

The surgeon sighed. *How bitter it is,* he mused, *that I must so humiliate my dearest childhood friend, but what other recourse remains to me, since his sickness compels him to destroy me?* "My Lord," he said slowly, "we were swimming—naked—as boys. We imbibed some wine later, and I succumbed to sleep. I awoke, your Excellency, and found him making love to me. We fought and I picked up a rock and—"

Flaminio paced back and forth in front of the prosecution table, faster and faster as his anxiety mounted, while his heart pounded so violently that he feared he would suffer a stroke. "Absurd," he shrieked, his voice rising with hysteria. "He lies. My Lord Cardinal, he lies."

"I speak the truth, Lord Cardinal," said Gasparo sadly. And then, after pausing, he added, "Besides, he claims I operated on a heretic, a Huguenot. Where is the evidence?"

"You make a point," said Bandini. "Where is your evidence, Fra Vulpi?"

Flaminio felt a wave of dizziness gripping him. "My Lord," he said, struggling to appear calm, "he is not available."

"Where is he?"

"When we came for him at Doctor Tagliacozzi's home, he was gone. We searched everywhere. He had disappeared."

"Disappeared?"

"Yes, my Lord Cardinal."

"Why haven't you informed us of this before?"

They cannot know, Flaminio reassured himself, holding the table for support. *There is no proof.* And, aloud, he said, "We were certain we would apprehend him."

"It would be far more fitting if we had the evidence."

"I have the evidence, my Lord Cardinal." In the audience, a friar in white gown and black hood leaped to his feet to deliver this astonishing statement.

Papa Gregory will sit enthralled as I tell him of this trial, mused Bandini. And, in a ringing voice, he asked, "And who, may I ask, are you, Father?"

"I am the evidence." The friar stepped forward, walked dramatically to the rostrum, and removed his hood. "I am the Frenchman—the Chevalier de Saint Thoan."

The spacious auditorium buzzed with anticipation, townspeople on the wooden benches craning their necks to stare at the Frenchman in friar's habit, who turned to face the papal Vice-Legate. Cardinal Bandini sat erect in his elevated chair, eyes quizzical beneath the red skullcap embroidered with white trim, to his rear the giant mural of Madonna and children warmly together, below him the teams of Inquisition officials, to the left the accused, and farther left, in the archway, seated Church and university dignitaries, Giulia tensely in their midst, flanked by the handsome black Scipio, the beautiful Caledonia, and the fiercely scowling Lorenzo, standing at attention, scrutinizing the Frenchman with sober mien.

"My Lord Cardinal," proclaimed the Chevalier de St. Thoan, rich baritone voice booming out to fill every corner of the immense hall, "I left your fair city on foot and escaped on horseback to Leghorn."

"Leghorn! And you returned?"

"Yes, my Lord Cardinal."

"Leghorn is a port for people of all religions," said Bandini. "Why did you come back?"

"To defend my friend and benefactor."

"You knew the danger. Why did you risk your life?"

St. Thoan stood straight and tall, his deep-brown eyes burning with a passionate fire, his chin thrust out in challenge and in pride. "In Leghorn, a land of freedom where everyone can worship as he pleases—Catholic, Huguenot, Jew, Turk, Muslim—I was not free. My conscience plagued me. Alas, I could not feel free until the doctor was free."

Haggard, pale, eyes mirroring alternating sensations of fear and anger, Flaminio Vulpi stalked restlessly around the prosecution table, beside himself with his need to attack the Frenchman. But it was Cardinal Bandini who insisted on pressing the interrogation, and Flaminio could only writhe in agony, wringing his hands, chest muscles constricting, blood pounding, as the Pope's representative asserted the prerogatives of his rank.

"You never confessed to a confessor while you were in the City of Bologna?" asked Bandini.

"No, my Lord Cardinal."

"Are you a Huguenot?"

"No, my Lord."

"Are you are a Turk or a Muslim?"

"No, my Lord."

"What are you?"

"A Jew!"

"A Jew?"

Simultaneously, Gasparo and Giulia had sighed, relief pouring from them on disclosure that St. Thoan was not a Huguenot; but the revelation that he was Jewish brought distress back to their faces, and they glanced covertly at each other, as if in mute signal or as if communicating a wish for an answer to the unanswerable. Throughout the assemblage the murmuring built to an uproar, and the more superstitious townspeople crossed themselves again and again, in repetitive spasms, hurling themselves upon their knees in frantic prayer, beseeching the protection of the Lord.

"A Jew?" repeated Bandini, waving for silence.

"Yes, my Lord."

"A Jew? A soldier?"

"A Jew, yes, my Lord," said St. Thoan, and his voice, melodious and resonant, rang out over the chamber, a hymnal, a benediction, a song of peace and love. "Jews were always fighting for peace. But I am no soldier."

"Who are you then?"

"A man of the cloth."

"A rabbi?"

"Yes, my Lord Cardinal."

"How did you come by your misfortune?"

"Protecting another human being."

"A Jew?"

"A Christian."

"You mean a Huguenot?"

"Yes, my Lord Cardinal. It was at the time of the Massacre of Saint Bartholomew. Hundreds of Christians, Huguenots, were slaughtered. One Huguenot, a friend of mine, Chevalier de Saint Thoan, sought refuge in my home. I protected him, but Catholic soldiers broke down my door. Saint Thoan escaped through the window. He was caught and murdered. A Catholic soldier returned. He beat me and cut off part of my nose with his dagger."

"Unbelievable."

"It is the truth, rest assured," said the Rabbi. "I would be happy indeed to discuss any aspect of the Bible with you, my Lord Cardinal."

"I do not think that will be necessary, Rabbi—"

"Rabbi Ben Lurian, my Lord Cardinal."

Bandini leaned forward, frowning as he contemplated this new complexity. "Now, let me see—"

"There is much to see, Lord Cardinal. I defended one Christian against another. I am sure there is no doubt in your mind that my purpose as a man of the cloth was to protect the life of a human being from another's brutality. It was my responsibility to prevent the bloodshed of war that has plagued mankind—that has no place in the spirit of fulfillment of man."

"Yes, I know, Rabbi."

"I was driven out of Paris and found refuge in Leghorn, a land of freedom. Here it was, my Lord, that I heard of the brilliant work of Doctor Gasparo Tagliacozzi. I had viewed the result on a man from Leghorn, a merchant whose goods were hijacked on the road to Florence. He was held for ransom by the bandits, your Excellency. They acquired their ransom, sire, but mutilated the merchant nevertheless. He was brought back to himself in God's image through the genius of Doctor Tagliacozzi. I loathed my abominably deformed nose and journeyed to this city for assistance."

"And you knew of the papal decree forbidding Catholics to operate on non-Catholics?"

"I knew of the decree," said the Rabbi. "I knew, my Lord Cardinal, that one Christian disfigured me for aiding another. I knew another, equally important decree, a decree for another Christian— a blessed Christian—to restore me to God's image. I knew what you know, my Lord, the greatest decree in existence, the decree of man's conscience in his search for self-respect to restore the self-respect of other human beings, in rendering assistance to a brother."

The thunder detonated again, crackling fiendishly from the ink-black sky. The concussion was savage now, a corps of Turkish cannon belching salvos upon the enemy, a roaring rapids bursting in an avalanche of foam upon the shore, fireworks igniting to sputter chaotically at a festival of ghosts. The earth was seized by a spastic internal convulsion, shaking with delirium, as in fever, and dozens of shrieking townspeople were hurled from their benches by the upheaval, there to lie, eyes wide with apprehension, as the lightning burst down from the enraged heavens, streaking jagged through the air, slitting the belly of the atmosphere with surgical precision, making incisions in the blackness, lighting up the barking, eruptive background, and in the distance, the Apennines, outside the City of Bologna, bleak and menacing in the heat. The thunder and lightning merged in a symphony of harshness, cymbals and trumpets crashing and bellowing at the frightened people clutching amulets of theriac, raising faces desperately to inhale the fumes of vinegar and incense.

"It is the end," cried out one poor soul. "The day of judgment is here, and Our Lord invokes His wrath to chastise us for our wickedness."

And then the rain commenced to pound down, lashing bitingly through the lightning, drenching the earth, driving relentlessly onto the roof of the Castello San Angelo. The lightning flashed wildly outside, illuminating the violent stampede of rain, while inside the stone building, in the dim torchlight, people knelt in prayer, women counting their beads and murmuring of their good deeds. The thunder blasted in rancorous encore, its reverberations drowning out the impact of the rain and the cries of the fearful. In phalanxes, the precipitation besieged the earth, stinging the grass, crumbling dirt into mud, bouncing up and out in deep puddles, unleashing its animal fury without mercy, untamed, licentious, almost depraved in its brutality.

"The thunder, my Lord Cardinal," proclaimed Rabbi Ben Lurian, "is the voice of God asking his children to stop wars, all wars, to seek human fulfillment, to arrive at the ideal trysting place for suffering humanity—the brotherhood of man." The Rabbi pulled out from under the friar's habit something suspended on a string around his neck. "It is a ram's horn," he said reverently.

"It is the shofar?" asked Bandini. "For the Jewish Day of Atonement?"

"Yes," said the Rabbi simply, and once, twice, three times he blew the horn. "The horn says *the time is now for the brotherhood of man.* May the sound of the ram's horn summon us against the forces of evil within our hearts and in the world. Oh, hasten the blessed time when all dwellers on earth shall harken unto the sound of the ram's horn and shall worship as one brotherhood at Thy holy fountain, O Lord!"

Lustily, he blew the ram's horn, the sound echoing and re-echoing in the air.

And then silence.

"The time is now," said Bandini. "Quite so, my friend." He rose from his chair and walked slowly past the groups of Inquisition officials to stand near Rabbi Ben Lurian. "The time is now, to usher you, Rabbi Ben Lurian, into the sunlight toward the port of Leghorn."

Flaminio Vulpi, Censor of Books, had seated himself, head bowed, at the prosecution table, shivering in the heat. He had heard little of what the Frenchman had said, reconciling himself to defeat after Bandini had insisted on directing the interrogation. Gasparo's public accusation—that he had tried to love him carnally—had filled his mind with guilt and, self-conscious, he imagined that everyone in the courtroom was whispering about him, that his innermost secrets were common knowledge. *The Devil has consumed me,* he acknowledged to himself, *and Gasparo tells the truth for, indeed, I still love him.*

"And you, Doctor Tagliacozzi," said Bandini, facing the accused, "you are free."

Numbly, Flaminio had turned inward. He was not really in the courtroom at all. He was in the country and the sun was beating down on his naked body as Gasparo, also nude, passed him the wine bottle and lay back on the blanket. Then, of a sudden, he realized what the Cardinal was saying. "No," he screamed. "He cannot go. I love him. Yes, I love him."

Bandini appraised Flaminio, uncontrollably shrieking now, with compassion. "I request that you, Captain General Buoncampagna," he said softly to the military commander, "see that your soldiers escort Fra Vulpi to the Dominican monastery to be under the protective custody of the Mother Church."

"He cannot go," howled Flaminio, struggling to twist away from the pair of soldiers who had seized him, sobbing and raging in his grief and humiliation. "He cannot go. I love him. No, my brethren, he must burn. The Devil has taken possession of his soul, and he must burn."

His eyes solemn, sympathetic, Bandini watched the soldiers of the Church remove the writhing, hysterical Censor of Books from the courtroom. Then he turned to Gasparo. "Doctor Tagliacozzi, you are free to go with your family to the port of Leghorn."

The surgeon paused before answering. "My Lord Cardinal," he said, "I feel indebted to my loyal friends in this fair city and have decided that my freedom is here, where I was born."

"So be it," said Bandini, and he took Rabbi Ben Lurian by the arm. "Come with me, Brother."

Crying with relief, Giulia rushed to embrace her husband, burying her face in his neck, tears moistening his flesh.

"You must cease your wailing," he said, as if in jest, "for your eyes will drown me in their rivulets."

"No, no, my feelings must not be dammed up. Not now, my love, when they overflow with joy and gratitude. For I feared the worst, I do confess, and no laughter will ever comfort me as do these woman's tears."

Hungrily, they embraced again, clinging to each other with the desperation of urgent need fulfilled.

"It is a miracle," said Giulia then. "The thunder and lightning are no more, and the rain has vanished. The sky lightens, my love, and there, look, patches of blue appear. Softness and sweetness return, and, yes, the sun comes back to give us warmth."

Chapter 26

The surgeon left the courtroom of the Castello San Angelo accompanied by Giulia, who, fearful that she might injure his bandaged hands, clutched his elbow. Walking in the sunlight with his wife, he felt exhausted and yet a sense of pride sustained and energized him.

The fresh air tasted like a mellow wine, the rumbling of carriages over the cobblestones sounded like music, and the aromas of the marketplace invaded his nostrils with a heady fragrance.

Swarms of noisy students, led by Lorenzo and his wife, escorted them to the street Delle Lame. Other supporters of Tagliacozzi joined in the procession; it was an incongruous entourage, including Scipio Africanus Borzani, Ghisella, the courtesan, and Jacopo Buoncampagna, the military commander. The buildings in the public square seemed to glisten, and the ninety jets of the Fountain of Neptune spurted water into the air as if applauding Gasparo's release.

He felt overwhelmed by the strength of his feeling for Giulia. The tender touch of her hand under his arm filled him with a deep gratitude, and he experienced a sense of rebirth, escaping the cold harshness of the tiny cell to return triumphant to their home on the street Delle Lame. Together, they walked through the front door and into the consultation room, where, kneeling, they prayed before the silver crucifix. Alone, they looked at each other with joy and sadness, kissing gently, as if for the first time, and Gasparo, even in his weariness, felt a resurgence of youthful hope.

Later Rabbi Ben Lurian arrived to say good-bye and the two men, weeping, embraced like brothers. Then the Rabbi left for Leghorn.

Gasparo felt rejuvenated by the simple act of lying in bed again, close to his wife, content with the joy of reunion. He placed his leg under her leg and crossed his foot over hers. While in prison, he had not dared to realize how much he missed her. He placed an arm under her neck and she snuggled her head on his shoulder, face close to his. They did not talk, drifting aimlessly, satisfied, kissing softly now and then.

She arched her breasts against him and her fingers rested lightly on his cheek. Their feet were still intertwined—it was as if they were kissing—and they drifted into sleep.

At dawn, the surgeon strolled into the garden, wandering under the tree, looking up at the branches. His hands were not so sore, so he had taken off the bandages. In his mind, he could see his father removing a small tree branch and transplanting it into the earth; he re-experienced wonderment on recalling how he had formulated the concept of grafting skin from the arm to cover a facial defect. Why did he think of Flaminio at this moment? Was it in association with the tragedy befalling his father? Vulpi would never regain his sanity; he was a lost soul, doomed to a life of emptiness and negation.

After breakfast, he walked and walked. For weeks imprisoned, he felt liberated at regaining freedom of movement. At the Mercato di Mezzo, he turned into the Piazza Maggiore, bordered by the Lambertacci Palace and the Cathedral of San Pietro, overlooked by the Prendiparte Tower and the Asinella.

A huge crowd was gathered in the public square, watching a troupe of acrobats. Nearby, townspeople boasted amulets of theriac to ward off the plague and the Devil, and prostitutes used the theriac to protect themselves from syphilis. Soldiers and students, in various stages of intoxication, some drugged by opium, were flirting with the girls; there were also noblemen on horseback and Dominican monks crossing themselves and praying to God. Duglioli passed by clutching his amulet of theriac. He was followed by his wife and handsome little boy.

The acrobats exited, and a pair of gaudily attired itinerant charlatans staged a grand entrance, regaling spectators with tales of their incomparable prowess.

The first charlatan discoursed upon a elixir. "For ten centesimi, my friends, you may purchase a bottle of this precious fluid, distilled by me for the purpose of arresting incipient insanity."

His partner extolled the virtues of a love potion. "I guarantee virility to the old and the young and the sick and the well and the fat and the thin. This potion, whose formula is known only to a chosen few, will revitalize those suffering from backache, insomnia, painful urination, and constipation. Higher and lower persons, members of the titled nobility, ladies and gentlemen, it will exalt your desires of the flesh and launch you into the orbit of the goddess Venus."

Is there no progress? Gasparo asked himself. *Is everything as in the past? The superstitions, the violence, the chicanery, will these phenomena repeat themselves to eternity, like a recurring nightmare? Where is the great Michelangelo today, towering above his fellows, opting for the sanctity of human aspiration? Has he vanished forever? Or is he still in the crowd, whispering to an unheeding mankind of its potential for growth?*

Is there a change from yesterday? he wondered. *Of course. The little boy, the son of the candlemaker, born with a harelip, is a normal-looking child and will become a fine adult. Is there progress? Of course. The Grand Duke of Tuscany has created Leghorn, a haven of peace for those fleeing persecution, a symbol, an augury of universal brotherhood.*

Gasparo, exhausted from his ordeal, half asleep, imagined that Brown Pigeon fluttered down from the sky to alight on his shoulder. He addressed the bird as if it were one of his students, and they entered into dialogue.

"Signor Brown Pigeon, the world undergoes a drastic transition, from hatred to brotherly love. It is not what you *are* that matters but what you are becoming."

"You have hope for mankind?"

"Yes, Brown Pigeon, for what is hope? Hope is what you are becoming. In these violent times many worry about the fate of the human race. But is this not an individual consideration? Is not the crucial issue what becomes of each human being?"

"This is true, Professor, for my studies tell me that the philosophers engage in disputation among themselves."

"Action may be more fundamental than thought, my dear friend, for you must do more than *think*. You must *act*. To achieve self-respect, you must demonstrate courage and persistence in the face of adverse conditions. One must do battle to arrive at reasonable objectives and to reach one's true stature and dignity."

"But behold the mobs giving credence to the itinerant charlatans everywhere, who do a brisk trade throughout the continent."

"True, but man, in his groping fashion, will strike out toward realization of his potential. Daily, man must give, share, grow, honor, he must eradicate hate and evil through such valiant efforts. Indeed, the hope of the human race lies in the striving to become and to do good for others. Do you agree, Brown Pigeon?"

"Progress is slow, Gasparo, and it creeps on shaky underpinnings."

"I must admit this. But ponder on the miracle of Leghorn, a place for the brotherhood of man. Here people are granted the right to progress and to justice. In the precious haven of Leghorn, they learn to deal sensibly with life and to yearn for improvement in their conditions. A few lead the way, others will follow."

"A wonderful dream."

"*Become* a reality. Leghorn is an inspiration, my friend. It is a cherished symbol, roaring out to the world, 'The time is now for fulfillment of human needs and for the brotherhood of man.'"

Fortified by the imagined conversation, the surgeon walked back to the street Delle Lame.

Three days later, celebrating the surgeon's acquittal, the public square vibrated with joyful carnival spirit. Indeed, seldom in the history of the University City had such a colorful spectacle been staged in honor of one of its citizens.

A quintet of trumpeters summoned the townspeople to congregate, huge bearded men wearing turbans of red sable, the leader a gigantic fellow with enormous shoulders, dressed in a multicolored gown engraved with arabesques, his ample waist girdled by a blood-red sash.

Soon the square was jammed with Tagliacozzi's personal friends, students from the university, city officials, a sprinkling of faculty members, the more enlightened townspeople—and many of his enemies.

The procession was dazzling, an opulent display of the exuberance that in volatile fashion characterized post-Renaissance Italy, for this was an age and a country in which, emotionally, flamboyantly, ecstatically, men celebrated life and death and knowledge and ignorance, marching in obeisance to creativity and destructiveness, truth and superstition, peace and war.

Ablaze with color, intoxicated with ceremonial, the City of Bologna was in love with movement. Around the public square, in rings surrounding one another, its citizens promenaded; on the outside perimeter, thousands of cheering celebrants strutted in formation, past the buildings fronting the huge open area. The inner ring of bristling, elegant humanity paraded after a wheeled float shaped like an elephant. This ring consisted of dignitaries, including magnificently robed senators and university professors, the Governor of Bologna, and noblemen, including Count Taddeo Pepoli and Count Lorenzo Desiri, the latter in bright-red suit, astride a prancing brown stallion. Behind Lorenzo was Scipio Africanus Borzani, holding aloft a fiery black-and-red banner. In all, four rings of marchers circled the public square in a mobile riot of color, the columns including multiple floats in the form of emblematic animals—unicorn, goose, snail, or elephant—revelers in whites and blacks and yellows and reds, on foot and on horseback, carrying banners of diverse hues and shapes, wielding long, sharp-pointed spears. Included in the outside ring were hundreds of students from the university, chanting slogans and singing hymns, waving enormous placards spelling out ardent messages: LIBERTY FOR TAGLIACOZZI IS LIBERTY FOR ITALY; TRUTH IS SCIENCE; THE TIME IS NOW.

At one end of the square the five trumpeters, accompanied now by a lute player and two drummers, blasted out vigorous martial tunes propelling the participants round and round in concentric formations. Near the musicians a trio of acrobats in tights turned somersaults and cartwheels, building to pyramids, and jested with the marchers. From the buildings lining the square, thousands of spectators viewed the proceedings, crowding archways, windows, doorways, and rooftops, applauding the paraders and shouting encouragement to them.

Not that the carnival spirit was shared by all. Viewers showed their disapproval in many ways—crossing themselves, clutching amulets of theriac, counting beads, lifting heads high in supplication of God for mercy, whispering to neighbors about the dangers of sorcery, the curse of the Evil Eye, and the sordid machinations of the Devil and his disciples.

Still, even some old-time foes of Tagliacozzi joined in the massive celebration, and one could not say whether it was the noise, the color, or the verve of the revelers that most marked the pageantry. In the background, the buildings and towers were draped with gaudy banners; from these vantage points the spectators were also participants, filling the air with confetti, lighting firecrackers and hurling them high to explode overhead, and playing musical instruments. Afterward, there were spirited boxing matches and duels and, later still, more fireworks and music, with wild dancing in the streets until after midnight.

The fun was not confined to the public square. There were small private parties on the university campus, in taverns, and in homes of the surgeon's supporters. The most boisterous of all was at the house of Ghisella, the courtesan.

This great lady was so overjoyed by the liberation of her personal savior that she renounced all the vows she had announced so fervently during the trial, nay, if anything, she added dimension and scope and intensity to her sinful life-style.

"There will be no fee today for services rendered at my establishment," she announced grandly to any passer-by who would listen (and many did), "to commemorate the restoration to honor of the greatest man who ever lived, the incomparable surgeon who repaired the hideous wound in my lovely cheek. And, my dear friends, this is additionally a festival day for observing another glorious anniversary, for it is seven months to the day since the death of the lecherous, immoral, thieving scoundrel Enrico Gradenigo who—and I reveal this most reluctantly—lost his penis at an early age during an eclipse of the moon."

The news of Ghisella's offer spread, and quickly her house was mobbed by the passionate and the penurious. Scuffles erupted among the bargain hunters lined up in front of her doorway, as the whooping, hollering males jockeyed for position, and the line extended around the block and beyond. The bald-headed Duke of Cremona, exultant conqueror of impotence with the aid and abetment of the opera singer from Milan, was strolling along, jauntily twirling a cane, when, half a kilometer from the brothel of his dreams, he sighted the pushing, shoving mass of humanity trampling Ghisella's immaculate front lawn. Horrified at the prospect of assuming an unaccustomed identity as Number 253 in relation to the favors of his beloved, he initiated an ill-advised maneuver toward the front door and was clubbed unconscious by a burly medical student, who, bored with his studies of vipers, wished firsthand experience with female anatomy. The ranks of the Ghisella-watchers swelled with the arrival of survivors who had endured a dozen circlings of the public square and who, after quenching their thirst at the city's taverns, charged headlong into the waiting mob. At this, the battle was joined. Hundreds of warm-blooded, hot-tempered, lecherous males punched and kicked one another on the lawn of Ghisella, the courtesan, and when a Pepoli sighted a Castelli, both pulled swords from sheaths in reflex and this triggered a series of duels that bloodied Tagliacozzi Day. Soldiers arrived to restore order and to arrest troublemakers, including the bald-headed Duke of Cremona, who, regaining consciousness, had instinctively struck out with his cane at the first object in his path—the military commander, Captain Jacopo Buoncampagna.

It was a memorable day in Lorenzo Desiri's rollicking life. He and his wife had commenced celebrating the evening before, sharing a quart bottle of wine, gorging themselves on heaping platters of veal and sausage and mushrooms and peppers, washing down the meal with more tumblers of wine and large, succulent blue grapes, and then retiring to their bedroom for a night of the flesh.

In the morning, buoyant, Lorenzo dressed for the pageant in the public square. Then, after honoring his friend Gasparo, he returned home with Caledonia to dine and make love. Satiated, his wife was sleeping soundly and when, a half hour later, Lorenzo, feeling the thrust of another erection, attempted to rouse her, she murmured something drowsily, buried her head in her pillow, and started snoring.

This was too much for Lorenzo, infatuated with his soaring powers. *It is insufferable,* he thought, *that this splendid feeling should not achieve satisfaction in action.* Grasping Caledonia roughly by the shoulder, he shook her, but she remained insensible and continued to snore. *How can my wife be allowed to so frustrate me?* mused Lorenzo. *It is not to be tolerated. Does this not violate the very purpose of life?* Bitterly, he recalled the week Caledonia had denied him by visiting her sick mother in Rome. *An act of inconsideration,* he concluded, *an abomination.*

Very well, he would exercise his prerogative as a man of character and visit Ghisella, the courtesan. Certainly this was the only honorable course to follow. The fantasies multiplied in his mind—Ghisella naked on the bed, her breasts heaving as he bent to kiss her pink nipples, writhing in rhythm to the heat of his penis of steel; Ghisella— Then the fantasies changed direction, for he had heard of the exotic qualities of the black girl with orange hair from Morocco and— Count Lorenzo Desiri could bear it no longer. He leaped to his feet and hurled on his clothes. "I love you, Caledonia," he whispered, leaving. "But, after all, I am a man."

But, as he strode vigorously from the house, banging the front door, three men eased from the shadows to trail him from a distance—a brother of the late Enrico Gradenigo and two hired assassins from Sicily. Singing loudly, the chief of the Pepoli *bravi* walked down the street, boots clomping on the cobblestones. Waving to an acquaintance, he turned down a dark, deserted street. Barely in time, he wheeled as his enemies attacked from the rear. He pulled stiletto from sheath and, lashing out, stabbed the brother of Enrico Gradenigo in the stomach, killing him, and then launched himself upon one of the hired assassins, wounding him severely. But the other assassin seized the opportunity while Lorenzo was thus engaged and, moving swiftly, thrust his dagger into the soldier's heart.

Desiri died instantly. It was ironic that, a moment before, he had been singing, his sexual powers at their lusty peak, his pores reservoirs of vigor, his nature bold, ardent, selfish, loyal, boorish, courageous, and thoughtless. He had lived without fear. He died brave and undaunted. Did the violins play for Lorenzo on his death? Did the angels sing? It did not matter. Lorenzo had lived to seize the day; he had never recognized the reality of the morrow.

Gasparo had relaxed with his family. Appearing briefly at the celebration in the public square to express his gratitude to the cheering throngs, he had hastened back to his house, where he could sit in the garden and talk to his beloved Giulia. He was still exhausted from his ordeal, and it was a pleasure to idle away the time. Later, he was startled and terribly saddened to hear of Lorenzo's death, and Giulia and he visited Caledonia to offer consolation and to help with the funeral arrangements.

As the days passed, the surgeon noted a change in his son, now sixteen years old. The boy had not attended the trial, but he was beginning to understand its implications in terms of principle and of his father's motivation in his work. Not that Gasparo learned this from conversations with his son—the two found communication difficult—but Giulia relayed to him the substance of *her* discussions with Giovanni Andrea. In a direct way, the boy showed his new attitude at meals, nodding hello to his father in a timid, friendly fashion, glancing at him now and then with respect, volunteering to pass him the platter of bread.

Gasparo was touched at these signs of reconciliation, but pained that he could not find anything to say to his son and that Giovanni Andrea was tongue-tied in his presence. How could he break through this impasse? His wife informed him that the lad was making friends, finally, but between father and son a silence reigned as vast and unconquerable as the fortress of the Apennines.

One day the boy left to take a walk and, overcome by an ungovernable impulse that he could not suppress, Gasparo followed at a distance. Proudly, Giovanni Andrea walked through the streets, head held high even when strangers crossed themselves and clutched amulets of theriac. He strolled past the university and the Fountain of Neptune, and at the public square he turned to a tower and commenced to climb the stairs.

Astonishing, reflected the surgeon, *for it was from this tower that Lorenzo and Flaminio and I launched pebbles down at pedestrians in the street.*

On another impulse, he decided to trail his son up the winding stairs. Somewhat winded at the first landing, he was thoroughly exhausted when he reached the top of the tower.

The two looked at each other, Gasparo panting and heaving with the overexertion. "I followed you here," the surgeon said simply.

"I know."

He must have looked back and seen me, thought Gasparo, but he could say no more.

Giovanni Andrea asked himself what he could communicate, but no words would flow from him. *What is this eternal quiet between my father and myself?* he wondered. *And how can I penetrate the gulf separating us? For I was a child, an ignorant fool, to spurn him, but, though wiser, though the need burns hotly within me, still I cannot talk with my father.*

Gasparo, too, was puzzled. *My son grows taller and more handsome, and at last he grows in stature as a person. I begin to respect him and to feel that he will do well in affairs of the world. Yet am I a most backward father in that my tongue is useless. Even here, looking out over the city, I cannot tell him what is in my heart. But why should this be so? Do I punish myself for my inadequacy? Should I not feel compassion for myself in the uncertainties of my human condition? Should I not accept my gropings, clumsy though they may be, because they are sincere? Then, perchance, may I bury our past miseries in the tomb of time, reaching out to the flesh of my flesh to open lines of communication between us, however fragile.*

I hate myself, thought Giovanni Andrea, *for the terrible things I said to you, Father. Can I forgive myself for my ignorance as a child? I called you a sorcerer. May I retract this nonsense?*

Haltingly, the father spoke. "What stroke of fate directed your steps to this tower, my son?"

"Mama told me how you and your friends, as children, played here. I wanted to see for myself. Was it a mad idea, Father?"

The surgeon laughed, overjoyed that his son was conversing with him. "We are all mad; my friend Girolamo Cardano used to tell me this. My dear son, in civilized society people devour one another like lions but, since refinement is required, they dab their mouths afterward with a genteel napkin."

"I was ignorant and childish. I realize now that your work is admirable and that you have dedicated yourself to the betterment of humanity. Truly, Father, I hope that you can find it in your heart to forgive me for my stupidity."

Tears flooded Gasparo's eyes, and he could barely trust himself to speak. "I do more than forgive you. I bless you for what you have said, for it lightens my burden and fills my heart with joy. In truth, my son, I have found it exceedingly difficult to converse with you and have condemned myself for my inadequacies as a father—rightly so, for establishment of proper communication is preeminently a parent's responsibility."

"I, too, have been unable to talk to you—"

"I know, and humbly do I beg your forgiveness."

It was Giovanni Andrea's turn to feel tortured by pangs of guilt. How could he enter into the world of his father without giving him worry or embarrassment or cause for self-reproach? And then it occurred to him that perhaps he might relate to Gasparo's world when he was a child. "You came to this tower when you were ten years old?"

"Lorenzo and Flaminio and I climbed here, feeling that we were on top of the world, and we rained pebbles at pedestrians in the street. There was an old man with gray hair and beard and stooped back, and Lorenzo pelted him pitilessly. Lorenzo was young and ignorant, unaware that this was the great Michelangelo, the spark who ignited our illustrious Renaissance."

"Did you like Lorenzo and Flaminio, Father?"

Memories of his childhood burned brightly in the surgeon's mind. "Flaminio," he said, "was a sweet, sensitive youth, my closest childhood companion, but he was unable to love a woman and, my son, his desire was to be my friend forever. When this wish was frustrated, he struggled for power, but when he gained it, he tried to use it to destroy me, for my existence threatened him. As for Lorenzo, he was a bold fellow who pursued the dictates of his body. He outboxed every other child in the neighborhood and bullied anyone standing in his way. I do not understand why God cannot exercise more mercy, for today Flaminio is insane and Lorenzo is dead."

What may I do, Giovanni Andrea sighed, *to lift the sadness from my father's heart? Can it be lifted? By me? how? Or was I born to multiply his burdens and immerse him in misery?* "I am sorry," he said. "I am very sorry."

A chill running up and down his spine, the surgeon looked directly into his son's eyes. *Yesterday,* he mused, *I looked away and, lo, today you are proud and as strong as an oak and your eyes mirror a new feeling stirring magnificently. You begin to feel a sense of the complex realities of life, and with it you breathe a fresh heady air, composed of self-respect and compassion, and, my son, you tread on hallowed territory sacred to the angels and to Our Lord.* He moved to embrace the son from whom he had so long been estranged, and the boy came running into his arms and unabashedly both were weeping.

Standing on the platform atop the tower, Giovanni Andrea marveled at the landscape spread out like a banquet before his eyes. "I am a new person," he said, "with a new father. Gazing at the Apennines, I see what you felt as a boy; I see beyond the street Delle Lame, beyond the mountains to a new world, and happily will I set out in this world to bring glory to our illustrious family name."

Together, they descended the tower stairs, but the surgeon's joy was diluted by an overpowering fatigue washing through him. *It must have been*, he reasoned, *the long walk and the ascent of the tower.*

Two years later, a courier arrived with an invitation from Ferdinando, Grand Duke of Tuscany. A celebration was planned to commemorate the anniversary of the founding of the port of Leghorn as a haven for religious freedom and a sanctuary for the brotherhood of man.

Gasparo accepted and left shortly in his horse-drawn carriage, accompanied by wife and son. The trip was uneventful, mostly down the same road to Florence traversed so many times during his lifetime. The surgeon recalled these memories, but his reminiscences centered on Vincenzo Gonzaga, now Duke of Mantua, and on the Chevalier de St. Thoan—no, the Rabbi Ben Lurian, he reminded himself.

He was anticipating the forthcoming meeting in Leghorn with Vincenzo and had written the Duke about his manuscript on plastic surgery published in the aftermath of the trial. He had dedicated the book to Gonzaga and would present him a copy during the festivities at the glorious port city.

As for St. Thoan-Ben Lurian, the Rabbi was infinitely dear to his heart. In operating upon the Frenchman, he had done more than remove the man's outer scar; he had removed the inner scar hardening his son's heart. For Giulia told him how for the first time Giovanni Andrea had understood the humane motivation underlying his father's work and how far this sense of purpose transcended the physical pain endured by patients. *Man exists in three worlds,* reflected Gasparo, *body, mind, and spirit. The brave Frenchman was mutilated in all three worlds. He required help in the world of his body to repair his mind and his spirit. And, miracle of miracles, when he was healed in his three worlds, my son was healed in his two deformed worlds—in his mind and in his spirit.*

These thoughts cheered the surgeon, seated in the bouncing carriage alongside Giulia, glancing now and then at tall, handsome Giovanni Andrea. But his state of health depressed him. Constantly, he attempted to reassure himself that he really did feel well; surely the daily fatigue that enveloped him was a temporary phase, a result of strain arising from his arrest, imprisonment, and ordeal at the trial. But many months had passed since the trial, and the energy of his youth had vanished.

At Leghorn, the boisterous festivities were under way. On display in the harbor, the fleet of the Grand Duke of Tuscany was to stage simulated battle maneuvers. The flag of each ship fluttered high in the breeze, while multicolored banners and wreaths of flowers decorated the decks, on which sailors in dress uniforms, standing at attention, were cheered by revelers. Then the giant guns of the fleet roared out their joy at the anniversary, spectators hurled masses of confetti into the air, and the mock battle began. It was, perhaps, a contradiction of the spirit of peace and brotherhood, but it was free of violence and destruction, and the combatants enacted their roles with playfulness.

The public square of Leghorn was also a scene of colorful pageantry. The list of events was almost endless. First, announcement of the program by the town crier. A parade followed, then an address by Ferdinando, Grand Duke of Tuscany, and a long string of entertainments: horse racing, boxing matches, performances by acrobats and jesters, enactment of plays.

In the evening the celebration continued, with wine flowing freely, dancing, and detonating fireworks lighting up the sky with colors of the rainbow.

The surgeon was sad that Lorenzo would not be able to attend the lavish ball sponsored by Grand Duke Ferdinando in honor of the anniversary of the founding of Leghorn. The death of his childhood companion had filled him with sorrow, but he brightened at the thought that soon he would be seeing his old friend Vincenzo Gonzaga and the Rabbi Ben Lurian.

In the palatial grand ballroom the Duke of Mantua rushed to embrace Gasparo. "I congratulate you, my dear friend," joked Vincenzo, "on passing *your* trial."

"It was, by comparison, a simple affair," laughed the surgeon, "for

I was permitted to retain the protection of my shabby prisoner's clothing."

"You have taken medicine into virgin territory," said Vincenzo.

"In the area of virginity, your art is unparalleled; the world salutes you. And it is an honor, my Duke, to present you with a copy of my book."*

The Rabbi Ben Lurian had arrived. "Never have I tasted such happiness," he said simply. "You are my savior."

"And, my good Rabbi, you are mine."

The orchestra was playing a waltz and the surgeon and his wife glided over the smooth marble floor. Giulia was humming gaily, but suddenly Gasparo's mood was sober, for once more an exhaustion seemed to press down on his body. *I shall visit Girolamo Mercuriale shortly for an examination,* he thought, but he felt that he would be all right and, not wishing to deprive his wife of the pleasure of waltzing, continued to lead her around the ballroom.

Then, abruptly, an agonizing pain tore down his left shoulder, running down the arm to bite into his fingers. A severe pain like this had alarmed him shortly after he had been forced to stab Morisini (and once before this), but it had disappeared almost instantly. Now it overwhelmed him and he stopped dancing, begging Giulia to fetch a doctor. She saw the agony on his face and, horrified, scurried off. *Forgive me, God,* he prayed, *for using the skin of people's arms to correct their facial disfigurements. Do you thus, O Lord, punish me in this manner—an arm for an arm? Oh, but I feel so tired. It is an unjust punishment, Lord, for my desire was to help people, can you not see this?* The pain was still more intense and he realized that he was dying. He thought first of Giulia and then of his son and was immersed in despair. In a series of overlapping images, the substances of his life raced through his mind: childhood adventures with Flaminio and Lorenzo; the business trip with his father and their arguments over his vocation; Michael Servetus, hideously in flames; his mother, Isabetta, mop in hand, eternally cleaning the house; marrying Giulia Carnali and the joy of their honeymoon; the afternoon in the country with Flaminio, and Vulpi's lifelong struggle to destroy him; the battles of Lepanto and Vienna; walks to and from the university, past the hostile townspeople; coun-

* *The Surgical Treatment of Mutilations by Graft,* published in 1597 in Latin.

: 408 :

seling the Prince of Mantua during his trial; his operations on Scipio, Lorenzo, Virginio Orsini, Ghisella, and the Chevalier de St. Thoan- Rabbi Ben Lurian; recognition from Grand Duke Ferdinando; the horrible revenge of Morisini; imprisonment, trial, and acquittal, thanks to the moderation of Cardinal Bandini. The images of people and feelings and places interpenetrated one another kaleidoscopically, a chaotic merging of impressions without beginning or end. *Lord, in my confusion and terror, have I done good for humanity?* His last thoughts were of Giulia, for he had adored her and worshiped at the shrine of her beauty and goodness.

All at once he crumpled into an inanimate heap on the floor. Screaming, Giulia rushed to him, too late, for his eyes were glazed and unseeing. The doctor trailing Giulia examined the surgeon and pronounced him dead.

"No," she cried out. "No, it cannot be."

But it was so, one of the totally unacceptable, intolerable realities, and for the moment no euphemism could shield it from the consciousness of those in the ballroom. Gently, Vincenzo Gonzaga and the surgeon's son pried the hysterical woman from her husband's lifeless body and led her, sobbing uncontrollably, to an anteroom in a wing of the palace.

The Rabbi Ben Lurian, weeping, stared unbelievingly at the eminent surgeon, struck down by superstition and ignorance and blind hate at the age of fifty-four, on November 7, 1599. In death, Gasparo's face was pale but calm, and the Rabbi folded the surgeon's long, sensitive, bejeweled fingers over his chest.

Vincenzo Gonzaga, Duke of Mantua, had returned to gaze upon the corpse of his friend. "He assisted me in regaining my honor at a time when the world laughed in my face."

"He was a splendid father," whispered Giovanni Andrea, "and I thank you, O Lord, for sparing him until I was able to understand this and begin to appreciate the sweetness of his nature."

No minister or priest was present in the distinguished assemblage. Grand Duke Ferdinando of Tuscany, in ceremonial white-striped doublet, wearing the robe of the Grand Master of the Order of Santo Stefano, eyes somber beneath a crown ornamented with the Florentine lily, addressed the Rabbi Ben Lurian, requesting that he administer extreme unction.

"O Lord," thundered the Rabbi, "this man was blessed by his deep regard for the sanctity of human life. He was not a shallow believer in the brotherhood of man. Lord, this man *practiced* the divine principle and for this reason do I commend him especially to your loving care."

The funeral cortege proceeded to the City of Bologna, where the body of Gasparo Tagliacozzi was to be laid to rest.

Giulia sobbed intermittently throughout the journey. She could not believe what she had seen—Gasparo tumbling to the floor, eyes vacant, his body and his love for life gone forever. It was too much. *Would that I, too, were dead,* she prayed. *O God, strike me dead in my tracks, please do me this beneficence, so that I may rejoin my beloved husband in Heaven.* But it was not to be, and in her grief and loneliness, submerged so deep in despair that she feared she would never escape its quicksands, she surrendered to her tears. *God, no longer do I wish to live,* she moaned to herself. *Please, be merciful.*

In her house on the street Delle Lame, she had cherished the portrait of her husband, by Tiburzio Passarotti, son of Bartolomeo. It was a fine likeness and, returning, she rushed to see it. The eyes of her beloved husband stared back at her. It was not endurable; she retreated hastily from this ghostly image of her loved one.

Mourned by wife and son and friends, Gasparo Tagliacozzi was buried in consecrated ground of the Church of San Giovanni Battista in the City of Bologna. His funeral was attended by leading civic officials of the University City and by former academic colleagues, and even Cesare Aranzio honored him with his presence.

Flaminio, under the protective custody of the Mother Church, was absent. Of the three childhood friends, he was the sole survivor. He prayed constantly to God, beseeching Him for support against the temptations of the Devil, and in his mind, flames crackled and sizzled and the Devil laughed mockingly.

The funeral oration was recited by the humanist Muzio Piacentini of Friuli. He eulogized the achievements of the surgeon, comparing him to Hippocrates and others. "Never," he said, "will they boast of a physician equal or even similar to the great Tagliacozzi." And, he added, only through emulation "can we hasten after his death from this human habitation to that divine abode, going by the straight pathway and without stumbling."

Time would attest to Tagliacozzi's unquestioned status as one of the great surgeons. But he was more than a superb technician. He was a bold creative genius, a man of courage who battled the forces of darkness, and, indeed, he may rightly be called the father of modern plastic surgery. Tragically, though his cause was honorable and humane, the strain of the ordeal proved too much. Did he not sacrifice his life for it?

The Rabbi Ben Lurian attended the funeral and returned to the Tagliacozzi residence with Giulia and her son, staying overnight. He offered what comfort he could to the bereaved widow and son.

Giovanni Andrea was submerged in guilt. "I killed my father; while he was alive, I gave him naught but heartache," he sobbed. "He revived *you* and I destroyed *him.*"

"You must forgive yourself," said Ben Lurian. "Do not hate yourself. You were young and lacked the understanding that comes with maturity."

"I called him a sorcerer. How can I forgive this?"

"You were ignorant, like all youths, who have not had time to learn from life. But you must find your self-respect and heal your wounds with the balm of compassion."

Ben Lurian occupied the same bedroom as a whole man as he had as a patient. He could not sleep, and through the night he could hear the weeping of Giulia.

He saw the forces of light working for Gasparo and for all mankind even after the surgeon's demise. Reeling under a flood of memories, pacing the room in darkness, he recalled his initial entrance into this residence and, moving in and out of the bedroom, he re-experienced the agony of Tagliacozzi's decision and his own suffering during the operation. With a hand on the crucifix he opened the secret door through which he had escaped the soldiers of the Church, recollecting the urgency with which he returned to testify. *He transformed me from a monster into a human being,* he reflected, *an image in God's image.*

In the early dawn, Ben Lurian strolled into the garden. There, before the tree where the surgeon had conceived the idea of grafting skin to help the deformed, he stood for a moment in silence. He acknowledged that Gasparo was his brother.

A brown pigeon soared overhead and fluttered down into the garden. The Rabbi recognized him as the prosecution witness so friendly to Gasparo at the trial.

"Our friend is not dead, Brown Pigeon. He lives in the hearts of all of us. Let us pray in his behalf."

It was the dawn of a new day, the dawn of a new year, the dawn of a Day of Atonement, and near the tree the Rabbi prayed in Hebrew in memory of his brother.

"I remember thee in this solemn hour, my beloved brother. I remember the days when we lived together in happy companionship and thy loving friendship was my delight. Though thou hast gone from me, thine image abides within me. I think of thee with gratitude and bless thee for all the devotion thou didst show me. May the Lord bless thee with everlasting joy, may He have thee in His keeping and grant thee eternal bliss. Amen."

Yes, it was the dawn of a new day and a new year with its Day of Atonement, and, in the garden, standing near the tree, the Rabbi raised the shofar to his lips, blowing lustily upon the horn to awaken the world to the possibility of the brotherhood of man. Once, twice, three times, the sound of the ram's horn echoed and re-echoed in the early-morning air.

The brown pigeon had vanished and, after offering condolences to Giulia, Rabbi Ben Lurian departed for Leghorn.

Epilogue

Several months after the burial ceremony, a new wave of superstition poisoned the air. The nuns of San Giovanni Battista reported hearing eerie noises emanating from the surgeon's grave, unearthly voices chanting in the night that Tagliacozzi was a sorcerer and a wicked magician. Was this not a premonition of evil? asked the Sisters, and the Inquisitor General ordered that Gasparo's remains be exhumed and reburied in unconsecrated ground.

A new controversy erupted. Giulia and her son were enraged. Seething at the terrible injustice perpetrated upon the good name of his father, Giovanni Andrea, a handsome young man of eighteen, dashed off a note to Gasparo's friend, the Rabbi Ben Lurian, who visited the Duke of Mantua and the Grand Duke of Tuscany.

Then Ben Lurian returned to Bologna. He informed the Senate of Forty that this insult would not be tolerated and that if justice were not granted to Tagliacozzi's corpse, the armies of Vincenzo Gonzaga, Duke of Mantua, and Ferdinando, Grand Duke of Tuscany, would lay siege to the city and burn it to ashes. That this was no idle threat was conveyed in stern epistles by the powerful dukes, while Jacopo Buoncampagna addressed a letter of protest to the Pope in Rome. Simultaneously, restless students at the university, demonstrating and counterdemonstrating, marched on the city to burn down a church building as evidence of the methods to which they could resort.

Scipio Africanus Borzani had been in mourning since the death of his benefactor. Indeed, the black man's deterioration since exhumation of the body had been horrifying. Each evening, frustrated, icono-clastic, he would stumble off to a nearby tavern and drink until, in a state of insensibility, he would stagger back to his house and collapse, stupefied, on a cot. Then one night, at the tavern, he overheard a fellow saying that a cousin of Aurelio Morisini had gone, in the mid-dle of the night, to the church where the surgeon's corpse had been buried and that *he* had made the terrifying noises, causing the Sisters to feel they would be doomed to perdition were not the body ex-humed and deposited in unconsecrated ground. Scipio, devoted to the memory of Gasparo, felt rage growing until he feared he would leap upon the gossiping man and strangle him. He suppressed the instinct and went immediately to see Captain Buoncampagna, and the military commander, with a contingent of soldiers, proceeded to apprehend the cousin of Morisini. Rousing him from bed, they in-duced him, cringing with terror, to confess, and they escorted him posthaste to the Prendiparte Tower.

The Senate of the City of Bologna was enormously relieved to acquire this intelligence. Alarmed at the threats of besieging their city and squirming under the belligerent demonstrations of the infu-riated students, they had resolved to send a courier to the Pope ask-ing for advice in dealing with this crisis. But with the confession and jailing of the culprit, the decision was easy: the eminent surgeon would be reburied in consecrated ground.

The following day, Tagliacozzi's body was reburied in its original site at the Church of San Giovanni Battista—in consecrated ground. A small select group attended the ceremony: Giulia, Giovanni An-drea, Rabbi Ben Lurian, the Governor of Bologna, and members of the Senate. The proceedings were brief but dignified. And for all time the surgeon's remains would rest in their permanent home.

Ben Lurian climbed on his horse once more. The animal was trot-ting toward the rising sun, toward the universal port city of Leghorn, an oasis for peace lovers in a violent world. In his mind, he addressed Gasparo warmly, quoting from Genesis: *"Let there be no strife between thee and me for we be brethren,"* and his companion responded, *The time is now, my dear friend, for indeed we must sanctify this prayer and embody it in the illustriousness of our performance.*

His horse was galloping now, dirt flying from hooves, dust obscuring the atmosphere and enveloping rider and animal as the pair thundered toward Leghorn. Ben Lurian became aware that he was not alone. The brown pigeon was following him, circling and swooping down, flapping its wings and trailing him onward. What could this mean? Outside the gates of the City of Bologna, he reined in to allow the horse a few moments' respite. The pigeon stopped flying and hovered in static position above him.

Again, the horse was sprinting along the road. The Rabbi glanced up at the sky. The brown pigeon was keeping pace. *Does the pigeon wish to tell me something?* he wondered. *Is the bird trying to elicit a reaction from me?* Did it represent not only the surgeon's conscience, but the conscience of man? Was it a bird of peace?

Then, instinctively, Ben Lurian realized that the pigeon was waiting for him to blow on the ram's horn—the shofar—hanging down onto his chest from a string around his neck. *Yes,* he said to himself, *the time is now to blow the horn of peace for Gasparo, still alive in the hearts of his friends everywhere.* The sound of the horn punctured the stillness of the country air. Once, twice, three times, it rang out, an insistent call for peace and brotherhood in a world ravaged by violence and vendetta.

As if in signal, the brown pigeon flapped its wings and circled low around Ben Lurian. Responding to the symbolic statement, the bird wheeled one, two, three times around the Rabbi.

And then the pigeon pointed its beak skyward. Higher and higher it soared. Its mission was accomplished; fittingly, it could now go home. Brief but purposeful was its flight back to the University City of Bologna. There it nestled in a small garden in back of a house on the street Delle Lame.